continued . . .

Ace Books by Lyn Benedict

SINS & SHADOWS
GHOSTS & ECHOES
GODS & MONSTERS

GODS & MONSTERS

A SHADOWS INQUIRIES NOVEL

Lyn Benedict

ACE BOOKS, NEW YORK

THE BERKLEY PUBLISHING GROUP
Published by the Penguin Group
Penguin Group (USA) Inc.
375 Hudson Street, New York, New York 10014, USA
Penguin Group (Canada), 90 Eglinton Avenue East, Suite 700, Toronto, Ontario M4P 2Y3, Canada
(a division of Pearson Penguin Canada Inc.)
Penguin Books Ltd., 80 Strand, London WC2R 0RL, England
Penguin Group Ireland, 25 St. Stephen's Green, Dublin 2, Ireland (a division of Penguin Books Ltd.)
Penguin Group (Australia), 250 Camberwell Road, Camberwell, Victoria 3124, Australia
(a division of Pearson Australia Group Pty. Ltd.)
Penguin Books India Pvt. Ltd., 11 Community Centre, Panchsheel Park, New Delhi—110 017, India
Penguin Group (NZ), 67 Apollo Drive, Rosedale, Auckland 0632, New Zealand
(a division of Pearson New Zealand Ltd.)
Penguin Books (South Africa) (Pty.) Ltd., 24 Sturdee Avenue, Rosebank, Johannesburg 2196,
South Africa

Penguin Books Ltd., Registered Offices: 80 Strand, London WC2R 0RL, England

GODS & MONSTERS

An Ace Book / published by arrangement with the author

PRINTING HISTORY
Ace mass-market edition / May 2011

Copyright © 2011 by Lane Robins.
Cover art by Shane Rebenschied.
Cover design by Lesley Worrell.
Interior text design by Tiffany Estreicher.

ISBN: 978-0-441-02038-6

ACE
Ace Books are published by The Berkley Publishing Group,
a division of Penguin Group (USA) Inc.,
375 Hudson Street, New York, New York 10014.
ACE and the "A" design are trademarks of Penguin Group (USA) Inc.

PRINTED IN THE UNITED STATES OF AMERICA

10 9 8 7 6 5 4 3 2 1

GODS & MONSTERS

1

Wrong Place, Wrong Time

FOR ONCE, WHEN PEOPLE STARTED DYING, SYLVIE LIGHTNER WASN'T at ground zero. When things went wrong, really wrong, she was fifteen miles away from the crime scene, haggling with a werewolf bitch over her finder's fee.

Five days ago, Sylvie had asked Tatya to keep an eye out and a nose up for a woman who'd gone missing from Alligator Alley, figuring she could turn Tatya's nightly perambulations through the Everglades to good use. Delegation had paid off: Three days later, Maria Ruben was no longer a missing person. Dead, but no longer lost, and that was something. Finding her body could bring its own resolution to the family and was worth every penny.

So Sylvie had met Tatya at the scene, called the cops, and split without waiting for them to show, spooked.

Maria Ruben hadn't been alone. There were four other dead women, drowned, pushed beneath the duckweed surface of an Everglades lagoon, and left to sway slowly in the dark, stagnant waters. Maria's short dark hair stuck out like a frightened puffer fish, showing the shock her slack face couldn't. A pink barrette—cheap plastic butterfly—

floated free, trailing a long bronze lock of hair belonging to a woman barely into her twenties.

All of them were young, Maria likely the oldest, and all were Hispanic. Someone had particular tastes. Sylvie swallowed disgust, studied the other three women by the sullen gold of the setting sun. Their ethnicity and ages might match up, but their clothes argued they came from different parts of the city: Maria's casual business wear; swimsuit and sarong; halter top and skirt; demure blouse and khaki skirt; and one who reminded Sylvie of her sister—a budding fashion plate.

That was the moment Sylvie had called the police. The moment she felt over her head. This was someone's sister. Sylvie might have a reputation as a vigilante, but she knew when to leave a crime scene the hell alone.

Tatya wanted a finder's fee for each woman. Sylvie didn't object on any moral ground—never mind that their agreement only covered Maria Ruben—but finances dictated haggling. Five hundred dollars had been half of the fee Sylvie had charged Maria Ruben's husband, but $2500 started eating into rent. Sylvie would be willing to take that financial risk, but her business partner, Alexandra Figueroa-Smith, wouldn't. Sylvie wanted to keep Tatya happy—the werewolf was a good source as well as a quasi friend—so the discussion lasted longer than Sylvie liked, culminating with Sylvie's writing an IOU for another thousand, payable the next month.

Once the rest of the women were identified, Sylvie could see about spreading around the cost of doing business. There might be a reward or, more likely, a client who'd want her to investigate how their loved one had ended up underwater. Now that she had an in with the local cops, courtesy of her making nice with Detective Adelio Suarez, she could be a useful liaison to a grieving family. And she thought that the police were going to be struggling with this one. The scene had felt . . . charged, a spark in the still, hot air that tasted of the *Magicus Mundi*.

Maria Ruben's car had been found abandoned beside the road, the battery run down, the driver's door hanging open. Her husband had reported his wife's last words via cell phone, *Salvador, you should see this. A two-headed alligator. I'm stopping for pics* . . . and nothing more.

Whatever had happened that night had seen Maria Ruben transported nearly fifty miles, her camera bag gone, her forehead marked, and her body left in a crowded and watery grave. It smacked of ritual murder.

Those women hadn't died natural deaths; that much seemed evident. The question that lingered was—how unnatural had they been?

* * *

BACK IN SOUTH MIAMI BEACH, SYLVIE PUT THE KEY IN HER OFFICE door, the phone shrilling on the other side of the glass like a race clock timer counting down. She forced the key to turn, slammed into her office—all haste, no caution, rushing to hear what Suarez had to say about the 'Glades scene, cursing him for calling the office instead of her cell—and fell into a nightmare.

A cobweb brush of sensation lingered and jittered on her skin, the sign of a spell laid over the doorway. A trap she'd bulled right on through.

Stupid, she thought, and froze, trying to control the only thing she still could: herself.

Her office changed around her, warped by powerful magic, an inferno blossoming. The illusion worked all her senses—drowned her vision in flickering flames that crackled and hissed, licked around and out of electrical sockets. She tasted acrid plastic; the chemical burn of it seared her nose and throat. Only furious control kept her from coughing, flailing for air.

Heat scalded her every inborne breath, dried her lungs. Her skin prickled, tightened, felt puffed with heat. Stretching a cautious hand forward resulted in blistered fingers.

Even with the memory of the telltale sensation, that

cobweb cling across her face and throat, she nearly believed in the illusory fire turning her office into a maze of heavy smoke and hellish light.

Believing in an illusion gave it power.

Illusion could kill if you accepted it as truth.

Her little dark voice fed her a nasty thought: *What if the spell is layered over a real fire? What if you burn trying to prove it isn't real?*

That moment of doubt cost her. Smoke choked her, tightened her lungs and throat, scouring her insides; her hair stank of burning. Sylvie fumbled for the door handle, just behind her, so far away, backing up and not finding it. Was she even moving?

Faintly, she heard the ringing of the warning bell on the main desk. A singing chime, growing faster, shriller, an audible sign that magic was saturating the air. It steadied her, gave her a focus. If the bell was still ringing, then the charred wreckage of the desk was illusion. It was *all* illusion.

And it was centered on her. Even if she fled, the flames would follow.

Meant to send you screaming outside, into traffic or the ocean, that internal voice muttered.

If she didn't flee? She risked being an anomalous death, a woman dead of smoke inhalation in an untouched office.

This, she thought grimly, was what came of playing by the rules. Of leaving the bad guys alive. If she'd killed Odalys the necromancer instead of seeing her arrested, if she had punished Patrice Caudwell for returning from the dead instead of balking at the complications involved—if, if, if. If Sylvie had disposed of her enemies properly, she wouldn't be one step from having her lungs ruined by imaginary smoke.

Anger surged. *Hell with that.* It wasn't a mistake worth dying for.

She broke the paralysis the illusion had forced her into. The illusion might be cleverly crafted, the mark of a talented if malign witch, but Sylvie refused to yield.

Sylvie's lips drew tight over her teeth, snarling. Hot air rushed into her mouth, drying it. Three ways to break an illusion spell for a non-magic-user. *Kill the caster. Wait the illusion out. Or overwhelm it.*

Sylvie would gladly put a bullet in the witch's brain, but the coward had struck from a distance. Waiting wasn't an option; not when it was a struggle just to keep breathing, to override her body's instinctive panic. But the ringing bell on the desk was a protective spell, defensive magic. . . .

She thought cool thoughts about AC, about health-giving air, about freshwater cascading over her skin, then stepped into the thickest gouts of flames. The fires licked her flesh, gnawed her hands, singed her jeans, her jacket, turned her gun to a hot brand against her back. Sylvie pushed it all aside.

The bell rang on, her guiding beacon. Sylvie moved by memory and sound, trusting her will above her body and mind. Control. Calm.

She slammed her hand down on the bell—agitated metal quivering against her skin, cool stone containing it, and the unyielding strength of the desk beneath. Her world erupted in an entirely new wave of heat/pain/magic. The offensive and defensive magics warred, her body the battlefield, the choice of weapon—fire. Pain ran liquid through her body; her blood sizzled as if it boiled within her.

Her hair streamed upward, rising like smoke, her eyes blind to both illusion and reality—completely vulnerable; then it was over, and she stood panting and aching in her office, on a balmy and peaceful South Beach evening, the only scent of fire in the air that of the restaurants searing freshly caught fish and shrimp. The warning bell was slagged silver in a cracked marble bowl, and beneath them, the desk was crocodile-scaled with char.

Wonderful. Just after she learned she had a powerful witch gunning for her, she destroyed the one piece of magic that would warn her of an attack.

She just wondered who it was that wanted her dead.

The list was regrettably long—the sorcerous *Maudits* community; the ISI, America's government spook squad; even a miffed Greek god or two. If Sylvie had to choose, though, she'd pick Odalys Hargrove, the necromancer she'd managed to get slapped behind bars two days ago. Odalys wasn't the type to suffer in silence. Sylvie had managed, with the help of the Ghoul, to prevent Odalys from fulfilling her vicious business plan: destroying teenagers' souls and selling the newly emptied bodies to hungry ghosts looking for a new lease on life. Odalys was exactly the type to have contingency plans lying around.

· · ·

SYLVIE CHECKED THE CLOCK ABSENTLY—10:00 P.M.—THEN TOOK A second, disbelieving look. Fury rose all over again. That ridiculous attack had cost her nearly an hour. An hour trapped in battle with her own senses. An hour gone. An hour . . . in which she hadn't heard anything at all from Lio.

Since she'd given him the heads-up on the bodies in the 'Glades close to two hours ago, she felt justified in her impatience.

While she doubted she'd have heard the phone ring, neither her cell nor her office phone had any messages, though the office phone's caller ID listed the call she'd missed as from Salvador Ruben, his nightly check-in on her progress.

Until today, Sylvie had had none to report. Now that she did, she had to wait on Suarez.

She said, "Dammit," aloud, and the dry rasp of it hurt. She leaned against the kitchenette counter, drank straight from the sink faucet. Lukewarm water had rarely tasted so sweet. She wiped at her damp mouth and cheek, thinking dark thoughts about police cooperation.

Detective Adelio Suarez would still have Maria Ruben as a missing person without Sylvie's help. He'd better not be cutting her out of the loop. Their relationship was supposed to be a two-way street, dammit.

The phone rang again, and she snatched it up, hoping it was Suarez continuing his habit of calling the office first. He was one of the long line of people who'd rather talk to Alex than Sylvie.

"Ms. Lightner?"

Sylvie cursed herself for not checking the ID. Salvador Ruben. The last person she needed to talk to just then. "Mr. Ruben—"

"Have you heard from your friend yet? Did she find anything? Did she find Maria?" Sylvie imagined that Ruben would have a nice voice when it wasn't pitched high with stress and hope. Now it quivered with so much tension, she felt her back and neck lock up in sympathy.

She let out a careful, soundless breath, stared out at the soothing flow of South Beach traffic, the glow of headlights and taillights, the glitter against the dark. She could lie, tell him she hadn't found anything, let the cops break the news; but he was her client. She had a responsibility to tell him the truth. Or at least as much of it as she could without jeopardizing the police investigation. "Mr. Ruben. It's not good—"

"Oh god," he said, reading her tone accurately. "Is she dead? Did someone do something to her?"

"Yes," Sylvie said. "I expect you'll be contacted by the police soon."

"You're sure?" he asked. "You saw her? It was her? The picture I gave you wasn't very good. Maybe it's someone else. . . ." A last hope thinned his voice, turned it to a whispered prayer, a man asking for a miracle.

Sylvie had dealt with gods; she knew miracles didn't come cheap.

"The police will answer your questions," she said.

"But you'll keep looking? For whoever did this thing?"

Sylvie hesitated. She shouldn't. It was a police matter now, not hers. But something about the scene nagged at her, left her with the same jittery discomfort in her bones that came from being around inimical magic. "I will."

It took her another few minutes to verify that he wasn't

alone, that he had a friend who could wait with him for the news. For the inevitable call that would shatter his world. A few minutes of evasion, not telling him exactly what had happened to his wife.

They felt like the longest few minutes of her life.

She set the receiver down, crossed to the couch, and slumped onto it with a creak of stressed leather. The air vent above cooled her skin, her agitated nerves. She wasn't good at patience. She wasn't good at offering comfort. She wished that Alex or Demalion had been around to take that call. But Alex was done for the day, and Demalion was . . . finding himself in Chicago, trying to see what he could salvage of his old life in the new skin he wore.

Sylvie kicked at the armrest, a brief spurt of frustration, then dug out her cell phone.

Suarez wasn't getting off the hook so easily; if he wouldn't call her, she'd call him. She couldn't make him pick up, though. It went straight to voice mail.

"Call me, Lio," she said. "I've got a client who's waiting on official word about his wife."

The ceiling above her striped light, dark, light with passing cars; the plate-glass window beside her grew cooler as the day's heat faded. Sylvie flipped the phone, checked the time again. Almost ten thirty. She'd spent most of the day on the road, meeting Tatya, then taking an ATV down bumpy trails and hiking through saw-grass paths, then doing it all in reverse; she'd have to find out when Alex left. It might give her a vague idea of when the illusion trap had been laid. If it was after working hours, the odds of a witness dropped.

There was a sweet spot Sylvie herself had taken advantage of when breaking into businesses. That gap of time between people heading home and heading out to dinner. If she were the witch, she'd have laid her trap then.

Of course, if Sylvie were the witch, she'd have sent goons in to take Sylvie out while she struggled with the illusion. Sylvie believed in being thorough.

She forced herself off the couch and folded the phone

away, fighting the urge to redial Suarez. The kitchenette light flickered, bringing to mind that there were leftover enchiladas in the little fridge, just the thing for a bite before she went home to her apartment and its perennially-in-need-of-groceries kitchen.

While she nuked the enchiladas, munching absently on the cold corn chips stored in the fridge to avoid attracting palmetto bugs, she clicked on the local news. The microwave dinged, but she didn't notice.

Breaking news and local news, and it was full of streaming lights, red and blue, and searchlights shining down on flames against a grey-green backdrop.

Everglades, she thought. Guess Suarez hadn't called because he was too busy dodging the media.

There hadn't been flames when she left.

The news bar across the bottom of the screen made her heart jolt: *Three policemen killed in Everglades.*

She hit the volume, listened to the newscast, trying to filter the controlled hysterics of the news anchor for actual fact—everything was urgent these days; everything was imminent doom on Channel 7. As far as she could tell, it *was* her crime scene, but what had changed? When she and Tatya had been there, it was as quiet as death; there hadn't even been mosquito hum in the air. Now the newscasters mentioned bombs and ambushes in a single breath, followed it with a totally inane recap of how many helicopters were circling the scene, and a self-referential media report.

Sylvie muted the set, hit redial on her cell phone. "Lio. Give me a call if you're all right—" Stupid message, but she felt the need to try something more than just waiting to see if the news anchors would broadcast the names of the dead.

Her office phone rang again, and Sylvie grabbed it, chanting *Be Lio, be Lio* in her head.

"Shadows Inquiries," she said.

There was silence on the line, a silence of words, not breath. She heard a rasp of controlled air, a clogged sound that might be a stifled sob, and her hand tightened on the receiver. "It's Sylvie. Who is this?"

". . . Lio wants you," the woman said, just when Sylvie was about to reluctantly let the line go dead again. "You come. You see him. Then you get away from my family."

"Lourdes," Sylvie said. Adelio Suarez's wife. She skipped the questions rising to her lips—*Was Lio all right? Was he hurt? What happened?*—and homed in on the information she needed right at this moment. "Where are you?"

"Jackson Memorial," Lourdes spat, and slammed the phone down.

. . .

SYLVIE LOOKED IN ON ADELIO AND WINCED EVEN AS RELIEF STARTED trickling into her system. He wasn't in critical care, didn't have anything her TV-trained eyes would assess as indicators of serious injury—no cannula, no morphine pump, no looming machinery surrounding the bed. But he didn't look good, either. Both his eyes were so swollen that they made one bruised lump across the sharp bridge of his nose. A long row of stitches lined his jaw, and there was enough stitchwork, still shiny with recent cleaning, on his arms to make her think of quilt patches. The hospital room, clean as it was, smelled of smoke and blood.

Lourdes, seated beside Adelio on a visitor's chair, rosary dangling from her fingers, looked up, and the expression on her face convinced Sylvie the woman would be adding Hail Marys for uncharitable thoughts to her post-confession routine next Thursday.

The woman got into Sylvie's space, pushed her back into the hallway in silent, bulldog outrage. Sylvie, conscious of the damage she'd done this family, allowed herself to lose ground before a woman twice her age and half her size.

She throttled down the angry dark voice inside her that didn't care for obedience or politeness or anything at all beyond its own survival, and let Lourdes tear her a new one, half in Spanish, half in English, all of it conducted with the careful, quiet fury of a woman who knew exactly how much noise would get unwelcome attention. Eventually, her words trailed off, fell apart under fear and hatred; her last sally was a broken, "You're a bad person, Shadows. You killed my son, and now you try to kill Lio."

"If I were such a bad person, would I sit here and listen to you?" Sylvie said. "Let me talk to Lio."

"He's sleeping."

"He can wake up," Sylvie said, and stepped forward decisively. Lourdes gave ground, then, in a sudden resurgence of fury, spat at Sylvie's feet.

Sylvie studied the shining spot on the worn linoleum and thought it was lucky Lourdes Suarez was a good Catholic and not a *bruja*, or Sylvie would be fighting off a curse in the midst of Jackson Memorial's inpatient wing. Instead, she just stepped around the sputum, marked it as a new low in her life, that a nice little Cuban housewife wanted to spit on her, and pushed her way back into Adelio's room.

He can wake up, she had said, and it sounded easy then. Not so easy to lean over him, searching for an unscathed place to press gentle fingers. Even washed up, he stank of smoke. His hair was burned to stubble on one side. Not so easy to wake him from blissful unconsciousness into pain. But she needed to know.

She settled for tapping the pillow beside his face, a quick rat-a-tat of fingernails and pressure. He snorted awake, thrashed a bit, then stilled as events caught up with him. Through his puffed eye sockets, the narrow slit and shine of his eyes, she could see him remembering *hospital*. Remembering *Sylvie*.

He angled his head on the pillow, trying to get any view of her he could. "Not a bomb," he said. "I didn't get hit by shrapnel. The chart is wrong."

"Okay," she said. She sat down, hitched the visitor's seat close, *screek*ing it over the linoleum. "What was it, then?"

"Bear."

It was a meaningless syllable to her at first, glossolalia brought on by painkillers, then the word clicked. "You were attacked by a *bear*? At a crime scene swarming with lights and cops?"

It just didn't make sense. There were bears in northern Florida, but not in the swampy parts of the Everglades. And even those bears were smaller, more peaceful than the western bears.

Adelio let out a long breath, took in another, a careful marshaling of strength. "I know what I saw. I know that it is possible. You told me so yourself when you showed me the orchids that once were people. Transformation—"

He broke off, fumbled a hand toward his stitches, suddenly panicky. Sylvie caught his hand in hers—large, chilled, shaking—and let it go once he'd calmed. Orchids. Transformation . . . After Odalys's arrest, Sylvie had taken Suarez to the Fairchild Gardens to visit a special collection of orchids, a group of thirteen rare plants that had once been the satanic coven who'd killed his son. Suarez had been skeptical, and Sylvie had spent more time explaining the mechanics of magical transformation as she understood it than she had ever thought she would.

"Am I going to change?"

"Into—"

"A bear?" Suarez's eyes glinted, shiny with panic. Sylvie felt like she was grasping at water, something that shifted and changed and fled her understanding.

Suarez groaned. She said, "C'mon, Lio, tell it to me from the beginning. One piece at a time. Tatya found the women, I called you, you went out to the 'Glades with a team—"

"Nightmare," Suarez said. His voice was gravelly with shock and lingering disorientation. "Outdoor crime scenes. A dump site for a serial killer. The Everglades. Takes forever. Just to get the bodies photographed in situ, the scene, and finally out of the water—it got dark. We set up lights, kept working. The helicopter came. Wind everywhere. But not on the water. No waves at all."

"Not in the lagoon?" That same stillness she and Tatya had noted.

Suarez shifted a shoulder. "Like glass, smothered ripples. They started loading the first body—"

"Maria?" Sylvie asked.

"No," Lio breathed. "*La rubia*, the blond woman, in the swimsuit. Closest to the shore—

"She burned, Shadows. Burned like rocket fuel. Blue and white flames, red flames, so hot, and they had her loaded. The forensic team burned . . . and then so did the bird. That's what exploded. The helicopter. Not a bomb. The helicopter and the pilot and the forensic team." Wetness streaked from one eye. Sylvie let him rest, but when she thought he might get lost in mourning his dead, she pushed again.

"Magic?" Sylvie closed her eyes, tried to recall the scene she had left. Tried to remember why she had been nervous there, why she had thought Lio would be calling for her advice. She was a city girl at heart; her visits into the Everglades had been school field trips to Anhinga Trail to count animal species, and the more recent excursions to see Tatya. But even without familiarity, she had marked the lagoon as too quiet. The lagoon had had the shaky, stretched feel of a world altered by force, and the wildlife had fled before that metaphysical earthquake, leaving deadness behind. So yeah, maybe magic. But it hadn't struck her as a spell waiting to happen. Hell, she wouldn't have called Suarez out if that had been the case. She would have called a witch to clear the area first. Magical SWAT. Something.

Maybe Lourdes was right. Maybe Sylvie was to blame for this.

"Can't tell about the fire," Suarez murmured. "God only knows. Could have been an incendiary inside her. But I don't think so. Not with the bear."

"Yeah, the bear," Sylvie said. "I'm still not—"

"I was in the water, thigh deep, worried that a gator was going to take me off at the knee, when the fire started.

I tried to get to them, then I saw the body move before me."

"The burning—"

"The other one. The one closest to me. The wildlife photographer. Your client's wife. Maria Ruben. I thought— she was alive. I reached for her, and she changed. All claws, and teeth, and fur. Charging me. Her claws . . ."

His hand flailed at his stitches again, and Sylvie got it this time. "The dead woman changed into a bear?" It was so hard not to sound skeptical. Even knowing about the *Magicus Mundi*, even knowing about shape-shifters.

Shape-shifters didn't play dead very well—too much animal. But they also didn't come back from the dead.

"Am I going to change—"

"No," Sylvie said. "It doesn't work like that. Either it's a genetic ability, or it's a sorcerous one. It's not a disease."

Given that there was death involved, Sylvie assumed sorcery. True shape-shifters were creatures at least partially bound by natural law: They lived, they bred true, they died if you killed them, and they stayed dead. Beyond that—Maria Ruben was straight-up human. Had been, at any rate.

The wild card might be the tiny percentage of shape-shifters that were curse-related, but those were rare enough that she felt comfortable erasing them from the map of possibilities. Didn't take too many generations of magic-users to learn that cursing your enemies to change them into beasts was more of an "oops" than a "ha!" Witches and sorcerers could make a tasty meal for a pissed-off shifter with a grudge.

Lio was quiet, more of those silent tears streaking his cheeks. Relief, this time, she diagnosed.

"They all changed," he whispered finally. "Wolves and a big cat with a lashing tail."

"The bodies?"

"Their eyes in the fires. Shone."

"What happened to them?"

"We were dying," Lio said. "Jorge was screaming— haven't heard men scream like that. Since the Gulf."

Sylvie caught his hand in hers again, held it tight until the shaking eased.

"*Los monstruos,*" he said. His eyes closed, shields against the intolerable. Bruises on bruises. Emotional and physical. "They left us there."

"'Left,'" Sylvie parroted. It was an odd choice of words. Didn't seem to apply to a group of fleeing animals.

"Retreated," he said. "All the same direction."

No matter how she questioned Lio, she doubted she'd get much more sense out of him. His skin was grey, beaded with sweat. His throat worked, holding back sickness, pain, fear. She didn't have a clear idea of what had happened in the 'Glades; but then, the real question was, did she need to? She'd investigated other cases with less to go on.

"Sylvie," Adelio said. "Find out. The only bodies in evidence now are police. Find out what happened, and stop it."

"Okay," she said.

"Do you have a plan?" he pushed, unwilling to take her word.

"Monster hunting," Sylvie said. "I'm waiting until morning, and I'm taking magical backup."

Dead women who changed shape? Dead women who came back to life? Sounded like necromantic magic. Luckily, she had a new acquaintance who liked to pal around with death magic. Tierney Wales, the Opa-locka Ghoul, was going to find himself rousted bright and early for a field trip.

. . .

SYLVIE MADE HER WAY ACROSS THE CROWDED PARKING LOT— hospitals always seemed to be doing a booming business no matter the hour—homing in on her truck and its clawed hood gleaming beneath a streetlamp. She thought of Suarez and his patchwork of sutured flesh with regret. He was going to scar as badly as her truck.

Footsteps sounded behind her, quick-moving, and she turned, always on alert, but saw only a woman searching for her keys in a cavernous leopard-print bag. Disorganized, Sylvie thought. The woman had the common sense to move quickly through the quiet lot but not enough planning to pull her keys ahead of time. She was asking to be mugged. Especially while leaning up against a steely grey BMW.

One of the sheep, her little dark voice suggested, *dependent on a careless shepherd.*

Hush, Sylvie thought at it. Bad enough when it preached misanthropy; it made her downright nervous when it started to verge on theology. The voice was the leftover bit of Lilith's genetic legacy carried down through generations, an all-too-active form of ancestral memory. Sylvie had killed Lilith when they met; she didn't need to keep Lilith's madness alive in her own blood.

Sylvie left the hospital behind with the usual diesel cough from her truck and a belated protest from her stomach, which chose that moment to remember the abandoned enchiladas. Burned women, hospital visits, dead cops— part of being a pro meant it didn't even faze her appetite. Not anymore. Which, considering the rate that the *Magicus Mundi* was invading Sylvie's day-to-day life, was a good thing. She'd have starved otherwise.

She checked her mirrors, checked the streets, trying to remember what restaurants were open and nearby. Mia Rosa's, she thought, was only two blocks back. She checked the streets once more, looking for cops, then hung a U-turn. During the day, she wouldn't have made it. At this hour, it was a little tricky, best done at speed, but definitely possible. Behind her, horns honked loud and long, and too late to be directed at her. She glanced back to see that another car had made the same maneuver, though the woman driving looked a little wild-eyed. Sylvie hmmed thoughtfully, and when she parked the truck, she unlocked the glove box and took out her gun.

She didn't like being followed.

She especially didn't like being followed when she had a killer witch after her.

The hostess at the door greeted Sylvie with a stiff smile, a pointed reminder that they were closing at midnight, and sat her among a group of tables with the chairs put up. Subtle, they weren't. Sylvie didn't care as long as the food was hot, plentiful, and quick to arrive.

She had just sent the waitress off with her order when the door opened again; the hostess moved to intercept another last-minute diner. Sylvie narrowed her eyes, and the dark-haired woman in the doorway waved at Sylvie and waved off the hostess.

The woman from the hospital parking lot threaded her way through the tables, her ridiculously large bag still hanging from her shoulder and clunking against upended chair legs every few feet. The same woman who'd made a U-turn to keep up with her, pushing her ancient Jeep hard to make enough speed to keep from being t-boned. She homed in on Sylvie, and Sylvie kicked out the chair opposite her. "So, that business with the BMW, was that play-acting or wishful thinking?"

"A little of both," the woman said. "It was a nice car, wasn't it? And if I had approached you in the lot, you would have walked away."

"Still might," Sylvie said. "I don't like strangers following me."

"I'm Caridad Valdes-Pedraza," she said. "And you're Sylvie Lightner. You're a PI who's always on the scene, and I'm a freelance reporter looking for a scoop. I've been waiting to see Adelio Suarez; you just came from seeing him. Feels like fate."

"Fate's an excuse for people who don't want to make an effort," Sylvie said.

"Interesting," the woman said. "I'd have marked you as

believing in destiny." She hefted her purse to the tabletop, dropped it with a *clatter*, and pulled out a notebook and a pen.

She scribbled in it, and Sylvie had to ask, "Are you writing that down?"

"Hey," Caridad said. "I like to take notes on my subjects."

"I'm not a subject," Sylvie said. "Ms. Valdes-Pedraza—"

"You could call me Caridad if you want. I know the other's a mouthful."

Sylvie let her breath out in a steady gust. She wasn't in the mood. If she hadn't seen the sullen waitress approaching with her meal, she would have just given up. Walked away. Caridad's expression was friendly, pert, that of a would-be newscaster. But there was something harder beneath it. Intelligence, ambition, and something deeper still, betrayed in the tension in her jaw: need.

"My friends call me Cachita," she said. She shot Sylvie a demure glance, one step away from flirtation. It was a good front, a good act, no doubt got her into a lot of conversations with her targets; but it was only an act.

Sylvie made her voice flat, no weakness. "Ms. Valdes-Pedraza, we're not friends, and we're not going to be friends. I'm going to eat a long-overdue dinner, and you're not welcome at my table. If you have something to say, say it and go away."

"Fine," she said. Caridad sat up straight, pressed her curling hair out of her face, drummed her nails on the table, a quick rumba, and said, "Tell me about the bodies you found in the Everglades."

"Police made a statement," Sylvie said. "There were no bodies, only mannequins. It was a trap, and three officers died."

"You know what police statements are? Sop for reporters too lazy to do their own digging. Too lazy to do anything but print a preapproved story. They trade integrity and a real interview for easy bylines."

"So you're what? A crusader for truth?" Sylvie spiced

her words with as much mockery as she could manage
when she was tired . . . and dammit, the woman was drawing her in.

"Is that a bad thing to aspire to?" Caridad asked. "There's
an awful lot of truth that gets ignored or denied out there.
I want to open people's eyes."

"Good luck with that," Sylvie said. "I get paid to find
things out, and people still don't listen."

"Doesn't it just drive you crazy?" Caridad said. "Make
you want to shove it down their throats? Me, I get so frustrated, I could scream. I turn in reports, and it's all, 'But,
Cachita, where's the point of—' "

Sylvie growled, took a breath, and said, "You know
something else that drives people crazy? Intrusive reporters. Go away. I have nothing to tell you."

Caridad leaned back in her seat, took her hands from
the table, made herself smaller. Dammit, this reporter was
good at reading people, at manipulating her own body language, her meekness only another path to taking control
of the conversation, to keep the dialogue open, to derail
Sylvie's anger.

Sylvie felt a wolfish grin stretch her mouth. Maybe that
kind of thing worked on regular people, but Sylvie had
anger to spare.

Caridad's eyes narrowed, pale eye shadow crinkling
beneath dark brows. "Women have been disappearing from
the city. The police aren't talking about it, and even if they
did, they'd be talking about a serial killer. Not a monster.
But that's what it is. You can help me. You found its playground, didn't you?

"I've got sources, Sylvie. They tell me that someone
called in five bodies that they found in the Everglades.
Another source tells me you left the scene. You're not
police, and you wouldn't be welcome at a crime scene—
so you must have found them. What made you look for
them in the first place?"

"Do you really expect me to talk to you?" Sylvie took
another bite of her "special"; it was some sort of creamy

pasta and seafood, barely lukewarm and sour with her irritation. "You said it. I'm not real popular with the police. You think they'd be happy if I shot my mouth off to a reporter?"

"I think you're *dying* to. I do my research, Sylvie. I know my subjects. I know about you. You've got to be sick of the injustices, the fact that people are getting away with murder. You could help me."

Sylvie said, "I usually get paid for helping."

"I expected better of you," Caridad said.

"What are you, my mother?" Sylvie said. "The only approval I need is my own."

She pushed her plate away, appetite gone. Her personal approval rating wasn't at its all-time best: Her dreams, in what fitful sleep she'd managed since the confrontation with Odalys, had been angry and focused on the one person who'd gotten away clean with murder: Patrice Caudwell, one of Odalys's revenant ghosts, who'd managed to keep the teenage body Odalys had provided. At least Odalys had had to lawyer up, had her world disrupted. Patrice? She was sipping *cafecitos* poolside and working on her tan. Impatience and irritation flared; Sylvie stood. Caridad grabbed her wrist, faster than Sylvie had thought she'd be, and a lot more willing to get physical.

"You aren't listening."

"You're not saying much," Sylvie said. "You want me to piss off the cops by sharing stories out of school. You want me to confirm your theory about a monster who's stealing women. Even if I played along, then what?" Sylvie shook her head. "Crazy talk's not going to get you far as a freelancer. You'd be better off peddling predigested stories."

"I'm disappointed," Caridad said. "I thought you'd respect the truth. But you're just another cover-up artist."

Where the previous attempt at scolding hadn't stung, this one did.

"Tell me something," Sylvie said. "You know Maria Ruben?"

Caridad's eyes went wide, sensing some sort of chance in the air. She chewed her lip, flipped through her mental files, raised her chin. "Should I?"

Sylvie sighed. Maria Ruben was the missing person most likely to be newsworthy—her husband saw to that with his ranting about alien abduction. If Caridad Valdes-Pedraza hadn't put her name on her list of missing people, she was no kind of reporter at all and a waste of Sylvie's time.

When Caridad stood, preparing to follow Sylvie from the restaurant, Sylvie snapped, "Sit. I'm leaving. You're not."

"We could be allies, Sylvie," Caridad said. "Help each other."

"You sure you want to volunteer? My most recent ally's in a bed at Jackson Memorial, torn all to hell."

2

Looking for Trouble

SYLVIE WOKE THE NEXT MORNING, MOUTH DRY, PANTING WITH ANGER, with a headache born of another night of fitful and furious dreams, trying to solve real-world problems in her sleep.

She hated when daytime frustrations bled into her dreams. It could wreck the whole next day.

Sylvie slapped at the light-blocking blinds, got a quick view of bright, morning sunlight—past time to get up. Time to go get Wales, go look for trouble in the swamps.

She thunked back against her pillow, crooked her arm over her face.

She'd slept like crap, and, while she was tempted to blame late-night indigestion caused by bad pasta, she knew it was all her own doing. Most of the time, she was glad of her own stubborn determination to see a problem through to the bitter end. *Most* of the time. That same determination turned ugly when the villains went free. When her youngest employee, Rafael Suarez, had died, her dreams had been nothing but her brain chewing on the injustice of it, a hundred different revenge scenarios, ways she could find them and make them pay; she hadn't actually slept well until his killers had been dealt with.

In the aftermath of the Odalys mess, she'd *expected* to sleep poorly. Four teenagers had died. Her *sister* had nearly died. And the mess with Demalion and Wright was nightmare fodder all on its own. Two ghosts, one body; only Wright's unexpected sacrifice had led to Demalion's survival. For which she was grateful down to her toes, but it needed adjusting to. How did you deal with your lover walking around in another man's body, when everything that should have been familiar was strange? Sylvie was still trying to work that one out

She'd gotten a bit of breathing room when Demalion retreated back to Chicago with his own plans and goals. First, he told her carefully, aware that it was going to be a sore point, he wanted to rejoin the ISI, wanted to be recruited all over again. Sylvie was too glad to have him back to argue.

Besides, his second goal was one she agreed with. Demalion wanted to make sure Wright's wife and son were taken care of. "No pension for his death," Demalion had said, "not while I'm wearing his skin."

How that translated to his pretending to be Wright for a time, Sylvie wasn't sure. She had ideas of her own. Demalion had grown up without knowing his father. He didn't want Jamie Wright to do the same.

Sylvie closed her eyes again, trying to figure the damage. Worse to think your father abandoned you? Or worse to see him turned into a stranger?

She started to drift off, dipped into her dreamscape again, and jerked awake, breath fast in her lungs. Again with the violence. Right back where she'd left off the first time. Trying to kill Patrice.

Her dreams had been chaotic things—vivid, distorted images and a strange, wild growling, the scent of blood and corruption. The dreams centered on Sylvie tracking Patrice Caudwell through the city, scouring the dreamscape for sight of Bella Alvarez, the teenager whose body Patrice had taken for her own. But Patrice proved as tricky to deal with in dreams as she was in the real world—

Sylvie emptied clip after clip of bullets into her smug face, but the woman refused to die.

That was when her dreams had gone weirder, when a voice rasped over her shoulder, a hand closed over hers, felt but not seen. *Like this,* her little dark voice said. *For vengeance. Like this.* Her gun shifted to a blade, her hand guided along a bloody pattern as Patrice fell apart before it.

It had been deeply satisfying in her dreams, less so when she was awake and faced with the reality of the situation. Bella Alvarez's death was only on the tally Sylvie kept; as far as the police were concerned, the girl was alive and well.

She would have to do something about Patrice. Pity the world was determined to keep her otherwise occupied.

It wouldn't take long to shoot her, leave her dying in the body she killed for, her little dark voice suggested. Sylvie swallowed back the rage before it could really get started, accepted the thought instead of arguing all the reasons shooting Patrice would be problematic, and moved on with a mental wrench. It was Alex's idea—a plan to defang the danger that lurked beneath Sylvie's skin.

A plan to tame you, the voice growled, and Sylvie had a harder time shaking it back: It was true. She had promised Alex she'd try it, but she thought it was doomed to failure. The little dark voice, Lilith's rage at the status quo, had survived generations and generations; Sylvie didn't think it could be shut off and ignored like a kindergarten bully. Alex said the voice was part of Sylvie, and therefore hers to control. Sylvie agreed because it was always easier to agree with Alex; but in all honesty, the voice felt separate, a piece of her but not part of the whole. Something extra.

As opinionated as the voice was, it wasn't always right, and it didn't make allowances for real-world considerations. Shoot Patrice in Bella's body and do what with the body, the inevitable investigation? At the moment, it was just too much risk.

Patrice, as little as Sylvie liked it, could wait for Sylvie to come up with a plan. It was simple math. One known murderess roaming free, sampling the joys of being flesh once more, or shape-shifting dead women who could and would kill cops.

Showered, dressed in time-smoothed khakis, boots, and a long-sleeved green T-shirt, she faced the day, knowing that as soon as the dampness from the shower left her skin, sweat would start. But if she was going to be hiking through the 'Glades again, covering up was a necessity. Snakebite, saw grass, and sunburn were a miserable trifecta.

She grabbed a couple of protein bars from the back of the cupboard, made sure she had an extra clip in her bag, and clattered down the concrete risers. That early, the parking lot beside the complex was a tangle of people leaving for work, jockeying for the single exit onto the highway. Sylvie munched her protein bar—*mmm, sandy*—and bided her time.

Her cell phone rang as she was reaching the main entrance to the Palmetto Expressway, and she fumbled it to her ear. "Yeah, Alex."

"You're not at work," her partner said. "I brought coffee and everything."

"Not at the office," Sylvie said, "but I'm working. You catch the news last night? That bomb in the Everglades?"

". . . You're not a cop, Sylvie."

"And it wasn't a bomb," Sylvie said. "Five dead women, one of whom burst into flame hot enough to blow up a helicopter, and another turned into a bear—"

"Okay, okay, it's definitely your case," Alex said. "What can I do?"

"Hunker down and get ready for company. Seriously, Alex, this whole bomb cover story is thin. Lio thought they'd have Feds descending on them for the bodies in the 'Glades—serial killer in a national park. But once this happened—"

"ISI," Alex said. "Those bastards."

"Yeah," Sylvie said. The Internal Surveillance and Investigations agents were never fun to have around. They coupled the usual government-agency attitude with levels of manipulation and secrecy that made them about as trustworthy as the average con man. They talked a good game about controlling the *Magicus Mundi*, but people still ended up dead. "That's one of the reasons I'm headed out to the scene today. I want to get there before they do."

Alex let out an exasperated sigh that Sylvie nearly felt through the phone. "Sylvie. The scene's going to be swarming with cops and press, and even if it's not—dead shapeshifters who can't be all that dead if they're tearing into people? I don't like you going alone."

"Didn't say I was going alone," Sylvie said. "I'm picking up Tierney Wales on the way out of town."

"The *Ghoul*? Like that's any better—"

"Later, Alex," Sylvie said. "Actually, wait—you want to look up monster myths in the Everglades? Just on the off chance that I'm dealing with something more monster, less magic."

"Swamp apes, chupacabras, three-tailed gators," Alex said. "Cryptozoology? Be still my heart." The words were delivered flat, deadpan, but Sylvie thought there might be a genuine thread of excitement in Alex's tone. Alex did so love the out of the ordinary.

"Just don't get sucked too much into monster geekdom."

Alex sighed. "Fine, fine. You sure about the Ghoul? I thought he was small-potatoes magic, a collector, not backup material."

Sylvie changed lanes, slipping around an obstructionist driver puttering along in the fast lane, garnering curses and blaring horns. It was getting too hard to hear Alex chattering away.

"I think Tierney Wales is a lot smarter and a lot more sneaky than I gave him credit for," Sylvie said. "At least, I'm hoping so. I don't have a lot of credit left with the local witches, and I need a researcher."

"And you think you've got credit with him?"

Sylvie hung up on Alex, content in the knowledge that

she could blame it on traffic later. She doubted Wales would be glad to see her, but she thought she could still make him see things her way.

· · ·

PARKING IN OPA-LOCKA DURING THE DAY WAS NO LESS NERVE-wracking than parking at night. Young men hung out on the corners, too bored, too restless, too angry to be anything but a threat. And they were far less dangerous than the watchers she couldn't see. Sylvie parked as close as she could to Wales's apartment, bumping the truck up over the broken curb and bringing it to a halt in the scrub grass and gravel. She showed off her holster as she swung herself out of the truck cab, moved with purpose and intent, and, though the men catcalled her briefly, they didn't rouse themselves to more.

Even so, wariness tightened her shoulders and chest; if Wales was going to stick around in south Florida, he was going to have to move. She ducked peeling paint as she went through the doorway, maneuvered her way up the cluttered staircase, avoiding the detritus, the empty soup cans, the empty bottles, broken glass, snarls of fishing line, all of it designed to trip a careless visitor.

The last time she'd come to see Wales, it had been dark, and the halls had been shadowed corridors with burned-out bulbs. Daylight made no difference. The shadows were the same, and the smell was worse with the heat of the sun seeping through the plaster.

Second floor—Wales's one-room apartment, and Sylvie pounded on the door, keeping a wary eye on the hallway, peeling paint the least of the blight visible in the gloom. "C'mon, Wales, I know you're home."

Lie, of course; she *hoped* he was home. Hard to tell. Last time she'd shown up unannounced and pounded on the door, Wales had slapped her into soul shock with a Hand of Glory; she'd woken tied to a chair. She thought they were on better terms now. Or maybe he'd just had second thoughts about using necromantic talismans after the whole mess with Odalys. Maybe he'd had second thoughts about staying in the city at all, and she was kicking a dead dog.

She stopped knocking, stopped calling his name, and just listened.

Scuffling from the other side of the door. Rat? Particularly large roach? A soft murmur that might be a voice in distress or one whispering threats. A chill brushed her skin, a drift like an air conditioner kicking on where there was none. Sylvie drew her gun; the door opened soundlessly before her, ushering her in.

Wales was pressed face-first against the wall, a young man leaning into him, skin-close, blade in his hand. Either the attacker was deaf or insanely determined because he didn't bother to turn around. Then again, Wales was a necromancer, and it was never a good idea to release a magic-user once you'd started threatening them.

"Hey," Sylvie snapped.

The young man forced Wales around, kicked his legs out from under him. Wales went down hard on his bony knees, wincing. Wales might be magically talented, but he wasn't physically strong. His pet ghosts took care of physical danger. So where were they? Sylvie licked dry lips.

The man's knife stayed tight on Wales's throat, a strange weapon when guns were easy to come by; but then, the attacker was a strange weapon himself. He dressed like the men outside, but he wore their clothes like a costume. His eyes were cold, purposeful, and calm, with none of the formless anger she associated with the Miami gangs. The knife, now that Sylvie could see it as more than a quick shine, had symbols etched into its blade.

Tread carefully, her dark voice suggested. This was magic versus magic, and she had a gun. Sometimes, that was like quenching a fire. Sometimes, it was like touching a lit match to black powder.

Sylvie let out a steady breath, and said, "Did I come by at a bad time?"

Wales said, "Depends on if you've got a lighter on you."

His long-fingered hands reached toward her, and the knife man jerked him back. Sylvie got a quick look at something Wales had wanted her to see: the gape of his jacket pocket—and the Hand of Glory within it. A tool that could drop the attacker in a second. Of course, it would drop Sylvie, too. Even if there were some way to light it without turning Wales's shirt into a torch.

The knife man dug the very point of his blade into Wales's neck, skin and blood swallowing the tip. The temperature in the room dropped precipitously; the knife man's teeth chattered once, then the symbols on the knife began to glow. Wales shuddered, face going grey with more than pain; whatever spell he was attempting was fighting him.

"Call it off," the knife man said, gritting his teeth. Sylvie could see his skin raised in goose bumps from five feet away.

"Marco," Wales breathed.

The air warmed; the knife's glowing symbols faded back to scratches in the metal. "Good choice," the knife man said.

"Better than yours," Sylvie said. "Attacking a necromancer in his own home."

"Lady, just walk away. The Ghoul is going to send a message for me."

"I'm not the walking-away type," Sylvie said. She narrowed her gaze. It was going to come down to bullets. Something about the way he said "message" made her think that the words were going to be written with Wales's blood and bone. It made the risk smaller for her. If Wales was going to die whether she shot or not . . .

"Shadows—" Wales slurred. He was listing to the side, and the blood was still sliding down the edge of the knife, a crimson drizzle on the floor. Not a bad injury, but he looked shocky. Maybe it was the spell on the knife; maybe it was simply fear. Either way, she thought, time was getting short.

"*You're* Shadows?" the knife man said. "Then listen. Odalys has a message for you."

Sylvie raised her gun. She had no interest in anything Odalys had to say.

"If she can kill a necromancer from a jail cell, what do you think she could do to your sister, Zoe?"

Fear and fury ran twin bolts of sensation through her body. Her finger twitched on the trigger. Both Wales and the would-be assassin flinched. Zoe was already protected, Sylvie thought, and backed herself from the edge. After the first night alone—post Odalys—Zoe had decided that staying with Val Cassavetes at her well-warded estate where she could learn more magic trumped the need to show she could be independent.

"Don't bother," the knife man said. "I'm protected."

"Yeah?" Sylvie said. She studied the talisman he indicated with his chin, a stone amulet with more of the same carved symbols that decorated the knife. She felt the grin spread wide across her face, all toothy nastiness—she recognized that talisman, knew what it was good for. And what it wasn't.

Sylvie fired; the tense hush in the room exploded, and when the echoes of the gun and the knife man's shout faded, a new tension took hold. The knife man slammed down to one knee, a hand clamped over his shoulder; his knife hand dangled, the blade dripping steadily onto the floor as if it were an oversaturated towel. Wales pushed away from him like a swimmer leaping into blue waters, skidding forward, and showing sense enough to stay out of Sylvie's line of fire.

The knife man cursed, anger and fear and outrage all mingled together.

"You should know your tools better," Sylvie said. "That talisman is protection against the *dead*, protection against *necromancy*. This gun? Is all real-world."

The knife man pressed himself against the wall, his blood adding new swirls to the already stained wallpaper. His fingers tightened on the knife, considering coming back at her, at Wales. Definitely a pro. Sylvie liked big-caliber guns, liked the way they knocked men down and kept them there. This guy was used to being knocked down but not out. She aimed again, and said, "Don't. You delivered her message. Now deliver mine.

"Odalys needs to stay away from my life, my family, my friends, and my city. If she knows what's healthy for her, she'll stay tucked up nice and tight in prison and behave herself."

"She's a witch; she'll eat your heart—"

"Someone's been watching too much Disney," Sylvie said. "Go on. Get out. Give her my message."

He rose; she tracked his movement, kept the gun leveled at his heart. "By the way, leave the knife."

He growled, dropped it, and she shifted stance enough to let him sidle around her, hand white-knuckled on his shoulder. Sylvie kicked the door closed after him.

"You got careless," she said. Wales glared up at her, untangled himself from the heap he was in, and folded himself into a seated position.

"I'd noticed, thank you," he said. "You put Odalys in jail? Guess that means you saved the day."

"Something like that," she said. "Get up, Wales. We gotta go."

"I'm all packed," Wales said. His voice shook, as did the hand he pressed to his neck. The blood seemed to have stopped, though, and Sylvie felt her shoulders relax.

"So you are," she said, allowing herself the luxury of looking around now that there wasn't a knife-wielding assassin taking up her attention. The room had been bare the last time she saw it—furnished with a single table, a chair, a futon, and decorated by a dozen or more Hands of Glory dangling from the ceiling. Now the mobile from hell was packed away, only small hooks showing that anything had once hung from the ceiling, and the futon was covered with taped-shut cardboard boxes. "Leaving town?"

"That was the plan," he said. He pushed himself to his feet, a scarecrow rising, making the room seem suddenly smaller. "Thought I might have made myself unwelcome."

Sylvie's response faded before she voiced it. The puddle of blood—Wales's and the assassin's mingled—was disappearing, small half circles curving inward, revealing the linoleum squares in damp spots. "What the hell—"

"Marco," Wales murmured.

Sylvie grimaced. Marco, the murdered convict. The ghost associated with Wales's favorite Hand of Glory. "I thought they snacked on souls, not blood."

Wales didn't look at her, let his gaze fall to his blood-spotted hands. "Some ghosts like both."

"And you just let them wander loose?"

"Marco and I came to a new agreement."

"Well, it doesn't seem like a good one. Where was he when you were attacked?"

Wales raised his head, grinned. "Doing the only thing he could. Letting you in. Amazing what a little independence in a ghost can get you."

The blood on the floor began disappearing again; Sylvie was torn between being creeped out that she couldn't see him, and grateful. Her imagination was bad enough, showing her a man kneeling facedown in a puddle of blood and licking pale lips.

"Get your shit and let's get out of here," she said.

"Where'd the we come from, Shadows? I'm leaving. You're not invited."

"Stop fussing and be grateful. I just want a consult on a case. It's right up your alley. Dead people."

"It's been two days!" he said.

"You've been hanging around the dead too long. Life moves fast," she said. "C'mon, I'll let you store your boxes in my office. I'll even buy you lunch."

She hefted the first box—distressingly light and rustling— eight boxes in the room, and she had to have picked up his box with the Hands of Glory. . . . But she'd lose her momentum if she dropped it and danced around, shaking off the squeamish.

He growled. "Y'know, Shadows, I thought Southern women were supposed to be sweet and courteous. You're pushier than a damn wheelbarrow."

"Yeah, yeah, bitch too much, and I'll take you to Mickey D's instead of someplace good. Time's a-wasting, Wales."

He caved all at once, his scarecrow body easing from the stiffness he'd been holding tight.

"Fine. Fine. But it's going to cost you more than a lunch. I want a consult fee."

"Everyone's greedy," she said. "Hurry it up, Wales. And hey, do we bring that knife or what?"

Wales looked back at it, his aggravation swapping back out for remembered fear. "Only if you need a knife that can hurt ghosts."

Sylvie shook her head and laughed. "Odalys. Christ. She would have been better off just sending someone to shoot you through your window. There's a convenient roof right across the way. That's the problem with you magic-users, always reaching for the esoteric answer."

"I'm so glad you've thought of ways to kill me," Wales said. He kicked the knife toward the wall and stalked out.

"Don't take it so personally," she said. "It's my job. Besides, it's not like she didn't have a go at me already." Even as she said it, she was wondering. Why would Odalys bother to send a messenger to threaten Zoe when she'd already sent a witch to kill Sylvie? Threats only meant something if there was someone alive to feel threatened.

While Wales loaded boxes in her pickup, Sylvie took the opportunity to call Zoe. There was a small but quantifiable difference between knowing her sister was safe at Val's, and *knowing* it. Zoe picked up just before the phone went to voice mail, and said, "Too early! Call me later," and hung up. Sylvie doubted she'd ever really woken up. Zoe liked her sleep. But hearing that familiar whine had soothed the worst of her nerves. Sylvie called Val also, got the machine. No surprise there. Even if Val had agreed to take care of Zoe, to teach her Magic 101, AKA how not to get yourself killed in a truly freakish fashion, it didn't mean things were copacetic between Sylvie and Val. That was going to take some time.

"Hey, Val," Sylvie said. "Just a heads-up. Odalys sent a magically armed thug after Wales, and he made noises about coming for Zoe, too."

Wales returned, sweating, pushing his hair out of his face, and gave her a dirty look. "We'd be out of here faster if you'd help."

It took them three silent trips to get the rest of the boxes into the truck, and Sylvie spent the time thinking about Odalys with increasing grimness. She'd known that jail wasn't going to be the end of things if they even managed to get Odalys convicted. The charges Suarez had arrested her on were approximations at best, real-world analogues for magical misbehavior, and hell, Suarez hadn't even had jurisdiction. A single wrong step, and the entire house of cards would fall, setting Odalys free. Sylvie had been willing to wait and see. That no longer looked like an option.

The problem was that the bars imprisoning Odalys also protected her. Odalys had contacts she could reach on the outside, but Sylvie's only friend on the inside was in the hospital and out of the loop. Still, something had to be done.

Sylvie didn't know if it was just a bad idea, or a *really* bad idea, that made her think she had a solution.

But first . . . she battened down the last of Wales's boxes and slung herself into the truck's cab. The Ghoul was a sullen presence in her passenger seat, idly tapping his fingers against his inner jacket pocket.

Like her, wearing a jacket in the Miami heat was more a matter of practicality than comfort. Sylvie used her collection of Windbreakers to help disguise the gun she carried at the small of her back. Wales used his ratty leather jacket for much the same reason, though in Miami, her gun was less disturbing than what he carried. She eyed the bulge over his heart, and said, "So, why cart Marco's Hand around? Thought you came to a new agreement. Gave him independence."

He looked at her for a long moment, a narrow, unwelcome gaze, before he deliberately settled on an answer. "I find his presence comforting," he said.

She licked her lips, and said, "That's payback for the sniper comment, isn't it?"

"You tell me, Shadows. Since you know me so well."

The boxes slid as she made a turn onto the highway, and she sighed. Time for a little Alex diplomacy maybe. "Sorry. I don't like Odalys's threatening people I care about." She kept it vague, let him wrap himself into one of those people if he chose.

He let the leather seat cradle him more firmly, his spine losing some of its rigidity. Apologies could do that even if they weren't sincere. It was the veneer of civilization— the hope of rational discourse. It worked more often than Sylvie cared to let Alex know.

Thing was, she did care about Wales more than she wanted him to know. Alex had done more digging in the days between their first interaction and this one, and had pulled up enough on his past to let Sylvie know that Wales was pretty much like her. They'd both been normal once. Both cared about their friends and family, were the designated problem-solvers, the ones who just couldn't sit by and let trouble happen to other people. Then they'd run into the *Magicus Mundi* and learned a whole new world of trouble existed.

Their paths had forked at that point. Sylvie had picked up a gun; Wales, like a child, had been formed by what he'd seen—the CIA and Hands of Glory. In other words: necromancy and paranoia.

She could have wished he'd gone a kinder, fluffier route, except the *Magicus Mundi* didn't reward gentle tactics, and she knew better than to rue things that couldn't be changed. If she ever started that, she'd be useless, left mired in hopeless nostalgia for an easier time, when she lived in ignorance. No one should ever strive to live in ignorance.

"Where we going?" Wales asked. "You said you had a job?"

"I'm not sure what I've got other than an unholy mess," Sylvie said. "You follow the news at all?"

Wales shook his head. "News feeds the fear."

"There's something new and nasty in the Everglades—"

"And it involves necromancy?"

"It involves dead things waking up and savaging people."

"Zombies?"

"Bear," Sylvie said. "Or so I was given to understand."

Wales patted his pocket again, that nervous tell. Sylvie put her attention back on the road, suddenly quite sure that he'd told her nothing but the truth; that Marco's severed Hand was a comfort to him.

With Wales's worldly possessions sliding gently in the back of her pickup, with the reminders of his personality flaws—things she'd glossed over in her memories since she needed him—she decided that stopping at the office was not only desirable but an absolute necessity.

If she dragged Wales straight out to the Everglades, all his stuff still boxed, after her unfortunate comments about shooting him, he'd probably assume she was clearing out one more necromancer from the city. He looked like he expected betrayal at any minute.

When Sylvie pulled the truck to a stop outside her office, Alex was waiting in the doorway, framed nicely by midday sun, and with Sylvie's thoughts still running on Odalys and on sniper shots, the sight sparked aggravation and concern. Alex had the self-preservation instincts of a lemming.

3

Monsters

ALEX MADE WAY FOR THEM AND THEIR PARADE OF BOXES, PROPPED herself up on the desk, and watched as the boxes stacked up in the kitchenette. "Is that Tierney Wales?" she asked on one of Sylvie's trips in that coincided with one of his exits.

"Yeah," she said. "That's the Ghoul."

Alex frowned. "He's skinny."

"So feed him a sandwich. Just don't adopt him," Sylvie said. She dropped the box she held, listening to the rustling of dried flesh scrabbling at cardboard; she'd picked the damn short straw again. She kicked the box toward the closet, wanting to wash her hands of an imaginary contamination. And Wales carried these things in his pockets.

Alex was still rubbernecking, watching Wales stack boxes outside the door. "He doesn't look like a necromancer. He looks like a stressed-out grad student."

She caught Sylvie's scowl and flushed. "Okay, okay, necromancers don't wear black robes and chant all the time. I get it. Just . . . he looks . . . scared. I didn't think necromancers got scared."

"Yeah, about that," Sylvie said. "You up for a vacation?"

"What?" Alex narrowed her gaze. "You're trying to get me out of the way again."

"Better me than Odalys," Sylvie said. "Someone tried to flambé me in the office last night."

"Is that what happened to the bell?" Alex asked. "I saw it had gone all melty."

"And you just stuck around?"

"I figured whatever happened had happened, and I knew you were all right. So it didn't seem that important."

"It's important," Sylvie said. "I think it's Odalys. She sent someone out to slice and dice Wales. There was even some mention of taking out Zoe. Thank god for Val." She grimaced at the welling of gratitude in her breast. Not her usual sentiment when it came to the witch. But after Val had seen Zoe's occultly stained hand and forearm, she'd decreed that Zoe needed protecting.

"And you, you've been caught in the magical cross fire before, Alex. You need to be more careful."

Alex waved a dismissive hand. "I am careful. Besides, Odalys doesn't even know I exist. Sucks about Zoe and Wales, though. What are we going to do to protect them?"

That was Alex all over. An abundance of caution. For other people. Reckless trust in her own safety. It made no sense at all. It wasn't like Alex had led a charmed life even before she'd become Sylvie's partner.

"Zoe's in no trouble right now," she said. "Not tucked under Val's wing. The Cassavetes estate is proof against pretty much anything but nuclear magic."

"If she stays there," Alex said. She surged off the desk and opened the door for Wales, helped him steady the last few boxes. "Hi. Tierney, right? I'm Alex. Sylvie's partner and all-around researcher."

He blinked at her, her bleached-blond hair, her bright makeup, the pink-nailed hand held out toward him the moment the boxes were down, and took a step backward. "Hi?"

Figured, Sylvie thought. Give him death, give him antagonism, give him trouble, and Wales was mouthy and cynical. Face-to face with a friendly smile, his personality locked up.

"So did Sylvie tell you what was going on? Bears? That's new. I mean, I get werewolves, I'm used to werewolves at this point, but bears?" Alex chattered easily, pushing Wales toward the kitchenette. "Guess it's 'cause we don't have bears around much. You think there are more shape-shifting bears in the West? Were-bears? Like Care Bears, only not?"

Wales looked back at Sylvie, eyes wide and entreating as they hadn't been even when faced with a knife-wielding assassin. Sylvie smothered her desire to laugh and didn't step in to bail him out. Wales gnawed his lip, then said, "I don't know. I'm mostly about necromancy. I don't . . . Shape-shifters? Shadows, I don't know anything about shape-shifters. If that's what you brought me here for, then you're wasting my time and yours."

"I do know about shape-shifters," she said. "I know they don't play dead well enough to be body-bagged before they wake up and change shape. These women were dead. Cold and dead. You need to pay better attention, Wales. I told you that on the road."

His response was a petulant huff better suited to a teenager than an adult and was followed by another spew of backchat that made Sylvie wish he was as tongue-tied around her as he was around Alex. "Well, you'll have to excuse me some since I was still thinking on the man that came to knife me. Normal people need recovery time for that sorta thing."

Alex's eyes widened in sympathy, and her urgings that he sit down and have a *pastelito* and a coffee overrode Sylvie's reflexive snort of, "You're holding yourself up as normal now, Ghoul?"

When Alex's fussing looked like it might drive Wales away, Sylvie said, "Alex." It was more than a reprimand; Sylvie had Odalys to deal with, and her idea didn't look any better now than it had earlier, but it was all she had.

"You need something?" Alex said.

"You still got . . . Wright's contact info?"

In the kitchenette, Wales shot to attention, nearly dropping the paper plate Alex had pressed on him. "Hey, I nearly forgot about your possession case. You got rid of his ghost all right?"

Sylvie snapped, "Mind your own business. Alex, you got it?"

"Yeah," Alex said, slowly, a drawl that nearly matched Wales's natural speech and was alien in her mouth, a mark of her uncertainty. "But didn't you . . . I mean, you've got it, too, right?"

"You're the one who's going to call, though," Sylvie said. "Just let him know about Odalys's bid for power, would you?"

She wanted to call; her fingers itched for the phone. She wanted to hear the cadences of his speech in Adam Wright's voice. But Demalion had a job to do—two jobs, neither simple. Better to wait until he'd dealt with one or the other. ISI or Wright's family.

Wales shook his head. "What do you think a Chicago cop can do about a Miami necromancer? You're grasping at—" His gaze narrowed. "That ghost of his was from the ISI. You gave the body to the ghost?"

"*Gave* isn't the word I'd use," Sylvie said.

"Christ," Wales said. "And the man inside, the man who owned the body? What'd you do with *his* soul?" He set the plate back on the counter, the pastry untouched.

"It's none of your business," Sylvie said again.

"Death magic is my business, and if I'm going risk myself in the swamps with you, I'd like to know that you're not going to sell me out for your own—"

"She *didn't.*" Alex stopped them both. She slammed herself into her seat, her coffee mug onto the desk. It sloshed but didn't spill. "It wasn't her fault. Wasn't anyone's fault. Wright died. Demalion got the body, but there was no taking or stealing or anything like that."

"Were you there?" Wales asked. "Or is that what she told you?"

Sylvie gritted her teeth. "Alex. Call him. See if he can

get a word to the ISI gossip chain; see if they can be bothered to take an interest. Maybe we can make her their problem. Wales, I'm going to say this once more. Leave this topic alone."

"He came to you for help," Wales pushed.

Sylvie said, "I did what I could." Her throat felt tight, a little ragged, but the conviction shone through, surprising even her. The guilt she'd been afraid of for days crumbled. It was true. She could grieve for Adam Wright's death; she could be uncomfortable seeing his body walking around with a new owner; but ultimately Wright had chosen to die as he'd lived: helping people.

If she could summon his spirit back from whatever afterlife he'd found, she thought that Wright's regrets would be sharp but few. It might be self-serving thinking—Wales clearly believed she was to blame—but Sylvie was going to cling to it. She was tired of grief and guilt.

"So, monsters and dead things that kill cops. You ready, Ghoul?"

Alex said, "Call Suarez first. He wanted to talk to you. Wouldn't leave the message with me. You might let him know that I'm in on the big stuff; it makes message taking a lot easier."

"Hey," Sylvie said. "Caution's a nice trait. 'Sides, you ever think that it wasn't you he was worried about but whoever might have been listening in on his end? Cop who talks about magic like a real thing might get a bad reputation pretty quick."

She dialed as she spoke, hoping that Suarez's call meant he was out of the hospital, hoping he'd be more lucid, could give her more to go on. She was willing to go out to the Everglades and play monster-hunter, but she'd prefer all the information she could get.

The phone clicked over. Lourdes answered. Sylvie bit her lip, and said, "Adelio Suarez, please," hoping if she kept it short, kept it professional, there'd be a chance that the woman wouldn't recognize her voice. Lourdes sighed but passed the phone over.

"Shadows?" Lio asked. "Are you at the site?"

His voice was sharper than it had been yesterday, less blurred by shock, pain, or drugs. Agitated, though. Sylvie regretted calling; she knew how this was going to go. Cop stuck in bed when there were problems to solve—he wanted to backseat drive.

"Not yet," Sylvie said. "Did you remember anything else?"

"Make sure you're not seen. By the cops, or the damn strange suits that showed up. And the press is swarming, so stay out of their way also."

"Lio—"

"And don't use my name if you get caught, or call on me for help. Odalys's lawyer is screaming, and my name's not what it should—"

"Suarez! I get it. Call me if you have something new to tell me."

"Tell me what you find." Suarez got out a final demand just before Sylvie disconnected. Her nerves felt stung and jostled; she loathed being treated like an idiot, like a subordinate. Lio needed to remember he was her client, not her boss.

"Do you need any stuff before we head out?" Sylvie asked Wales. He jerked as if she'd caught him doing something other than eyeing Alex sidelong, then flushed brick red across his pale cheekbones.

"Stuff?" he asked.

Alex grinned, and Sylvie reminded herself to have the talk with Alex. No dating necromancers. She took another, more objective look at Wales. No dating necromancers even if they were halfway to good-looking by daylight.

"Magical tools?" Sylvie said. "To help at the scene?"

"Now, see, let's chat about that for a bit. What exactly do you want me to do?" He held up a hand, said, "Not that I'm saying I won't help. I just want to know what you expect of me."

Sylvie sat on the desktop, swung her feet for a second, thinking. It was a fair question. "To be honest, Wales, that depends on what you can do. At bare minimum, I'd like you to take a look at the scene and see if you can sense and/or identify whether necromancy was used and what its purpose was."

He frowned, twisted his hands over, stared at his knuckles. "Yeah," he said. "I can do that."

"Special equipment?"

"Just me. And Marco."

"Marco?" Alex asked.

Sylvie said, "You want to show her Marco?"

Wales rose abruptly and went outside, stood squinting up at the sun.

Alex wrinkled her brow, gnawed her lip. "So what'd I say?"

"Marco's his pet ghost," Sylvie said. "He carries Marco's Hand around in his pocket."

"His . . . Oh," Alex said. Her lips tightened. She pushed her coffee cup away from her as if the cream and sugar had gone bad.

"Necromancer," Sylvie said. "Not a clean magic. Something to remember, Alex." She pushed off the desk, ambled out into the sunlight after Wales, and left Alex with something to think about.

Necromancy left a bad taste in Sylvie's mouth, more so than any of the other branches of human magics she'd come across. It seemed . . . cannibalistic in a way the other branches didn't. Witchcraft and sorcery were all about turning the world to suit yourself. Necromancy was about the unhealthy mingling of life and death, going so far as to elevate the dead above the living.

Sylvie climbed into her truck and found Wales waiting for her, Marco's Hand in his lap. The sight of it—withered and dried flesh drawn up tight over muscle turned to jerky, the fingers curled tight against the palm, the nails rusty gold with the remnant of old flames—made her already tightened jaw clench until her teeth creaked.

"So, new deal with Marco. Anything I need to know about that?"

"Marco and I can interact at will now," Wales said. "He doesn't sleep anymore. Is that what you wanted to know?"

"Jesus, Wales. Does that mean he can soul-bite people at will? I can't let—"

"No, no." Wales shook his head in extra emphasis. "I still light him up for that. Just . . . he's around now. That's all I'm going to tell you."

Sylvie licked her lips, tasted cool air on her tongue, and wondered with a shudder if the chill was Marco's influence or her laboring air conditioner. "You must have been crazy lonely when you thought that mod up," she said, and got a glare in response.

"Look," she said. "You didn't approve of Odalys's modifying the Hands. What am I supposed to think when you start messing around in the same—"

"I'm not her," Wales said. "I know what I'm doing." And that was the first taste of sorcerous arrogance he'd ever given off. Pride in his abilities. Interesting.

Sylvie pulled the truck out into traffic, and said, "So you're more powerful than you like to let on. That's fair. I understand the urge to fly under the radar. Got a question for you, though. Can you yank a possessing ghost out of a body?"

"Thought you didn't blame your man—Demalion, was it?"

"Not him," Sylvie said. "Odalys had one success. There's a teenage body walking around Coconut Grove with an old murderer in her skin."

"Double-souled?"

"No, the original's gone. Devoured."

"So, you just want to drop her dead in her tracks? But you'll let your boyfriend keep his new body?"

"He didn't kill anyone to get it. Look, can you do it or not?"

Wales shrugged. "Depends. A soul that's crossed death shouldn't fit all that well in living flesh. But it adapts. Like a new organ, rejection's a risk, especially in the beginning."

"Can you eyeball that? Get me an idea of how fragile she is?"

"I ain't killing her," Wales said. "I got some sense of self-preservation. I don't want the cops coming up with my name when they've got a body they can't explain."

Sylvie said, "Fine." She could work on changing his mind later. Hell, he'd been angry on Wright's behalf —how much angrier would he be once he saw Bella? Or the body that had been Bella. Wales was a man and a Texan at that. Young, attractive . . . murdered? She bet Bella would push all his buttons.

"All right. We're going to give the cops and the press a little bit longer to get out of the Everglades. We're going to swing by and visit Patrice. If I'm paying you a consulting fee for the day, I'm going to get my money's worth."

• • •

SYLVIE PULLED UP JUST AS PATRICE WAS LETTING HERSELF OUT OF her house. It was worthy of a photo shoot, the young woman in a sheer sundress on a picturesque front stoop, all smoothed Mexican-tile steps, wrought-iron banister, and flowering bougainvillea.

Patrice saw Sylvie's truck and hesitated, her hand on the door latch. Then she closed the door behind her, stepped out into the sunlit day, and turned her face up as if to bask in it, a gloat that she was alive to enjoy the day. Silver hoops dangled from her ears, small rubies glinting at the bottoms of the curves.

Sylvie climbed out of the truck; Patrice cocked one hip, leaned up against the banister, and waited for Sylvie to reach her.

"Shadows," she said, taking the battle directly to Sylvie. "I could have a restraining order taken out against you."

"So why don't you? Afraid your new parents wouldn't understand? How's that working out for you . . . Bella? You all still a happy family? Or do they get it, deep down, that you're not their daughter? You're the woman who killed her." Sylvie's voice was thin and tight, a thread of rage well controlled. Patrice could in fact have a restraining order signed out; the Alvarezes were rich, well connected, played golf with an entire courtroom's worth of judges and lawyers.

Wales stepped out of the truck, impatient, graceless, drawing Patrice's attention. Patrice stiffened all over as if she recognized Wales. Or at least the threat he might pose to a newly embodied ghost. She relaxed when Wales lounged back against the side of the truck, squinting at her.

"You know," Sylvie said, "you're a cliché, Patrice. An old woman clinging to youth, and really? A dress that short? At your age?"

Patrice growled, a rattle in her throat that sounded like Death given voice and nothing like a teenager.

"Having trouble keeping up the part?" Sylvie asked. "You're not a good actor. How's the body fitting? Chafing? Coming loose around the edges?"

"Is that your plan?" Patrice said. "Shake me from my flesh? It *is* mine. I've taken precautions to keep my soul in this flesh. This very lovely flesh. So your pet necromancer can't do squat. I don't think I ever enjoyed my body this much before. When I was a teen, it was the thirties. Good girls didn't get spray tans, hair extensions, bikini waxes. . . . And the cosmetics are to die for." She pulled a lipstick from her pocket, glossed her lips, and blew a kiss at Sylvie.

She shot a quick glance at Wales, who dropped his chin in a reluctant nod. Patrice was telling the truth. She'd stolen that body, and now she'd strung it tight with antitheft security.

Her temper flared as red-hot as the lipstick. Sylvie snatched it away from Patrice, then found herself possessed by a wicked inspiration. "Trusting to magic to protect you? Let's see what it can do against this." She sketched a bloody symbol with the lipstick across the yellow enamel paint of the front door. A rough, enigmatic image, two flat circles, two attached triangles, a line binding them together.

Patrice drew back, her breath slipping through clenched teeth as if waiting for an axe to fall.

When nothing happened except Sylvie throwing the ruined lipstick at her feet, Patrice laughed. "What's that supposed to do?"

"You'll find out," Sylvie said. "Watch your back, Patrice. I will be."

She turned, dragged Wales away from his brow-wrinkled contemplation of the lipstick sigil, and drove them off.

It was a mile or so down the road that he spoke. "So what all was that about? What'd you try to bring down on her head?"

"Nothing at all," Sylvie gritted out. "It was a bluff. She just pissed me off. If I can't kill her, and you can't evict her—"

He shook his head. "She's wrapped up good and tight in some type of protection spell. I don't have the magic to even slow her down."

"Then the least I can do is scare her, maybe make her day run rough."

"A bluff?"

"It's a petty victory," Sylvie said. "I know that." God, did she know that; her internal voice was still demanding bloodshed, hadn't been appeased at all. Its appetite had only been sharpened by the brief fear on Patrice's face. "Sometimes," she told Wales. "Sometimes, just making 'em flinch feels good."

Another several miles, and he said, "Are you sure it was random? It's just . . . It kind of struck me familiar like. Something I've seen before."

Her hands tightened on the wheel. It felt familiar to her, too. Not the look of it, but the creation, the motion of it. It mimicked the blade work her little dark voice had guided her through in her dream.

"Probably," Sylvie agreed. "It's not like I wander around memorizing random magical sigils. It's probably some company's logo. I've probably just invoked the wrath of Starbucks on her ass."

Wales's lips twitched, creased in a smile. "Starbucks is a curse all on its own."

. . .

BY THE TIME THEY MADE IT OUT TO THE EVERGLADES, THE SUN WAS AT full zenith, and the road before them was smudgy with heat mirage. Sylvie wondered if it was the idea of slogging through the heat of the day or a fear of the unknown that made Wales relax into a tiny smile when the nearest access point to the crime scene was still jammed with cars—cops and press alike.

"Don't get your hopes up," Sylvie said, driving by. "We're going around back. The route Tatya took me." She cast another glance over her shoulder at the huddle of press drinking sodas out of their cars, AC cranked high, and thought maybe Cachita had a point. Reporters should be like Kipling's mongoose, filled with the need to "Go and find out."

He sighed, and said, "You sure about this? It's not wise."

"Client wants what the client wants," Sylvie said. It was easiest to think of Suarez that way. She owed him a favor; he had things he wanted explained. Therefore: client. Though she'd better set Alex on to a bunch of the littler cases—spouse shadowing, background checks, and the like—or they wouldn't have enough money to pay Wales and Tatya, not to mention the rent and themselves.

Bright side was, keeping Alex out and about made her less a sitting duck should the nameless witch make another attempt on the office and Sylvie. Downside, Alex would bitch. She hated doing research on the run.

Sylvie turned off the main road two miles farther on, trading asphalt for dirt and limestone gravel, a sandy, weedy stretch of lane just wide enough for her truck.

"They won't notice us coming 'round the back?" Wales asked, found his own answer as the track they were on curved abruptly, taking them away from the scene of the crime. Sylvie continued the drive for another few minutes until she spotted the tiny yellow flag planted near the base of some scrub.

She pulled the truck over and cut the engine; it gave a diesel cough and left them in silence. "ATV track. We'll have to walk it, but it should bring us up pretty close, then we can just wait for them to clear out."

He whined in his seat, and she said, "I brought snacks?"

He opened the door, and said, "Hope you brought water. Hot as fuck out there."

"A Texas boy complaining about the heat?" Sylvie said.

"A Texas boy smart enough to make a career in Web design. Indoors. You know. Before."

Before the *Magicus Mundi* stuck its fingers into his life, changed his path.

"There's water in the lockbox; never travel without it." She chucked the keys at him. "Come on, Tex."

"Tex?"

"You rather I go back to calling you *Ghoul*?"

The walk they took was quiet, almost pleasant—the scuff of their shoes in the trail dust, carefully carved along what passed for high ground in the 'Glades. Wales wasn't a chatterer, just slunk along beside her, studying the landscape—all grey-green and gold—with the curiosity of a man who spent the better part of his life between four walls. There was water moving nearby, some slow tidal wash created by something moving through the river marsh. Turtle, maybe a soft-shelled slider, all push and glide. Her school field trips were years and an entire world away.

Even the heat wasn't too bad, not yet; Sylvie felt her bones relax like caramel beneath the sunlight's weight.

It took her long minutes to realize that the sun wasn't doing its job any longer, that despite the peace and quiet and the pressing warmth that urged languor, the muscles along her spine were slowly tightening, the sweat-damp hair at her nape prickling.

Beside her, Wales's head was up, looking around with more intent than before. No longer a tourist in a strange world but prey sensing a predator. His lips moved silently, some conversation not meant for her ears. Meant for his ghost companion, maybe.

Sylvie swallowed, her throat dry with more than heat and exertion. The sounds about them—plop of water, rustling grass, the cry of distant birds—just reminded her of how much was unseen around them. She settled a hand on her gun, the other locked tight around a water bottle, and tried not to think about alligators or panthers or any other predators that might be out there.

"Wales?" she said.

He shook his head briefly, and she wasn't sure if it was in response to her implied question or if he was still focused on Marco and hadn't heard her at all.

Sylvie checked her mental map. They were nearing the crime scene; some of the bird-cry sound might actually be human voices twisted by distance and the wind over the water. She licked her lips, thought, Go back? Give up because she got spooked? She felt like something was watching them—so what? That was the state of the world. Nature was nosy.

She stiffened her shoulders, twist-tied her empty water bottle to a belt loop to get her hands free. "Pick up the pace," she said, and moved on. She didn't give up, and she didn't turn tail without good reason. Sometimes, not even then.

They smelled the scene before they saw it, Wales wrinkling his nose against the stinging, acrid scent of burned metal and gasoline. Sylvie thought that was darkly funny. The Ghoul, thinking a little bit of char was bad? Then the breeze shifted and brought the underlying scent to her—burned flesh. She dropped her gaze and concentrated on breathing, trying not to think of the cops who had died.

The ground at her feet was growing dark and damp. They were leaving the ridge of the ATV trail, and the water level was rising. The saturated soil had taken on an oily sheen, contaminated by the explosion. It made the foot-

ing more slippery than it should have been, like a tattered
carpet laid over grease. The bird cry of voices stabilized,
became the sporadic chatter of men and women trying to
piece together a puzzle they didn't understand, frustrated
outbursts that allowed single words to drift in Sylvie's
direction.

Not finding any signs of a bomb.
Is that an alligator tooth?
Should have brought a porta potty.

Wales said, "So, what's the plan?" His voice was a
whisper, and even then, she twitched at the sound of it.
The sense of being watched was still strong and sharp in
her blood.

But there was nothing in any direction that she could
see. The slough ahead of them, ground ceding to water.
The hammock to their distant left, a low smudge of trees
on the horizon, crackling with birds.

Be careful, her little dark voice murmured. *Some things
don't need eyes to see.*

Sylvie shut it down. One paranoid companion per ex-
pedition was enough. Another last glance—saw grass, hammock, slough, the seeping track behind them, and sounds
of life everywhere: frogs, birds, the rustle of quick lizards.
Maybe there had been something or someone watching.
Something that had been still enough not to spook the
wildlife. Or maybe it had been and gone, and the only
spectators they needed to worry about were the police.

Stay careful.

"You getting anything at all?" she asked, keeping her
voice to a hush. "You picking up anything death-magical?"

"From this distance? No."

"So we wait for the cops to leave, then." Sylvie hesitated. Waiting had sounded okay in her office, but in the
actual 'Glades? For one thing, they weren't that well hidden, not by the landscape, anyway. But if they retreated,
they could miss any narrow window of opportunity that
might present itself.

"They look pretty damned entrenched to me. I'm not really in love with the idea of waiting until past dark to do my look around."

"You and me both," Sylvie said. The idea of lingering out there, exposed in the tall grass, was bad enough in daylight. In the dark? "We've got to get closer."

"All right," he said.

He drew out Marco's Hand and his lighter, and Sylvie said, "Wait, what?"

"What'd you think I was going to do?" Wales asked. "Put on a suit and pretend to be a cop? Sorry. I got just one spell that'll get us up close."

Sylvie growled. "You want me to ignore the fact that lighting up Marco is going to result in soul shock for people who already feel fragile? Some of those cops are cleaning up bits of their colleagues."

Wales shrugged. "Then you should have brought a different type of witch," he said. "One who could send them off chasing a will-o'-the-wisp or give them the compulsion to go back to the station. But you pissed off the local witches, and now you've just got me."

You could have called on Zoe, Sylvie's little dark voice whispered.

That was enough to steel her spine. Bad enough her little sister had gotten a yen for practicing magic, worse that she showed talent enough she had to be trained, worst of all would be Sylvie's *encouraging* her.

Two types of pragmatism warred in her, and, finally, she just shook it all off. "You light Marco, and I go down, too. I've had enough soul shock for a while."

Wales frowned. "There is that." He set Marco's Hand down on the grass, fumbled through his pockets some more. Sylvie kept a close eye on the Hand of Glory. Last thing they needed was some random raccoon running off with it. Problem with nature. It was always lurking, always hungry.

"Ah," Wales said, drew out a pocketknife, a convenience-store special, the kind that lived in plastic bins beside the dollar lighters. "Blood'll do it."

"Yours or mine?" she murmured, but the question was already answered. Wales dragged the thin, brittle blade across the heel of his hand, left a bloody smile slowly forming. He wiped the blade on his jeans, shoved it back into his pocket, then dipped his fingers into the blood.

"Hold still," he said, brought his fingers toward her face.

She shied back. "Blood goes where exactly?"

"On your skin," Wales said. "So Marco knows you're part of me."

"Marco was *licking* your blood earlier—"

"He won't lick this," Wales said. "Trust me."

He touched her cheeks, two quick strokes and a squiggle, some symbol she couldn't see; the temperature of her body, the heat of the day, was such that she didn't feel the dampness at first, only smelled the old-penny copper of it.

Then it started to trickle sluggishly down her skin, nothing like sweat, sticky and already going rank. She had to force herself to hold still for the next two touches, marking her forehead and chin. No point in doing this half-assed, and she really didn't like the idea of having her soul munched on by a ghost who wasn't all that fond of her.

The last time she'd seen Marco—more than just his remnant Hand—he'd gotten in her face and told her he killed women like her.

If there was anything that would break the deal between Wales and his pet ghost, it would probably be her: Recidivism was more than just a word, after all, and while alive, Marco had made a habit of killing women.

She was trusting Wales on two fronts here—that he knew what he was doing and that his word was good— and that made her nearly as edgy as the hunt they were on. She watched him, her vision narrowing until the flick of the lighter, his long, pale fingers, and bony knuckles, the quick and tiny spill of sparks, got eaten by the wash of the Hand of Glory coming alight.

The last time she'd seen Marco, they'd been confined and close in a single room. The last time she'd seen ghosts, they'd been focused on their victims. Both events left her utterly unprepared for the speed of Marco now.

Her breath went out in a rush, and Marco breezed through the small crowd of policemen and technicians, bending close, sending them into unconsciousness with a kiss—*a bite*—before they could even realize something was happening.

Marco moved like wind, a grey shape in the air, unfettered by human requirements of energy or space. He blew through the equipment, set one machine to shrieking an alarm, and took out the technician before she had time to turn her head. The woman crumpled, face-first, and Wales hissed in disapproval.

"What is it?" Sylvie said.

"Hurry up, *hurry up!*" Wales muttered more to himself than her, then broke, running with graceless haste through the slough, going knee deep in places, forcing his way through, leaving a muddy wake. Sylvie, finding a drier path, finally saw what Wales, with his greater height, had seen: The female technician was facedown in the water.

Marco hadn't changed at all since his death. Sylvie wished she could be surprised.

4

Magic and Monsters

SYLVIE PICKED UP HER PACE, FELT THE SAW GRASS LASH AGAINST her legs, heard the low hum of it rasping against her clothes; she got there as Wales manhandled the woman out of the water, checked her airways.

"She all right?" And wasn't that a careful distinction of *all right*? Was the soul-shocked woman still breathing? Morals and the *Magicus Mundi* didn't line up all that well.

"She is," Wales said. Marco shrugged, an insincere *oops*, "They all are," he said, nodding decisively as if saying it made it so.

"Yeah, let's just do this," Sylvie said. She directed her attention to the scene, trying to splice the two images together in her mind. When she'd been there last, it was a peaceful scene—minus the dead women, naturally—glimmering waters, green duckweed, saw grass stretching out toward the sloughs and the hammocks.

Now there was char everywhere, scraps of metal in the process of being collected; scorched grass, oily water, the detritus of investigation, and a double handful of dropped cops. Sylvie wandered over to the collected evidence bags, reading labels. Might as well start there.

There were two men fallen near the bags, dressed in Fed-standard suits, in Fed-standard colors—one blue, one black. Miami detectives had more sense, wore khakis and short-sleeved polo shirts. Sylvie pulled out the first man's ID: Dennis Kent, ISI. She burned his face into her memory. Odds were, she'd be seeing him again. Dark hair, grey flecked, a Roman nose. Soft hands.

The second man—dirty blond, smooth-skinned, a babe in the woods—was Nick O'Neal, and definitely the junior of the pair.

Strange suits, indeed. Lio's rumor mill had been right.

But these two looked more like an exploratory team than the first wave of an ISI incursion. Someone wanting to make sure that this was worth their time. Sylvie grimaced.

Using the Hand of Glory on them would probably go a long way to convincing them that this was ISI-interesting. Couldn't win for losing, sometimes.

In the background, Wales held a furious, whispered conversation with Marco, a series of snake hisses on the breeze. Sylvie tipped her head, let the air cool her skin, drying the blood on her face until the streaks pulled uncomfortably. She reached up to scratch, then saw Marco studying her, his hollow eyes eager even from twenty feet away, and dropped her hands. *Yeah, better not.*

She put their IDs back, flipped through the evidence bags.

"You sense anything? Find anything?" Sylvie asked. She was coming up blank, blanker, blankest. Yesterday, the landscape had held that strange charge to the air, the sense that magic had been used, had altered reality. Today, it was just heat, breeze, sun, water, smoke, oil. Nothing out of the ordinary at all. She slapped at a mosquito that made a heat-slow sortie at her exposed wrist and pulled her sleeves back down.

"Nothing much," Wales said. "Bit of a ghost presence. The dead cops. The burned woman. But they're only traces,

and they're fading fast. They're so far gone, holding 'em
back'd be nothing but an act of cruelty."

"You could do that?" Sylvie asked. "Pull them back?"
That made her twitchy. It wasn't just that he could keep
them there, but that Wales—scarecrow klutz of a man—
could pull their souls *away* from whatever gods lay waiting to claim them.

"Could. Won't," Wales said. "They can't tell me much
more than they already have, whispering about confusion
and being lost."

"You can hear them?"

Wales turned away from the empty space he was studying so intently that she knew he saw more than she could.
"You don't know much about necromancy, do you, Shadows?"

"Never needed to," she said.

Wales hmmed thoughtfully, then spotted an open cooler
of drinks, ice sparking against the sun, and said, "Thirsty?"

"Yeah," Sylvie said, caught the icy soda he tossed her
way with relief, set the can against her nape. "So we're
done here?"

"Nothing of death magic happened here," Wales said.
"At least, nothing powerful enough to linger. And you said
five dead women? That should have lingered." He raised the
can to his lips, lowered it without taking a drink. "You sure
they were dead?"

"They were underwater," she said, but she was thinking
of different angles. "They weren't breathing, weren't moving."

"Did you try to revive—"

"Wales, I took a look and got the hell gone."

He gnawed his lower lip, knelt among the charred rub-
ble that had been a police 'copter. He tilted his head as if
he were listening.

"They weren't dead," he said.

Something slow and miserable churned in her belly, a
flutter of guilt and professional embarrassment. She hadn't

even checked. She'd just seen the surface of things. And she knew better than to take things at face value.

"They weren't dead," he said again, and if she hadn't known better, she'd have assumed he was rubbing salt in the wound. But it was an echo in his voice, patiently repeating something he heard. Something a ghost was sharing.

He stood, staggered a little, and said, "Okay. The burned woman is the only one of the five women who is actually dead. Jennifer Costas."

"Could I have—"

He shook his head. "No. Jennifer burnt up because the spell binding them broke. It feels like a contingency plan of some sort. A magical if-then command. The others?"

"Fled," Sylvie said. "According to my witness, they got up and walked away."

"But Jennifer was restrained," Wales said, turning as if he could see the helicopter that her body had been strapped into. "Trapped."

"She was the only one who burned," Sylvie said. "If the spell broke—"

"She was the only one who couldn't get free," Wales said. He paced back and forth, raising clouds of soot, stumbling over metal fragments, making his mark on the scene. There would be no pretending that they hadn't been there. "She tried. Twisting. Tangled. Hot like spell fire in her veins. It's strange magic, Sylvie. I don't get it, and she only knows what she felt."

"Necromancy?"

"I don't know," he said. "There's death in it. Sacrificial death of some kind, but old." A shudder ran through his body. His eyes unfocused, listening. "She's so afraid. She's dead, and she's still afraid it could get worse. She's . . . It's all . . . hunger and torn hearts and fear in her mind." His voice gave out, going thready, then silent.

Sylvie waited. He was motionless, as if listening to the dead allowed him to take on some of their deathly calm. A moment passed, with his tight breathing and the distant slurp of moving water the only sounds.

He shook it off all at once, body moving from ghost languor to his more normal hunched shoulders and twitchy nerves. "It's . . . necromancy and sorcery and witchcraft and . . . it's a tangle of magics. It's layered, and it's really ugly."

"So the other four women are . . . what? In some type of magical suspended animation?"

"They were," he said. "Until Jennifer was pulled from the water."

"Lio said the other women changed shape."

"See!" Wales gesticulated broadly, pointing at nothing but his own aggravation and confusion. "That doesn't fit either. Shape-shifting's not necromancy; it's closer to biology."

"And you said you didn't know anything about shape-shifters," Sylvie said.

"So I hear things. So what?"

She let that slide. Wales wanted to keep his breadth of knowledge on a need-to-know basis? She could live with that. For now. There were other, more pressing problems. "How would that work?"

He shrugged. "Suspended animation? Hell, maybe it wasn't magic at all, just more of the government fucking around in our lives, using us as—"

"Wales," Sylvie snapped. "Take off the tinfoil hat and focus. It wasn't pure necromancy, fine. I believe you. Can we get out of here now? Let these people recover before a snapping turtle starts nipping off fingers?"

Wales nodded. "Yeah. Good point."

They backtracked to the ATV trail, Wales sticking to drier ground this time, and once they'd reached a point where the grass would cover their presence, Wales brought out a little packet, tipped it into the stagnant waters. Sylvie watched the water go the color of old bone, swirling white and cream, and said, "Powdered milk?"

"Don't knock it; it works," Wales said, and dipped Marco's flaming Hand. "And a hell of a lot easier to cart around."

It was one of the things she hated about magic. It made these rules for itself—the purity of milk could put out an evil flame—and then bent or broke them at the user's will. Grocery-store milk? Powdered milk? Where was the purity in that? But it was working.

Marco faded away. Behind them there was silence, then shouting, as alarmed police found themselves waking, groggy and scared. Sylvie bit her lip as she and Wales moved away. The ISI would understand what had happened even if the police didn't. Odds were, they'd come looking to her for answers first.

She hadn't thought this through at all well, had let her eagerness to clear the debt she owed Lio send her rushing out to the scene, and for what? They hadn't found anything. No monsters. No dead girls. Hell, if Wales was right— her stomach lurched once again.

"They're *alive*," Sylvie said. "Christ. I could have saved them if I'd called a witch instead of the cops yesterday. I freaked out, saw the scene, and thought I didn't want to be found near it. I fucked up."

Wales, thankfully, didn't say anything, a veteran of the kind of second-guessing that paranoia bred. After another moment, Sylvie said, "So, can *you* help the women? If we find them? Even though it's not necromancy?"

Bitterness laced her question, made it accusing, blaming the nearest magic-user for the actions of another. Wales blinked, paused in his steps, and she flipped a hand at him in apology.

Just . . . why did it always have to come down to magic? What had happened to the days of point and shoot, and problem solved? At this rate, she was going to have to have a full-time witch around, and Sylvie just didn't trust them that much. Not Wales. Not Val. Hell, not even Zoe, whose first actions in the *Magicus Mundi* had been shortsighted at best.

"Magic's not that different, branch to branch," Wales said. "Sorcery, witchcraft, necromancy. We're all built of the same thing. We just . . . specialize."

"Is that a yes?" Sylvie said.

"It's a maybe. Don't make me theorize without evidence."

"Now you sound like a witch," she said.

He stalked along, squelching, his jeans collecting dust and mud, and finally said, "So, let me guess. A witch told you about magic. Painted witchcraft as team Good. Let me tell you what. It's all the same at the core. Greedy scavengers stealing power, growing stronger every year they survive, and rearranging the world to suit themselves."

"Yeah?" Sylvie said. "So why isn't there a word for a good necromancer? Everything else has a good versus bad. White witch. Mambo. Shaman."

"Because we don't need the ego stroke. Deal with death enough, and you'd be surprised how little you care for human approval. I think you'd understand that. Besides, good, bad, benign, malign—it's all about who's making the judgment."

"Bullshit," Sylvie said. "Enslaving the dead's a magnitude worse than a witch's glamour."

"Even if the witch spells someone to fall in love? Erases their self-will? It's not just the stuff of novels, Shadows. Witches talk a good game, but they use the same magic we do. And let me tell you. Witches do far more damage than your average necromancer. Yeah, we can turn a man into a zombie, keep him as a servant until he falls to pieces, but it's really not all that useful. They take effort to create, they're hard to control—too stupid to really get complex ideas across—and they can't communicate even if they aren't dumb as a sack of bricks. Brain death really means something, y'know.

"And in the time that a necromancer does that? Your average witch will have sold, traded, or dealt out enough spells to destroy a dozen men. Witches like their comforts. Or has your friend Cassavetes never used magic to get her point across?"

Sylvie shrugged, wanting to deny it, but she couldn't. Val was, or had been—before her powers got nuked—all about the little irritants. Sylvie had seen her whisper a confusion spell through the phone when an unlucky solicitor had dialed her one time too many. Val had said the spell was temporary.

Wales said, "I knew a priest once who made awesome zombies. Mixed in a witch's poppet spell, broke out his own teeth, and bound them into the zombies' skulls. It was like he had an entire group of servants who responded to his every whim."

"So, what, that makes it worth the effort?" Sylvie said. "That how you made your new deal with Marco? Tied a bit of yourself into him?"

Wales shuddered. "No. A thousand nos. The priest I mentioned? That witch spell was based on the law of similarity. Like to like. It let him control 'em with minimal effort. Problem was he drew that similarity so tight it went both ways. He started to rot."

"Gross," Sylvie said.

"At least he only injured himself," Wales said. "Your average witch could do that to any man on the street."

"Careful," Sylvie said. "You make your point sharp enough, you'll end up impaled on it."

When he paused, she said, "I already distrust magic-users. You really want me to have another reason to tar you all with the same brush? Keep comparing yourself to the *Maudits* and bad cess witches. Give me a reason to go after—"

Sylvie stopped midthreat, shaking it off. Wales wasn't a witch, but he just might be as clever as Val at getting his own way. Locked in their argument over semantics, they'd headed absently back toward her truck.

She had other ideas.

"The ghost girl," she said.

"Jennifer," he said.

She waved off the name. She knew it, but who the girl had been was currently less important than what she was now. "Can you get her to track the other women?"

Wales opened his mouth, caught her expression, and sighed. "Yeah. Probably. If she's not too afraid."

"So. Do it."

Wales scrubbed at his face, at his wayward hair, and said, "Yeah, okay. It's just weird."

"You were talking to her before," Sylvie pointed out.

"In the place she died. That's like . . . going to interview someone at their home. This is like cuffing them and bringing them down to the station. She's going to be unhappy."

Sylvie said, "Talk, talk, talk. Not getting it done." Briskness was best, the only antidote to Wales's dwelling on a fear that wasn't his.

He sank down to a spider-legged crouch; his shadow drew away from him, spraddled long and dark over the grasses and waters. He scraped charcoal from his boot tread, piled the chunky ash and soot into Marco's turned-up palm, folded himself over the Hand, whispering, his breath stirring the dust and ash. "Marco, bring her here."

A spur of glacial cold racked Sylvie's bones for a millisecond, then passed through her, leaving her with a taste of danger in her mouth and a rocketing heart. Wales shrugged uncomfortably. "Marco doesn't care for you overmuch," he said.

"He's not the only one," Sylvie said. "Just keep him under control."

The brush of cold came back; this time she sidestepped the majority of it. She was a quick learner if nothing else.

"Is she here?"

Wales ignored her, head cocked slightly, gaze turned inward, lips moving in soundless speech, coaxing, commanding. He shivered, either for being bracketed between ghosts or for fighting off Jennifer Costas's fear.

"Wales," Sylvie said. "Her pain. Not yours. Her fear. Not ours."

Wales nodded, head up, gaze following something invisible to Sylvie. If she squinted hard, concentrated, she thought she saw a shimmer walking ahead of him, something like a blur of smudgy heat. Jennifer Costas.

A coolness in the air—the lurking Marco—got her

moving also, thinking wryly that this was the single most gruesome game of hot'n'cold she had ever played, directed by ghosts in the search for bespelled women.

· · ·

WITH THE GHOSTS GUIDING THEM, THEY CAREFULLY MOVED OFF THE track into the pure wilderness. Sylvie tried to pick her way over the grassiest ridges, tried to stay out of the water. At least she didn't have to worry about animal life—the ghosts were better than hounds at flushing game. Everything fled before them. Anhingas rose up on dark wings, clacking beaks. Snakes oiled through the grass, left dark wakes on the water like miniature sea serpents.

Only the mosquitoes stayed persistent. She slapped another one from her cheek, drawn there by the bloody symbols Wales had put on her skin. She lifted her shoulder, rubbed at the stickiest spot, and left smears on her clothes.

"Don't suppose she has a time frame," Sylvie said. The sun was high and hot, would stay that way for hours yet. Didn't mean she wanted to spend the entire day in the swamp.

"Look on the bright side," Wales said. "At least we're off the radar for Odalys and her crew."

"Small comfort," Sylvie said. "Very small."

Wales grinned, surrounded by ghosts and utterly at ease. Necromancers were just plain different from regular people.

"You just want to shoot something," he said.

"It is cathartic," she agreed.

She slipped off the next hummock, splashed down into dark water to her calf. Shaking water out of her shoes, she thought, Yeah, shooting things was better than this.

Between one breath and the next, her irritation fled. Her spine tightened up; her skin went clammy. She wanted to blame Marco for it, a ghostly bump and run, but Wales had gone just as rigid.

She drew her gun, the rasp of it leaving the holster loud in the sudden silence. Wales, beside her, was whispering into the wind, or Marco's ear, or Jennifer's, seeking re-assurance or explanation.

The question—*Is something there?*—hovered on her lips, unasked. The answer was evident. The thick heat of the day had gone unwholesome, unhealthy. Sylvie licked her lips and tasted something in the air, something foul and earthy like a poorly skinned hide left out to cure.

Her palm sweated on her gun; she changed hands and wiped the other against her jeans.

Wales said, "We're close."

"You think?"

He shot her a pissy look, which she gave back in spades, and he shrugged a single shoulder in reluctant agreement. "To our left. Magic. A lot of it."

"Necromancy?"

"Not exactly," Wales said. His face creased in concentration; his eyes closed as if he could get the feel of the area better with one sense cut off. Sylvie, thinking of dead cops and bespelled women, preferred to keep her eyes open, watchful. "It's not not-necromancy either. I don't . . . I don't like it. Marco doesn't like it. And Jennifer—she's so scared. I'm letting her go now."

Jennifer wasn't the only one scared; Wales's voice wavered. He tucked his hands into his pockets, tangling Marco's dead fingers in his own.

Sylvie felt the trembling echo of his fear in her own bones, transmitted like a virus. This, this was why she preferred to work alone. It was hard enough to face the *Magicus Mundi* on her own; she didn't need someone to infect her with their fears.

"We could go back," he said.

"Or hey, we could do the job I brought you here for? Investigate?"

"We don't even know what we're walking into," he said. "I like caution. Caution is good."

"Caution had me calling the cops last night," she said. "Caution killed Jennifer Costas and three policemen. Injured a friend of mine. This job doesn't reward caution."

She took a steady breath, refusing to choke under the weight of whatever saturated the air. She had resisted aversion charms made by one of the best witches in the state; she could withstand this growing miasma of fear and wrongness. She let her breath out, pushed Wales's fear out of her bones, and took the first step toward trouble.

The next one was easier.

Wales followed on the fourth step, so tense that she felt his presence like a live wire, something to be wary of, something that could lash out, unexpectedly, in any direction.

"Are we getting closer?"

When he didn't answer, she glanced over her shoulder, irritated that she had to do so—the ground before them was growing marshy again, treacherous.

He nodded stiffly. "Straight on."

Straight on, like there was even a path. Sylvie soldiered onward, stepped into a deceptive puddle, and found herself suddenly knee deep, a plume of mud swirling through the previously still water.

Wales said, his voice tight and small, "Marco says we're close."

"Well, if Marco says so." She shifted her grip on her gun. Didn't know if she would need it. So far, the day was quiet. Creepy and fraught with magical tension, but quiet. But then, that was how it had been yesterday, and Lio had been mauled.

Her skin goose-bumped. She didn't know if she should use the gun, even if attacked. Odds were, any attackers would be the shape-changed women, not the wildlife that fled their path.

But she knew herself and knew that she would shoot in a heartbeat. If necessary. She hoped it wouldn't be.

Water slipped into her jeans, nearly blood temperature, and wicked upward, filling her senses with swamp. A vibration in the water ahead sent ripples stroking slowly back her direction.

Sylvie squinted against sun gleaming off the water. There was something up ahead, a paler patch in the water, the sway of something that wasn't reed. "Wales," she breathed, and picked up her pace, still scanning the area but moving off to investigate that pallid gleam. Sand maybe?

Given that Wales looked as happy to be in the water as a house cat, she doubted it was anything so natural.

Sylvie hastened the last ten feet, her pulse echoing in her ears, her breath in her chest, and splashed forward. She stilled, staring down at the choppy water, trying to see. She could reach through the water, touch . . . but even the kaleidoscope image she could piece together looked distressingly like flesh. If she reached, would she end with cold flesh in her hands?

Or worse, if this was one of the women, would touching her break the spell in the wrong way? Create another burst of lethal flame, boiling her and Wales alive?

Wales said, "Sylvie?"

"I found . . . something," Sylvie said.

"So did I," Wales said. He waded a gentle circle around her and the lagoon. His mouth drew tight. "You said there were five women?"

"Were five. Now four."

"Five," he said.

"What?"

"I count five. A pentagram. Jennifer's been replaced."

Sylvie waded over to him, following his path, dismay overriding the cold dread in her bones. She studied each face, blurred by water, trying to pick out which one was new.

Six women and only two names known. One of them elicited from the woman's ghost. Her city had enough problems without women being dragged into the 'Glades and turned into mannequins.

The bodies swayed gently in place, as if tethered. Despite Wales's assurance that they lived, they looked dead. Abused and dead. Grimacing, Sylvie reached into the water. Blood temperature near the surface, cooler and subtly slimy deeper down. Beside her, Wales hissed out a warning breath.

"Easy, Tex," she murmured. "I'm just getting a closer look."

"Just be careful," he said. "I think the water is an insulator. Like silk. Magically inert. Pun aside, it might be a dampening field. Helps maintain the stasis they're in."

Sylvie nodded. "What if I keep most of the body beneath the surface?"

"Why mess with them at all?"

"Pictures," she said. "I know Maria Ruben. The others are still unidentified." She grasped the woman's shoulders from behind, her palms pressing flat against clammy shoulder blades. The woman—girl, really—felt dead. Heavy and inert, unpleasantly limp, free from rigor. Her blond hair slithered over Sylvie's forearms like a swath of clinging weed. She swallowed hard and gently raised the woman's face; the water rolled back, baring open contact-green eyes with fixed pupils. A symbol was carved into her forehead, blanched white and bloodless. The skin furrowed.

"Do you know this symbol?" Sylvie asked.

"No," he said, after a glance.

Sylvie braced the woman's shoulder against her hip, took out her camera, and clicked. One down.

"That's enough," Wales said. "Put her back."

"Sense something?"

"I don't know," he said.

"It's a yes-or-no question," she said. "Do you sense something?"

"Yes, then. Don't know what. But something's paying attention. Do the others fast."

"You could help. You're the necromancer. You're the one who's supposed to be grappling with corpses."

"That's the point, Shadows. They're *not* corpses, remember?"

"Picky, picky," she said. She repeated the picture tak-

ing with the other women, careful not to raise them too
high, careful to get clear shots, not only of their faces, too
pale, too slack, but the symbol on each of their foreheads.

She stared down at Maria Ruben's dark eyes, the color
of the mud beneath her, and said, "Maria doesn't look too
good."

"There's a good?"

Sylvie said, "There's definitely a bad." Maria looked . . .
withered. Dry. Even in the water's embrace, her skin looked
parched. Her mouth looked chapped, the edges split. Her
fingertips looked charred; reddish black streaks climbing
her hands. More symbols nestled in her upturned palms.

Too close to the woman who went up in flames?

Or something worse.

Wales hissed when he joined her.

"What do you think?" Sylvie asked. "Collateral damage or intrinsic?"

Wales tilted his head, listened to Marco, his body slowly
tightening. "Marco says she's close to death. The spell —
it's too much energy to contain. Even like this."

"What's the spell for?" Sylvie said. "It's an awful lot of
work to go to if we just have a sicko sorcerer who likes
his girls passive."

"I don't know," Wales said. "It's not . . . It seems non-
sensical. If I can figure out what the symbols represent, I
might be able to get a better idea. But I can't do that here.
All I can tell you is that the magic feels strange. Like it's
trying to do two things at once. The power's both coming
and going. Like . . ." He crouched, put his hands into the
water, licked swamp off his fingers while Sylvie felt her
nose wrinkle in disgust. Necromancers. Always with the
organics.

"It feels like some kinda exchanger," he said. "Like a
person breathing. Changing oxygen to carbon dioxide. Some
type of magical chemistry. It's—" He jerked upright,
wiped his hands on his pants, and said, "It's too complicated not to be fragile. I think we should get ourselves

gone before Marco or I have an adverse effect on the holding pattern."

Sylvie studied the women; she hated like hell to leave
them behind. But she'd known that was a possibility the
moment she began snapping pics: That wasn't the kind of
thing you did if you expected to solve the problem then
and there. Their options were so limited. They hadn't come
prepared to camp out, hoping that the spellcaster would
return. They could try to disrupt the spell. . . .

Wales was obviously following along with her thoughts;
he shook his head. "We've got no guarantee they wouldn't
just burn if we broke the stasis."

"Can you break the spell completely?"

Wales grimaced. "Not without making a few mistakes
first. Which would kill most of them."

Sylvie tapped her gun barrel, thinking. "If we leave,
and you figure out what the symbols mean, what all the
spell's actually trying to do—"

"I might be willing to give it a try," Wales said. "Even
if I can't break off the spell, I'm a necromancer. I can
encourage it toward entropy. Encourage it to break itself."

Sylvie blinked. "You can *kill* a spell."

"Theoretically?"

She sucked in a humid breath, tasting her own frustration. "How long's Maria got, you think?"

Wales had another one of those whispered conferences
with Marco. Sylvie turned away, staring out over the still
water that held the women like flies in amber. A drawback
to working with necromancers. Hanging out with the person who looked like he had an imaginary friend. Negative
points on the discretion factor.

"Best guess? Four days, maybe." Wales ran a damp
hand through his too-long hair; he left dark streaks behind
on his cheek. "It's like . . . stress, right? Too much stress,
and the body rebels. For all intents and purposes, Maria's
having the world's slowest heart attack. The spell can't
hold it off forever."

The women bobbed gently in the water, imprisoned without a cage. Sylvie thought of Maria's high-strung husband, so lost without his wife, of what Lio would say, and her stomach soured.

Her voice was clipped when she said, "Fine. We're out of here."

She took a last, frustrated look at the innocent women she was leaving and stalked off back toward her distant truck. It felt . . . wrong. Like she was walking away from a fight.

Sylvie never ran from a fight. It wasn't in her blood.

5

Symbology & Sources

RUSH-HOUR TRAFFIC SLOWED THEIR DRIVE HOME TO A CRAWL AND helped Sylvie give herself a tension headache from grinding her teeth so hard. But the first time she'd let loose with a volley of profanity and the horn, Wales had gaped, and asked, "Kiss your mother with that mouth? Christ, Shadows. I know sailors who'd balk before saying half of what just came out of—"

"Shut up," Sylvie said. "I wouldn't be so pissed if you'd—" She cut herself off; he *had* done his job. It wasn't his fault that he didn't have the instant solution she wanted.

His jaw was tight when she glanced over, locking back his own need to argue. She'd decided he was right. Silence was golden. Otherwise, she'd be a road-rage statistic.

By the time they made it back to the South Beach office, Sylvie wasn't a lot happier, but she was calmer.

That lasted until she stepped inside, squinting at the transition from tropical sunlight and soaring sky to fluorescent bulbs and low, dark-painted ceiling. When her eyes adjusted, she found that Alex wasn't alone.

Alex sat on the reception desk, swinging her feet, and across from her, sitting on the couch, Caridad Valdes-

Pedraza was striped in the sunlight that seeped through the miniblinds.

"Get out," Sylvie said.

Alex said, "Sylvie! Be polite! This is—"

"We met last night," Sylvie said. "She's a reporter, Alex."

Wales growled, pushed past her, and raided her fridge, pulling out an icy bottle of soda. He pressed it to his face, his long neck, the open vee of his worn T-shirt. Alex watched him, belatedly responding to Sylvie.

"Duh." Alex raised a binder, flipped it open to show a sheaf of paper about twenty pages thick. "She's doing a story on missing women."

"Her research is for crap," Sylvie said.

"Looks good to me," Alex said.

Caridad had the grace to rise and look shamefaced. "I know I'm intruding," she said. "But it's important. You know it is, or you wouldn't have spent the day in the Everglades."

"Alex," Sylvie hissed.

Alex shrugged. "I didn't tell her. But you're both sunburned, muddy, and stinky. Hardly a stretch."

"I know we got off on the wrong foot," Caridad said. "But give me another chance."

"Why should I?" Sylvie said. "If you really wanted to help these women, you'd be haunting the police station, not me. You just want the damn story."

"It's not like the police will listen to her. Not when she's talking about monsters," Alex said. "Besides, think about it this way. You and Cachita find the women, it's a win-win. You save them, Cachita writes about it—we might get more business."

"Whose side are you on, Alex?" Sylvie said. Alex shrugged a narrow shoulder.

Wales slumped onto the couch. "Do you really need more business? Ever since I met you, it's been go, go, go."

"Sylvie gets bored," Alex said. "You wouldn't like her when she's bored. She does shit like—"

Sylvie coughed, cocked her head in Caridad's direction, and Alex shut up.

"Cachita," Alex said. "Maybe you'd better go." She took in Wales's scarlet nose and cheeks and dug out the first-aid kit with a resigned huff. "I think we've got some aloe gel in here."

"All right," Cachita said.

Sylvie thought her jaw might drop. Caridad hadn't been anywhere that docile the night before. But before her surprise could turn to pleasure, the woman paused, running her nails thoughtfully along the seam of her jeans. "Sylvie, you saw the news report about the monster, right?"

Sylvie closed her eyes. She'd known it wouldn't be that easy. "What monster?"

Caridad dropped back into the seat she'd just vacated, brought her briefcase up, and popped it open. She dug out her netbook, flipped it open.

"Caridad, I don't want a PowerPoint presentation," Sylvie said.

"Cachita, please," Caridad said. "Here." She cued up a video. The local news. Morning edition. When people were credulous and not looking for more than sound bites to flavor their coffee.

She must have made a face, because Caridad mirrored it. "So the source is dubious. The report is real. I've got the police reports to back it up—"

Sylvie waved a hand irritably. Bad enough she was caving to this nonsense; the least Cachita could do was let her listen in peace. The perky newscaster, some pleasing mixture of black and Latina, leaned forward, pasted a serious expression on her wide-eyed face, and said, "Local patrons of a favorite restaurant claim to have seen a monster coming to dinner. . . ."

Stripped of the mindless banter between anchors, the story was simple, the start of a joke. A man walks into a bar and turns into a monster.

It could have been a joke, but the punch line was bloody. Whatever had happened after that—and the anchors

weren't sure, parroted comments about knives and shattering glass—seven people went to the hospital to have their
wounds stitched.

The anchors made inane comments about gang initia-
tions, quoting urban legends about car headlights and homi-
cidal quotas as if they were fact, and Sylvie turned them
off. She was thinking about timing.

The police had disturbed the bodies in the swamp on
the same night the man pulled his "stunt" in the restaurant. The women had changed shape. So had he.

A thin connection, maybe even no connection. There
were werewolves who made their home in the city, and
there was nothing to say that one of them hadn't simply
had a temper tantrum. But it was worth checking out.

Caridad smiled, toothy with victory. "I told you."

"Smug isn't a good look on you," Sylvie said.

"I've got an appointment to talk to the staff in an hour.
You could come."

Sylvie looked at Wales. "Symbology?"

"Go," Alex said. "I can help him." She put a last glide
of aloe gel across his cheekbone and smiled.

Wales hesitated, slipping a few more inches between
him and Alex, but finally nodded.

With that less than ringing endorsement, Sylvie followed Cachita out into the evening.

· · ·

IT WASN'T A LONG DRIVE, NOR AS UNPLEASANT AS SYLVIE HAD
feared. With only Sylvie as her audience, a willing one at
that, Cachita stopped being so fiercely cheerful. She tuned
the radio to a Latin station, all dance beats, drummed
along on the steering wheel, and said nothing at all.

Her face in repose was oddly stern. For the first time,
Sylvie found herself considering the woman seriously as
something other than an ambitious reporter willing to step
outside the bounds of the norm in search of a story to call
her own.

The restaurant light was turned off, the lot blocked

with a sawhorse. Cachita pulled up; Sylvie hopped out, canted it aside, and let Cachita drive past.

She followed on foot, approaching the restaurant slowly. Whatever had happened had broken out at least one of the front windows. A series of plywood sheets was nailed over it.

Sylvie dropped her gaze. The lot was asphalt, sun-baked, the lines worn, and overlaid by tread marks. Nothing animal would have left tracks. There was no real greenery around. To the right of the restaurant, down Aragon Ave, palms studded the sidewalk, and small planters sprouted trees and flowering bushes. To the left, down Merrick, there was a green space shoehorned in between a shopping center's parking lot and the Casa de Dia's.

Then again, if it had been a shape-shifter, presumably he'd had a car parked somewhere near.

Cachita paused in the doorway, briefcase dangling from her hand. "See something?"

"Just getting a feel for the area," Sylvie said. She'd hoped for a paw print, cheesy as it seemed. Lio said Maria turned into a bear. A bear print would be a better link than a wolf print.

She spun once more, slowly, looking for security cameras. She didn't expect to find one, and she didn't. If there had been cameras, the cops would have had the tapes, then the ISI would have stepped in, and they'd have the restaurant under wraps.

Inside Casa de Dia, the promise made by shattered glass was fulfilled. The restaurant wasn't quite in shambles, but it was close. A young man in an apron was steadily sweeping up shattered dishes; another was following his smeary path with a mop. Several tables listed to one side, courtesy of broken legs, and a pile of damaged chairs made a strange tangle.

Cachita set down her briefcase on one of the remaining tables and beelined in on the older woman staring over the mess. Her hair was tied back in a long braid, and it whipped around like an angry cat's tail when she turned on Cachita and Sylvie's approach.

"You the reporter?"

"Yes," Cachita said.

"What do you want of us? I won't have my staff ridiculed."

"We just want to know what they saw," Sylvie said easily. She leaned up against the edge of a booth, checking first to make sure it was still sturdy. Three long rips in the red leather drew her attention. Claw marks. A cop might interpret them as knife marks if they were inclined to look for an answer that made sense and not for the truth.

The *chink-chink-chink* of swept-up china stopped. Both young men were listening.

"Gloria, it's all right," Cachita said. "We won't hang you out to dry. We just need to know. We think this monster's kidnapped and killed women, and there's a woman who never came home last night."

Sylvie stopped running her fingers through the tears. Cachita hadn't said anything about that back at the office. She might be making it up—Sylvie thought Cachita was comfortable with saying anything to get her story—but there had been a new woman in the 'Glades today.

"He came in. He exploded," the boy pushing the broom said. "One moment, a man. The next, fur and teeth."

"A wolf?" Sylvie said.

"Mezcla," the mopper said. *"El monstruo. Gato y oso y lobo y hombre. Como una pesadilla."*

"Con dientes grandes," the sweeper said. He stuck his fingers in his mouth, drew his lips back, and snarled.

"A mixture of animals, a nightmare," Cachita repeated.

Both boys nodded.

"With big teeth."

That wasn't right. The *Magicus Mundi* had its share of monsters and chimeras. There were gods who could take any damn shape they wanted. But this . . . Going from human to a patchwork quilt of animals.

It sounded more and more like sorcery to her. False shape-shifting. Something bought with blood and pain and easily warped.

"People screamed," Gloria said. "I screamed. And he just started flailing, biting, and clawing." She hesitated, then pushed up her colorful sleeve. Beneath it, her arm was mottled black-and-blue, skin drawn tight beneath stitches. "He grabbed me, dragged me toward the door." Her breath rattled in her lungs; she folded her arm across her chest, and the boy dropped the mop to lean up against her.

"People were panicking," she said. "They crashed through the window, and it startled him. I pulled, and he let go. He ran into the street, then ran into the dark. Out of the light. He howled. . . ."

"Una pesadilla, verdad," Cachita murmured. "You were very brave. Then and now."

Gloria shrugged. Unwilling to take praise for simply surviving. She pinned Sylvie with her dark eyes. "Are you a reporter, also?"

"No," Sylvie said. "I'm a monster-hunter."

"Bueno," Gloria said, and disappeared into the kitchen.

Cachita whirled on Sylvie. "What? I come to you with monsters, and you give me shit about being crazy, but her? You just *tell* her you're a monster-hunter?"

"She didn't annoy me," Sylvie said.

Cachita blew her hair out of her face in aggravation. "I've been nothing but forthcoming—"

"You didn't tell me another woman was missing."

"You didn't tell me who Maria Ruben was."

"You're the one who wants to make nice," Sylvie said. "You've got the motive to share. And so far, you haven't. You've got a list of missing people you could give me."

"But you won't let me work on your team. You'd have shut me out tonight if I had let you."

"It's for your own protection—"

Cachita's lips twisted. "You know what? You can get your own ride back. I've got things to do." She clutched her briefcase, headed into the women's room. Sylvie propped herself on a table and waited.

She wanted to shake the names out of Cachita but thought the woman was reporter enough to bite her lips and keep silent. Didn't matter. Sylvie had pictures and Detective Adelio Suarez. She could get the names another way.

Cachita came out of the bathroom, dressed to kill—bright green blouse that dipped low in front and cut out in back. She wore a tight black skirt, bright yellow heels; her hair had been tousled into curls. She rocked back a bit when she saw Sylvie, licked newly red lips. Everything about her was designed to draw attention, down to the leopard-print bangles on her wrists.

"Hitting the streets?" Sylvie asked, pure bitchiness, then paused. Cachita had blinked agreement before her mouth said, "It's none of your business."

"Holy shit," Sylvie said. Pictures of the spellbound women flashed across her memory. All young. All attractive. All Hispanic. "You're putting yourself out as bait."

Cachita raised her chin, tossed her hair out of her face. "If the cops won't, I will. I want him found."

"And what if you do find him," Sylvie said. "Or more to the point, what if he finds you? Then what? You'll whip out your pen and write at him?"

"Better than doing nothing," Cachita said. "You could always come with me. Lurk in the shadows. Ready to run to my rescue. Oh wait. I'd have to pay you first, wouldn't I?"

They had attracted an audience, and Sylvie grabbed Cachita's arm. Tried to. The woman evaded her. Sylvie finally threw up her hands in defeat. "Fine."

It was irrelevant, really, she thought with a pang of guilty relief. Five women to power the spell, and there were five women she'd left behind. If Mr. Monster was the sorcerer, then Cachita could play monster chum all she wanted, and he wouldn't bite.

It wasn't much—there were all-too-human monsters out there—but Cachita was right. It was none of Sylvie's business. It still felt a little like leaving the spellbound women behind, that guilty discomfort twitching in her veins, when she went outside and called a cab.

· · ·

THE OFFICE WAS BRIGHTLY LIT AGAINST THE NIGHT WHEN SYLVIE entered, and even better—it smelled of dinner. She sniffed, trying to be discreet, and Alex grinned. "Cuban sandwiches, black beans, and rice. Yours is in the fridge."

"Thank you," Sylvie said.

"Petty cash paid for it," Alex said. She dangled the key to the tiny lockbox from her fingertips, then dropped it back into the desk drawer, kicked back, and put her feet up.

Wales was draped across the couch, barricaded behind the enormous screen of his laptop. Sylvie drifted over, peered behind it. "You know, that's pushing the definition of laptop," she said. "Any luck? I'd expected to find you surrounded by occult books by now. You haven't even cracked a box? Dinner that exciting?" Despite herself, she couldn't help but let her gaze drift between Alex and Wales suggestively.

Alex laughed.

Wales went scarlet. "I'm a man on the move, Shadows. It's all in the hard drive. Every occult book I've ever laid hands on is scanned in this baby. When you're wanted by the CIA, you might not get time to pack."

Sylvie eyed the boxes still piled about the office. "So what's all this, then?"

"Nonessentials," he said. "Just because I can winnow all my necessities to one bag doesn't mean I don't like having other stuff."

Alex headed into the kitchenette, dished up Sylvie's food, and nuked it.

Sylvie swallowed, belated hunger catching up with her.

She snagged it out of the microwave before the timer had run down, ate rice and beans while they were still lukewarm, and said, "So, Tex, the symbols?"

"They're old," Wales said. "It's a strange thing, magic. Trends occur in it, too. This is an old form of symbology. I've got two alchemical symbols—" He turned the computer screen toward her, highlighted the images, etched in skin.

"The thing that looks like a calligraphic F on a plain attached to a lowercase y? That's fusion. This one? The tilted V with loops? Purification."

"What about the lumpy swastika-looking thing," Sylvie said.

"It's not a swastika; it's a lauburu," he said. "It's a Basque symbol, but it's older than that. It's a little hard to be sure, but given context—shape-shifting—I'm going to assume it's Paracelsus's symbol for animal healing."

Sylvie frowned. "Purification and healing—"

"Yeah," Wales said. "I think our sorcerer's sick."

"He put women into magical comas and left them in the Everglades. We knew he was sick," Sylvie said. "Sorcerers tend toward depressingly good health, though. Sick could mean cursed." It would fit with the man that Gloria and her sons had seen—a sorcerer who lost control of his borrowed skills at shape-shifting.

Alex said, "Tell her about the eye."

"The bull's-eye with a line through it," Sylvie said. "The one Maria Ruben has on her forehead?"

"It's pretty basic," Wales said. "It's a blinding spell. To keep his deeds hidden."

"It doesn't work, then," Sylvie said. "Tatya found them, I found them, the cops found them, we found them again." She traded the rice for the sandwich, wanting to bite and rend at something. Even when she thought they'd gotten a clue, it was useless. "Are you sure you're interpreting it right?"

"You're missing the point, Shadows. That blinding spell ain't aimed at us. It's a specific blinding spell. Our sorcerer's got an enemy."

Sylvie blew out a breath. She couldn't tell if that was good news or bad. The enemy of her enemy was her friend.

But that only worked in black-and-white worlds. In the real world, there were endless permutations of evil.

The sorcerer who had abducted, enchanted, and bound the women was evil—that, she didn't doubt. The man he feared?

"What's the last symbol?" she asked. "The linked ovals."

"Transformation," he said. He traced the lightly sketched symbols with his finger, his nails ragged, bloody at the edges. He'd been chewing them, internal anxiety clawing its way out.

"Problem?"

He twitched, opened his mouth, let it close. Fidgeted. Alex leaned closer, said, "What is it? You can tell us. Even if it's weird."

"Not one of your clients," Wales reminded her.

"Then don't play coy," Sylvie said. "My clients always hide things from me. Or try to. What's rocking your world?"

"Two things," Wales said. "I think I know what he's doing. Broad strokes at least. Not the why, not even the specifics, but—"

"Tex—"

"It's like a power filter," he said. "Transformation. The power that's coming in isn't the same as what he's getting from it."

"Like a plant," Alex said. "Turning carbon dioxide to oxygen."

"More like money laundering," Wales said. "Turning power that's actively trying to injure him into power he can use to protect himself. Using the women's lives as filters. He'll have one of these sigils carved into his own skin, the better to link himself to them. To feed off them."

Sylvie grimaced. "Ugly."

"It gets worse. I think I know who's doing it. Except I never thought he was real. He's a sorcerer's bogeyman. The soul-devourer."

"The soul-devourer?" Sylvie repeated. "You've seen this before?"

"Not this; if it were this, I would have said at the scene.

But it reminded me of something. Got back, started looking at the symbols, and it twigged. There was a kill zone in the Louisiana bayou. A pile of women's bodies found, their hearts torn out. Some local sorcerers took a look but said they couldn't even summon the murdered women's ghosts. That their souls were—"

"Devoured, got it," Sylvie said.

"I remember that," Alex said. "That was just after Katrina. They thought it was a serial killer."

"Serial killer, sorcerer, potato, potahto," Sylvie said. "Where's the link, Tex? Our women aren't dead."

"There were symbols carved into the flesh," Wales said. "The police started asking around. And in Louisiana, they don't make any nonsense about asking the magical folk. If this binding spell is truly a filtering system, the last step would be to kill the women."

"And steal, bind, or devour their souls," Sylvie said, flatly. Her shoulders felt heavy, her breath leaden. She loathed magic. Loathed necromancy, which denied the dead even their final rest. "Don't suppose you can fix it, now that you've recognized it? Can you call for help from the others in the community? Your *good* necromancers?"

"They'd be more like to never speak to me again if I brought them to the soul-devourer's attention. And if I mess with his spell, believe me, I'll be a shining beacon for him."

"Can you do it? Unbind the women before they wither away or get dragged off to have their hearts yanked out?"

Wales lifted a single shoulder, his gaze avoiding both Sylvie and Alex. "No. Maybe? I might be able to slip each of them out of the binding. Thing is, breaking the stasis doesn't mean I can free them from the power pouring into them. Or the power from changing within them. Those symbols were carved into their skins. They're black holes for the power."

"I'm lost," Alex said. "Who's pouring all the power into them? Why?"

"It's a curse," Sylvie said.

Wales raised his head, caught by surprise, and his eyes were wary and wide. "Yeah," he said. "That's my thought. The blinding spell? The soul-devourer is putting some serious effort into hiding his presence. Which implies—"

"Someone's putting nearly an equal amount into finding him," Alex said, pleased with herself. Then her triumphant expression froze, faded. "Wait. The soul-devourer's a sorcerer's bogeyman."

"Yeah."

"And he's hiding from someone his equal or worse?"

"Got it in one," Wales said. "We've just stepped into a grudge match between seriously amped sorcerers, and I for one would like to go home and beef up my security."

"You moved out of your apartment," Sylvie reminded him. "You're homeless."

"That's what hotels are for," he said. "I'll call you if I get any leads." He collected his computer, a change of clothes, the box with the Hands, and headed for the door.

"Hey, Wales," she said.

He looked back, raised a shoulder. "Yeah?"

Sylvie said, "The ghost girl—Jennifer Costas. She'd be able to tell you more, don't you think? Who's hunting him? Why? If you can get her to calm down."

"Yeah," Wales said. "She'd know. Guess I'm going to be talking to her tonight." He didn't look happy about it, his shoulders stiff, his arms tightening about his boxes so hard the cardboard dented.

Sylvie didn't feel that good herself. Jennifer Costas should be on her way to her afterlife, claimed by one god or another, whisked away from mortal concerns, and Sylvie kept conspiring to keep her from her rest.

"Wales?"

"What?" he snapped.

"You're gonna pay for the hotel room, right?"

"You gonna pay me now?"

She hesitated.

"Yeah. Thought as much. Besides, I prefer to stay under the radar," he said. "And the Hands need to be fed." At her grimace, he said, "Don't ask if you don't want to be told."

She flipped the latch after him and took his place on the couch.

Alex perched on the desk, and said, "Soul-devourer? That really doesn't sound good."

"A necromancer so secretive and vile that the other necromancers won't name him? Not good is an understatement. Christ," she muttered. "I hate necromancers."

"Not Tierney," Alex said. "He's helping. He helped you earlier, and he's helping you now—"

"Ease off," Sylvie said. "I'm not bad-mouthing him. He's all right. For a ghoul."

"I think he's sweet," Alex said.

Sylvie said, "Alex? Just hold off on falling for him until we get this resolved? He's twitchy. You jump him, he's gonna run. Let's finish the case first."

Alex grinned. "Can't be too long. You guys have a plan."

"Plans so rarely survive contact with the real world," she said. She poked listlessly at her sandwich. It was tasty, but she lacked the appetite now. Wales's pulling the ghost back was dangerous, even if he hadn't made a big deal of it. Dangerous and repugnant. And necessary.

Sylvie's thoughts circled. When did *necessary* stop being an acceptable excuse? When did the means stop justifying the end?

Her little dark voice growled, *Someone has to do what's needed.*

"So I called Demalion," Alex said, and successfully derailed Sylvie's morbid speculation. She swallowed the first thing that came to mind, the eager question of *How was he?*

"He going to help with the Odalys issue?" Sylvie sat up on the couch. Alex fidgeted, her gaze on her brightly colored sandals.

"Sort of," she said, when Sylvie let the silence linger.

"Sort of?"

"He wants you to call and ask," Alex said.

Sylvie let her breath out. "Well, I guess I don't need to ask you how he's doing. That's classic Demalion." Her traitorous heart jumped in her chest at the idea of talking to him. Anxiety, excitement, something of both. She dragged herself off the couch, headed up the stairs for dubious privacy.

She closed the door to her private office, sat down, and stared at her phone for a long while, then dialed. The phone rang, and she was concentrating so hard on her lines that she forgot what his would be.

"Wright." The voice was familiar and not. Demalion's cadence in Wright's tenor. It twisted her stomach and made her mute.

"Alex?" he said, then more surely, "Sylvie."

"Yeah," she whispered.

A breath let out, a rush of relief in her ear. "I wasn't sure you'd call."

"You basically blackmailed me into it," she said. And maybe this wasn't so hard after all. They were falling right back into their usual patterns.

"I know you, Syl. You were going to try to cut me off while I . . . accustomed myself to a new life, then you'd get weird and decide it was better not to call. And time would keep passing."

A smile tugged at her lips, warmed her from the inside out. "You learn all that in high school? Either you had a lot of bad breakups, or you didn't have any."

"Hey," he said, "I was suave for my age. Very. You can check my yearbook out if you want." The background noise around him swelled: people shouting suddenly, a fight going from zero to sixty and ending just as fast.

"Where are you?" she asked.

"Police station," he said. "Seemed simplest to just walk Wright's beat for a while. Gets me out of the apartment anyway. Gives me an excuse to stay late."

Yeah, she thought, an excuse to stay away from Wright's wife and son. She wanted to know how that was going, didn't want to know at the same time. That was another reason she hadn't called. She felt like someone's mistress.

"So, Odalys," she said, ignoring the whole mess, retreating to the safety of business. "You still have any way of getting info to the ISI?"

"I can't believe you want me to," he said. "That's an about-face."

"She's a threat," Sylvie said. "And I don't have time to deal with it."

"You all right?"

"I'm working with the Ghoul on a case," she said. "My client is Adelio Suarez, and the body count is already at four, three of them cops. Oh, and the ISI is sniffing around again."

Silence from his end, then, "I can be back in Miami by morning if you need me."

Oh, she was tempted. They brought out the best in each other, worked well together. Did other things well together. She bit her lip hard, said, "Just get Odalys off my back. I'd do it myself, but oddly, it's as hard to get into a prison as it is to get out."

"All right. I know someone who can pass the information on."

"Thanks," she said. She hesitated. She should hang up now; their business was concluded. "You doing all right?"

"Miss you like hell," he said. "And I'm in way over my head, but I'm coping. Mostly."

"Anything I can do?"

"Stay alive," he said. "It's too weird if no one else in the world knows who I really am."

"There's always Alex," Sylvie said, teasing.

"Alex knows my name. Not me." His voice was nearly the right pitch now, roughed and deepened with emotion, hushed through the distance. It made her ache.

"I get it," she said. "Demalion, be careful. You came back from death once. Don't blow it on some pissant traffic stop."

"Yeah, yeah," he said. "Go easy with the case, huh?

Watch your mouth. Play nice with the necromancer if he's going to watch your back."

"Playing nice isn't as much fun as winning," she said, and disconnected on his laugh.

6

Delegation and Negotiation

SYLVIE CLATTERED BACK DOWN THE STAIRS AND FOUND ALEX TIDYING up the dinner dishes.

"So?" Alex said. "You talked to him?"

"He's going to deal with the Odalys issue—"

"Yeah, not what I meant. Did you *talk* to him?"

"He's fine," Sylvie said. "I'm fine."

"I can't believe you sent him away. Unless . . . what? Does he not do it for you anymore now that he's all body swapped? Got something against blonds?"

"Alex!" Sylvie said. "Would you just think before you talk tonight? Wright's *dead*. He was flat broke when he died. He's got a child, a wife who's working full-time to cover her student loans. Wright died, saving Demalion."

Her throat hurt, thinking about that close call; she'd been slow, caught up in saving her sister, in fighting Odalys. If it had been left to her, Demalion would have died. Again. "We owe Wright. I can't do anything to help them out. Demalion thinks he can."

Alex's face shuttered; she winced. "Sorry. I didn't . . . I thought . . . He told me he was trying to get back into the ISI. I thought maybe you'd dumped him for that—"

"I try not to make the same mistakes twice," Sylvie said. "I don't like the ISI. I don't trust them. But I trust *him*."

"Good," Alex said, still quieter than was her usual wont.

Sylvie sighed. "Look, I had to leave those women in the 'Glades at the mercy of their abductor. It makes me cranky. And we're going back tomorrow, and I still know nothing about him. Except that he has a rep as the soul-devourer. It just doesn't look good."

"You can take care of it," Alex said. "This is your world."

And wasn't that a lovely thought. That she belonged to the *Magicus Mundi*. She shook it off, and said, "All right, then. If he is a sorcerer, he'll have a reputation somewhere. Can you hit up the contact list and see if anyone knows of a sorcerer with a penchant for killing shape-shifters for his own gain? Link it up with alchemy. This guy, if Wales is right, is old-fashioned."

Alex reached for her computer, heading straight into research mode. Sylvie put a hand on the screen, and said, "Take it home with you."

Alex met her gaze head-on. "You're getting me out of the line of fire."

"It's getting late," Sylvie said. "Besides, you can research from home just as easily, and we don't get a lot of drop-ins. Odalys hit me here once already, and now the bell is dead. I don't want you caught in the cross fire."

Alex worried her lip, and said, "If I work from home, you'll keep in contact?"

"Promise," Sylvie said. "Go home."

"You're not going to sit here all night and play bait, are you? Demalion said I should watch out for you."

"Demalion has problems of his own to worry about," Sylvie said. "Don't encourage him to focus on mine."

Alex shut the laptop down, pulled the cord, and started packing up. "Sorcerer, alchemy, shape-shifting. Check. You want me to look for more incidents like Cachita found? I mean, I know we've been busy, but he can't have been around here for that long, or we'd have noticed. If we can track where he's been, maybe we can ID him. I mean, he might be *Maudit*."

"Unlikely," Sylvie said. "The *Maudits* are bastards, but they're modern in their habits. I can't see them going back to alchemical scribblings, even ones that work." She poked at a peeling sticker of Chibi Cthulhu on Alex's laptop. "I don't know, Alex. I got a bad feeling about this one. It's all so thin."

"We'll find him. There's no way a monster sorcerer goes completely unnoticed. We'll find him, and you'll shoot him. End of problem."

"I live in hope," Sylvie said.

She saw Alex out, hit the phone again. Lio wasn't in the hospital any longer, which was a plus, but it also meant that Lourdes could play gatekeeper a lot more efficiently. She hung up on Sylvie before she'd gotten three words out.

Sylvie sighed, flipped through the images of the women on her phone. They were all youngish, midtwenties. They were all Hispanic. They looked like they would have been healthy if they didn't look so . . . dead. Made sense in a sorcerous sort of way: If the sorcerer was using them as receptacles for an overabundance of corrupted magical energy, healthy people would last longer.

That they were all *women*, all *attractive* women, implied that no matter what the sorcerer's magical use for them was, he was indulging himself. He wasn't desperate; he was picking and choosing.

She really hoped Alex was right, and this one could end with a single bullet. The Everglades could hide a dead sorcerer just as well as the ocean could. She and her little dark voice contemplated the idea with a shared hunger that lingered until a car honked outside.

Sylvie flipped the phone closed, rose from the couch, smelled swamp and dirt, and grimaced. So past time for this day to be done.

Unfortunately, the world disagreed. She had just closed

and locked the door when she turned to find Salvador Ruben coming up the sidewalk.

· · ·

"SHADOWS!" HE SAID, HIS VOICE TIGHT WITH STRESS AND NERVES. His suit coat, open, rumpled, flapped as he hurried toward her. He tripped on the curb, stuttered in his question, but didn't stop. "Wh-what the hell is going on? You said she was . . . You said the cops would call—"

Sylvie held up a finger—*give me a moment*—unlocked the door, and hauled him back inside her office. "Have a seat," she said, busied herself with Alex's ridiculous coffee-maker. He subsided onto the couch, clutching his knees. Anxious but obedient.

She wished the brew time were longer, wished that it required more of her attention: She needed every moment she could get to figure out what she was going to tell him. Maria was alive. That was a plus. But she was close enough to death that giving him hope might simply be cruel.

"Here," she said, passing him a cup of coffee heavily adulterated with sugar. Good for stress, sugar. He wrapped his hands around it, brought it toward his chest as if the coffee could ward off some internal chill.

"What's happening?" he asked again. Pleaded. Salvador Ruben was the kind of client she wanted to help most, the ones who might break under the weight of the world without her. "I called the cop you mentioned, but he's 'not available,' and no one knows anything about Maria. Is she dead or not?"

Sylvie sat next to him on the couch. She was bad at offering comfort, but she could pretend. "Salvador. It's complicated and strange. I want you to listen to me. Just hear me out."

"Is she dead?" he asked. His mouth quivered like an old man's. He twisted the ring on his finger. He and Maria had been married for eight years, been friends since they were twelve. More than half his life was bound up in this woman, and she was . . .

"She's not dead, yet," Sylvie said. "I'm going to do my best to save her. But it involves getting her away from a very dangerous situation. I thought the police could help. They can't. They nearly died, trying."

"Aliens," he said, his knee-jerk response to anything extraordinary.

"No," Sylvie said. "Sorcery."

"What?" His breath gave out entirely. Sylvie fished his inhaler out of his suit coat pocket, handed it to him, watched him suck in air.

"She's under a spell," Sylvie said. "Like . . . Sleeping Beauty. Only not so nice. The spell's draining her."

"So break it!"

"I've got a specialist working on it," she said. "We're doing what we can. I hope we can save her. But, Salvador, you have to understand, it may be too late."

He turned away from her, put his face in his hands. After a minute, he turned back, all his distress forced back. "You're . . . you're telling me the truth. Magic's real."

She nodded, wondering if the man who believed in little grey men could accept this in its place, wondering if he'd go running directly to the cops. She doubted it. He hadn't gotten on too well with them in the first place.

"Is she . . . Is she hurting?" he asked. "You said she's sleeping?"

"She is."

"Can I see her?"

"No," Sylvie said. "It's not that much like Sleeping Beauty. You can't kiss her awake. The spell's fragile. Disrupting it has killed one woman already."

He nodded, a man used to taking the advice he paid for. An easy client. "So what do I do?"

"Go home. Wait. Pray if you like."

"We're atheists," he muttered.

"Good for you," she said. "C'mon, Salvador. I'll walk you to your car."

When he stood, he did it like an old man, stoop-shouldered, curled around pain, staggering with it. She took his arm and walked him out, biting back the urge to tell him it would be all right. There was no guarantee it would.

. . .

HER APARTMENT COMPLEX, LIT AGAINST THE TWILIGHT, GLIMMERED whitely; the pool gleamed blue, proving once again that dim lighting was the best decorating technique of all. In the uncertain light, the cracks in the stucco, the weeds in the pavement, and the sheer bizarreness of the sculptural accents were easy to overlook.

There was dim light, Sylvie thought, then there was in-adequate light. The stairs to her floor were deeply shad-owed, the fixture at the base of the stairs dark. She took the first step, felt glass grate beneath her foot, and hesi-tated. Burned-out bulbs were common around her complex. Broken ones . . . not so much.

Her gun was back in her hand, held close and low to her side—no point in scaring the shit out of her down-stairs neighbors if they looked out at the wrong moment. Or worse, courting their questions. College students. So nosy when it was least appropriate.

She took the stairs steadily, without much worry. The stairs were a straight shot up, open on the sides, no room for someone to lurk. A benefit to her apartment complex being built more along the lines of a beachside hotel—a lot of open space. Not a lot of nooks and crannies. Hell, it was one of the reasons she'd chosen to live there in the first place.

The light near her door was out, too.

Overplayed, she thought.

Take out the first light, and it made her careful. Take out a second light, and it stirred the atavistic sense to get in, get safe, get out of the dark. . . . Or run headfirst into a trap. Like an animal herded into a deadfall.

She slowed her steps further, approached her door cau-tiously.

Trap, her little dark voice agreed. The air was charged,

the taste in the air sour and sharp, a roil of nausea in her stomach. A quiver of out-of-place energy. Another spell laid over another door.

She decided she was offended. The *same* trap? She might have fallen for it once, but not again.

Still, recognizing a trap wasn't the same as disarming it. A witch's spell had to be attached to something; if she found the trigger, it'd be pretty much like cutting the power.

Val Cassavetes liked cobwebs. Easy to overlook, easy to leave behind. It was a classic, and probably what had gotten Sylvie the day before.

Miami was full of spiders.

But it could also be a spill of sand or a scratched pebble. She swept her gaze over the door, the frame. Cobwebs, dust, clumps of mud. She wasn't exactly house-proud, and it was coming back to bite her.

She pulled off her Windbreaker, ran it around the frame, cleared everything out of her path—there was a scatter of sparks, a hiss like a snake slipping by. She swore, slapped at her calf with her Windbreaker. Spell backlash—

The wood frame above her head splintered.

Sylvie whirled, tried to drop the Windbreaker from around her fist, tried to get her gun back up.

The gunman was closer than she thought he'd be, coming out of her next-door neighbor's apartment. She slammed her door open, slammed it tight, latched it, gun in hand, breathed hard.

It wouldn't hold. Not long enough for the police anyway.

Illusion spell plus bullets, she thought. Who said the bad guys couldn't learn?

A back window might give her an escape route—if she didn't break her leg on the landing.

The door burst open, right off the hinges, a rocket of wood that slammed into her shoulder, spun her gun out of her hand. He loomed in the doorway, looking as surprised as she felt about the broken door. Cheap material, or spell taint—she didn't know. Didn't have time to care.

She lunged forward, not for her gun, but for his knees.

If he fell just right, she'd have him out of her apartment and even better—over the railing.

He grunted as she tackled him, snarled a hand in her hair, trying for balance, only succeeded in falling forward, the opposite direction she wanted. His weight crashed down on her, the heat and sweat and fear-stink of him. Sylvie squirmed beneath him, her goal crystal clear—

Get his gun.

She wasn't a trained fighter, but she was strong, determined, and fought dirty. In the distance, she could hear her neighbor screaming. She got his gun hand beneath her body, cringing and praying that his finger had slipped from the trigger. He punched, aiming for her kidneys, hitting her hip, and she gouged hard at the nerves in his forearm.

He rolled, trying to expose her belly, to get his hand free, and she dug her nails in and raked, felt skin gum up the space beneath her nails . . . The gun wobbled in his grip; his breath went out in a hiss. She got the gun free, jerking it from his loosening grasp with a crack that she thought might be his finger.

They sprang apart. Sylvie twitched the gun into a proper grip. He canted a glance at the destroyed door, at her gun a few feet away from him; he looked like he was about to make a judgment call. Could he finish the job before the police arrived?

Sylvie made a judgment call of her own.

She pulled the trigger. He crashed backward—finally out of her apartment. She followed him, gun ready. If he wasn't down, she'd have no problem shooting him again.

Dark blood bubbled through his T-shirt. Not arterial, but not insignificant. His eyes were closed, his features drawn tight with pain and shock, aging him.

Now that she had a chance to assess instead of react, she thought he was of the same ilk that had attacked Wales: youngish, dressed to blend in, but without even a protective charm to his name. Guess that might have broken the illusion if she'd been trapped in it.

Her downstairs neighbor, a college student named Javier,

staggered up the stairs. Beer night with his buds, she thought. And yeah, there was the milling of footsteps beneath, young men who weren't sure they wanted to get involved beyond calling 911.

He gaped at her. "You all right? He all right?" He didn't wait for an answer but looked down at the gunman. "Should we try to stop the bleeding or something?"

"If you want," Sylvie said. "He attacked me. I'm not feeling forgiving enough to play paramedic."

Javier dithered, and she said, "Why don't you check on Christina? He came out of her apartment." She jerked her chin in that direction, and he obeyed. Shocked but willing. A good kid.

Sylvie crouched down beside the gunman. "Who sent you?"

He groaned, turned his head, his breathing labored and thick.

"Confession's good for the soul," she said. "Think about it. You wake up in the hospital, talk to the cops. Of course, if you talk to me, your odds of reaching the hospital alive go up." She tapped the gun muzzle against his shoulder; his eyes widened.

"I don't—"

Sylvie said, "I'm not playing. And you didn't know what you were getting into. I've killed worse than you and gone to sleep with a smile—"

"Odalys," he said. "I used to smuggle things into the country for her. She asked me to do this."

"Good," she said. "Just remember to tell that to the cops when they ask."

She dropped the gun when the police lights flashed into the lot and resigned herself to another couple of hours before she got that shower she wanted.

. . .

MIDNIGHT HAD COME AND GONE BEFORE SHE WAS DONE ANSWER-ing the police questions. Judicious use of Adelio Suarez's name, and the clear evidence against the gunman—a shattered door, the traumatized neighbor who'd unwillingly hosted the bastard until Sylvie got home—meant Sylvie got to answer questions in the dubious comfort of her own apartment.

She gave the police a list of every possible place she could be reached in the near future and waved them good-bye. Ten minutes after that, she helped apartment maintenance nail plywood sheets over the gaping hole in the door and headed back out into the night.

Alex would open her doors to Sylvie; but then, the options were sharing her couch with the German shepherd who drooled or the futon with Alex, who kicked and twitched, as active in her sleep as she was during the day.

She called Wales. "Tell me you snuck into a hotel room with two beds."

He groaned protest but gave her the address and room number.

Thirty minutes later, she was pulling into one of the Holiday Inn Expresses that dotted the Florida landscape. Tapping on his door yielded a grumble and a series of oddly careful footsteps.

He opened the door, leaned across it, blocking her entrance, and said, "I could have been sleeping, y'know."

"What kind of necromancer sleeps at night? Isn't that against union rules or something?" she asked. She squeezed in, blinked in the dimness, took in the scent of old tallow and spices. Not the usual hotel scent. Wales had been playing with the occult in the dark like the good, creepy Ghoul he was. "Tell me the room has a coffeepot."

"Yeah."

She lingered in the little square space beyond the door, trying to figure if she really wanted Wales for a roommate. Even for a night. If it had been a suite, maybe. "You know, if you're going to sneak into a hotel, why not pick something nicer?"

"Reservations," he said. "Theirs, not mine. I took this room out of the system, but at an expensive hotel, someone would throw a stink. More odds of discovery."

"Surprisingly sensible," she said. "Do you still have clean towels?"

He flipped on the light, looking at her. "D'you have a black eye?"

She touched her face; it wasn't particularly tender. "Just dirt, I think. Bruised ribs, shoulder, and hip, though. Odalys sent one of her bullyboys to my home. Kicked my door in."

"You shoot him, too?" Wales grinned.

"Yeah."

He stopped smiling. "Seriously? I thought your rep was all about shooting monsters. Not people. That's two in one day, Sylvie."

"I've learned to make exceptions," she said. Sylvie ducked under his arm and trespassed. She stopped two steps later and looked at the room. Basic layout—two beds, dresser, TV, a table, and two chairs—except Wales had spent some time rearranging. The chairs were piled on the dresser, a tangle of legs, and the table was squished into the narrow space between the second bed and the wall, clearing a space near the window.

He'd also let the Hands out of their box. He'd made a circle of them, palms up, and stippled them with some pungent herbal ash that made Sylvie's nose wrinkle and her lungs itch as she approached.

"Pennyroyal," he said. "Helps ward off curses. Be a hell of a thing if I went to all that trouble to get Jennifer back here, and it killed me."

"I thought you were going to talk to her, not drag her back. Just talk."

Wales shifted, antsy under his skin. "I wish. If I were wanting to know about her past, what her favorite color was, her best memory—I'd just ask. But death's traumatic as hell no matter how it happens. We don't like to have our toys taken from us, and life's about the biggest toy there is."

"And trauma leads to muddled thinking," Sylvie interrupted.

"Especially when what you're wanting to ask about is their death. Then it's all metaphor and scrambled words. Like talking to someone who got their Happy Meal with a side order of LSD. If I want to learn anything from her death, she's gotta come back. And that requires more than a bit of thought."

"Plus backup, or are you just using the Hands as ashtrays?"

Wales snorted. "Martha Stewart would have my hide. Nah, they're going to be a fence of sorts. Hem her in. In case she tries to escape."

Sylvie edged past the piled-up furniture, crawled onto one of the beds. Necromancy. A lovely way to victimize the dead. But they needed more to go on. As if he had had this same argument with himself, Wales said, "If she could understand what was at stake, she'd *want* to help us. Save the other women."

"That's sweet," Sylvie said. "But I've always found that human nature involves a lot of 'Fuck you, I've got mine.'"

Wales cracked a thin smile. "Truth. Are you gonna hang around for this shindig?"

"Nowhere else to go," Sylvie said. The bed was comfortable beneath her. She might have won her battle with her attacker, been checked over by the EMTs and pronounced okay, but her side ached, her hands ached, and she thought there might still be splinters in her hair from the bullet hitting the door frame. Here was good. Even if it meant playing witness to coercive magic.

Plus, this way she could keep an eye on Wales. He might be more competent than he had pretended to be on their first meeting, but dealing with ghosts just made her skin crawl.

Dead things should stay that way, her dark voice commented.

Demalion, Sylvie rebutted. The dark voice sulked and slunk away.

Wales took a breath, flipped out his lighter, and Sylvie coughed. "Smoke detector?"

He clambered up with a shame-faced wince and yanked the wires. "Thanks."

"Had enough excitement for tonight," Sylvie said. "Hate to add hotel evac to the list." She dragged a pillow to her chest, curled around it; the bruising ribs on her side appreciated the support. She felt like a tween on a sleepover—all they needed was a Ouija board and some Gummi Bears to replicate her seventh-grade birthday party—and patted her gun for moral support.

Wales lit a small brazier of herbs; they didn't stink as strongly as the pennyroyal did, but they made a strange smoky trail that coiled not-quite-aimlessly through the circle of Hands. Where the smoke brushed up against the Hands, ghosts shimmered in grim outlines.

Yeah, this was going to be ugly. Drag a dead girl's soul back through the ether, interrogate her, study her, and slap her in the center of a hard-eyed ghost ring of murdered ex-cons.

Wales tossed a piece of jewelry into the brazier; it sank under herbs so fast that Sylvie only had time to register the gold shine of it. It looked like a pendant charm.

He rattled off a long stream of words that could have been anything, a quick blur of vowels barely contained by a consonant here and there. Alex would have been making zombie-language references—all groan and moan and tongueless words. Whatever it was, it raised the fine hairs on Sylvie's arms, made her clutch the pillow tighter.

Not fear, she told herself. *Discomfort.* It didn't sound like something people should say.

The smoke reacted to it, eddying back from the edges of the magical ghost circle, twining up Wales's legs, creeping through the air like a snake tracking a rat's scent.

"Jennifer Costas," Wales said. Back to English, and it should have been a relief. But the Texas drawl was gone from his voice; he sounded crisp and hard and clean. It was a tone a stage actor would envy, meant for carrying cleanly to the rearmost seats. It was a sound to wake the dead.

"Jennifer," Wales said again.

The smoke thickened, bunched like a swallowing snake, pulling at something Sylvie couldn't see.

Belatedly, she wondered if she'd see anything at all, or if she'd be stuck watching Wales talk to more invisible people, trying to read success or failure in his body language.

Fire crackled in the smoke, a sullen flicker like a banked fire being poked. Sylvie thought of Jennifer Costas, burned up in a spell backlash, and found herself whispering the closest thing to a prayer she was capable of. *Please, let her not spend the afterlife eternally burning.*

It depended, she supposed, on whichever god had laid claim to her soul. Some were more merciful than others. Some were indifferent. And some were downright cruel.

The smoke closed in, engulfed the flame, giving shape to the intangible. Jennifer Costas was formed out of smoke and distant fires, her long hair like fiber optics, glowing dully at the ends, drifting.

Why?

Her voice was a wisp, a child's plaint.

Sylvie smothered guilt. *Sooner done, sooner she'll be released.* For once, she and her inner voice agreed.

Wales swallowed, let the hard edge leave his tone. "Jennifer," he said.

The ghost girl turned her head, and Sylvie decided she preferred the smudgy shimmer the girl had been in the 'Glades to this phantasm, whose eyes gleamed with lambent flames. Jennifer shouldn't have been threatening— lost, scared, dead—but panic lent strength to any creature.

Sylvie shifted on the bed, running over anything she knew on how to banish a ghost. Just in case.

Jennifer shuddered in response to one of Wales's questions. Like a child, she repeated it, *Was I first? No. She and she were there. White eyes under the water, and he pressed me down under the water, a knife blade in my skin, crimson rivers flowing. . . . He gave us to him like a poisoned sweet, and he lodged in our bones. In our blood. We burn.*

The fire crackle beneath her smoke skin doused itself, faded into silence. An utter silence. Utter stillness. Death in a smoke shell. A hollow core of memory and pain.

Sylvie shivered. She almost wished the flames were back.

"Do you remember the words he used?" Wales asked. "Can you tell me?"

Wales was dogged; Sylvie gave him that. Still concentrating on the spell that bound the rest of the women. Trying to figure out a way to safely unpick the knot they were in. Still trying to make sense of someone else's malignancy. But his shoulders were tight, his eyes jittery, and she wondered how long he could hold Jennifer there.

Chains. More chains. Jennifer mourned, turning about in the circle. *Trapped. I want to go home. I must. He calls.*

Beneath the stillness, a tension. Sylvie thought of tides pulling back before tsunamis, of the silence before an earthquake.

"Wales," she murmured. "Hurry it up." Dangerous to interrupt, to divert his attention, but she couldn't help but feel that time was short. A new sound grew beneath the smoke, something distant, repetitive, vaguely familiar. Something that made her edgy.

"What was his purpose?" Wales said.

The smoke shape turned her palms upward, wordless answer or a confused shrug. The sigils carved into her palms meant the motion could be either.

To hide. To grow strong at our expense. At his. He calls.

Sylvie peered through the haze of ghosts playing fence, tried to see what Wales might be seeing. All it was to her was featureless grey-black, a roil of distress.

"Hide from whom?"

Jennifer flashed in the circle, a rush of smoky movement, crashing up against the hedging ghosts, trying to escape. Her face, built of smoke and terror, was visible through the gaps; her lips moved soundlessly. The word was clear, though.

No. No. No. I don't want to. . . .

Wales frowned, his face tight and stern. "Tell me," he commanded. The ghost wept flaming tears.

Sylvie wondered if Alex would still find him sweet now. She didn't dwell on it. That sound came again, just on the edge of her hearing. A displacement of expelled air. An explosive sigh, but with anger beneath. The bed shivered beneath her. She dropped the pillow, held her hands out before her. Steady as a rock. The trembling wasn't her. It was something else. Something approaching. Something sniffing them out. Sniffing the ghost out.

A power filter, Wales had said. Power went in, changed, came out again. That kind of thing left a mark on a soul. That kind of thing could make a ghost a tasty morsel for anything powerful enough to sense it.

Another thought crossed her mind, sent her heart into rocketing overdrive. *He gave us to him.*

It wouldn't be the first time a sorcerer had bartered with a god for power. If the soul-devourer had given these women's souls to a god . . . if Wales was keeping Jennifer here when a god was expecting her.

He calls.

"Wales!" Sylvie snapped. "Send her back. Do it now."

"Just a minute more," he crooned, equal answer to Sylvie and comfort to the ghost. "Just a moment, now." He circled the ghost, scribing a circle within the ghost circle, and Sylvie's nerves seized with a sudden realization.

Wales was inside the ghost circle. Contained as much as the ghost he summoned.

Too late, Jennifer whispered. *He comes.*

Sylvie rose, paced the outside of the circle in an echo of Wales pacing the inside. The cold barrier of the Hands kept her at bay.

Leave him, her dark voice suggested. *Run.*

The air hummed, seethed in the room like locusts, something fiercely alive, something terrifyingly hungry.

The entire room trembled around them, a localized earthquake. In the hall, people were beginning to cry out, a hastening of footsteps running for the exits.

And the explosive grunting cough was getting stronger.

God, Sylvie thought. A god, coming to see what was keeping his newly gifted soul.

"Wales!" she shouted. "End the spell!"

Wales's head came up, only then catching on to his danger. His expression went blank with shock; Jennifer's burning gaze was tilted upward, terrified, waiting, a huddled creature in the glare of a headlight.

Sylvie gritted her teeth, sucked in willpower, hoped there were enough remnants of Wales's protective spell on her skin, and reached through the ghost barrier.

Ice and cold and vertigo; her arm went dead to the shoulder, but her hand hit what she was aiming for, closed tightly around Wales's thin forearm. She leaned back and yanked.

He barreled out of the circle, shouting protest; Sylvie only yanked harder, pulled them both down between the beds. Light exploded into the room after him—the spell breaking on two fronts.

The room shuddered; Sylvie scrabbled for her gun, got Wales between her and the floor, and stared into the heart of the light, trying to see what was coming for them. For Jennifer.

Something clouded the light, a dark mass, the shadow of a god reaching out toward them. The air in the room stung Sylvie's skin, magic crawling over her body, jangling every nerve all at once. Again, she heard that hungry, moaning grunt.

Jennifer's ghost blazed with heat, flames rushing outward, crawling the ceiling, the walls, the floor.

Sylvie rolled, trying to angle herself for a shot. Took it. Hit nothing but the wall. Got another roar of complaint. *We're fucked.* Too late to run.

She ducked, curled tight around Wales, choked on oven-hot atmosphere, her ears throbbing with pain as that animal howl went on and on, too loud for human comfort, Jennifer's shriek mingling with it.

Heat on the back of Sylvie's neck, a supernatural shadow

drifting over her skin, Wales a bony, quivering mass beneath her. Jennifer's scream cut off like someone had flipped a switch. The heat in the room subsided.

That angry moan sounded again, close enough to rattle her bones. And then . . . nothing. The shaking stopped; the light blinked out; her ears rang tinnily; spots danced before her eyes.

When she was convinced the god was gone, not merely playing with them, she rolled off Wales. He was out, eyes sealed shut, bruising beneath it. Yanking him through the circle hadn't been a good idea. But it had been the only way. Ending spells, like starting a spell, took time that they hadn't had.

She manhandled him onto the bed, fell back against his side, and gaped at the room. She expected destruction. Cracked plaster, scorch marks, the like. But there was almost nothing. The mirror over the dresser, glimpsed between stacked-up chair legs, had gone dark, smoked, as if it had gotten a better glance at the intruder than she had and burned from the inside out, incapable of reflecting it back.

A god, she thought again. And they were lucky. It hadn't manifested completely. Hadn't done more than cast its shadow on the mundane world. She spared a brief, belated thanks to the god of Justice: When he'd walked the earth, he'd contained his godly strength as best he could. This god didn't care enough to do so.

She got up on shaky legs, and something crunched beneath her feet. Bone. She let her gaze drop, held through the swinging dizziness that caused, and let her eyes focus slowly. A skeletal hand. One of several.

The Hand of Glory had transformed from a withered, yellow mass of flesh and bone to a hand stripped completely to bone and charred black all the way through. Like Pompeii's victims had, when she touched the hand, it disintegrated to a crisp pile of brittle ash.

Guess they'd finally found a way to destroy the Hands of Glory in one swoop, Sylvie thought wryly. That could have been useful a week ago. Now it was only a *huh* and a footnote in the supernatural files her memory kept.

She kicked it aside, away, staggered into the bathroom, ran the water cold and clear in the sink, and scrubbed at her face and nape. She felt more human at once. Another cloth, wetted down, still dripping, came with her back into the main room. She slapped it across Wales's forehead, watched him flinch with some relief. *Just out, then. Not dead.*

She folded the comforter—scratchy, floral polyester— around him, cocooning him. He muttered, ducked his face into it, and dislodged the washcloth. He flailed a spastic hand in complaint as water ran down his neck and spine, then gave up, passing out or falling asleep. One or the other.

Sylvie dug her bullet out of the wall where it had lodged, dumped the misshapen thing into her pocket. That was the final straw as far as her own energy levels went. She staggered over to the other bed, face planted in the abused pillow, and was out before she could do more than wonder if housekeeping would wake them in the morning.

. . .

SHE WOKE TO HER PHONE RINGING SHRILLY, TO WALES'S GROANING something that might be *Make it stop*, to fading dreams of someone growling in her ear, and to a body gone stiff and sore. Bastard, she thought. She hoped the gunman's wound got infected. She'd ill-wish their godly visitor, too, if she had a name to fling her curses toward.

Fumbling an arm across the stretch of clean sheets brought the phone to her hand. She flipped it open, "What?"

"You didn't call me back," Lio said.

"Your guard-dog wife hung up on me," Sylvie said. A moment later, she put her face in her pillow and groaned. She'd intended to talk to Lio, but after she'd inhaled enough caffeine to be reasonably civil, at least to the point of not insulting the man's wife.

Lio was silent for an angry second, then sighed. "Did

you find anything?" He sounded good. Lucid. Impatient. Cop on the mend.

"Found everything," Sylvie said. She sat up in the bed, shoved her hair out of her face. "It's complicated."

"Magic?"

"Yeah," she said. "Good news, bad news? Good news is the women aren't actually dead—well, except for the one who burned up—Jennifer Costas was her name, by the way.

"The rest are in mortal danger, but alive. At least if I don't screw around too much. They're kind of on a time limit. More good news? I found them again. Bad news? I left them there, and you can't send anyone out to move them. They have to stay *missing* until we fix this."

"What?" All the irritation he'd suppressed earlier came out in one sharp bark. "You what?"

"Look, Lio, I don't like it either. But right now, I don't have a choice. I could tell you where the women are, but that would just lead to a repeat of what put you in the hospital."

They argued for a few minutes longer, repeating the same material—*How could she? This was why he didn't like private investigators. This was why she didn't like cops. They didn't understand the risks*—until Wales shut her up by hurling a pillow into her face and slinking into the bathroom. "Make coffee," he snapped, and slammed the door.

Guess he wasn't suffering too much damage from spell shock, then, if he was lucid, irritable, and hogging the shower.

"Look, Lio," Sylvie said. "I do have some info you can work on, even from home. I took pictures. If you can match them up with missing people . . . No, I'm not telling you how to do your job." She tugged at her hair in increasing frustration and finally hung up. They were never going to be easy allies, but dammit, she needed him to keep the cops occupied, to distract the ISI.

She threw the phone down on the bed, fisted her hands in the sheets. It just pissed her off. A government agency designed to deal with the supernatural, and they were so bad at it that she couldn't just tell them where the women were and trust to them to fix the problem. A government agency that was so bad it didn't even realize how fucked-up it was. They'd poke, and pry, and drag out some low-level witch or psychic who'd preach caution. Then they'd ignore him or her and bull on ahead.

She heard clattering and chatter in the hallways—the maids talking about the shaking last night, talking about crazy guests, and Sylvie took it as a sign. She might not be ready for the day, but it was more than ready for her.

First up, the office and faxing the pics to Lio. He might be pissed at her, but he was homebound, bored, and far too decent a cop to let the information go just because it came from her; he'd look into it.

Wales stumbled out of the bathroom, towel slung around narrow hips and looking like he'd been on a three-week bender. Dripping, he started coffee, leaned over the pot as if caffeine steam was a panacea for what ailed him.

"So what the hell happened?" he asked. He frowned at the charcoal splotches on the carpet, all that was left of the Hands. "Last thing I recall, you were dragging me out midspell. You do like to live dangerously."

She made grabby fingers at the mug of coffee he poured, and with a growl, he handed it over. "So . . ."

"So, next time listen to me when I say stop the spell," Sylvie said. "Then you won't get a magical concussion. Did you get anything more out of the conversation with Jennifer than I did? 'Cause I heard mostly gibberish. Before she got yanked away." He looked like he was going to demand more answers, answers she wasn't ready to give yet. Talking about gods before breakfast was just . . . inhumane. She took a deliberate sip of coffee, mmmed happily though the coffee didn't deserve it.

As an early-morning distraction, it worked.

Wales followed her second sip with a hooded, hungry gaze, then poured himself a cup. "I was closer to her, got some of her memories relayed up close and personal."

"Ugh," Sylvie said. "Glad I missed that. Get anything useful to go with the horror show?"

"Yeah," he said. As usual, he qualified his first positive response. "Maybe. I might be able to peel back at least one layer of the spell."

"Break the stasis? Kill the spell like you suggested?"

He shook his head. "After losing the Hands? Best I can do is buy the women some time, weaken whatever's draining them."

"That's not nothing," she said. "You going to be up to a trip to the 'Glades?" Sylvie asked. It wasn't quite the question she meant. She meant was he up to trying another tricky life-endangering series of spells after the magical backlash he'd suffered last night.

He poured a second cup of coffee, killing the pot, and said, after a long, scalding swallow, "Reckon I'll find out."

7

III-Met

THE SUN WAS BRIGHT AND HIGH AS THEY SET OUT, EVEN IF THEIR moods weren't. Their trip to the Everglades had been delayed while Wales took the time to pack up the sad remains of his Hands of Glory, brushing up the ash with careful attention to detail. When she'd raised a brow in inquiry, Wales had said, "Caution always pays off."

Sylvie had asked, half fearing the answer, "Marco wasn't one of the ghosts guarding the circle, was he?"

"No," Wales said. "He's safe."

Safe, Sylvie thought. Not the first word she'd use to describe Marco. Not even the tenth. But it was a little like the affection between a boy and his snarling, mangy junkyard dog—not something you wanted to come between.

"Good," Sylvie lied. Marco might be a useful tool, but he made her nervous.

Wales had merely shrugged, finished tidying ash into the plastic laundry bag supplied by the hotel, and headed for the truck.

Then she broached the subject again. It wasn't that she cared—as far as she was concerned, the Hands of Glory were abominations—but an upset necromancer just seemed like a bad idea. "They're at peace now," she said. "Not slaves any longer. You got 'em away from the CIA, took care of them, and—"

"Jesus," Wales said, "I ain't mourning them. I'm freaking the fuck out. We could have been killed last night."

Sylvie clicked her mouth shut and turned her attention back to the blacktop unrolling beneath her tires. They were out of the city proper already, had seen an alligator or two sliding into watery ditches alongside the road. "Oh. Sorry."

"Should be," he muttered. "You got any idea of what it was that came for us? 'Cause I've dealt with death guardians before, creatures that hold the souls of the dead to their proper planes, but that wasn't—"

"I think it was a god," Sylvie said.

"God," Wales said.

"Yup," Sylvie said.

He stared into the sun dazzle reflecting off the watery ditches alongside the road. "Any particular god?"

"An angry one?" Sylvie said. At his flat look, she elaborated. "I don't know. One that doesn't care overmuch for keeping a low profile. Not one of the big ones, or we'd be a smear on the wall that the maids would be quitting over. Still, its shadow did enough damage, don't you think?"

"Don't know. Missed most of it," Wales said.

"Hopefully, you won't get another chance," Sylvie said. "Gods on earth are bad news. They're . . . disruptive just by their presence. Monsters and cataclysms. A hurricane in Chicago—"

"That was a god?" he interrupted.

"Yeah," she said. "Several, actually. Political infighting. The smaller ones—the demigods—aren't so bad in comparison. They fuck things up when they're down here, but not to that scale. Mostly, they just get people killed."

"Gods? I don't want to play anymore," he said. "I like my life."

"Then you're smarter than the soul-devourer," she said.

He cocked his head at her, frowning as if he almost remembered what she was talking about.

"One of the things Jennifer said," Sylvie explained. "That she'd been given to him. That he was coming for her."

Wales groaned. "Stupid, arrogant bastard. Made a deal with a god. Bartering for borrowed power from a god to take out an enemy. I really, really want to leave town."

"Tough it up, Tex," she said. "You drew the short straw. I need you."

"Lucky, lucky me," he whispered.

"Just . . . try to stay under its radar," Sylvie said. "Keep a low profile for a while. No ghost summoning."

"Not a problem," Wales said.

GPS pointed out they were there, and Sylvie pulled the truck off the road, coasting to a bumpy halt on the dead-end access road.

Wales looked out into the heat shimmer, clutched his satchel tight, and licked his lips. He opened the truck door but didn't get out. Sylvie walked around the truck, looked in at him.

"You up for this?" Sylvie asked.

"Don't got a choice," Wales said. "We can't leave them there again. I've got to try. "

Sylvie grabbed his satchel, slung it over her shoulder, gritted her teeth, and bore it as the edge of it pressed up against her bruises. She was tough. Wales . . . wasn't. The sun had driven out some of his pallor, but he still held himself like he hurt.

He was right, though. They didn't have a choice.

* * *

THIRTY MINUTES LATER, SYLVIE DROPPED THE SATCHEL INTO THE mud, heart sinking even faster than the bag.

This was the place; she could still see the flattened grass where she had skidded yesterday and gone to her knees. A long streak of turned earth, the tread of her boot.

A fish leaped at a hawk's shadow as it fell over the water, set off a chain reaction. A turtle ducked its head, glided into motion; a snowy egret hunched its neck; a long ripple cut the surface as a water moccasin slid by.

Life.

Sylvie slapped at a mosquito absently.

"They're gone," Wales said. He gaped at the water's surface as if it had betrayed them. As if it were responsible for their disappearance.

Sylvie considered it an evident statement and made no response. It wouldn't have been polite anyway. Guilt sizzled through her veins, laced with a healthy slug of rage.

"Can you find them again?" she asked.

"I could try—"

"Go for it," Sylvie said.

Wales said, "I'm not a dog, Sylvie. I don't jump on command."

"If I say 'pretty please'? C'mon, Tex," she said. "It's not just for me. Those women need our help."

Wales said, "I'm not promising anything. Marco's built to override defenses, magical or otherwise. He's not meant to hunt necromantic magic."

"You were the one talking about sympathetic linkage," Sylvie said. "Can't you use that?"

"They're not dead. Marco is. But I'm going to give it a try. You got a pen on you?"

Sylvie dragged one out of her pocket, a half-sized Sharpie that Alex mocked her for carrying, but as Wales started marking alchemical symbols onto Marco's Hand, Sylvie sent a mental *Take that!* to Alex's techno-love that would send Sylvie into the field with a PDA instead of ever-useful pen and paper.

Wales finished the designs, tilted Marco's grey-skinned palm to show Sylvie the symbol for fusion, repeated twice, one on the palm, one on the back.

"Is it working?"

"Patience?"

"Never had it," Sylvie said.

Wales closed his eyes. The breeze that passed over him reached Sylvie with the faint chill she was beginning to associate with ghosts added. Despite the humid heat that weighed her bones, she stepped away as best she could, checking her path. When she looked up again, Wales was twenty feet away, blindly following Marco's urging.

Sylvie gritted her teeth, thought of a will-o'-the-wisp leading men to their deaths, and hastened after him.

Wales set a rapid pace over hummock and limestone, over knotted grass and through muddy puddles that spat frogs at their approach; sweat trickled down Sylvie's spine, damped the hair at her temples and nape, greased her palm around the handle of her gun. An anhinga rose on a flap of dark wings and something large slid into the water nearby. Alligator, Sylvie thought, and clutched her gun tighter. They were common enough in the city, but the difference between seeing them as you drove by and walking pell-mell into their territory made her heart rocket.

It would be a crap way to die; deathrolled in shallow waters, as horrible as anything the *Magicus Mundi* could dish out.

Wales stopped all at once. Around him, the mosquito cloud flitted away from Marco's cold presence.

"There," he said. A breath of air.

Sylvie joined him; beneath their feet the soft ground grew gritty, limestone gravel forming a path—a narrow access road.

On it, wider than the gravel, pressed tightly against the encroaching vegetation, a black van with a man closing the rear door. Sylvie got a glimpse of pallid, limp flesh, and drew her gun.

"Don't move," she said, trying to spot his companion. Black van, man in a suit, taking up a crime scene—ISI seemed likely, and they didn't work alone.

But Wales's response—tongue-tied pallor—suggested otherwise. He hated the government, but he didn't fear it.

This was fear.

"It's him," Wales stammered. "The sorcerer."

She jerked her attention back to the man leaning up against the van. "Soul-devourer?" Her gaze centered, picking out a target. His tie, his smoothly shaven throat, the handkerchief in his breast pocket, the space between his dark eyes. He seemed utterly at ease, lounging back as if to allow her all the time in the world to choose her shot. A far cry from the flailing man-monster at the Casa de Dia, all claws and terror.

"I've never liked that soubriquet," the man said. "But it will do for an introduction, I suppose. You are . . ." He tilted his head, doing the strange *I talk to spirits that you can't see* thing that was beginning to look familiar. Necromancers.

"None of your business," she said.

"Sylvie—" Wales said, a near-breathless warning. She could forgive him showing his fear openly, but to use her name when she'd just denied it to the sorcerer—that was something else. She'd expected better of Mr. Paranoia.

"Sylvie?" the sorcerer said. "Shadows, if you're out here hunting me. The new Lilith." His tongue came out, quick, oddly reptilian, brushed his lips, retreated. Had there been scales on it? The longer she looked at him, the less convincingly human he seemed.

The more *wrong* he seemed.

Sylvie wasn't magically inclined, but she was good at sensing magic, that subtle shift in the feel of the world. Everything about him screamed *unnatural*, something held together by magic and willpower. The suit he wore bulged rhythmically, as if the flesh it covered was in flux.

Maybe not so controlled, after all.

He pressed himself away from the van, moved toward Sylvie. A wave of wrongness preceded him. She pressed her finger on the trigger, felt the tiniest of gives. "Don't."

The sorcerer never stopped smiling, a sliver of white teeth between blood-flushed lips. "Don't? Don't what? I'm doing nothing—"

"What are you, five? Stop moving, or I'll shoot you."

Wales made a creaky sound of protest, and Sylvie thought briefly about shooting him. "What?" she snapped.

"That's no good," Wales said. "The spell—"

"He's right," the sorcerer said. "The binding spell works

both directions. Should you shoot me, you risk destabilizing it."

He didn't need to say more. When Jennifer Costas had been trapped, she'd burned. The five women in the van were equally trapped. Equally at risk.

"A deal, then," Sylvie said. "You unbind the women from your spell. I don't shoot you today."

"Give up my little harem? No. In fact, I'm going to keep them closer than ever." His lips curled into a smile. He had a disturbingly pretty mouth. It made what he said that much more off-putting. "Too many people were touching them. Like the ancient sultans, I require my women to be mine alone."

Sylvie's finger twitched. Wales whispered fiercely, an argument held with someone spectral, and the man on the roadway laughed. "Listen to your ghost, boy. I'm more sorcerer than you want to tangle with."

"I'm not your boy," Wales said. "And Marco says you should be dead." Wales might be thin, scared, and brittle; but he was dangerous for all of that, still a necromancer. The sorcerer obviously agreed; his eyes sparked green-white phosphorescence like an animal's.

Even with the trigger mostly depressed, Sylvie was too slow, hampered by calculations; protect Wales, endanger the women, or . . . Her voice howled furious protest, drove her finger down on the trigger. Her bullet went hopelessly wide. The sorcerer leaped the distance between Wales and the shore, slapped Wales with a careless hand. Wales spun away, blood spurting from his cheek, his shoulder, spinning into the water. He crawled out, coughing, draped himself over a tuft of grass, and passed out.

Crouching, the sorcerer flexed his hand, showed her an animal's paw, a cat's claw, ivory nails curved and wet with blood. "Now that he's down, perhaps we can talk."

Her second bullet missed him by millimeters; he rolled with an animal's grace, rose, and threw sand into the air before him.

The world erupted into a scouring riot of sand devils

stinging her flesh, stirring into her lungs, her eyes—she blinked furiously, let the voice chastise her into seeing the truth. It was an illusion, only an illusion.

And she didn't give in to illusion.

She cleared her sight, found the sorcerer within arm's distance. She threw herself backward, avoided the claws coming at her face, but his other hand, seemingly human, struck her gun. It crumbled beneath her grip, the metal gone friable, pattering into the sand.

Not an illusion this time.

She kicked back, got herself out of his reach, panting, reaching for a fist-sized stone, for a branch, for anything she could use against him.

He breathed hard, contorted, his entire shape changing, warping. Cloth ripped, that fancy suit giving at the seams. Going monster. Maybe she'd hit him, or maybe the spell was weakened by whatever he'd done to allow the women to be moved.

She surged to her feet. Grabbed Wales's shoulder, tried to drag him to his feet. If she could get him to the van, get behind the wheel—

The sorcerer leaped between her and the van, more monster than man, bulked to twice his original size, mouth distended by teeth better suited to a saber-tooth, piebald fur of different lengths and textures poking through. He drooled, growled, blocked her path. There just wasn't room on the narrow road, and Wales was deadweight in her grip, a reminder of how hard the sorcerer could hit.

He sucked in a breath that sounded like the final rale of a dying man, then slowly, painfully, returned to human form. He patted his hair, smoothing it into place, a tiny vanity.

"I don't like the deal you offered," he said. It started out distorted, as alien as a voice synthesizer, and ended the same smooth baritone he'd had before. His internals slower to recover from shape-shifting than his externals? Or was it vanity again, the sorcerer's priority. It didn't matter in the grand scheme, she supposed, but it helped cement in her mind the kind of man he was.

"I don't like dealing with sorcerers," she said. "You're lucky it was as generous as it was."

"Still, you're open to dealing," he said. "Which is more than you could say about the first Lilith. That woman was rabid in her focus."

"Maybe she just didn't like men who used power as a weapon to oppress innocents," Sylvie said. Her voice was strung tight; nothing good ever came of being compared to Lilith. Much less being called the new Lilith. "I think you'll find I have more than a few things in common with her. I don't kowtow, I don't play nice, and I have a bad attitude."

"And you were created to kill the unkillable. Believe me, I know what you're capable of. I'm depending on it." He seemed wary and tense behind that ever-present smirk. He rolled his shoulders; his skin rolled with them, a blurring of his features, an unnatural distortion that turned her stomach. She'd seen werewolves shift; she'd seen the furies shift shape. They had been alien and strange, but they had their own beauty. This—whatever it was that roiled his skin—was nothing but ugliness. He managed to hold back the monster this time.

"Still, I believe we can find a way to agree," he said. "You want the women freed? I want to be freed."

"What the fuck do you mean, 'freed'?"

"I want you to break a curse for me. I'm not unreasonable. Just doing the best I can to stay alive." His teeth were too long, forcing his lip into a false pout. He shook his head, turned purely human again.

"I'd be more likely to spit on you," she said. "I don't care about your curse. I bet you deserve it."

Wales groaned, drawing her attention. His long limbs flailed briefly.

"You all right there, Tex?"

"I'm facedown in a swamp," he muttered. "You get the bad guy yet?"

"Working on it," Sylvie said. *Working on it with no gun, no nothing.*

"Work faster." He pushed himself up to a crouch; his face was swelling, and blood masked his jaw and mouth. Daylight didn't erase the horror-movie look. She winced.

The sorcerer growled. "You will pay attention to me."

"Only if you say something I want to hear," Sylvie said. "Release the women, and I might be willing to take your case. You know. Maybe next year. Maybe not."

He growled, fury twisting his handsome face into a gargoyle's mask. "If you don't help me, those women are ash. The curse you don't care about will ensure that. Do I have your attention now? If you want to save them, you'll have to save me first."

The sorcerer had enough sense to finally dim his smile when she didn't immediately shoot him down. Enough sense to try to hide his triumph when she said, "A curse," in a bid for more information. She wasn't going to work for him. But she needed to know what she was up against.

A few feet from her, Wales sat up, his expression full of furious focus, even while his eyes were glazing over. That blow the sorcerer had dealt him had been a hard one, enough to knock him out. Concussion, she diagnosed. She was just lucky he wasn't puking his guts out. Instead, he was doing his best to follow along, doing his best to help her out. Wales was tougher than she'd given him credit for.

"Get on with it. Tell me about the curse. Tell me what it is." Her teeth wanted to chatter; she felt cold to her bones. She wanted to blame it on Marco, but there was a lacy pattern of frost forming over the puddle that Wales was sitting in. And the blood on his lacerated cheek was fading, wiped away in careful, invisible strokes. Marco was otherwise occupied.

"It starts, as so many of these things do, with an accident. I killed the wrong man."

"He tripped and fell on your spell?"

That wash of anger on his face again, and he hissed, "Don't you presume to judge me, Lilith. If you had no blood on your hands, you wouldn't be fit to be her successor."

"But you're the one who needs something from me. I get to judge," she said. "Deal with it."

"I killed a man with a powerful friend," the sorcerer said. "He cursed me."

"If he cursed *you*," Wales said, "why are the women the ones getting hurt?" He was tracking better than Sylvie had thought, enough that he wasn't going to let the sorcerer slip that one by.

"I am a shape-shifter," the sorcerer declared. "I have the power to alter my shape, to take on the guise of a bear, a wolf, a great cat."

Sylvie scoffed. "Liar. You're no shape-shifter, and I'm not that new to this game. You're a human sorcerer who stole the power by killing true shape-shifters. So tell me, which one had the powerful friend? Bear, wolf, cat?"

He ignored her. "The cowardly sorcerer refused to fight me face-to-face. Instead, he cursed me with the inability to control my form. I am become a monster."

"Ugly, too," Sylvie said. She grinned when his face went scarlet. If he needed her, she could make him sorry for it.

His lip drew up, and he took a deliberate step toward Wales. "I might require your aid, but his—" He held up his human hand in threat. Should have been less intimidating than the bloodstained claws, but Sylvie's disintegrated gun argued that even a single touch could be deadly.

"Fine," Sylvie said. "Cut to the chase. What do you want me to do? Find this sorcerer of yours and bring you his head?"

A hot light burned behind his eyes, a hunger she could feel. Wales hissed, a warning sound that she didn't need. The sorcerer made her want to pump his skull so full of bullets that it could be used as a rattle.

"That won't be necessary," he said, "but it would be enjoyable. All you need to do is . . . convince him to lift the curse. I'll leave it up to you to decide how to convince him." He gave her a long once-over, gaze traveling toes to crown, and leered.

She shuddered. He hadn't. The disgust in her belly, the twitching of her trigger finger argued he had. She'd met a lot of bad guys, but this one was winning in the sheer skeeze factor.

Wales staggered upright, sagged, a sad scarecrow in unyielding daylight. "You're using the women to deflect the curse. To keep your shape stable. Mostly stable."

"I am," he said. "You're cleverer than I thought, little necromancer. But I could still rip out your throat before you muster a single defense. I'm refraining as a show of good faith."

Sylvie said, "We get it. You're bad. You're scary. Tell me where to find this other sorcerer. What I have to do to break the curse."

"He calls himself Tepé."

"And he lives where?" Sylvie said. "I'm not leaving you loose in my city while I run your errands."

"He'll be here soon. He follows me. Always just out of my sight. Gloating. This spell you think is so cruel . . . is the only way I've found to weaken him."

"Nice to know you hold your life so high that you'll use innocents as a shield," Sylvie said. "You're not making me want to do you any favors."

"Every time I change without intent, without control, it's as if acid is poured beneath my skin. I burn. . . ."

"Not feeling sorry for you. Just so you know."

He gritted his teeth; his jaw deformed on one side, thrust forward; his cheek twisted and sprouted whiskers before slipping back to *GQ* smoothness. "Make no mistake, Lilith. I am in control here. It's a devil's bargain I offer you. But you cannot afford to say no. These women will wither and die. Tepé's curse is strong, and they are human. Help me. Save them. If you delay too long, they will die, and I'll be forced to find replacements.

"Think of that, if nothing else. Me, loose in your city. Can you protect every woman who meets my needs? It's an enormous city, Shadows. Do we have a deal?"

"How do I contact you?"

"You don't. Break the curse, and I'll vanish as I came. The women will wake and return home. Always assuming you were quick enough that they survive."

"I know your rep," Sylvie said. "Soul-devourer. You've left a trail of bodies."

"You'll just have to take it on trust," he said. He slipped alongside the van, climbed inside.

Sylvie yanked Wales around. "Can you do anything right now? Can you help those women? Wake them? If so, do it!"

Wales shook his head, nearly tilted over, and Sylvie clutched his shirt in her fists as the soul-devourer drove away, his "harem" still intact. Swaying, Wales put a hand to his head, and said, "Can we get the hell out of here?"

"God, yes," Sylvie muttered. She wanted away with a force that nearly sickened her. Away from the scene of her defeat. Away from the sorcerer's unclean magic. Away from her agreement to aid him.

It wasn't quite the rapid retreat Wales wanted. She made him sit first, studied his pupils—reactive, the same size, able to follow her fingertip—and declared him hardheaded.

"I've heard that before," he drawled.

The blood was mostly gone, courtesy of Marco's cleanup, and what was left, Wales mopped at with the edge of his sleeve. The gash on his cheek had coagulated; the one on his shoulder was glued shut with fabric. The two in between were reddened lines on the thin skin of his throat—a reminder of mercy. The sorcerer could have ripped Wales's throat open, and from the way he fingered those small tears, Wales knew it.

. . .

SYLVIE LET WALES INTO THE SOUTH BEACH OFFICE, GESTURING HIM ahead, and already looking over her shoulder. Attempted murder tended to make her a little paranoid. Wales, of course, lived in a state of controlled paranoia.

She shut the door; he was peering out through the blinds, his mouth drawn tight. He looked tired, strung-out; he'd dozed fitfully most of the way back, jerking awake every so often, eyes frightened, hands flailing. It all argued that it hadn't been sleep that held him last night but simple unconsciousness. Two days in her company, and she'd worked him into a frazzle.

Alex wouldn't be happy.

"You know you got men scoping your shop? They're not subtle." His voice was pitched low, as if he feared being overheard.

Sylvie took a look, miniblinds spread around her fingers, and sighed. "There's the ISI. Figures. They don't hunt the bad-guy sorcerer, no. They come and camp on my doorstep. They're cheats. Something bad happens, they like to try to copy off my test paper."

"I didn't sign up to deal with the government," Wales said, still in that same half mumble. Trying to avoid a parabolic mike.

"Untwist your panties, Tex," Sylvie said. "You've got Marco, remember? They get too close, you disappear."

She let the gap in the blinds shut, kept the sign on the door to CLOSED, and headed upstairs, fighting the urge to stomp her feet like a child. She hadn't missed the ISI and their spying one bit.

Her little dark voice said, *You should have taken care of Odalys yourself.*

They would have been back, no matter what, she argued with it.

Think they were watching when you were attacked? Watching and waiting to see if you'd take care of the assassin yourself? Watching while the assassin held your blameless neighbor hostage?

"Wales!" she snapped. "Stop gawking at them and start some coffee."

"Not the boss of me," he shot back. But she heard him drop the blinds with a snap.

Her upstairs office was a mess. Leftover paperwork from the previous case, still incomplete for more than just the time it would take to code things properly. If the ISI was on her ass again, it was more important than ever to keep her case files innocuous, cloak the magical in the mundane.

But these files were also waiting on Odalys, on Patrice, on justice to be done. Sylvie dumped the files into her drawer and rested her head on her hands. It was hard to start the hunt for this mysterious Tepé when she knew the one benefiting from her actions would be the soul-devourer.

She opened the safe, took out the newest backup gun, and sorted her feelings out by loading it.

There was a sudden burst of conversation below, the rattle of the door closing, then Alex wandered upstairs, sipping coffee from Etienne's.

"Working from home?" Sylvie said. "I know you're here a lot, but home's the thing that has an actual bed in it."

"Got a futon, not a bed," Alex said. "Besides, practice what you preach, Syl. I was just driving by, and I saw your truck."

"Just driving by?"

"Okay, so I bet myself one of Etienne's beignets that you'd be in." She held up her free hand, then deliberately brushed powdered sugar onto her jeans. "So Tierney seems kinda pissy today. And hurt. I told him I'd get the first-aid kit, but he sent me up here, instead."

"ISI's back," Sylvie said. "He doesn't like the government overmuch. Go home, Alex."

"Don't you want to know what I found out?"

"Phone, e-mail—"

"Oh, but face-to-face is more fun." She draped her lanky self over the spare chair, kicked her flip-flops off, and hooked her feet in the rungs. "Are you going to ask?"

"Alex," Sylvie said. "We met the soul-devourer. I'm not in the mood."

Alex stiffened all over. "What happened? Is that how Tierney got hurt? What did he want?"

"He wants me to work for him," Sylvie said. She filled Alex in; by the end of it, she was pacing the room, angry and sick all over again. "He's holding the women as hostages. He said they get closer to death the longer I take. Wales agrees."

"You can't work for him," Alex said, focusing in with her usual talent for rubbing salt in the wound. "He's the bad guy."

"I have to work for him. But I'll make him choke on it before I'm done. For me to do that, I need to know who he is. Where he came from. What his weaknesses are."

"Okay," Alex said. "Okay, I can maybe help—" She pulled out her laptop, flipped it open, and said, "I did some preliminary research. I skipped the soul-devourer part. Tierney's right. That's a giant dead end. The necromantic community knows he exists but nothing else about him. Hell, turns out they weren't even sure it was a man, just defaulted to it. So I went back to the simple facts. What you and Tierney got from the symbols: old-fashioned magic, Basque magic, a linkage to alchemy."

"Alchemy? He disintegrated my gun with a touch."

"Oh yeah," Alex said, eyes lighting with wholly inappropriate enthusiasm. "Alchemy's all about the transformation of one thing to another. Bet your gun didn't just disintegrate; bet it became some other type of metal first—"

"Alex. He *disintegrated* my *gun*. Tell me you got something," Sylvie said.

"Not something," Alex said. "But something that might lead to something. A nineteenth-century man they called the Basque Alchemist. Eladio Azpiazu. Supposedly he had the power of a wolf, and he scared his neighbors so bad that rather than drive him out, the town picked up and moved."

"*Nineteenth* century? Not our guy, Alex."

"I've been thinking," Alex said. "It's like the *Maudits*. They seek out apprentices—"

"You say apprentice; I say slave," Sylvie murmured, but she got the gist. "You think it's a lineage. A pattern of teaching."

"Yeah, and a strict one if this modern sorcerer is still using the same techniques as his ancestor. That'd be like me still using quill and ink. It works, but there are better methods now. Why should magic be any different?"

"Anything else?" Sylvie asked. "I'm greedy."

"One ring-a-ding prize maybe," Alex said. "I farmed out some of the research. I thought, if the town moved, that would leave a record. Or if the town just disappeared. I know a grad student at UM, a local history buff. She looked into it, confirmed that there was a town that disappeared, and this is the important part—one of the key reasons people left? A series of grisly murders where people were found with their hearts torn out. Sound like the soul-devourer? I'd say that our modern sorcerer was following the family line all the way down."

"Alex, you're amazing," Sylvie said.

"So what's my prize?"

"More research," Sylvie said. "Look into his enemy. A sorcerer called Tepé. Tepé cursed him but good. An enmity that strong should draw notice."

Alex sighed. "Good work makes more work. So damn true."

Sylvie said, "I strongly doubt that's his real name, anyway. Sounds more like a handle than a given name. Like   " She raised her head. "Like the Ghoul."

Wales flipped her off as he joined them. He leaned against the doorjamb, and Sylvie waved him in. The landing was narrow, the stairs were steep, and Wales still didn't look any too steady on his feet.

Alex moved to get out of her seat, and Wales shook his head. His earlier fear had given way to a sullen sort of irritation. He had come upstairs, Sylvie thought, to pick a fight. Give himself a reason to storm out of the office and the city.

Usually, when people wanted a fight, Sylvie was willing to oblige. Not today. She turned her back on Wales, took her seat again, tried for calm. "You going back to the hotel?" she asked.

"Unless you have something else you want me to do today. Boss," he said.

"Better leave the necromancy be for a bit," Sylvie said. Wished she hadn't the minute the last word left her mouth.

"You think?" he snapped. "Want to tell me to not play in traffic, too? Or hey, how about not shooting up?"

"You look tired is all. Not in shape to watch your back."

Wales shot her a grin that was all teeth, offense, and not a lot of humor. "Guess it's a good thing I got Marco for that."

In a hasty attempt to disrupt the argument ready to break out, Alex said, "I checked out Patrice on the way here. She was macking on some goth boy at a coffee shop." She huffed under her breath, said, "You have to be really dedicated to work full goth gear before 9:00 a.m. Of course, later in the day it's too hot for that much guyliner—"

"You did what?" Sylvie said.

Alex looked up from her amused memories and blinked. "Um."

Sylvie took a deep breath, ready to shout, caught sight of Wales's smirk, and let her breath out. When she did speak, it was far more moderately than her original intention. "So instead of working at home where it's safe, you went out and chased a dead girl around."

"I did work at home. Then I hit a dead end, decided to clear my mind, and since you got up in Patrice's face yesterday—yes, Tierney tattled—"

Sylvie blinked again. When the hell had Alex had time to squeeze in a chat with Wales? But she should know better than to underestimate Alex's ability to gather information.

"—so I figured you couldn't follow her around, and she doesn't know me, so, I sat outside her house and followed her to the coffee shop—"

"Where she hit on a goth boy, got it," Sylvie said.

"Cute one, too, if you like that type. Long, lanky, the kind of bony shoulder blades that make me think of wings." Alex's gaze was resting on Wales's clavicle, visible through the thin shirt.

Wales's cheeks darkened steadily, but he said nothing, only hunched his shoulders and made himself small. At least embarrassment had eclipsed his anger.

"Great," Sylvie said. "She's got the new life, and now she's slumming it."

"Can't be slumming it too bad," Alex said. "Not if he's buying five-dollar coffees and ten-dollar pastries. And they're planning on clubbing tonight at Caballero, so there goes another chunk of change."

Sylvie shook her head, disgusted. Patrice offended her on a very simple level. She'd stolen a new life and was doing nothing new with it, tracing the same self-indulgent lifestyle she'd had before.

You could still shoot her, the little dark voice suggested.

Rather than listen to it, Sylvie headed back downstairs.

The sunlight seeped in through the closed blinds, thin lines of brilliant gold that exposed every dust mote in the office and made her sanctuary into a prison of shadowy bars.

Sylvie yanked the blinds open, blinked in the glare, and sent a rude gesture in the direction of the ISI nursing their coffees at the crowded pastry shop across the street. They wanted to watch? Let them.

It was going to be another scorcher. Sylvie hoped Patrice's goth boy melted and ruined her day. Hell with it, she hoped Patrice melted.

Likelihood was, the only one who'd be suffering from the heat was Sylvie. Odds were, she'd be out pounding the pavement for hours, looking for the black van that the sorcerer had used to take the women away. She envied the cops and their ability to just slap an APB or BOLO or whatever acronym floated their boat on a vehicle.

The idea made her thirsty just thinking on it. She raided the fridge, cracked a water bottle, took a healthy slug of cold—

The pain surprised her. It was sudden, all-encompassing, breathtaking. Like knives lodging in her throat, her stomach, her chest. She let out a strangled cry and found blood speckling her lips. She thrust the bottle away, though she knew it wasn't to blame.

A spell. Finding its target.

No.

A *curse*.

Her throat itched, ached, and burned. She couldn't breathe through the agony of it, found herself crumpling forward, losing all control of her body save the most important one.

She wouldn't cough. Wouldn't cry out. Whatever the spell was, it was tearing the hell out of her throat.

Her hands were wet, icy with spilled water.

She tried not to breathe. Not to move. Not to make it worse.

This wasn't illusion. This would kill her whether she believed it was happening or not. Her unaccountable resistance to magic could only last so long. Blood blossomed hot, slippery in her throat.

Footsteps came down the stairs so fast they were nearly falling. Alex shrieked, high and distorted, Wales's shouting back, all but incomprehensible, torn between fast words and the Texan drawl.

"Hold on, Sylvie," he said. Or she thought he said.

Icy fingers threw her backward, pressed her down. She clawed up, felt only fog, malevolence.

"Don't fight him," Wales said. "He's trying to help."

Cold fog iced over her lips; something that tasted of rot, of cold, clotted blood. Marco, she thought, and was amazed that she still had energy to be squeamish.

Marco sealed her mouth with his, blew death and ice into her chest. She stopped breathing. No. *She* didn't stop. He stopped her. Killed her. The deadly cold in her lungs spread outward. Her hands struck at nothing; the pain in her chest and belly fought back.

Her bones were ice, too cold even to shiver.

In the background, Alex sobbed.

Just when Sylvie thought she must be encased in ice, a new cold pressed into her belly, so frozen it burned. So cold, that if she'd been breathing, she'd have expected to see ice.

Her lungs ached; her vision dimmed, but she saw the impossible. A floating clump of red-smeared pins rising through the skin of her stomach. Passing through her flesh, held in Marco's invisible fist.

She blacked out.

When she came to, the lips on hers were warm, breathing life, not death, and shaking with fear. "C'mon, Sylvie," Alex whispered. "C'mon."

Sylvie's heart gave a giant lurch, stuttering, then pounding furiously, shaking her lungs into action. She coughed, felt pain, tasted copper, but nothing like before, and curled onto her side. Alex slumped beside her, rubbing her spine.

"Tierney sent the ghost after the witch," she said. Her voice was hoarse. "Said Marco's gonna force-feed her the pins. God, Sylvie—"

"'S okay," Sylvie breathed. It wasn't.

Pins. That was ugly magic, a far cry from the illusions she'd been attacked with earlier. Hell, she preferred the gunman to this. And she didn't know how it had been triggered. Line of sight? A poppet? A triggered spell attached to the bottle she'd so carelessly picked up?

She hadn't expected Odalys to try something so messy and violent. Something inexplicable enough to rouse serious attention. Something so old-fashioned. Odalys was a modern witch.

For the first time in a long while, Sylvie felt in over her head. She was crazy to do what she did. To face off against the *Magicus Mundi* with a gun and nothing more. She was going to have to cave, have to crawl to Val and Zoe and get the defensive magics back on the shop and their homes.

"Don't talk," Alex said. "He's pulling the truck around. We're going to take you to the ER. The ghost got the pins out, but—"

"'S okay," Sylvie whispered again. This time it was. She felt . . . all right. Like crap. Sore. Like her throat and lungs and stomach had all been sandblasted. Like she could brush forever and never be rid of the taste of Marco's tongue moving between her teeth. But nowhere near the kind of pain she expected from shredded tissues.

"Help me up," she said.

Alex shook her head, mulish. Still trembling. Sylvie reconsidered. Alex didn't look like she could get herself off the floor, much less aid Sylvie.

Sylvie rolled forward, going from her side, tucking her knees, and ended up in a half crouch, half-kneeling position, her hands braced before her.

Alex squeaked in worry.

Sylvie hung her head for a second, let the blood rearrange itself in her body, then pressed upward. Yeah. She was going to be fine. She knew it because the little dark voice was snarling, ready to make someone pay. Her blood thrummed with rage.

Wales had acted fast enough, and she'd not panicked, and Marco, disgusting and deadly though his touch was, had been gentle. Alex looked up at her, her makeup smeared, and shaking hard enough for the both of them, and Sylvie thought that feeling okay wasn't going to keep her from a hospital trip.

Wales came barreling back through the door, rocked back when he saw Sylvie on her feet. Mutely, he handed her a wax doll, the length of her palm, blurred with his sweaty agitation. The doll might be formless, but the braided strands of hair atop the waxen head were brown. Were hers. A silver shadow lingered in the poppet's chest; she nudged it out—a final pin pulling free—and felt an answering twinge in her body.

"I'll melt it down for you," Wales said.

She spat out a last mouthful of blood, a scarlet splotch on the white and black linoleum, and said, "Thanks." She pinched the tiny braid off the doll, rolled it between her fingers, and finally stuck it in her pocket. Just to be safe.

"Truck's running," Wales said.

"The witch?"

"Dead," he said. "The ISI's having a conniption fit over it. Apparently, she was seated in the café next to them. A nice little *abuela* with a bagful of knitting."

"Hospital now, talk later," Alex said.

Wales nodded, bobbleheaded, gave Sylvie another wild-eyed glance, and dragged them both into the cab of the truck.

Sylvie resigned her afternoon to hospital paperwork and a careful explanation. *A witch cursed me and transported pins into my stomach* wasn't going to go over well with the docs.

Alex shivered against her in the close confines of the truck cab, and Wales put his foot down on the gas. Sylvie, sandwiched between them, closed her eyes, the better not to see Wales's truly frightening driving skills, and to focus. Now that the first flush of triumph had slowed, she felt nearly as freaked-out as Alex looked.

She was fine. She shouldn't be.

8

Bad Guys

SYLVIE MANAGED TO BARTER DOWN THE HOSPITAL IN EXCHANGE FOR a friendly clinic. Getting X-rayed, probed, and told she was a lucky woman took the better part of five hours. She was honestly surprised to find Wales still hovering nervously in the parking lot. With the ISI in play, his own injuries, a dead witch on his conscience—she'd expected him to be a vapor trail on the horizon.

Instead, he was slumped down low behind the steering wheel, studying any car in the lot that looked suspicious. A plus for the clinic over the hospital, Sylvie thought. The ISI drove high-end sedans, carefully maintained.

Sylvie clambered into the truck, said, "What'd you do with Alex?"

"Took her home, came back," he said. "You're running low on gas."

"Thanks," she said dryly. It was marred by a fit of coughing. She checked her palm. No blood. She wouldn't have said no to a lozenge.

"Where to?" Wales asked.

Sylvie paused. "Did the witch say anything? Say who sent her?"

"You didn't say a lot with your belly full of pins. Neither did she. She just died. Marco killed her." He swallowed hard. "*I* killed her. Didn't even think about it. I was just . . . angry and tired. I could have told Marco to drop the pins. I'm not that guy, Shadows."

"This world brings it out in all of us," Sylvie said. "Can't say I'm sorry. Not about the witch, anyway. How'd you know what to do?"

"Poppet magic," Wales said. "Had a brief resurgence in popularity in Texas some years back. Had a grudge against a cattle ranch. Drained the cows. Lamed the workers. Finally, fed the owner a bellyful of death, and the ranch died with him. That's witchcraft, mind you, your *cleaner* magic."

"Charming," Sylvie said.

She leaned her cheek against the air-cooled window, closed her eyes.

"Something wrong?" Wales asked. He sounded about ready to drag her back inside the clinic.

"Just . . . surprised I guess. Pins and poppets are messy and old-fashioned. Odalys likes lethal. But she also likes subtle. Low-profile."

"She's in jail," Wales said. "And she's a snob. That kind of woman loses friends fast. She might not have a lot of choice for allies."

It made sense. Made the inexplicable less so. "Hey, Tex?"

"Yeah?"

"Get out of my seat."

Once they'd traded places, Sylvie said, "Hotel for you?"

"Not like I have anyplace else to be. Not like I need to find a new apartment or anything."

"You don't want to look for one now, anyway," Sylvie said. "Wait a few days. The ISI's attention span isn't that long if you're not me." She found a sudden laugh in her throat, black humor forcing its way out.

He shot her a questioning glance.

"Just . . . I always knew they'd sit and watch while I died. Lazy bastards." Her stomach ached dully, kept her amusement brief and bleak. She hoped that Demalion had managed to get the word out. Her life would be just that much easier if she didn't have to worry about Odalys's attempts to kill her every few hours or so. Sylvie didn't mind a challenge, but she had five women depending on her.

"Don't suppose you know any defensive magic," Sylvie said.

Wales shook his head. "Marco mostly takes care of that for me. Shouldn't have pissed off your witchy friend."

Sylvie chewed on her lip. She was bad at groveling. Even if she went to Zoe instead of Val, there was no guarantee that Zoe had learned enough magic to make herself useful.

Once she's brought in, her little dark voice suggested, *it can't be undone.*

She turned her attention to the traffic. No. No to groveling. No to asking her baby sister for aid. For now, she'd rely on the simplest method of survival. Keep moving. Make herself hard to predict, hard to hit.

Steer clear of the office, her home. Wales was going to have a bunk mate in his hotel-room squat. As if tuned in to her thoughts, he said, "If you come knocking tonight, bring dinner."

"I think I might be late," she said. Odalys was out of her reach; she had no leads on how to find the soul-devourer, much less fight him. Tepé was still an utter blank, and maybe not even in town yet. But Patrice was, and Sylvie—thanks to Alex—knew where the woman planned to spend her evening.

She dropped Wales off at the hotel, headed to her parents' home. If she was going out, and her apartment was a potential minefield, she was raiding Zoe's closet.

An hour later, she looked into the mirror, grimaced, and called it the best of the lot. Black slacks, boot cut, the hem ripped loose to make up for the extra inch or two Sylvie had on Zoe. One of her sister's tank tops—black, shiny, stretchy, but not too strappy. Sturdy enough in a fight.

She found a leather jacket lurking in the back of her sister's color-coded, season-sorted closet, and pulled it out with an appreciative smile. Not Zoe's usual taste at all. The leather was dark red, but the cut skewed motorcycle instead of fashion plate. Sylvie shrugged it on, strapped the SOB holster back on, checked the look, and called it done.

Caught in the fragrance of her sister's room—Chanel and cosmetics and the tiniest lingering hint of rot from her sister's foray into necromancy—it suddenly felt intolerable that she hadn't spoken to Zoe. Hell, she hadn't even heard back from Val about her warning.

She dialed Zoe, got voice mail, and called Val, expecting more of the same. Surprisingly, Val picked up. "Your sister's fine," she said. "I confiscated her phone so she'd stop texting her boyfriend while I was trying to explain magic to her."

"Of course she was," Sylvie said. "Where'd she find this one—"

"Sylvie. Stop calling. She's fine. *Stop calling,*" Val disconnected. Apparently, answering the phone didn't mean Val and she were friends again, just shared a weird sort of custody over Zoe.

An hour later, she was parking her truck on the streets outside Caballero. It was early still, as these things went, but she'd prefer to be in already when Patrice came.

She forked over a cover charge and headed in. Caballero had started out as a gay club but had changed over, slowly but surely, to a goth dive with a steady flow of European-styled heavy metal. Patrice was definitely slumming. Rich girls like Bella Alvarez, even while underage, frequented high-end clubs with long lines and bouncers that were there primarily to play fashion police. Rich girls like Bella Alvarez went to clubs where the clothes were Miu Miu, not Hot Topic.

At Caballero, Sylvie got waved in without even a sneer for her scuffed-up Docs. She found a decent vantage point and waited. She saw the goth boy Alex had mentioned first; he was hard to miss, even in a like-minded crowd. His hair, dead black, was plumed off his skull in a series of fluffy spikes that seemed more akin to feathers than human hair. Dead white skin, red stripe across his eyes— she almost missed Patrice tucked into his side. He felt her attention, winked, and nipped Patrice's neck with cheesy white vampire veneers. He worried at the ruby beads on her earring, and Patrice frowned.

Sylvie's hatred for Patrice kicked up another notch. Patrice had cheated death, and now she played with would-be vampires.

Patrice pushed him off with an irritated hand, saw Sylvie, and locked up.

Sylvie slunk toward Patrice, taking advantage of the crowd hemming her in, and grinned, trying to show as many teeth as Patrice's pet goth did. For some reason, Patrice didn't find the effect as pleasing in Sylvie's mouth.

She clawed at her goth boy's leather jacket, jerked backward, and Sylvie's smile faltered. This was more than concern. It was shock and panic.

It was surprise that Sylvie was alive.

It was awareness that she shouldn't be.

It was *fear*.

Sylvie laughed, loud and free and angry. "I blamed Odalys for it all, you know," she said. "The magical attacks as well as the physical. But it was you who set the witch on me, wasn't it. Tell me, were the pins your idea? Did you want to make me hurt?"

Goth boy laughed. "I like her, Bella my Bella. She's fierce. Can we bring her home with us tonight?" He ran black-painted nails up under Patrice's lacy black blouse, showed Sylvie that Patrice wore a belly chain, strung with silver charms. Magical or mundane?

Patrice slapped at his hands, her nails raking his skin, pinned by the crowd that held her in Sylvie's space. She backed up, and Sylvie closed the space between them, got her gun out, pressed it just under the curve of Patrice's rib cage.

Pushing things, she thought. That restraining order was going to be a sure thing at this rate. But the crowd was tight, and visibility was poor. The only witness was the goth boy, and his pupils were wider, blacker than even the dim club light could account for. Stoned close to insensible.

"Usually, I warn people to stay away from me and mine," Sylvie said. "But I'm not giving you that option. I will find a way to rip you out of that body."

The goth boy laughed into Patrice's teased hair, inadvertently pressing Patrice closer to Sylvie and her gun. "So tough," he giggled. The woman was shaking, fine tremors that traveled through metal and stirred Sylvie's predatory nature.

"Not if you're dead first," Patrice said. "You've been lucky so far. How long do you think you can keep it up?" Her trembling was rage, not fear. Not even rage. *Outrage.* The rich-old-woman personality coming out, furious that someone would dare question her.

"Ding-dong, your witch is dead," Sylvie chanted. "Got a bellyful of pain and died of it."

Patrice raised a brow. "What makes you think she was my only option?" She leaned back, let the goth boy support her. She reached up, petted the young man's pale cheek. "You don't think I picked Aron here just for his skill with eyeliner. . . ."

The goth boy smiled, ducked his head again, let the feathery spikes of his hair brush Patrice's skin. He never took his gaze from Sylvie. "It's true," he said. "I'm magic from my head to my tippy-toes."

Sylvie said, "I bet I can shoot her before you whip out a spell."

"You're not that stupid," Patrice said, a smile curving her mouth. It was a smile Sylvie had seen so many times before; Bella Alvarez, her sister's best friend. There had never been such a level of malevolence behind it, though. "Shoot me, Aron's good enough to keep me alive. And all these lovely witnesses will see you in jail. Maybe even alongside Odalys."

In the perpetual-motion machine that was a nightclub, their careful immobility drew eyes like a mountain set down on a beach. The bouncer, a tattooed Cuban cowboy in a wifebeater, waded in their direction.

Sylvie holstered her gun as smoothly as possible, but the bouncer picked up his pace; he'd recognized that movement. Sylvie slid her own hands onto Patrice's curving waist as if they were dancing. Patrice went rigid and still, but Sylvie had found out what she wanted to know. The belly chain wasn't magically active, wasn't the thing that kept Patrice safe, no matter the decorative charms.

"Hey," Aron said, pulling Patrice out of Sylvie's grasp, slipping her behind him. "You want to grapple with someone, try me instead." He insinuated himself into her space, so close she could smell his greasepaint and cologne. Acrid with a strong swell of musk and incense beneath. He closed his hands on her coat, pulled her against him; if the belly chain Patrice wore wasn't magic, something Aron wore most definitely was. Magic *burned* against Sylvie's skin, a ripple of energy as lively as a snake, even through two layers of leather jackets.

"Get off me," Sylvie said, her words tangling with Patrice's, "Let's get out of here."

A puff of laughter in Sylvie's ear, Aron's breath oddly hot on her nape. "I hear and obey. See you later, Shadows."

Just as the bouncer reached them, Aron backed away, taking Patrice with him, disappearing first into the crowd, then, on a wash of heated tropical air, onto the street. The bouncer glowered at Sylvie, and she held up her hands. "I just want a drink."

"No trouble," he said.

"Of course not," Sylvie promised. It was easy enough to make; trouble had just left the building.

She crunched her ice with growing anger. Self-directed. She hadn't thought that confrontation through at all. She'd meant to rattle Patrice's cage, and all she had to show for it was a woman more determined to kill her than ever.

. . .

AN HOUR LATER, SHE WAS STILL IN THE NIGHTCLUB, THOUGH SHE'D moved from the barstool to a booth, propped her legs up on the opposite seat, and dared others to sit down.

The music throbbed in her ears, loud, discordant, reasonably enjoyable for all that. Some rock fusion; metal in an eastern scale, twisty and rhythmic. Sylvie reminded herself to mention the band to Alex. She sipped her soda— if Aron the witchy goth boy was going to come gunning for her, it was no time for alcohol—and chewed the ice, and tried to decide what to do with herself. Wales was expecting her, but was it fair to take her troubles back to him?

He'd already killed for her once today.

She kept remembering him rubbing bruises into life beneath his eyes, that tired and shell-shocked brittleness to his voice. *I killed her.*

Wales had lost a lot when he started working in the *Magicus Mundi*; today, she'd helped him lose another piece of innocence. He needed some downtime to deal with it. She couldn't give him much time—they had to break the women free—but she could give him a single night.

"Sylvie," Cachita said. Shouted really, over the screaming, jangling guitar solo.

Sylvie looked up at Cachita. The woman was dressed to be sorcerer bait again, this time in a short white halter dress with a leopard-print belt. Gold jewelry. Red heels. Sylvie heard Zoe drawling, *ta-cky*, in her head, and bit back a grin.

Cachita pointed at Sylvie's feet, and Sylvie reluctantly tugged them back, opening up the other side of the booth. Cachita plopped down into it with a sigh more seen than heard. A man followed her to the table, some local businessman drowning his sorrows, his tie loosened, his suit jacket rumpled. He tried to squeeze in beside Cachita, and Sylvie propped her feet back up, blocking him from taking a seat.

"Aw, c'mon, I'll buy you drinks," he grumbled.

"Sorry," Sylvie said. "No room." She tipped her glass at him, and he stomped away. He retreated across the room, leaned back against the bar, and watched them. Cachita crossed her arms protectively across her chest.

"Pig," she said, then shook her head.

The band switched over to a softer tune, and Cachita said, "The problem with attempting to lure out a sorcerer with a taste for young women is that you also catch a bunch of mundane assholes."

"What would you do with the sorcerer if you ran into him?" Sylvie asked, her mind still dwelling on her failed attempt to scare Patrice.

Cachita smiled, her expression going wicked. "Taser him. I've been reading up. Sorcerers can be shot if you're fast enough. So I figure they can be electrified."

Sylvie reluctantly gave Cachita some credit. It was an ingenious idea. It might even work. The sorcerer might have a bulletproof shield of some type, but a Taser might be a loophole. Nonlethal. Maybe something that would penetrate the magical defenses.

"Then what?" she asked. "Say it worked?"

"I'd call you and say, 'Hey, Sylvie, got a sorcerer all trussed up.'"

Sylvie laughed. "Nice way to deal with your problem."

"I'm a reporter, not a vigilante," Cachita said.

"You're stalking the streets, hunting an evil sorcerer with a Taser," Sylvie said. "What's your definition of vigilante, again?"

Cachita flashed a smile, then grew serious. She leaned across the table, and said, "Actually, I came out tonight to find you. Your assistant said she thought you might be here."

"Alex's getting pretty talky around you," Sylvie said.

"Maybe I just know how to ask. Oh, don't get huffy," Cachita said. "We were getting along so well. Look, I brought you stuff." She put her purse on the table, a smaller thing than Sylvie had seen her carry before. When she opened it, it held only a few items. The Taser, a wallet, a digital recorder, her smart phone, and a memory stick. She held the memory stick out toward Sylvie, pulled it away when Sylvie reached for it.

"I'm not giving it to you," Cachita said. "But I want you to see what's on it."

"The missing women," Sylvie said. "You going to give me their names now?" She did want that information. Wanted it badly.

"Come back to my place," Cachita said. "I've got more than their names. I've also found a pattern of similarities among the missing women. And some other mysterious murders you might wanna see."

"One conspiracy at a time," Sylvie said.

Cachita rolled her eyes; the decibels rose exponentially, and Sylvie caved. There'd be no talking in the club.

Outside, the silence fell over them like a balm. False silence, really. The streets hissed with traffic; the bass followed them onto the street; people hung out beneath streetlamps and talked.

Sylvie scoped the area, and sighed. "You bring your car?"

Cachita shook her head. "Took the metrorail."

"All right. My truck. Now."

Cachita followed Sylvie docilely enough, but her eyes were busy. Sylvie saw the moment she got it; her brows closed in over her nose. "The man from the bar's following us. He doesn't look so drunk now. ISI?"

The woman really was too well-informed for her own good. Sylvie needed to warn her about the dangers of knowing too much; it attracted the wrong kind of attention. But not just then. Sylvie picked up the pace, aware of the probable agent on her tail, imagined she heard the soft slap of his loafers on her shadow.

She'd seen the gun bulge under his coat back in the bar, hadn't said anything, Cachita too much a wild card to confide in. While Sylvie had no trouble giving the ISI agents hell, she preferred not to do it around witnesses.

But she'd kept an eye on him, watched his dark-featured face grow more sober, more openly watchful as Sylvie and Cachita had talked. For an employee of the Internal Surveillance and Investigation agency, he was crap at surveillance, got so engrossed in watching that he forgot to be sneaky.

Maybe he didn't need to be, her little dark voice suggested. *Not if he was herding her toward something.*

ISI tended to work in teams of two minimum, four more often. That meant there were probably others around.

Beside her, Cachita was scoping the scene. "They're Feds. They work in teams, right? You think they're after you or me?"

"Don't know," Sylvie said. "You do anything they'd be interested in?"

Cachita shrugged, a nonanswer if Sylvie had ever seen one. From a woman as casually chatty as the reporter, that twigged alarm bells. Sylvie made a mental note. Get Alex to look into Caridad Valdes-Pedraza's history. Freelance reporter was a job description that could cover a number of sins.

"Our friend just picked up another friend," Cachita said. "You think they want to talk to us? Or arrest us?"

"I'm not in the mood for either," Sylvie said. "But if I had to say . . . a nice quiet talking-to in an undisclosed location."

Cachita tottered along beside her on those ridiculous heels, moving with a quicker stride than Sylvie expected. As they approached Sylvie's truck, a dark SUV popped its side door. It gaped blackly, an open mouth ready to swallow them up. "Shit," Sylvie said.

"I hate them," Cachita said. "They'll ruin everything." The venom in her voice surprised Sylvie, and it showed. Cachita elaborated. "They don't care about the women, or any of it. They just want to—"

"Ladies, a minute of your time?"

"Go to hell," Sylvie said. His face flushed beneath the streetlamps; Sylvie hadn't bothered to lower her voice and the passersby on the street were beginning to gawk. Not interfere, of course, but gawk.

Still, maybe that was good enough. Before she could put her hasty and crappy plan into action, Cachita stamped her foot suddenly, a sharp clack like gunfire echoing into the night.

The man drew his gun, jumpy, and the crowd mood shifted.

"We're over with," Cachita shrilled. "I told you and told you! I'm with Sylvie now, and you'll just have to— I got a restraining order. You're not supposed to get this close. Someone call the cops!"

Cell phones sprouted everywhere, and most of them were probably just filming so that people's Twitter feeds could be enlivened by someone else's drama.

Sylvie smirked at the suddenly wary ISI; they were screwed. Demalion had had the same problem when she'd met him. Secret agencies weren't allowed to just flash badges. She draped an arm around Cachita's heaving shoulders, shoved her toward the truck.

Sylvie opened the passenger door, slid across, dragged Cachita in after her. Key in the ignition, and Sylvie got the hell out of there before the ISI could really regroup. Cachita had been loud. And quite a capable actress.

Cachita flung herself up onto the seat beside her, grinning. "Take a left up at the light."

Sylvie huffed but did. Guess she was going to see what Cachita had to show her.

Cachita looked back over her shoulder. "Who would have thought?"

" 'Thought'?" Sylvie prompted, watching the traffic ebb and surge around them, a smear of red taillights and dark asphalt. She didn't see the ISI.

"They're not really very good at their jobs, are they?" Cachita asked.

"They're big believers in retreating to fight again," Sylvie said. "They'll be back. We're not done with trouble, yet."

9

The Girl Reporter and the God

CACHITA LIVED IN AN OLD TWENTIES-ERA HOUSE, ALL CURVED stucco arches and rounded corners, and the cracked tiles were soft and sandy beneath Sylvie's shoes. Cachita's heels made small gritty rasps as she led the way in. Sudden movement drew Sylvie's attention: In the tiny, overgrown garden, a cat streaked after a pallid gecko that made the mistake of touching ground.

As she watched, more sinuous forms took shape, slinking curls of shadows; every bush seemed to have a cat beneath it.

"My neighbor's a cat lady," Cachita said. She seemed embarrassed. "So of course, her cats use my yard as their litter box. If I were the house-proud type, I'd be on the phone to the landlord so fast—"

She flipped on the light, gestured Sylvie inside, and shut the door behind them. Paper rustled with their entrance, and Sylvie blinked.

Cachita might be computer savvy, but she *loved* her paper. The living-room wall was a shaggy mess of printouts stapled directly into the stucco.

Definitely not the house-proud type, Sylvie thought

with a hidden grin. Then she saw the subject of the files, and her smile faded. There were easily two hundred sheets stapled on top of each other, next to each other, overlapping, underpinned, a combination of photographs and text, and one entire row seemed dedicated to Sylvie herself.

Cachita even had a photograph of her, scowling into a paper cup of coffee. Sylvie recognized that moment; she'd ordered an Americano and been given a mocha. It was the morning she'd taken Detective Lio Suarez to see what had become of his son's killers. She'd been tense and cranky and apparently careless enough to miss someone snapping candids.

"Don't get weird," Cachita said. "I'm not a stalker. I just believe in knowing my subjects."

"I thought you were concerned with the missing women," Sylvie said. "Not a PI."

"Hey, you've got a rep," Cachita said. "You think I'd just walk up to you without knowing what to expect?" She tapped a cluster of papers, six deep, and said, "Testimonials, of a sort."

Sylvie yanked them from the wall, folded them tight, and shoved them into her bag. "Leave me out of your surveillance," she said.

"Paranoid," Cachita said. "Leave that alone and look at this." She kicked off her shoes, padded over to her laptop, and plugged in the memory stick.

Sylvie took a couple of steps toward her, then froze. A picture and a name. Jennifer Costas. A high-school glamour shot, all soft focus and dreamy smile. Sylvie thought of Jennifer screaming, burning beneath a god's touch, and looked away.

Guess her research wasn't that bad after all.

Sylvie moved to the next picture—unfamiliar—and the next—*familiar*. She compared the woman to her memory and made a match. Lupe Fernandez, one of the spellbound women. A college student at Miami Dade Community College, according to Cachita's notes, in the nursing program.

Lupe grinned in her photo, an arm slung around another girl, both of them wearing rainbow beads.

She looked at the wall again. If each row was a woman—

She swallowed. There were far more than five women missing. And Cachita hadn't had Maria Ruben on her list.

Christ, her city was under siege, and she hadn't even noticed.

"The first one, Ana Cortez, disappeared two months ago," Cachita said. Sylvie studied the picture, but it was unfamiliar. If Azpiazu's descendant had taken her, she was dead and gone already, her body sunk somewhere in the Everglades, alligator food.

"How many?"

Cachita lifted a shoulder. "There are seventeen women who've gone missing in the city that I know of. Out of those, thirteen seem like they might be related to this bastard. There's a type he goes for."

"Young, Hispanic, female."

"Atheist. At least, most of them."

She gestured at a cluster of photographs. Sylvie picked out three more familiar faces: Anamaria Garcia, student teacher; Rita Martinez, bartender, single parent—a secondary photo of a young girl was stapled beneath; and Jennifer Costas's replacement, stolen just the night before, Elena Llosa. The girl was ridiculously young, made Sylvie think of Zoe. Her hand fell to her cell phone in her pocket, but she refrained. What would she say? "Just thinking about you"? "Hoping you're careful"? At best, she'd get a huff of irritation. At worst, a pissed-off teenager asserting her independence.

"Atheist," Sylvie said. *That* was unusual. Most of Miami's Hispanic population were brought up in a dozen shades of religious. Everything from holiday devotions to daily prayers. Young women who were atheist enough to make it a real point in their lives were not that common.

It made sense, though, went with Jennifer Costas's ghostly lament. If Azpiazu was bartering with the women's souls for a god's aid, the women would have to be atheist. A god stealing another god's follower was more than a divine faux pas; it was an act of war that could ripple through the pantheons.

"I was hoping to find a smoking gun, something I could use to warn his next targets. But atheists are still a huge pool," Cachita said. "No way to get the word out, no way to home in on his next victim. And with this many, I have to assume there are going to be more."

Sylvie looked back at the older "missings" and shuddered. Cachita had found thirteen that fit the sorcerer's need. "He's burning through them. They're not lasting long enough."

"Burning—"

Sylvie bit her lip, and Cachita said, "Please, Sylvie. I need to know what he's doing."

"Why do you care so much?" Sylvie said. "You a *Magicus Mundi* junkie? Can't get enough of magical mayhem?"

Cachita yanked a photo from the older column; the staple stayed behind, a shiny scar in the soft plaster. Sylvie stared at it, and reluctantly took the slick paper. She let her gaze drift down. Elena Valdes.

Valdes.

Elena Valdes.

Caridad Valdes-Pedraza.

Sister? Cousins?

It was a common enough name, but Cachita's face was clenched tight, all her confidence washed away and replaced by misery. "She's been gone for seven weeks. I think she's dead. I *know* she's dead. She wouldn't leave her family otherwise. You said he's burning through them?"

Sylvie closed her eyes. Fuck, but she hated giving out bad news. "The sorcerer's cursed. He's using the women to control his curse. Binding them into the spell. Filtering the inimical power. The curse comes in, strikes the women, and he pulls out enough cleaned-up power to control his shape-shifting. But it's hard on them, and eventually, they . . ."

They didn't just die. He killed them. Took their hearts, devoured their souls. But why? How did that match with the assumption that he was offering their souls to the god?

It didn't.

Soul-devourer, Wales had said. He dealt with the dead. He'd be familiar with the leftovers after a god took a soul. No one called that soul-devouring. That was just the natural state of things.

The sorcerer was doing more than just bartering the women's souls.

Sylvie's stomach churned with fury. She was working for this son of a bitch. Helping him when he'd already killed more women than she could save.

"Is that how he's doing it?" Cachita murmured. "That bastard."

Her body was one tight shiver of emotion. Sylvie couldn't read it, but it looked painful. Cachita might be a crusader for truth, but that didn't mean truth couldn't hurt her.

"We have a lead on him," Sylvie said. She didn't mention that she'd met the sorcerer. The shame of it lingered in her skin. She was helping him. But not for any longer than necessary. If Wales could break the spell. If they could free the women. If she could put a bullet in his brain. "There's a sorcerous Basque lineage—"

"Eladio Azpiazu," Cachita said. "I know."

"How'd you find that name?" Sylvie said. "Alex tell you?" Bad enough that Alex had told Cachita where to find her. To share case info?

Cachita said, "You're standing in the middle of weeks of research. Do you think I need to crib info from your assistant? I have my sources. You made yourself unpopular with the sorcerous community, and Alex is well-known as your girl Friday. I'm an unknown. They talked to me."

"Share," Sylvie said. She pulled out a chair from the dining-room table; the wood scraped unpleasantly along the tile and made her tight nerves wind tighter. Cachita folded herself onto it, resting her hands on the heavy arms of the chair, leaned her head back.

"They say," Cachita said, "that the Eladio Azpiazu who's around now is the same Eladio Azpiazu who was around then. That there's only ever been one of him. A murderous power-hungry monster who experimented on and took the heart of every shape-shifter that crossed his path. The soul-devourer."

"It's not the same man," Sylvie said. "It might be the same name." Sorcerers weren't immortal. They weren't even particularly long-lived. Their lifestyle tended to be hard on them, and their apprentices usually turned against them.

"They say it is," Cachita said. "They say he got cursed by another sorcerer; that all his stolen power would back-fire and make him the monster forever. A punishment he richly deserved—" Her voice dropped to a growl. "And now he's pushing it off onto innocents!" The wall of photos should have withered beneath the heat of her gaze.

"It doesn't work that way," Sylvie said. "Think about it, Cachita. If sorcerers could grant immortality, don't you think they'd apply it to themselves first? Not their enemies."

Cachita's angry gaze shifted. "I'm telling you the truth," she snapped. Then she let out her breath. "Sorry. That's what they told me."

"Did they tell you anything about the sorcerer who cursed him? Tepé?"

Cachita chewed her lip, white teeth denting red gloss, taking on a bit of the color. "They say . . . They say that he cursed Azpiazu in the eighteen hundreds."

Sylvie frowned. That couldn't be true either. Not if Azpiazu expected her to deal with Tepé in modern day. Sylvie might have gaps in her *mundi* education, but that was one thing she was certain of: Immortality was bestowed by the gods, and *only* by the gods. Even the Sphinx wasn't immortal. Only impossibly long-lived.

Cachita looked up from beneath dark lashes, and said,

"They say that Tepeyollotl cursed him because Azpiazu took his last acolyte."

Sylvie went abruptly cold. *Acolyte* wasn't a regular word in the sorcerous community. Apprentice. Follower. Novice. Yes.

Acolyte was a godly word.

And Tepeyollotl was a far cry from the simple and fairly mundane *Tepé*. Sylvie knew that name from Mesoamerican history. Tepeyollotl was an Aztec god.

No wonder Azpiazu had been coy about his enemy. No wonder he had recruited her. The new Lilith. The one who could kill the unkillable. She hadn't been drafted to break a curse, no matter his claims. Azpiazu expected her to kill a god.

. . .

SYLVIE PULLED OUT ANOTHER HEAVY CHAIR AND DROPPED INTO IT. Tepeyollotl. A god.

She put her face in her hands. Going up against a sorcerer could be difficult enough. But a god . . .

"Sylvie?" Cachita said. She squeaked when Sylvie jerked to her feet, started pacing the room. The movement felt good, eased the shake in her bones. A god.

Maybe she didn't have to approach him as an enemy.

Yeah, right, her little voice growled. *He's not going to care about five mortal women.*

Depressingly true. It was like one of those damn SAT analogies. God is to man as man is to insect. Interaction was based on either ignoring the lesser creature, controlling it, or, occasionally, swatting it.

Still. He cared enough about a mortal to curse Azpiazu in the first place, Sylvie thought. Assuming Cachita's third-hand story had truth to it. Tepeyollotl might care that Azpiazu had found a loophole in his punishment.

Or he might be on the other side of the magical divide, mourning his glory days, too lazy to be bothered with human insecta.

Azpiazu had told Sylvie that Tepé would follow him;

but then again, Azpiazu expected attention, demanded it.
Sylvie had only met the sorcerer once, but she had that
much of his personality figured out. Sociopath. Attention
whore. It was all about him. Either his fear of Tepé was
inherent and false, or a frightening possibility. Gods ruined every party they crashed.

It still didn't make sense. If Azpiazu was cursed by
Tepeyollotl, bartering with another god couldn't happen:
"Curse" or "claim," the words meant the same thing in
divine circles.

There was no way that Azpiazu was bartering with one
god to keep another one at bay. But if he was dedicating
the souls to Tepeyollotl, if he was trying to appease the
god . . . That wasn't it either.

Somehow, Azpiazu was using Tepeyollotl's own power
against him. Using Tepeyollotl's strength to hide from
Tepeyollotl's curse.

The god wouldn't stand for that. He'd come searching
for his prey. Azpiazu had said as much.

"Sylvie?" Cachita said again. This time, when she spoke,
Sylvie ceased her pacing all at once, found her breath
rasping in her throat.

If Tepeyollotl were in the area, the world would bend
around him. When the god of Justice had walked the
streets, the world had rippled and changed according to
his will. And he'd been trying to keep the damage minimal.

If Tepeyollotl were in Florida, there would be *signs*.
Undeniable signs.

"Cachita," she said.

The woman jumped. The chair rattled against the floor
like a chattering of teeth, and Sylvie said, "You brought
me here to show me your files."

Cachita nodded. "The women—"

"You've got more on the board than just the women,"
Sylvie said. She'd get to the women later. Their information could be easily digested. Tepeyollotl required more
thought.

"Where they were last seen, that sort of thing."

"You've been hunting Azpiazu. How?"

Cachita frowned. "You *know* how—"

"How do you choose the clubs you do?"

"Oh!" Cachita said. "Weird shit happening around them. Like the Casa de Dia restaurant. A man who was a monster. Or a wolf seen in the streets. A street where all the lights failed at once. No explanation. Or other things that might be magic."

Sylvie graced the woman with an honest smile. Cachita wasn't Alex. Lacked the intuition that made Alex a gem. But she wasn't that bad. "Things that might be magic. Like . . ."

Cachita said, "Like a murder?"

"Are you asking?" Sylvie said. "Or telling me?"

Cachita shook her head. "Sorry. I meant, there have been some weird murders in the last couple of days. People with their heads torn right off—"

"That's . . . special," Sylvie agreed. "But not what I'm looking for." Murder was pretty direct for a god; she was expecting smaller, more pervasive things. World-warping things.

"You don't think so?" Cachita asked. "There are some strange circumstances—they were all killed behind locked doors."

"Were they bastards?" Sylvie said. "'Cause murder's easy. Sorcerers. Witches. Human hit men. Hell, corrupt cops can call a crime scene secured when it's not. I'm looking for really weird. Like *el monstruo*."

Cachita said, "I'll keep looking. It would help if you'd let me in on your epiphany. Tepeyollotl means something to you." Eagerness sharpened her voice. "You know something about him. Tell me. How do you deal with him?"

Sylvie dropped into a chair, studied Cachita across the table, trying to figure out how this was going to go. There was a quantifiable difference, Sylvie had noticed, between someone accepting the sorcerers and monsters of the *Magicus Mundi* and accepting the gods.

"If the stories you heard are true—if Azpiazu is the original recipe, then Tepeyollotl is a god."

Cachita's lips parted. She looked . . . rapt. "A god," she whispered. Sylvie fought off a shiver. Cachita was a junkie for the *Magicus Mundi*, which meant working with her was about as safe as working with a known spy. She could go double agent at the drop of a hat, or magical bribe.

"How do you deal with a god?" she went on to ask. "How do you talk to one? Do you think he'll help you?" Lip-lick. Dilated eyes. Could be fear; could be excitement. Could be both. Cachita seemed like the type to enjoy a scare. "Help *us*?"

Sylvie grimaced briefly. "Gods are bad news, Cachita. They don't make a habit of helping. At least not in my experience. Tepeyollotl cursed Azpiazu. I don't think asking him to remove the curse is going to go over well. Gods don't like to change their minds."

Cachita said, "But Azpiazu's not suffering. He's pushing it onto others. That's not what Tepeyollotl intended. He's probably furious. Probably ready to punish Azpiazu all over again. If he could find him. And if you, if *we*, tell him about the binding spell in detail, I bet he could find Azpiazu again. . . ."

"And the women?" Sylvie said. "I'm all for Azpiazu getting his just deserts, but Tepeyollotl won't care about the women. Their souls are already his; living or dead, it's the same to him." She wrapped her arms about herself, remembering the hotel room, hiding from that angry, hungry force coming to claim Jennifer.

"Look, Cachita, for all we know, Azpiazu's *curse* is specifically designed to feed souls to Tepeyollotl. Aztec gods are big on sacrifice. So, Tepeyollotl's hitting the mundane world's about as safe as standing at ground zero when a volcano erupts. People will die. Depending on how much power Tepeyollotl wields, a lot of people."

Something brushed against the wall, a rasp behind the paper, and Sylvie jumped, realized that Cachita had taped her files right over the window. She peeled back the nearest sheaf of files, and a cat leaped off the narrow sill, slinking back into the depths of the overgrown yard.

"That bad?" Cachita said.

"With gods, it's best to think worst-case scenario. Best to solve it ourselves and keep Tepeyollotl from even getting involved."

Cachita said, "You make it sound like kids cleaning up a mess before Mom gets home. How do you hide things from a god?" Cachita had finally caught Sylvie's growing fear. Her questions were whispers; her eyes flicked around the room as if she expected eavesdroppers.

"Azpiazu's apparently found a way," Sylvie said. "But mostly, it's about acting quickly and not getting their attention in the first place." She grimaced. *Don't get their attention.* Easy enough to say, but their entire plan—breaking the binding spell—hinged on doing something that would set off the equivalent of a neon sign flashing for Tepeyollotl's attention.

"The binding sigils," Cachita said. "Can I have copies of them? Maybe I can get some help?"

Sylvie said, "I don't have them with me." It was a lie, but the last thing Cachita needed was to start messing around with magic. "I've got someone researching them."

"The Ghoul?" Cachita asked. "He has them?"

Sylvie scowled. "Christ, you are a stalker."

"I just . . . Those women are in danger," Cachita said. "I want to help."

Sylvie sighed. As determined as Alex. She wanted to be useful. Sylvie wanted to use her. Problem was, Sylvie couldn't trust her. From the furrow in her brow, Cachita was picking up on that. The space between them, littered with names of dead or dying women, grew tense.

"Tell me about those murders, again," Sylvie said. It was a peace offering of sorts.

"You'll tell me what the Ghoul finds out?" Cachita countered.

"Sure," Sylvie said. She might. When Hell froze over.

Cachita might want to dive headfirst into the doings of gods and sorcerers, but she didn't know what she was asking for.

Gatekeeper's a thankless job, her voice reminded her. *And often futile.*

Sylvie ignored it. Cachita might be overeager, potentially treacherous, but she didn't deserve to get ground up by the *Magicus Mundi.* Later, when her first excitement had burned off, she'd thank Sylvie.

Cachita eyed her, as if everything she'd thought had been clear on her face, and she was deciding whether to let it slide or pick a fight right then, right there.

Sylvie leaned back in the chair, listening to the wood creak faintly, and put her feet on the table. "The murders?"

Cachita caved. "Three of them over the last two days. Two men, one woman. Heads—"

"—torn right off, I remember," Sylvie said. Interest sparked despite herself. Three people, two days. Someone was busy. And strong. Cut off could be done by anyone with a sharp enough tool and a strong enough stomach. Torn off was monster territory.

If they'd all been women, Sylvie might have considered Azpiazu for it, but Miami was a big city. Big enough for multiple monsters. She reminded herself that she wasn't a crusader.

"No one's freaking out about it because they weren't great people. A drive-by shooter who killed a kid. A rapist who preyed on schoolgirls. A woman who drove her car through a playground during recess. No one's really mourning them."

"Kids damaged each time," Sylvie said. A signature. But not Azpiazu's. She didn't know enough about Tepe-yollotl to make a judgment. She didn't think he was doing it himself, but gods could radiate influence. When Kevin Dunne, the god of Justice, had sought his missing lover, the police had turned all their energies to doing his will.

"You think it means something?" Cachita asked.

"Yeah. But not my something. Azpiazu's enough to deal with," Sylvie said. "I can't afford to be distracted." Easy to say, hard to do. She *was* distracted. Odalys threatened her friends and family. Patrice was trying to kill her.

Sylvie scrubbed at her face as if she could scrape off the day's accumulated frustrations. Outside in the garden, cats screamed, and Sylvie twitched.

Cachita said, "It's late. We can talk about it in the morning. Are you staying? I've got a guest room."

"Yeah, why not," Sylvie said. Ungracious, but she was thinking about being greeted at sunrise with Cachita's eagerness to go play with magic, as mindless as a puppy wanting to chase cars on the freeway.

Her ringing phone gave her an excuse to wave Cachita off; she picked it up, stepped out onto a back porch that stank of tomcat.

"So, Shadows, you dead or what?" Wales asked. His drawl clipped off most of the consonants, turned sarcasm into a tired slurry of words.

"Not yet," she said. His exhaustion was a weight on the line; it made her confession that much harder to voice. She never liked admitting she screwed up. "Hey, Tex? I slipped up. Let that damned reporter know about the sigils. She might come sniffing around, asking questions. For her own good, don't talk to her."

There was a long pause on the line, a heavy sigh. "You're worried about *her*?"

"You're cautious," she said. "You know what can go wrong. It's all shiny, new, and exciting to her. She wants to play—"

"Idiot," he muttered. "Keep her away from me. Lois Lanes get the good guys killed in the real world."

"Speaking of getting killed," she said.

"Aw fuck," he said. "No good ever came of a sentence begun like that, Shadows."

"You remember that Tepé the soul-devourer talked about?"

"You got a lead on him?"

"Tepeyollotl."

Wales was quiet a long moment, then said, "Isn't that an Aztec god?"

"The very one."

"Aw fuck," Wales said again. Breathless this time, no amusement in it.

"Thing is, Tex, he's probably not in the world yet. I'd like to keep it that way. And we might have sent up a flare earlier—"

"The thing that came for Jennifer Costas—"

"Yeah," Sylvie said. "Tepeyollotl come hunting a soul that was dedicated to him."

"So why is Azpiazu dedicating souls to him if they're enemies?" Wales said.

Sylvie sank down onto the rickety edge of the porch, dangled her feet over the dark, tangled grass. "I don't pretend to know how gods think, but if I were Tepé, wouldn't it be part of punishment? To force your enemy to consecrate souls in your name? A method of increasing your followers?"

"Except Azpiazu's devouring the souls instead," Wales said.

"Hence the problem," Sylvie said. "But the point of all this—stay out of the ether, Wales. Don't ghost hunt. Don't draw attention."

"What about you?"

Sylvie said, "I'm staying at Cachita's tonight. I think if I tried to get to yours, she'd only follow."

"I rescind my welcome," he said. "I could use some downtime anyway."

"Just you and dead Marco," Sylvie said. A week ago, that would have been a taunt. Now it was nearly affectionate. Wales might be a necromancer, but he was proving himself an asset. A necromancer, but a good guy. One step from being *her* necromancer.

"You know it," he said, and disconnected.

No sorcerers are good guys, her little dark voice objected. *Paranoia is healthy.*

Sylvie went back into the house, escaping her circling thoughts and the garden stink; Cachita startled away from the back entry, pasting a quick smile on her face. Sylvie gave her back a tight grin. "Eavesdroppers rarely hear good about themselves."

"Even when they're playing host?" Cachita asked.

"Sorry," Sylvie said. "I'm not so good at following rules."

10

Politics as Usual

SUNLIGHT GLEAMED JUNGLE GREEN AND GOLD THROUGH CACHITA'S kitchen window, a lacy pattern on the dusty floor. Over-grown trees pressed close against the glass, making the room feel dimmer than it should, the day later than it was. Sylvie checked her watch again—8:00 a.m., and Cachita was already gone, doing god knew what, leaving Sylvie to snoop through her house at will.

Pity of it was there was so little to see. Two bedrooms yielded two beds, and, in Cachita's closet, a handful of discarded clothes. The living room was empty of all furniture, and the dining room held only the table, two chairs, and the walls of paper.

Sylvie closed another empty kitchen cupboard and checked out a drawer that held a collection of dead spiders. She grimaced and slid it shut again. The refrigerator, bulb burned out, held a single take-out container with a fork and knife resting on top.

Hell, maybe Cachita had gone out for breakfast, and was on her way back, coffees to hand.

Her stomach turned over in hope. Her brain suggested she take advantage of Cachita's absence to get gone before she was saddled with an intrepid reporter for the day. She was tired; she was hungry; she was dressed in yesterday's clothes. None of that could be fixed by dawdling in Cachita's house not-so-beautiful.

Her phone rang. "Lio?"

"Sylvie, I need to talk to you. Now," he said. "My house. Hurry."

Then silence. A brief spurt of irritation flared, tramped out by worry. Lio had sounded . . . frightened. Maybe Odalys had turned her attention to the man who'd arrested her.

Sylvie gave up the search for anything edible and headed for her truck. She made a quick stop in the dining room, snagged the pics and files on Azpiazu's victims. Cachita would be pissed, but whatever. Sylvie could do more with the names and files than she could. Most protection spells worked better if they were specific to the person. Wales might be able to ramp up his unbinding spell if he knew the women's names. If they could find them again.

While the thought was sharp in her mind, Sylvie texted Alex. New research. Azpiazu's black van. Caridad's background. She clicked the phone shut, feeling accomplished all out of proportion.

Twenty minutes of driving brought her to Lio's house. Like Cachita's place, it was 1920s stucco, set on a small plot. Unlike Cachita's, it was immaculately kept. The grass was plush and green, the stucco white, the tile roof burnished by sunlight and care.

It looked serene, and Sylvie wanted to bask in it rather than step inside to conflict and stress. She wondered what Lio had gotten into that brought that note of desperation to his voice. Wouldn't find out by standing outside, admiring the lawn.

The white eyelet curtain in the door twitched.

Busted, she thought. As if her truck's diesel growl and its coughing sputter of a stop hadn't betrayed her arrival.

She stiffened her spine and marched up the gravel path.

The door opened before her, Lourdes scowling in the frame. "You took your time."

"Be glad I wasn't coming from the office," Sylvie said. "I'd be stuck in traffic for at least another half hour. What's going on? Is Lio okay?"

The hallway was dim after the brilliant sunlight outside, and the rooms beyond the shallow foyer weren't lit—Sylvie jerked back, got her hand on the gun, just as the Suit entered the hall.

"Sylvie Lightner," the Suit said. Mr. Tall, Dark, Angry from the bar. He looked like he was holding a grudge for the embarrassment of the night before. "AKA Shadows. AKA the New Lilith. Scourge of god. *L'enfant du Meurtrier.* Have I left anything off?"

"Scourge of god's a new one," Sylvie said. "I don't like it."

"Oh yes," he said. "Smart-ass bitch."

"You don't get to call me that on our first date. Hell, you never even bought me the drink you suggested," Sylvie said. Her back was against the door; she had the distinct feeling that if she turned, that quiet lawn and street would no longer be so empty. "So you have a name, or do I get to make up one on my own?"

"Don't make this difficult, Lightner."

"I'm good at difficult," she said.

Behind him, two more Suits lurked, a man and a woman, Lio sitting stiffly on the couch between them. He met her gaze briefly, looked away, his mouth pulled tight. Her simmering anger moved to a faster boil.

You have a gun, her little voice prompted. *Even a body shield in the form of one sturdy Cuban housewife.*

"Sylvie," Lio said, a rumble that carried desperation. "They just want to talk."

"I've got a phone," she said. "And I'm in the book."

"We're old-fashioned," the ISI squad head said. "We like face-to-faces to be on our turf. Don't worry. We can be gracious hosts."

It took more willpower than she'd expected to take her hand off her gun, to let the female agent take it from her, to let them surround her. She felt a little like a tiger in a big-cat press at the zoo, and from their wary expressions, they felt like newbie vet students.

But then, the ISI's numbers had taken a hit in Chicago. They might be as green as they looked. The woman patted her down, her touch tentative. "She's clean, Riordan."

The squad head—Riordan—opened the door, and she had been right. A black SUV had appeared out of nowhere; no doubt it had been burning gas circling the block, just out of sight. Sylvie took the passenger seat and dared the waiting driver to object. If she was going to be hauled in by the ISI, she was doing it on her terms.

Lio was handed into the back of the SUV, moving stiffly, his bandages evident. They were pristine white, recently placed, and with loving care. Sylvie looked out the tinted window, saw Lourdes slumped against the door frame, and when Lio said, "I had to call you," she didn't bite his head off.

"I know," she said. It wasn't forgiveness, but it was understanding. The ISI could be real bastards. She didn't think their threats were anything more than bullyboy posturing, but she couldn't blame Lio and Lourdes, immigrants from a Castro Cuba, for taking them seriously.

"Just next time, Lio? Give me a fuckin' hint."

The SUV growled into movement and Sylvie closed her eyes, wondering what the hell the ISI wanted this time.

There was so much to choose from.

• • •

SHE AND LIO WERE HUSTLED THROUGH A CLAMMY PARKING GARAGE, taken into a basement room big on white paint and cheap furniture, short on charm. They were locked in and left.

Lio swallowed. "Shadows, what's going on? Feds don't usually—"

"Did they tell you they were FBI?" she asked. "They're not. They're the ISI. Internal Surveillance and Investigation. They're all about the magic. Did they say what they wanted?"

Lio shook his head, winced, put a hand to the healing lacerations.

Sylvie paced, thought aloud. "It has to involve both of us, or they wouldn't have brought you along. You're no kind of leverage against me. No offense, Lio, but it's true."

"Lo sé," he said. "So, the ladies in the Everglades, then? Do you think they know you studied the bodies?"

"They do now," she muttered.

He grimaced. "Sorry."

"Ah, they probably knew. Though"—she raised her voice a bit, put an edge on it—"it's amazing how many things manage to happen right below their noses. Would you believe that a crazy immortal wandered in and out of their Chicago offices at will? And they didn't notice until she started killing them? I could tell you stories—"

Lio frowned, lost. The door to the room opened, and two agents came in. Agent Riordan from Lio's house, and a blond fireplug of a man with an ugly expression.

The blond leaned up against the door, crossed his arms over his thick chest. The dark man leaned over the table, tried for smooth and intimidating. Demalion had done it better. "I'm Agent John Riordan. I've been assigned to your case."

"Man," Sylvie said. "Sucks to be you." She met his stare head-on, keeping just enough focus on the rest of the room that when the blond agent rushed forward and slapped the table, Lio was the only one who jumped.

Riordan said, "Janssen." It wasn't quite a reprimand. Had the weary edge of a *We've talked about this—you said you'd do better* moment.

Silence fell over the room again. Lio, wincing, crossed his arms over his broad chest, gave the young agents a flat stare.

Sylvie said, "You know, I've got a complicated reputation. I'll admit that. But you know what no one's ever said? That I'm psychic. If you have a question, ask it. I'm not going to guess."

"Odalys Hargrove," Janssen said.

"What about her?"

"Tell us about her," Riordan said. "You two conspired

to put her in jail on charges that frankly don't stand up to decent scrutiny. What's the real deal?"

Lio said, "You're here for Hargrove? What about the women in the Everglades?"

"Not my case," Riordan said. Utterly disinterested. "You're my purview, Shadows. Not some magical serial killer."

Sylvie interrupted Lio's next comment, put her hand down hard on his wrist. His cheeks, beneath the dark patchwork of stitches, flushed to a brick color that made Sylvie think of strokes and heart attacks. "Odalys Hargrove is a necromancer," she said. She didn't usually approve of telling the ISI anything, but hell, she'd put this in motion by asking Demalion to pass the word. It wasn't Lio's fault they were there. It was hers.

And if she wanted them to do something about Odalys, she needed to make her case against the woman. Otherwise, bad-tempered Janssen and disinterested Riordan would have no problem leaving Odalys to the usual justice system just to spite Sylvie. "She started a nifty little business that transferred the souls of the rich and recently deceased into the bodies of teenagers. It killed the teens, and endangered a hell of a lot of other people in the process. Odalys Hargrove is not someone that jail will keep down for long. Necromancers use organic matter for their magic, and jails are full of that. A scrap of nail, a lock of hair, a bit of blood, and Odalys could take back her power, person by person. Odalys is—"

"Dead," Riordan said. He dropped into the seat opposite Sylvie; the tight anger on his face eased back, shifted toward skepticism. "You didn't know."

"No," Sylvie said. Kept her denial flat, her surprise minimal. He was ISI; he wouldn't believe any protestation she could make.

"Get up," he said. "I have something to show you."

Curiosity got her to her feet when irritation at being bossed around urged her to settle herself more firmly in her chair. Lio rose a beat behind and was waved back to his seat.

Janssen said, "Want to keep your shield, Detective? Take a seat."

"It's all right, Lio," Sylvie said. Better for him to stay out of it if it was even possible.

The Miami ISI headquarters had moved since the last time she'd looked for it. Given what she could see after a trip up in the service elevator—wide hallways, plush, patterned carpets, the sheer number of doors they passed, all identical, all evenly spaced—she assumed they had taken over the fourth floor of a Miami hotel. The ISI were big on having their offices among other buildings.

When Sylvie had asked Demalion about it, he'd said that it meant they had nothing to hide. Sylvie thought it meant that they had facilities they wanted to hide very badly, and this was their way of throwing off suspicion.

Whatever their reasoning, it made it surreal—her body keeping count of rooms, of familiar proportions—to find, instead of a hotel laundry room, a makeshift morgue.

It wasn't much of a morgue. Sterile, but small. More like a one-room research lab with a very hefty budget and very small space. Lots of technology; very narrow table in the center of the room. It actually looked more like a chest freezer than anything else. It hummed like one. A chest freezer with a plasticized white sheet draped over a human-sized form.

"They found her late last night in her cell," Riordan said. "Strung up against her bars, and"—he flipped back the sheets—"mutilated."

Sylvie swallowed hard, concentrated on keeping her face impassive. She had a reputation after all. *Hard as nails.*

She wished the word "nails" hadn't crossed her mind. They made her think of hands, and Odalys was down two of them. Sliced off cleanly at the wrists.

"Sends a message, don't you think?" Riordan said. "My question is from whom to whom? Can you shed some light, Shadows?" He wasn't as calm as he wanted to be. His fingers twitched; he stuffed his hands into his pockets.

Sylvie pulled the sheet back up over Odalys's con-

torted face; the woman hadn't died easy. A vicious wound
nearly bisected her chest, tearing through ribs and organs,
like the world's worst autopsy student had made a desperate last attempt to impress with effort if not competence.
Another agent might take it as a weakness on her part to
cover Odalys, but she thought Riordan was just grateful
he didn't have to do it himself. Besides, it bought her some
time to think.

Odalys's death was on her head. She knew that. She'd
asked Demalion to pass the word along; she hadn't antici-
pated them killing Odalys—though truthfully, she hadn't
thought it through. What had she expected them to do?

Demalion had passed the word along. The ISI had responded. And Odalys was dead. So why were they dragging her in and asking her questions that felt . . . honestly
confused?

"Shadows," Riordan said. "I'm waiting."

"I don't know what to tell you," she said. "She killed
some very influential people's children. That kind of thing
makes powerful enemies."

"*You* have a reputation for being a powerful enemy," he
said.

"Does my reputation give me the ability to walk into a
secured jail, armed with what? A machete? Hedge trim-
mers? Sorry, Agent. You'll have to look beyond me for the
killer."

He leaned back against the door, keeping her contained.
"That your only answer?"

"The only one I have that you'll like."

"I *don't* like it. You could try again. If you have any
plans for the day other than babysitting Odalys's body.
I'm curious. Do you think necromancers recover from being dead?"

"No," Sylvie said. "They're just dead." She studied him
again, began to get his measure. He might be Janssen's
boss, her new personal spook, but he wasn't much more
than a researcher, someone dragged out of the labs to fill
in a manpower gap.

Might even be the answer to why he dragged her in. Odalys's death provided him a chance to take a crack at her, something all ISI agents wanted.

"You could have gotten into the prison," he said, testing. "I've been following you. You associate with the Ghoul. Our files suggest he has the ability to break in anywhere, unseen and unstoppable. The CIA has him marked down as a threat to national security. You expect me to believe that he couldn't get you inside the jail?"

"Are you kidding?" Sylvie laughed. Wales spent all his time trying to keep a low profile. Magical murder behind prison bars was not low-profile. "Sorry. I think the bad guy you're looking for is much closer to home. You should be careful. You might be stepping on toes above your pay grade."

She turned her back on Odalys's corpse and reached for the doorknob. He put his hand down over hers; his skin was soft, unmarked. Definitely a newbie in the field. "What do you mean?"

"You said it yourself. The ISI watches me. They probably saw me dealing with Odalys. They probably recognized the threat right away. What do you think the higher-ups decided to do about Odalys's existence?"

"We don't kill people," Riordan said.

"You can tell yourself that all you want," Sylvie said. "Doesn't make it so."

He gave ground; she let herself out into the hall, breathed in the softer air of recently vacuumed carpet, slightly dusty light fixtures, and nothing of bleach and death.

Lio and Janssen broke off their staring contest when she opened the door. Janssen's face twisted into a scowl. Lio's didn't warm much either; in fact, he looked downright angry. "You done playing, Shadows? 'Cause Lourdes is going to be frantic."

"Yeah, we're going," Sylvie said.

Janssen said, "No, you're not—"

Riordan just shook his head. "Yeah, she is."

Lio pushed himself up out of his seat; the table creaked

beneath his palms. Still hurting, still sore. Sylvie reached to give him some support, and he jerked away from her touch, headed slowly out the door.

"Are you giving us a ride back?" Sylvie asked. "Or do I bill you for the cab fare?"

"I'll get you a driver," Riordan muttered. "Don't get used to it, Shadows. I'm still going to . . ." He trailed off.

"You're not very good at being threatening," Sylvie said. "Work on it."

Sylvie made her way back out toward the front of the hotel, found Lio there, blinking and swaying in the sunlight, and reached to steady him again. He shook her off. "Don't touch me."

"What's your problem?" Sylvie asked. "I should be the pissy one. You're the guy who turned me in to the ISI."

"You killed Odalys," Lio said.

"I did not," she said. "Christ, Lio, she was in jail."

"Don't blaspheme," he muttered. He paced, forcing some fluidity into sore limbs, gone stiff with his hospital stay, and the no-doubt bed rest that Lourdes would have prescribed. "Janssen said the killer took her hands. That she was tortured before she died. You did that?"

"I didn't," Sylvie said. "You have a hearing problem? I don't kill people."

"No," he said. "Maybe not directly. You have pagan gods do it for you." His voice broke, and in the crack it left, Sylvie saw fear.

She should have expected it. She had expected it days ago, back when she first started to explain the *Magicus Mundi* to him, had seen a glimmer of panic in his hospital bed, but this—this was the corrosive terror that meant he wasn't going to cope. He'd wanted to know, and the knowledge was going to break him.

She'd made a mistake telling him.

Into the silence, Lio said, "This is a democratic country. There's a contract that we keep faith with. We arrest people, we try them, we find them guilty or we acquit them. They are sentenced. Their punishment takes their time and their freedom, or a death that we make simple and clean. We don't torture for punishment or for proof. We don't sentence people before their trials. An eye for an eye leaves the world blind. Vengeance destroys what makes us human."

Sylvie growled. "You were pleased enough that your son's killers were destroyed. You are a hypocrite, Lio."

"Perhaps I am. But I didn't sentence them. You did."

A black SUV pulled up, smooth as silk, into the roadway before them; a dark-haired woman in a suit got out, and said, "So where am I taking you?" The question was directed at both of them, but the woman's focus was all on Sylvie.

"You're taking him home," Sylvie said. "I'll find my own ride." Best to give Suarez some space, some time to calm down. He'd lived through a Castro Cuba, earned citizenship by fighting in the Gulf, worked his way up the ranks in the Miami police. He was a tough bastard.

"Damn," she said. "I was hoping we could chat."

Lio eased himself into the passenger seat, closed the door with a solid thud. The driver lingered, standing on the curb, waiting for Sylvie's response. Sylvie blinked; she hadn't thought the woman's attention was anything more than ISI attitude.

"Doubt we have anything to talk about," Sylvie said. She badly wanted to be out of there, away from the ISI. And this suit in particular was beginning to set off alarm bells. It wasn't the woman's poise or confidence, wasn't the tough-girl vibe that made Sylvie convinced the woman was a brawler and a gunfighter. It was that she acted like she knew Sylvie.

"We could start with the favor I did for you. Or we could talk about Michael Demalion," she said. "But if you won't, you won't." She saluted Sylvie briefly, a quick twist of her fingers near her brows, a casual gesture that should have been mocking. But the woman's hand, drawn to Sylvie's attention, looked . . . bloodstained. A mottled, muddy crimson wash over her knuckles and palm, rising upward to her wrist and beyond.

It wasn't a birthmark or skin ailment. Sylvie had seen that mark before, and recently.

"Wait," Sylvie said.

"Too late," the woman said. "Don't worry. I'm sure we'll get together at some point."

The agent climbed into the SUV and disappeared into the steady stream of traffic. Sylvie, despite wanting to get away from the ISI, found herself meandering gently to the nearest bench and dropping into it. The metal slats were soothingly warm through her clothes, and she leaned back. Her head was going to burst. Ducks squabbled on the green surface of the nearby canal.

Too much information—murdered Odalys, Tepeyollotl, the need to find Azpiazu, Azpiazu's theoretical immortality, the falling-out with Lio, and now this ISI mind game?

Murderer, her little dark voice whispered, belatedly identifying the female ISI agent. Not by name, but by profession.

Even if she hadn't mentioned Demalion and a favor in the same breath, Sylvie would have known. She'd done some quiet research on her own since Zoe's incident, since that same magical scar showed up on her sister's flesh, trying to figure out what that scar meant. Rumors proliferated—the only clear truths she could grasp were that the scarring was rare and only blossomed on specialized killers. What made them special, no one knew.

Sylvie plucked at the gaps in the bench, drew lines between the bars, bridging the eternally distant, and gave in to impulse. She called Demalion.

It rang, but he didn't answer. She disconnected before Wright's voice mail could pick up, waited.

Her phone buzzed. "Shadows," she said.

"Sorry, honey," Demalion said.

"You're at work," she said. "And not alone. They think it's your wife calling?"

"Seemed easiest," Demalion said.

"You got the word out on Odalys?" she asked.

"Took some careful maneuvering, but I did find a willing ear," he said.

"Did you know they'd kill her?"

The radio sounds in the background, the tangle of voices, and the clatter of movement through a crowded room kept her from demanding an answer when he went silent. Her patience paid off; the background noise changed to wind and distant murmuring. "Taking a cigarette break?"

"She's dead?" he asked.

"Yeah, and I got hauled in for questioning—what's that about?"

Demalion's voice, even in Wright's husky tenor, sounded edgy. "Syl, the ISI's changed. After Chicago, the factions within the agency started getting more . . . outspoken."

"Let me guess. One faction's all about putting down the magical threat."

"Hey, Odalys deserved to be dead—"

"Not arguing that," Sylvie said. "Really not. But your perky little ISI assassin cut Odalys's hands off, and that worries me. What, one for the Hand of Glory, and one for a trophy?"

Demalion swore quietly and steadily; Sylvie had the feeling that if he weren't hanging out at the cop shop, pretending to grab a smoke, he'd be all hissing intensity, his eyes narrowed to angry slits. Finally, he said, "My perky little assassin?"

"That's what you focus on?"

"It's the only part that I don't get," he said. "I don't know the assassin. C'mon, Syl, you're the closest thing I know to an—"

"Five-eight; short dark hair, dark eyes, cheerful personality, and oh . . . red right hand. She seemed to think she knew you."

"You sure?" Demalion asked. "She said that?"

Sylvie said, "No. Not exactly. She said we could talk about you."

"Fuck," Demalion said. "Look, Sylvie, don't tell them—"

"'Cause I so often talk freely with the ISI," she snapped.

"It's not just them," he said. "I'm making ripples here. Wright's life doesn't fit me well. I can't afford the wrong kind of attention."

"I thought you were going to court the ISI."

"On my terms, yeah," Demalion said. "But it's not about them. Sylvie, the Furies killed me on the say so of their god. I'm pretty sure I was supposed to stay dead."

Sylvie's stomach dropped. "If Dunne finds out—"

"Don't use his name," Demalion said. "Using a name gets a man's attention. I doubt a god would be less attentive."

"Hell, I've spent all of last night and this morning talking about a god and got nothing. But at least I'm giving him a headache."

"You're not trying to summon our mutual—"

"No," Sylvie said. "An Aztec god. Casc."

"Sounds like your case got complicated."

"You've no idea. My evil sorcerer–slash–serial kidnapper–slash–killer? Also immortal."

"You managed to beat Lilith," he said. "You can take him."

"Hell, Demalion. I'm working for him." She closed her eyes against the sun, the sting of it penetrating through her eyelids, heating her face. It felt a lot like shame.

"You have a reason for it," he said.

"Five reasons," she said. "Maria Ruben. Elena Llosa. Lupe Fernandez. Rita Martinez. Anamaria Garcia. He's holding them as leverage."

"You have a plan?"

"Not so much," she said. "Know how I want it to end. Dead sorcerer at my feet. Five women going home."

A voice on his end interrupted their chat, a raised shout with Wright's name tacked into it. Demalion sighed, his breath a gust in her ear. "Work calls."

"You going to look into the assassin?"

"Not unless you have to have the information right

now," he said. "I'm trying to keep a low profile, and pushing Odalys cost me some cover."

"Understood," Sylvie said. She let the connection drop, gnawed at her lip. She had to let it go. Odalys was done and dealt with, and it wasn't worth risking Demalion.

Another black car pulled into the pickup loop of the drive, a wash of exhaust in her face, and three black suits came out of the hotel to claim it. Sylvie grimaced; she'd nearly forgotten she was sitting in the ISI's lap.

She called Alex. "Come get me."

• • •

RATHER THAN WAIT OUTSIDE THE ISI OFFICES, SYLVIE WANDERED down the street, such as it was. The downtown hotels were heavy on business, not so much on amenities. But a mile or so gave her a breathing space between the ISI and her, and brought her to a long-desired cup of coffee at a lone coffee shop that made its money catering to desperate visitors who didn't want to pay hotel prices for food.

She had finished three cups and a breakfast sandwich, barely tasting any of it, picking at the tangled problem of sorcerer, god, victims. It was like a shell game, but with explosives. If she freed Azpiazu from the curse—he wasn't trustworthy. Those women would be dead. If she didn't free him from the curse—he'd burn them out. They'd be dead. She had to free him, but she had to get the women out of his range, first. Which meant Wales, untested spellwork, and a rush job, trying to do it all before Tepeyollotl came hunting.

It felt like a loser's game.

Alex pulled up. Sylvie left the air-conditioned coffee shop, hotfooted it over the sun-soaked cement between the door and Alex's car.

She slammed in, grateful for the heavy window tint. Alex got them moving again, and said, "Your truck?"

"Outside Lio's house unless he's feeling pissy and had it towed."

"I thought you two had made nice," Alex said.

"Temporary setback," Sylvie said. She propped her feet on the dash. "You have time to check out anything else on Azpiazu?"

"The original or the—"

"All the same man," Sylvie said. "Or so Cachita tells me."

"You believe her? Little while ago, you were saying her research was crap."

Sylvie studied the road unfolding before her, conscious of Alex's darting glances in her direction. "It's like this," she said finally. "I don't have any real proof. What I do have is a sorcerer who feels . . . off. Who practices old magic like it's natural, and who's entirely too confident even for a sorcerer. If he's been cursed with immortality—there has to be a god. Hell, given the way my luck runs—I should just plan for code red every single morning and save myself the time and wasted optimism."

Alex took a turn a little too fast; Sylvie swayed in the seat belt's grasp, thumped the door, steadied herself. "It would explain some things," Alex said. "While I've been looking for the sorcerer, hunting for anything that can be attributed to him—shape-shifting stories, missing women, attacks on women, that kind of thing—I've found a lot of weird shit going on. Miami's bubbling, Sylvie. It's like the frog in the boiling water. We didn't notice because it's happening gradually. But . . . there are different types of events."

"You break it down into categories?" Sylvie asked. It was a rhetorical question. Of course Alex had. She might look scattered, act scattered, but she was ruthlessly organized. Sylvie'd been in the girl's apartment. Alex alphabetized her CDs, her DVDs, her bookshelves, her spice racks, her pantry, her refrigerator. Her enormous array of cosmetics was Velcroed to a makeshift color wheel that took up a wall of the bathroom.

"There was the attack at Casa de Dia, a few other sudden man-to-monster sightings. One about every fifteen to twenty days, discarding the de Dia attack, which was triggered by the cops breaking the spell. A woman went missing after each episode."

Sylvie swallowed. That was bad news. If Azpiazu lost control of his shape when his deflective spell broke down, then the regularity of it suggested that the burnout of his human components took less than a month. Maria Ruben had been missing for a little more than two weeks. Her time was running out.

"So that's Azpiazu," Sylvie said. "Cachita told me about some locked-room murders."

"Oh, Cachita said . . ." Alex griped. "I'm not enough for you?" At Sylvie's look, she dropped it. "The decapitations? Yeah, nasty. They're on my list. But they're not Azpiazu."

"No," Sylvie agreed. "Not the god, either. Forcible decapitation isn't much in their line of things."

Alex lifted a shoulder. "Voodoo vengeance, maybe. Those people hurt kids, Sylvie. That's a pretty strong taboo. And their cases were public knowledge. But . . . maybe. Indirectly. You said in Chicago that with the Greek gods roaming around, all sorts of people suddenly grew powers. Might be something like that. A would-be crusader who suddenly has the ability to make it happen."

"By the time that was happening, Chicago was really zippy," Sylvie said. "Magical hurricanes, transformations all over the place. We would have noticed."

"True," Alex said. "So I'll slap an unknown on that one. Also? Two cops found dead in their patrol car. News is keeping things pretty quiet, but something sounds weird about it."

"Keep following it," Sylvie said, "and the decaps. That might end up on my desk if it goes on too long."

"Other than that," Alex said, "we've got some Fortean stuff happening, small scale. A woman who claimed the cats at the animal shelter started talking. Localized earthquakes—"

"Been there," Sylvie said, thinking abruptly of Wales and his struggle to hold Jennifer Costas's ghost. "You heard from Wales?"

"Gave him a call," Alex said. "I was going to invite

him to breakfast. He didn't pick up, though. You think I came on too strong?"

"I think eating meals with necromancers is a really good diet plan," Sylvie said with a shudder. "Alex—"

"Don't date the help? I know. It's just. It's nice to meet a cute guy who already knows about the *Magicus Mundi*. Makes it easier to talk freely. Makes it less likely that he'll go to the restroom and never come back."

"You *tell* your dates?"

"I don't like to lie," Alex said. "If I lie, then he can lie, and I can't even be pissed about it. Anyway, small earthquakes. People hearing strange sounds in the dark. If there are UFOs, these are USOs. Unidentified screaming objects. A lot of 911 calls that lead nowhere. Feral-cat attacks. Weird shit like that. Only noticeable in aggregate. Cachita tell you about those?"

"Nope," Sylvie said. "You're still the champ. Let me know if we start heading toward a rain of toads."

"Flock of slaughtered ringneck doves?" Alex said. "The golf course was a mess."

"Like that, yeah." Sylvie leaned her head on her hands. They were nearing Lio's, the highway giving way to residential streets, and she said, "Okay. This is the deal. We've got to find Azpiazu and the women. Immortal sorcerer or not, he's also a man. And a man has needs."

"Yeah," Alex said. "Food, shelter, that kind of thing. But it's a damn big city, Syl."

"We've got three options as I see it. Profile Azpiazu. Find him where he finds his women. Problem with that—"

"He won't hunt until one of the women is dead," Alex finished. "Hardly the result we want."

"Yeah," Sylvie said. "Option two is to track Azpiazu by magic. Given that he's managing to keep a god off his trail?"

"Option three?"

"Back to the material needs. He's not on the grid. He has no existence in the eyes of society. He's not going to have a credit card, a bank, or a mailing address for cata-

logs. If Cachita's sources are right, Azpiazu's a loner to
end all loners."

"If she's right," Alex said.

Alex's jealous mutter sparked a loose thought into place.
Sylvie's hands tightened on her knees. She interrupted her
own instructions to veer to new ones. "Alex. Look into
Cachita. Look deep."

"Yeah?" Alex grinned.

"Cachita is very sure of herself. But a little careless.
She claimed she found out Azpiazu's name and history
from the sorcerous community."

"I didn't find anything," Alex said.

"Nor did Wales. From the same source. In fact, he told
me they didn't know anything beyond the soul-devourer
nonsense. And if he couldn't find it, and you couldn't,
Cachita didn't either. At least not from those sources. She's
desperate, though; who knows where she's really getting
her info."

"Desperate for the story? Jeez, she can find a new one
that isn't picking over other people's bones."

"Her cousin, Elena Valdes, is among the missing, pre-
sumed dead."

"Oh," Alex said. She studied the road, the ever-present
excuse of traffic to help hide her blush.

"Just look into her," Sylvie said. "As for Azpiazu. He is
a loner, but he has . . . let's call them dependents."

"The women," Alex said.

"Yeah," Sylvie said. "They need water. And privacy.
Someplace he can close off and control. "

"A private pool," Alex said. "Probably indoors. No
neighbors to notice. Sylvie? Maybe he left them out in the
open as bait? You said he was looking for you. Maybe he
made you find him?"

"Doesn't matter at this point," Sylvie said. "He's got to
be squatting somewhere." She closed her eyes, recalled
their meeting. Azpiazu had dressed for the occasion. Expensive suit, tie, fancy shoes, manicure. Well-groomed. "He's
a sorcerer, which means he's most likely a pretentious fuck

Wants the finer things in life and can take them at will. He'll be squatting someplace nice. Wouldn't surprise me if he'd killed someone for their house. You find anything on the black van he was driving?" She spoke faster as she saw Lio's house growing larger in the windshield.

Things were far too awkward for Sylvie and Alex to hang around outside Lio's place and talk business. Sylvie sighed. All the drama of a breakup and none of the fun.

"Stolen, dumped," Alex said, picking up some of Sylvie's conversational urgency. "But hey. Not too far from the golf course."

"Where the doves were killed?"

"That's the one. It might mean something. If the god is looking for him, maybe he's closer—"

"Let's hope not," Sylvie said.

Alex pulled up behind Sylvie's truck. "Okay. I'll hunt Azpiazu. Look up Cachita. What about you?"

"I'm going to talk to Val. Wales is good. But Val is better. Even if her magic's still burned out, she's got a hell of a lot of experience under her belt. Maybe I can convince them to work together—"

"When Hell's a skating rink, maybe," Alex said.

"She can't stay mad forever," Sylvie said. "It's juvenile, and Val prides herself on her civility. Besides, we need a new bell. I don't want any more sneak attacks at the office, and I'd like to go home sometime this century."

Alex reached out and grabbed Sylvie's wrist just as Sylvie opened the passenger door, holding her in place. "Syl."

"Just say it," Sylvie said, when Alex stared at her, trying to convey *something* in blinks of multicolored eye shadow and violet mascara.

"Val hates gods. She's scared to death of them. You going to warn her that there's one headed our way?"

"Yeah," Sylvie said. "But *after* I get her to talk to me. Once I mention a god, she'll be hightailing it for the Azores."

Alex let her go, leaned her face on the steering wheel.

"You ever think you might get back to being friends if you didn't manipulate her?"

"Oh look, we're here," Sylvie said, pointedly. She escaped Alex's car, and Sylvie juggled her keys in her hand before giving in and heading up Lio's front path. She knocked on the door, heard a grunt and a groan of effort that told her what she wanted to know, and considered just leaving. But she was already in Lio's bad books; she didn't want to add playing ding-dong-ditch to his list of her sins.

The door opened; he leaned on the frame and just looked down at her, face stubbled and tired, a frown settling in.

"Just checking they brought you back in one piece," Sylvie said. "That's all."

She walked away, and he didn't call her back. She hadn't expected it. Not today.

Alex was right; it was hard to find people who knew about the *Magicus Mundi*, harder still to find people you liked in it. Damn near impossible to find reliable allies.

She really needed to get back on Val's good side.

11

Gods and Powers

THE GATES TO THE CASSAVETES ESTATE WERE LOCKED, A SCROLL-work of wrought iron that encompassed several discreet protective wards. Behind that, a long white drive stretched forward surrounded by plush grass and tall, swaying palms.

Pretty.

Except when you were on the wrong side of the gate. Sylvie rolled down her window, reached out gingerly for the intercom. Last time she tried to talk to Val, it had been all aversion magic and sparks and burned fingers. She steeled herself, hit the TALK button, and said, "Hey, Val, you home? I really need a face-to-face."

She waited for the sparks, the magical anger, the rejection; instead, the intercom buzzed and the gate pulled back with a rumble of gears.

Sylvie put her car hastily into drive, headed up the long limestone driveway. She parked her truck, felt more than heard the massive front door open—a little gap in the protective cocoon of magics woven over the house. When she looked up, it wasn't Val silhouetted in the doorway but Zoe.

"Hey," Zoe said. She seemed subdued. She'd been that

way ever since Odalys had tried to erase her soul. "Glad you came."

"Yeah." Sylvie felt like crap. She hadn't come to check up on Zoe, only to ask for help. Her gaze dropped; Zoe shifted her arm behind her, too late for Sylvie to miss the reddish stain that washed her sister's skin from fingertip to forearm.

"Val's taking us out of the country," Zoe said, and distracted Sylvie from wondering what exactly the stain meant, what her baby sister and an assassin could have in common.

"No. What? Why? Do Mom and Dad know?" The AC, working full tilt, made her shiver with longing.

Zoe looked over her shoulder, checked that the hallway was clear, and ushered Sylvie in. The door frame shivered and rang around her, a bell felt in her bones. Sylvie said, "What was that?"

Zoe bit her lip. "Dammit. Val's gonna be pissed."

"Her default position when it comes to me," Sylvie said. "What was that? I've had a lot of magic bounced off my skin in the past two days. Not really in the mood for something more."

"It's a red alert," Val said, looming up behind Zoe. "What are you doing here?"

"Why are you taking my sister out of the country? You think to ask me first?"

"Your parents don't object," Val said.

"You bewitch them?"

"Only a little," Zoe said. She put her hand on Sylvie's arm. "I need to go. I need to learn, Syl."

"She's safer with me than with you, at any rate," Val said. "Consorting with gods again, Sylvie?"

"Not if I can help it," Sylvie admitted. "Don't suppose you can whip up any god-be-gone or some such."

"No," Val said. "Zoe, we're leaving in four hours. Are you packed?"

"Yes," Zoe said. It was a total lie. Sylvie knew it. Zoe never finished packing until the very last minute. Given

Val's tightening mouth, Val knew it, too. But she said, "Fine. I'll go finish up with Julian. Visit with your sister. Don't go anywhere with her. You're too vulnerable right now."

"Whatever," Zoe said. She dragged Sylvie into a room that was windowless, soundproofed, and covered with protective symbols. The only piece of furniture in it was a long table, covered with a cloth. A stranger might take it for a Wiccan altar, but Sylvie knew Val. Despite the fancy cloth, it was nothing more than a magical workbench, as secular as it came.

"So this is the deal," Zoe said. "Val says we're leaving because there's a god and a power in the city. She says that's a bad combination."

"The god's not here yet," Sylvie said. "I'm hoping to keep it that way. The power? He won't be a problem if I have my say in the matter. He's a cursed sorcerer who's got himself in the god's bad books and is using innocents as a shield."

Zoe frowned. "Val didn't think they were connected. A curse would be a connection. And I don't think she'd consider a sorcerer a capital-P power."

"Even one cursed with immortality?" Sylvie asked. "Azpiazu's not really human any longer."

"She doesn't think *you're* a power," Zoe said. "And you're the new Lilith."

"Hey, I don't call you names," Sylvie said. She was going to have to deal with that at some point. Find out what being the new Lilith meant before the rumormongers decided for her. Before more men like Azpiazu started getting expectations. "Look, if it's not Azpiazu—'

Zoe shrugged. "She didn't really say. Just a power."

"So what's a power when it's at home, then," Sylvie said. "Not a sorcerer—not a human?"

Zoe said, "I don't know. So far, Val's lessons about powers and gods consist of *Stay away from them.* But if I had to guess, those demigod kinda things. Immortals with magical abilities. Like the Sphinx."

"Like *Azpiazu*," Sylvie said. "Immortal. Sorcerer."

Zoe said, "Whatever," again. "Do you want my help or not?"

"Not," Sylvie said, knee-jerk. "I want you on that plane with Val. Safe."

Zoe's jaw tightened. "We had this conversation, Syl. I'm not a baby. I can take care of myself. Besides. That wasn't what I meant." She gestured toward the table. "I was thinking more along the lines of a new warning bell."

"You know it broke?"

"Val said it did. It gave her a headache. Spell backlash, you know. There was a lot of her in it." Zoe looked at the table, frowned. "Maybe not a warning bell. Maybe something better. A spell neutralizer. I know there's one around here somewhere."

Sylvie said, "Hey, Zo, how is Val doing? Magic-wise."

"Magicless? Kinda sorta?" Zoe leaned back against the table; the cloth wrinkled up behind her like a boat's wake on the sea. Every movement left ripples, Sylvie thought. She'd asked Val's help on a case, brought her face-to-face with a god; the result had been a textbook case of magical dynamics. What made a witch a witch was the ability to draw bits of power toward them—the scavengers that Wales called them. Val, brought smack up against the god of Justice, ended up like an ungrounded circuit after a lightning strike.

"Actually," Zoe said. She lowered her voice. "When that bell broke? She got a boost. A little bit of power coming back to her. The link remembered."

"Like a rut in the world," Sylvie said. That fit with what she knew of magical energy. It took on the flavor of its wielder. "So wait. If Val goes touring around, smashing up her old charms—"

"Yeah," Zoe said. "She's thinking maybe it'll kick-start her motors again. But that's why we're running. I mean, look at it from her perspective. She's just getting hope back that she can do more than teach magic, and a god's in town?"

"Coming to town," Sylvie said. "Maybe."

"Val seemed pretty sure," Zoe said.

"Val's biased," Sylvie countered.

Zoe poked at her own fingernails, clicking them thoughtfully against each other. "What I don't get . . Val said gods burn out witches. But I was doing a basic illusion spell last night. I was supposed to make a tabby cat walk across the room, and I got a jaguar that tried to take my face off. It actually smelled real, sounded real. Kinda cool once I realized it couldn't hurt me. But Val freaked. Said I shouldn't have that much power to draw on."

"Gods shed," Sylvie said.

Zoe said, "That's what she said. So why do witches hate gods? I mean, Syl. The jaguar was so amazing. I could see the carpet dent beneath its paws. Feel its breath. It felt so good and so easy. Why not just avoid the gods? Feed off their shed power?"

"Zoe," Sylvie said. "That makes you a parasite. No one likes parasites. Least of all the creature they're scavenging."

Zoe sighed. "Do you know how much cooler senior year would be if I could tap that kind of power on a regular basis?"

Sylvie said, "Zoe—"

"I know, I know," Zoe said. "No magic when I go back to school. But you have to admit, it would be amazing. Gives entirely new depth to daydreaming."

Sylvie's lips twitched against her will. "Just try not to cause a riot."

Zoe pulled the cover off the table, revealing a series of cupboards beneath; she opened one, said, "Aha!" and pulled out an amulet strung on a white satin cord. "Here."

It was a cold glimmer in Sylvie's palm, a thorny golden circle that, on closer inspection, turned out to be an ouroboros.

"A snake," Sylvie said. She didn't particularly like snakes.

"An ouroboros," Zoe said.

"I know that," Sylvie said. "Why that shape?"

"Purification," Zoe said. "Consumption and production. It cancels each other out. Hence—"

"A magic neutralizer," Sylvie said. She hefted it, then tucked it into her pocket. It was cold and heavy, had some of the same comfort as her gun. A tool to be used.

"More powerful if you wear it," Zoe said. "I promise, it's safe to wear."

"I trust you," Sylvie said. It was easy enough to say. Was even mostly true. "Could I get a replacement for the warning bell, also?"

"Greedy much?"

"Hey, long time since I've been enough in Val's good graces to be let in the door. Got to make the most of it. Besides, the warning bell works for more than me. Alex depends on it, too."

Zoe made her usual face at the thought of Alex but bent obediently to search. "It won't be as strong as the last one. Won't be keyed specifically to your place."

She dug out another tool, a single *baoding* ball. It chimed the moment Sylvie's hand closed around it, vibrated in her palm.

Zoe took a step back. "Syl?"

"What?" Sylvie snapped. "Why's it doing that?"

Zoe licked her lips. "The door alert went off, also. I just thought—"

"Zoe—"

"You've crossed paths with that Power recently. Closely. Enough that some of his energy stuck to you."

Sylvie sighed. Azpiazu had touched her, it was true, but she thought she'd gotten off lucky with just losing the gun.

Zoe took the warning bell, tucked it into a silk bag, silencing it, before passing it back to Sylvie. "Why don't you come with us? Get out of town?"

"Got a job to do," Sylvie said.

"I could stay," Zoe suggested. "Maybe help you."

"Val's keeping you wrapped up tight," Sylvie said. "There's probably a reason for it."

"I'm the youngest witch in the city. Apparently that makes me tasty." Zoe paced. "It's sort of like being grounded all over again. At least Val gets every cable channel known to man."

"What about that goth witch, Aron? He didn't look that much older than you, and he's roaming around unsupervised."

Zoe shook her head. "I've never heard of him. Val said *I'm* the youngest by a whole lot of years. I mean, besides Julian, of course." There was pride in her voice that made Sylvie twitchy. It *had* to be magic that her sister took a shine to.

"Aron's working for Patrice," Sylvie said. "Strong, a little crazy. Don't know his field, though."

"Some witches only look young," Zoe said.

"Yeah, that's going around," Sylvie said, thinking of Patrice, of Azpiazu.

Zoe said, "I'll ask Val about him, call you if I find anything out."

"Hey, Zo? Any way to find out if Azpiazu left anything nasty on me? I'd hate to be carrying around a magical time bomb, and I wouldn't put it past him."

Zoe gnawed at her lip. "I'm not supposed to do magic without Val."

"Just a quick look-see. C'mon, Zo. A little witch-sight. That's all I'm asking for."

"All right, all right," Zoe said. She closed her eyes, murmured a quiet incantation—for focus, Sylvie knew, not any intrinsic magic of its own—and then opened her eyes again.

Brown eyes flared wide; her pupils shrank to dots. "Christ Almighty, Sylvie." Zoe backed away, bumped into the bench, slid down the side, and sat. She closed her eyes tight, shook her head.

"Bad news?" Sylvie tasted dust, a sour sting of adrenaline. She jammed her twitching hands into her jacket pockets.

"No," Zoe said. "You're just . . . You're very vivid. Alive

in kind of a scary way." She shook her head again. "Okay. I saw what brushed up against you. It's dark, but it's not doing anything, and it's fading. Like mud getting brushed off as it dries."

"Anything I can do to wash it off faster?" She was going to ignore the other stuff. She was alive? She knew that. Felt it every time someone tried to kill her.

"I don't know," Zoe said. "Wear the ouroboros. Be careful."

"Back at you," Sylvie said. "Val means well, but sometimes running's the worst thing to do. Sometimes running just gets the attention of things that like to chase."

"And sometimes it's the only smart thing to do."

"Come on," Sylvie said. "Show me out before Val comes and kicks me out. That way, I can call this a successful visit."

Zoe grimaced. "She can really hold a grudge."

"We were friends for a reason," Sylvie said. "Like to like."

They stood there in the vaulted foyer, a little awkward in each other's company, that gulf of secrets between them exposed but not dealt with in any real fashion, still reluctant to part. Finally, Zoe frowned, and said, "Is that my jacket?"

"Not yours anymore," Sylvie said, ducked Zoe's smack, hugged her baby sister tight, and took off.

She had barely made it back onto the road out of Key Biscayne when Alex called. Sylvie, dealing with tight traffic, let it ring to voice mail. But Alex called right back, and with a groan, Sylvie found the nearest shoulder—a sloping sandy patch of straggly grass way too close to a watery ditch—and pulled over.

"What?"

"I think I've found Azpiazu," Alex said. There was triumph in her voice, and fear.

"Tell me," Sylvie said.

"I called Lio about the two dead patrol cops. They were

found near the dumped van, near the golf course. And in the center of all that—a lot of nice houses."

"You called Lio?"

"It was easier than trying to piece together decent info from the skimpy news reports. He's annoyed with you. Not me."

"Whatever," Sylvie said, and bit her lip. Dammit, Zoe's teenage speech pattern was as contagious as chicken pox. "What did he say?"

"The two cops died, officially of poisoning. Unofficially? Lio says that the coroner says they died from having molten lead replace their blood."

"Jesus." She shuddered. That would be one hellish death. She fingered the ouroboros amulet in her pocket and reluctantly pulled it over her head. If Azpiazu could do that, she couldn't afford to be squeamish about using magical protection. "What connects it to Azpiazu?"

"Sigils on their hands," Alex said. "The alchemical symbol for lead. It's transmutation. What with the women in the Everglades having sigils on their faces, and what he did to your gun, I thought it must be linked."

"Sounds like," Sylvie said. A heavy truck whizzed by, buffeting her in its wake.

"One of the last things the patrolmen did was check up on a missing person. A magazine editor for *StyleMiami* didn't show up to work a couple of days ago. When he missed a meeting, his coworkers called the police, and they sent a patrol car out to check his house."

"And?"

"Patrolmen reported that he was there, just down with the flu. But, Sylvie, they didn't take a picture or ask for ID. It was just a courtesy check. After that, they died."

"You think Azpiazu took his place. His house."

"You're the one who said he might do something like that."

"I did," Sylvie agreed. "I just didn't expect him to be so—"

"Stupid? Blatant?"

"Arrogant," Sylvie said.

"Sorcerer."

Sylvie sighed. "Your point. Got an address for me? Or are the police swarming the scene?"

"They're still trying to figure out what kind of freak accident replaces a man's blood with metal. You've got a head start. And, Syl? The *StyleMiami* guy, Serrano, his house backs up pretty damn close to the golf course where the dead doves were."

Sylvie looked at the clock in the dash, squinting in the sunlight. A couple of hours until sundown. If she could roust Wales from his sulk, collect him, the Hand of Glory— maybe they could sneak into Azpiazu's lair. Maybe he'd have come up with something special to free the women, something to pick apart the spells that held them. If Azpiazu could move them without breaking the spell into a flaming disaster, maybe Wales could do the same. Like a bomb, picked apart in precisely the right order. Maybe, maybe, maybe.

She wanted certainty.

12

In the Monster's Lair

AN HOUR LATER, SYLVIE, WITH A NERVOUS AND SULLEN WALES AT HER side, drove into Serrano's neighborhood. No wonder the police had been so willing to make a house call. Serrano lived on the distant edge of a golf course. The neighborhood was nice, professionally landscaped, spacious plats, two-story houses, expensive but not too expensive. Upper-middle-class; the kind of area where people still called the police instead of their private lawyers.

Sylvie had been concerned that it would be a gated community, but it was one of the holdouts—a wealthy neighborhood that didn't want to masquerade as an island resort. She took a last look at the real-estate paper in her hand: Jose Serrano's house listed an indoor lap pool. She sighed.

"Think we're wasting our time?" Wales said.

"Trying to figure our approach. If Serrano's home sick, like the cops reported, breaking in is a no-go. And using Marco to sneak us in—"

"If he's really ill, I wouldn't chance it," Wales said. "Marco's bites take a lot out of you."

"I remember," she said.

"Even if it is Azpiazu there, waking Marco is a risk,"

Wales said. "Azpiazu's familiar with necromantic magic."

"You think he can take Marco from you?"

Wales shook his head. "No. Marco's mine, for good or ill. But using necromantic magic in his vicinity? It'll be like ringing an alarm bell."

"Will Marco be able to knock him out?"

"Doubt it," Wales said. "You've gotten resistant to him with exposure. I'd imagine an immortal necromancer would be a sight more resistant than you."

"Then we're stuck playing cat burglar," Sylvie said. "And if Serrano's home?"

"You're a fast liar," Wales said. "I'll leave the talking to you."

"Thanks," she muttered. But she didn't see another option.

If this *was* an information misfire—if Serrano really was inside, sick with the flu, and the cops had brushed up against Azpiazu elsewhere—she couldn't afford to break a window and climb inside. She had enough of a reputation with the cops that she didn't want to add a B and E charge, especially since she was armed. That kind of thing could be difficult, if not impossible, to shake. Her life plans didn't include a detour for jail time.

Sylvie touched the ouroboros at her breastbone, tapped the warning bell in her jacket pocket, and headed around the back of the house, Wales a clumsy afterthought.

One thing she'd had proved to her over and over again in this career path was that people's idea of security was often more for show than fact. They made a big deal about locking the front door, the windows, put up security gates and signs, then left their back doors unlocked, unguarded, or shielded from all watchful eyes.

It made no sense to her, but the nicer the estate and surroundings, the more likely the homeowners fell into that kind of carelessness. They thought that privacy and space equaled safety when, in truth, what they mostly meant were no witnesses.

The lawn, thick and vividly green, denting beneath her

boots, made her steps as soundless as if she were walking on pillows. Behind her, Wales swore softly as he tripped over a sprinkler head.

The twilight moving in made her as close to invisible as a human could be without magical intervention, turned the world into moving columns of grey, purple, black. Her red jacket sucked in light, turned dark and shadowed, better than camo prints.

Rustling in the underbrush and a skink oiled out before her, slipping clumsily through the grass, two heads drawing it in different directions. She watched it, struck by the freak show of it, and stepped onto a path that crunched. The gravel was dark and pale at once, as patterned as a copperhead. The paler splotches gave beneath her feet with small cracks and pops until she realized they were skeletal frogs. An entire pond's worth.

Dead doves. Now this.

The last doubt in her mind that she might be blundering into some innocent's house crumbled.

Tepeyollotl might not be physically present, but something of him was seeping through the curse—his power fueling it, his power that Azpiazu was warping. God-power spilling out and messing with the world.

Several acres over, she heard a car pull up, a garage door churn into mechanical life. The neighbors weren't going to notice anything, focused on the homecoming transition. She wondered if they'd noticed any changes in their own little worlds, or if they'd just shrugged them off.

Recon, she thought. Take a look, get a grip on the situation, get Wales's take on it, then come back better informed and armed for bear.

Or monster.

The backyard, accessed by a quick climb over a stucco wall, yielded a gardener's paradise. Sylvie, used to seeing tropical gardens, was still impressed. The air was thick and damp and green sweet fragrant, the walls hidden with rosary pea and hibiscus; orange trees and woody jasmine bushes studded the walkways.

Wales landed in the grass behind her, grimacing.

She didn't think the pained distaste on his face was for his awkward landing. The closer she drew to the house, the less soothing the garden felt. Her little dark voice growled in constant warning, and Sylvie didn't think it was simple caution about housebreaking.

The weathered deck creaked gently beneath her steps, her bootheels muffled impacts that echoed in her quickening heartbeat.

Recon, she reminded herself. *A look-see. Nothing more. We aren't prepared for more.*

The house, seen through a pair of French doors, was dark, caught in that awkward space between being lit by daylight and not quite dark enough to require internal lights. The rooms she saw behind the glass looked as static and unpeopled as a closed movie set.

And, like a signal from the heavens, the alarm keypad she saw was flashing green green green. Unarmed. Unset. An open invitation.

Sylvie turned her head, looked sidewise, dropped her lashes, peering through the shadows she made of her vision. There. A glimmer on the glass, *within* the glass. Like the traceries of fingerprints and skin oils left behind, except that this was a magical symbol. Another tiny proof that made her believe Cachita's assertion that Azpiazu was the original recipe: He used magic instead of technology at every turn.

Even the *Maudits,* proud sorcerers that they were, tended to mix and match.

Still, her trip to Val's might have already paid off. Sylvie pulled the ouroboros amulet from around her neck, wrapped the cord around her wrist, and reached for the door handle.

Wales tugged at her wrist, a silent warning.

"You see something I don't, Tex?"

"You trust the charm that much?"

"Got to try it out sometime," she said. "Better now than in a face-to-face, yeah?"

She jiggled the door handle—locked—and waited.

No sparks, no magical result, no nothing. The magic made into nothing. The spell not broken but bypassed. Val did good work.

Wales let out a shaky breath.

Sylvie pressed close to the glass, looked down. Not even a dead bolt. Just the handle.

It was a moment's work and another scrape on her credit card to get the latch to flip. She eased the door open, and the hair on her body stood on edge as the house air washed over her. It carried with it the brittle hush of a sleeping household, the movement of slow, steady breaths.

"Sense anything?" she asked.

Wales edged past her, getting himself beyond the ouroboros charm's reach, then nodded. "Ghost. Someone's dead."

Sylvie frowned. Never good news. When the ratio of innocents to evil sorcerer was six to one, it was definitely bad news.

She closed the door behind them, easing the latch closed. She slung the ouroboros charm about her neck again, let it dangle on her chest.

Her breath, let out softly, warmed the air she moved through. Wales hunched tight, shivered. Her own skin goosebumped.

The entire house was frigid, the AC working at full capacity. Sylvie moved inward and tasted the hint of something foul and greasy on her tongue. Rot.

Someone's dead. Sylvie hoped it wasn't Maria Ruben.

She followed the scent, followed Wales, wrinkling her nose and wishing that the charm neutralized odors as well as magic. An adult's rec room, all plush carpet, pool table, wet bar, and HDTV, was ground zero for the meat-rot scent. She gagged, peered into each shadow, and finally found a man's body shoved out of sight behind the wet bar.

It had to be Jose Serrano, the home owner, since he was clad in pajamas and slippers; hardly the outfit for a visitor to the house. His ankles were swollen red-black with pooled blood. His eyes were fixed and filmed over, his skin livid and streaked, his entire body contorted. He hadn't died easy.

Grimacing, she knelt, turned his hands toward the light.

"Careful!" Wales said. He hovered behind her, looming over her shoulder.

"Tex," she said. "Watch the door, all right? Watch my back, not my *back*."

He huffed, but obeyed, leaving Sylvie to her inspection of the corpse.

Like a brand on his palm, a sigil charred the skin, wept a substance dull grey and soot black. Sylvie touched it with a fingernail, felt it dent beneath her touch. She scratched at it. It left a silvery streak on the edge of her nail.

Lead.

Azpiazu seemed to be a one-trick pony when it came to killing people. But that made sense. Even someone who didn't believe in magic would still get up and walk away from a man shouting a lot of mumbo jumbo ritual magic.

Every sorcerer she had met had a single, instinctive offensive spell. Often, it was a paralysis spell; but Azpiazu . . . He hadn't needed to kill the cops. They'd gone off content. It would have been days before the search for Serrano started up again. He'd killed them because they'd annoyed him.

And he had to have done it quickly, smoothly, and naturally. A handshake, given that the marks were found on the palms.

"Sylvie," Wales warned, just as the glasses in the bar rattled. One shifted far enough that it danced out of its rack; she put a hand up and caught it. It was icy slick, burned her skin.

"What the hell—"

"Serrano's ghost," Wales said. "He's pissed—"

"Tell him we're here to help!"

She set the glass down, rubbed the cold off on her jeans, and stood. Ducked the cue ball as it blew directly at her. Her hand tangled briefly in the ouroboros charm, but it had no effect on the items winging in her direction.

Ghost, right. Not magic.

Ghosts counted as fucked-up nature on their own. It was only once people started harnessing them that it became magic.

She dropped back to her knees, wincing. The carpet might be plush, but it wasn't that thick.

Wales whispered into the air, more of that not-quite language, and Sylvie dodged a pool cue, caught it as it flew past.

"Wales! Less coaxing, more commanding!"

"Not that easy," Wales snapped. "He's not exactly a normal ghost."

"Sic Marco on him."

"He's a victim here, not the enemy," Wales said. "And remember, we were trying not to alert Azpiazu—"

She dropped, rolled, came up on the other side of the pool table, aggravated, and smelling of carpet powder and rot. "Easy for you to say. He's not chucking stuff at you. C'mon, Tex—"

Wales let out his breath, stiffened his spine, jammed his hand out into the room—a flat-palmed *Stop!* "Enough."

A glass and two striped balls dropped midflight. The room, already cold, grew frigid. Frost laced across the flatscreen TV like a shatter mark. "Sylvie, bring me some of his hair."

"Serrano's?" It was a stupid question; she knew it even as it left her lips: Who else's?

She twined her fingers in his hair, thick and glossy still; the lead that had filled his blood had killed him too quickly for his hair to show the damage. She yanked, ungentle, uncaring. Serrano was dead, even though his bones creaked, and his head jerked back as if he felt the sting of her hurried fingers, her pinching nails.

She brought Wales the dark lock, pressed it into his free hand. "Now what?"

"I show him who's in charge."

Wales held the tuft of hair up, two hands out before him; the *halt* and a cupped palm, the hair resting in it like an offering. A wisp of smoke rose; Sylvie blinked. She hadn't seen anything like fire coming near it. The smoke grew higher, lit from beneath with a blue flame that burned like ice, cooling.

In the arctic mist blooming from Wales's hand, the ghosts took on a visible shape. Marco's looming, hollow-eyed presence, familiar, inimical, shoulder to shoulder with his necromantic partner. And Serrano. Or what Sylvie assumed to be Serrano. At first she thought his ghost had been cleaved in two, mutilated even after death—she knew Azpiazu was no respecter of the dead. Then she saw him more clearly. Not a ghost split in two, not a mutilated ghost, but a mutated one. One body, dividing midtorso to stretch two necks upward, two heads, one flushed dark with rage, one blanched with fear.

"What the fuck—"

"Your time is spent; your life is gone to dust and ash. I bind you and dismiss you from this plane," Wales said.

Serrano twitched and faded in chunks, left leg, angry face, torso, until the only ghost left was Marco. Wales closed his fist, let ashes dribble out, streaks against his bony hand, and sighed.

"That was ugly," he said.

"What was that?" Sylvie said. The frigid air faded to something approaching warmth by comparison. She doubted the room temperature made it to sixty.

Wales shrugged. "Harder to dismiss than he should have been? Something warped his ghost, broke him into—"

"I saw," she reminded him. "Ghost schizophrenia?" She remembered the double-headed skink outside, twitching and jerking its way forward, and surreptitiously ran her fingers along the line of her neck.

"Azpiazu's magic." Wales shoved his hands into his pockets, closed his body up, shoulders turned inward, chin tilted down. Thoughtful. Worried. "I think . . . I want to see that binding spell again."

"Why we're here," Sylvie said. She shook off the chill

that the room, Serrano, Wales's magic working had left in her bones, and headed back into the hallway.

Bedrooms, bathrooms were likely toward the back, more public rooms toward the front of the house. If she were a lap pool, where would she—

She opened doors gingerly, as if she'd open one to Azpiazu leering at her. As if he'd have done nothing while Wales cleaned ghostly house for him.

Each door opened revealed nothing out of the ordinary. Her nervousness grew. It felt like a game of Russian roulette, each innocuous room bringing her one step closer to the loaded chamber.

The tang of chlorine overrode the scent of death and guided her finally in the right direction. For a brief moment, entering the pool room, she found the scene not only peaceful but beautiful. The lap pool was lit softly from below, casting a wavering blue gleam over the ceiling. The women, curled into seated positions, looked more like spa visitors than victims, resting peacefully in a beautiful room.

Until Sylvie took that next step into the room, saw the lines of strain on their faces, the haggard pallor to Maria Ruben's skin; then it was all too easy to see the truth. It made Sylvie itchy under the collar, coldly furious.

Wales swore quietly. "Sylvie, we have to do something."

"You're the necromancer."

Wales closed his eyes, listening to Marco, listening to his own instincts. Sylvie watched him, seething with impatience and a slow, guttering anger. There had to be a way. Something she could do to free them. She'd walked away once and had been regretting it ever since.

Kill the sorcerer, the little dark voice said. *No sorcerer, no curse, no deflection spell.*

Hell, it would be the best of all worlds. Kill Azpiazu, and she wouldn't need to worry about Tepeyollotl's making the scene . . . or maybe she would. Gods could be cranky about having their punishments interrupted.

Worth the risk.

The water rippled, a tiny movement disturbing its glass-ine smoothness. Maria Ruben was quivering. Tremors so small that they seemed more felt than seen.

Maria Ruben's time was up.

"Think fast, Tex," Sylvie said. "I'm going in."

"What? Sylvie—"

"We don't have time. Maria's in trouble, and Azpiazu will be returning to harvest her soul."

Wales nodded. "Give me three minutes. Let me see if I can start wearing down the spell defenses. Keep them from shifting or flaming out, at the least." His eyes rolled back in his head, blind to anything but the power he was calling on. Sylvie shuddered. Shuddered again when he sliced into his hand and walked the perimeter of the lap pool, drip-ping his blood into the water, unerringly on target. Marco whispering directions to him, or magic at work?

Her curiosity got stomped hard when Wales began whis-pering into the room, nonsense words, broken syllables that somehow, upon repetition, crawled inside her head and translated themselves.

I am death the slowing drum the lassitude of bone I en-fold all and I am death the clinging shroud the beetles' breath the clock wound down . . .

She tuned him out in self-defense, waited for him to finish his slow circuit around the pool. The moment he did, she darted into action, clawing at the ouroboros about her neck. If Maria was about to die anyway, yanking her from the binding spell seemed like a worthwhile risk. The snake-scale necklace scratched her skin, snagged her hair, but Sylvie tugged it off, held the cord wide, and dropped it over Maria Ruben's head. The result was instantaneous.

The room hummed; the water bubbled as if someone had suddenly nuked it to boiling. Maria Ruben's eyes flew open, her mouth gasped, the tendons in her neck stood out like hawsers. Sylvie grabbed her shoulders, pulled—

The woman was heavy, as stiff in her arms as a corpse in full rigor; the other women were moving, too, eyes opening without awareness behind them, their skin flowing . . . sluggishly, like raw clay softening in the water.

Time ran short.

Azpiazu had to know, had to feel it. He would have felt Maria destabilizing, would already be on his way. One unbalanced binding spell, and somewhere Azpiazu was losing control of his shape, showing the world the monster he was on the inside.

Maria's breath shivered coldly on Sylvie's cheek, a brush of soundless words. *Help me. Help me.* The ouroboros around her neck tarnished from bright gold to something hot and dull, the magic being sucked from it. Overwhelmed.

She was going to lose Maria, Sylvie thought sickly. All the ouroboros was doing was bringing her back to awareness of her suffering and impending death. The sigil on Maria's forehead began to seep blood at the cut edges.

Wales dropped down beside her, hauled Maria out, muttering a spell that sounded like the hissing of snakes and pounded against Sylvie's body like the tide. Pushing, pressing. Sylvie felt like she was drowning and forced herself to let it slide by her, let it reach Wales's target.

Maria.

The woman gasped, breathed in harshly as if she'd been drowned and just had the water punched from her lungs. "What—"

"Let's go, let's go—" Wales said.

"The others—"

"He's *here*—"

A growl traveled through the room, a vibration that had Sylvie dropping the argument, and spinning around, trading Maria's jerking flesh for the hard steel of her gun. She rolled back, making space and taking aim—the trigger juddered beneath her finger.

"Run, Wales!" on an outborne breath, panted between shots.

He did his best to obey, burdened by Maria's slack weight.

A series of perfectly placed shots on an easy target:

Azpiazu twisted to monster form, a distorted patchwork of predators, wolf teeth and bear bulk and long, lashing cat tail, claws leaving marks in the tile, coming straight for her. She put the entire clip into his chest.

Azpiazu didn't even slow; her gun clicked on empty.

He howled, turned one gold eye, one black on Wales's retreating form, crouched to spring. His first lunge after Wales coincided with a sudden hiss in the air, a window shattering and spilling glass in a storm toward him.

Marco, defending his master.

Azpiazu rocked back, shook glass off like a spill of sharp-edged raindrops.

Sylvie grabbed the warning bell out of her pocket and threw that in his face. It rang wildly, raised a cascade of sparks, but Azpiazu batted it away with a savage paw.

The bell served its purpose, though, bringing Azpiazu's attention back on her and let Wales vanish to safety, Maria slung any which way over his bony shoulders. Sylvie scrabbled for a weapon, found metal to hand—freestanding towel rack—and slammed it into his chest and side. The metal crumbled beneath the impact.

She rolled away from the next attack, splashed into the pool, flailed away from the women who reached for her with slow-forming claws. As she clambered back out, a heavy paw slapped her between the shoulder blades.

Numbness, crashing pain. Dizzy speed. Sylvie slammed into the wall, as spread-eagled and ungainly as a landed starfish, breathless, blackness hovering.

She crashed to the tile, got her hands down in time to prevent her from cracking her skull, but her back screamed protest.

Six inches higher, and he would have broken her neck.

"Mine!" Azpiazu's voice was a guttural thing, a wolf's snarl, a cat's scream, a bear's grunt.

"No," Sylvie said, her voice inaudible. Didn't matter. She heard it in her head, felt it in her throat. Maria Ruben *wasn't* his. Not anymore.

The room swooped and swayed about her. She dodged

the next crashing blow, managed to shift her weight enough to kick Azpiazu square in the drooling, misshapen muzzle.

His jaw slammed shut, teeth severing the lolling tongue. Blood spattered her face, the floor, Azpiazu's patchy fur.

He howled, a gargle of blood and rage, and Sylvie shoved past him, all plans gone, traded for the basic need to survive this unexpected fight. Survive it long enough for Wales to get Maria away.

Azpiazu lunged after her, knocked her sprawling, crouched over her, growling, salivating. His mottled fur was unmarked; her bullets hadn't done any good at all. Metal wasn't going to do the job, she thought. Not in bullet form, not in any form.

Fucking transformationist necromancer, she thought. Hard enough to kill something that was immortal. Even harder to kill something that could change a weapon's composition to something useless.

"Kill me, and you'll be cursed forever," she rasped out. "Thought you wanted my help."

Being this close to him set her skin afire with magic, corruption of the natural order. It made her gag, made her recoil.

He lashed out with a bear's massive paw, claws nearly an afterthought behind the physical power that could break bones with a single blow.

Sylvie kneed him in the jaw, knocked him back, kicked him once more, hearing bones creak beneath her heel, before he wrapped a human hand around her wrist. *"Die,"* he snarled.

Her blood kindled; her skin burned as if it had been struck with a branding iron. He flung her back, and she curled around her arm, watching the symbol for lead rise on her flesh, scarlet and black, a burn welling up from the inside.

No, she said, *you won't be rid of me that easy.*

It wasn't really her voice, but the thing that lived within her. She gouged at the hot lash of the brand, tore at it, intent on ripping the magic out of her skin if necessary. Blood burst beneath her nails, hot, wet, crimson. Human.

Blood, but not lead.

The fire in her veins, the heat that throbbed at her temples, the fever—they all faded until she was left with the taste of metal in her mouth and a bloody wound on her forearm. She got up, shook her matted, soaked hair back, and stared into his eyes. "Come on. Want to try again?"

Faintly, beneath everything else—the flutter of broken water, his panting, hers—she heard a sound familiar and welcome: a garage door rising, a car engine working at speed. Wales and Maria were nearly gone.

He surged in their direction, and Sylvie, burning adrenaline, picked up a potted palm and hurled it at him, breaking his stride and his jaw. His muzzle was streaked with blood; his teeth were wet with it. His pelt grew gore-clotted.

She'd hurt him more with that than with an entire clip of bullets.

"Give it up," she said. "Maria's gone."

"Replaceable," he slurred.

He paused, still crouched, still drooling blood and teeth, the first glimmer of something human beneath the monster coating. The first hint of the cleverness she knew he had.

Azpiazu had manipulated her from the start. She'd stumbled over him, and he'd acted quickly, given her an impossible, deadly task—find the god—to keep her out of his way. To give himself space. And he'd used the women as bargaining chips.

His muzzle reshaped itself; ivory teeth sprouted from broken edges.

"You never really wanted my help," she said. "Your curse is your ticket to immortality."

He hunched tight; the space between them could be breached with a single leap. His long tongue worked; his jaw pushed back. Beneath the animal snout, he shifted to a human mouth. "Smarter than Lilith," he said. "No. I never wanted your help. What could I possibly want from *you*? An untalented blunt object."

Sylvie licked her lips. Apparently, they weren't going

to start duking it out again. She couldn't say she regretted it. Her head ached where he'd slammed her into the glass, and her back throbbed. Blood spilled down her arm, dripped from her nails.

"You wanted to use me to distract a god."

"A god?" he echoed, a growl in the room.

"I know you. I name you. You're Eladio Azpiazu. Cursed by the god Tepeyollotl. I know all of this is to avoid him."

"Not *all* of it," he said. "Some of it's for my pleasure." His weight shifted. Azpiazu lunged; Sylvie dodged, taking the slash against the thick leather of Zoe's jacket. A sigil sizzled against the coat, burned hide curling away from his touch.

"Missed me," she said, her voice clogged with anger. "Want to try it again? Get inside my space? I'll make you hurt." Never mind that the room was sparse on weapons; pottery shards would be enough for her at the moment. From the sudden caution in his eyes, animal wariness, the uneasy shift of that massive body, she thought maybe she'd hurt him more in the past five minutes than he'd been hurt in decades.

The thing about immortals was that they got divorced from human experience. From pain. From fear. They felt untouchable as the years piled up behind them. She was reminding him of those things, reminding him that immortal did not equal invulnerable.

And that she had a reputation for killing things.

He sucked in a breath, spun away from her. She let him put the space between them, leaping across the lap pool's width. He hunkered down beside the pool, ran his fingers through the water, licked the taste of it from his skin, his eyes always on her.

"Don't overestimate yourself," Azpiazu said. "You don't understand what you're dealing with. I'm stronger than you can imagine."

"And yet, you can't shake the curse," Sylvie said. "Immortal, yes, but miserable with it."

He laughed, spittle and blood streaking his chin. "Not for much longer."

"Yeah? Got big plans? Feel free to share," Sylvie said.

He swayed foot to foot, lowered his heavy head, looked at her like a wolf studying prey. It made the fine hairs on her neck stand up. Azpiazu was just so . . . wrong. The wolf brow, the human mouth, the bear bulk, the cat claws—a forced-together chimera working against itself.

There was no way in hell he'd want immortality in this guise.

For one thing, he was far too vain. For another, it hampered his magic. All of that energy going just to maintain himself. Like a car with a chronic oil leak.

"Get out, and count yourself lucky," he said.

"You never needed me, but you didn't want my attention on *you* either. You have my undivided attention now. I've got you in my sights."

"Get out," he snarled once again. This time, Sylvie's better sense prevailed. She really wasn't in any shape to take him down. Not and survive.

She straightened, backed out of the room, pausing to scoop up her emptied gun, and watching Azpiazu as long as she could.

Turning her back on the house and striding into the dark felt impossibly difficult, not just for the crawling fear that he was following her, ready to rip out her spine, or slap another sigil on her meant to boil her blood, but because there were four women she was leaving behind.

Saving Maria didn't seem like enough of a triumph to count the evening as a win. Their recon had been interrupted, their enemy made aware of it. Azpiazu was undoubtedly packing up his remaining harem right now, heading someplace new.

Times like this, she hated the ISI with a passion bordering on obsession. If she could just call them for help. If she could count on them to know what they were doing. If she could trust them to be as interested in saving the victims as in studying the wicked.

Instead, it was her and a cobbled-together crew doing their meager best. Sylvie cast an unfavorable eye on her gun, a dark shadow in the passenger seat. If metal was no good, if Azpiazu's transformation skills worked fast enough to make bullets benign, she was going to need a different weapon.

. . .

TWO CALLS—ONE TO WALES, ONE TO ALEX, TO PASS ON THE NEWS— had her pulling into the Baptist Hospital lot where Wales had taken Maria Ruben. He'd gotten far enough ahead and Maria's quasi-celebrity status as a missing person had gotten them sucked right in past the emergency room waiting area.

"Here for Maria Ruben," Sylvie said, slipping past the ER receptionist. Confidence counted here. She hefted her purse as if it were Maria's, and she was just taking her things to her.

"Room fourteen," the receptionist said. "We've got some forms that need—"

"I'll take 'em," Sylvie said. Nothing better than a clipboard to prove you had a legit reason to be in the hospital. When she reached out, the nurse's eyes sharpened, focused, seeing Sylvie as more than just an irritant.

"You're bleeding." Seeing her as a potential patient.

Sylvie looked at her arm as if it belonged to someone else. She'd taken the time to bandage it in the truck, but the gouges her nails had left ripping Azpiazu's sigil apart had reddened the white gauze.

"Not a lot."

"You come back up here if you decide it needs to be stitched," he said.

Sylvie nodded. She wouldn't. It didn't need sutures. Though it had hurt like hell, when she went to bandage it, the wound was less deep, less severe, than she had thought. Looked no worse than a staple-gun accident, complete with silvery streak that she'd had to peel out.

She found Room 14, the curtain drawn across the glass

but the door open. The bed was empty, and Wales was pacing in the quiet.

He turned, and his expression was pure surprised relief, eyebrows up, mouth slack but shifting toward a smile. "You got out alive."

"Took some doing," she said.

"Azpiazu?"

"Alive. Evil. Up to something. How's Maria?"

"She made it here," he said. "They rushed her up to a real room. Can we get out of here? I've already fended off more questions than I know how to answer." He jolted toward the door, then back toward the bed as if tethered. Sylvie knew what held him. There was a certain weight that came with rescuing someone. A responsibility. Wales had carried Maria out of Azpiazu's lair, and he couldn't let go, no matter how much his paranoia urged him to flee.

Down the hall, just past the swinging doors, a pair of police officers consulted with a nurse, who pointed toward Room 14, toward Sylvie and Wales. "Yeah," Sylvie said. "Let's go." These cops weren't here for them; even if a doctor had called them about Maria, they'd shown too quickly. Didn't mean they wouldn't stop and interrogate, given the chance.

She stepped out of the room, her bandaged arm crossed over her chest, head ducked. Wales put an arm about her waist, quick on the uptake. The best way to leave an ER unnoticed? Look like any other patient who'd been treated.

They met Salvador Ruben rushing in as they were rushing out—he homed in on Sylvie like a tracking dog. "Your assistant called. She said. She said . . ."

"Maria's alive," Sylvie said. "Weak, but alive. Go see her." His attention veered toward the intake desk, and Sylvie and Wales slipped away.

They got out into the lot, and Wales dithered. "Serrano's car?"

"Leave it," Sylvie said. "Not the first car I've abandoned in the hospital lot."

He hotfooted forward through the lot, came back when

he didn't see her truck right off, and took off again. Sylvie seized his sleeve on his second twitchy search, and said, "That way," gesturing.

When he nodded once and set off at a rapid pace that she was hard-pressed to keep up with, she said, "Hey, you okay, Tex? What? Hospital too ghosty for you?"

He didn't respond, only hovered around her truck until she opened the door for him. Once the hospital lights shone bright in her rearview mirror, he finally answered.

"Maria died, Sylvie. I shoved her spirit back in her body. I'm kind of freaked-out. I'm not sure whether that makes me a healer or if she's a revenant."

"Breathe," Sylvie said. "Her heart was beating; she was breathing, right? The doctors weren't running around in a panic freaking out about zombies? She's alive. You saved her, Tex. That's a win."

"Did I save her? I'm not all that sure I did. Azpiazu's marks are all over her body. Her face, her palms, her feet, her heart . . . What's to prevent him from reaching out and killing her for pride and—"

"For one thing, he's got to move the rest of his harem and find a replacement," Sylvie said. "We fucked up our recon, but we also fucked up his night. He's going to be a busy monster."

"But Maria—"

"We've done what we can. Is the ouroboros charm still with her?"

"She's not wearing it, but it should be in the same room."

"That'll help," Sylvie said. She said it mostly to watch Wales lose some of that vibrating tension that made her feel like his spine might start rattling at any moment. "Focus, Tex, I've got questions. Azpiazu's got bigger things in mind than just controlling the curse Tepeyollotl laid on him. I think he's got some idea of how to break it, and without the curse holding his attention . . ."

Wales leaned his head against the passenger window, staring blankly at the stream of headlights. "Without the curse, he'll be more powerful. He's had decades spent fighting magic, decades spent in chains."

"Yeah. He'll be raring to go," Sylvie said. "Thing is, I think there's something more going on. You have any ideas?"

Wales closed his eyes. "There's something about the way he's set up this curse-block, power-exchange spell. It's . . . complex. Bizarrely so. Even beyond the whole sleight of hand required to use Tepeyollotl's power to gain immunity from the curse."

"Explain," she said.

"Ritual," Wales said. "It's all in how you're taught. Me? I don't use a lot of ritual, you might have noticed. 'Cause really? I'm a mundane with a skill for improvising. The more I tried to train, the worse I got. For someone like Eladio Azpiazu? An alchemist first? It's all about ritual."

"You're the one who was bitching that it was too complicated—"

Wales sighed. "True 'nough. And I think I phrased it wrong. Magical rituals are like . . . statements of intent. I have a poppet, I have an enemy. I want my enemy to suffer the same fate as this poppet. Yeah?"

"That's 101," Sylvie said. "Skip ahead."

"So touchy," he muttered. "Depending on your nerve and your skills, you can layer your rituals. Like . . . oh, a witch who wants you to see an illusion. That's almost always a two-part spell. The illusion they want you to fall prey to, and a stay-in-place layered beneath. After all, an illusion is a fragile thing, really. If they anchor it directly to you . . . it loses plausibility. I mean, say they curse you to see a—"

"Fire?" Sylvie asked.

"Yeah," Wales said. "That's a good one."

"Not really," Sylvie said.

Wales was undeterred. "So you walk in a place, and it's suddenly on fire. You run, right? I mean, hell, it's not even human nature; it's faster than that. It's animal instinct. *Flee.* So that's wasted energy on the witch's part if you just walk away. But if they attached it directly to you, so it followed you—"

"You start to doubt it," Sylvie said. "Because it doesn't make sense."

"People like their real-world rules," Wales said. "Things that tell us the sun rises in the east, the moon waxes and wanes, and the entire world cannot be on fire. So the witch slaps an anchoring spell beneath the illusion spell. A stick-around suggestion."

"Cobwebs," Sylvie said. "They like to put illusion spells on cobwebs."

"Exactly!" Wales nearly bounced in the seat beside her, a researcher getting to share his passion. Springs creaked, audible even over the steady growl of the engine. "And that's ritual in itself. A stay-put spell on something sticky. Helps them layer the spells, helps them keep it sharp, keep it safe."

"So Azpiazu's layering his rituals, which means he's layering his . . . intent?"

Azpiazu's name dragged all that excitement right back out of Wales's body. He slumped. "That fucker. I don't know what the hell his intent is. The binding spell is part of it, but it's overkill. Even for a god. Why not just deflect the power coming at him? Some of the sigils I saw on Maria . . . they almost looked like magical lightning rods, like they were meant to draw the magic in."

"You said he was filtering it."

"And he is. To control his shape, I thought, and to fuel his spells so he can keep controlling it. A sort of magical loop that I don't even know how he got started. He would have needed some kind of boost. . . ." He trailed off, then his mouth twisted. "I can't think of any good ways."

"Soul-devouring," Sylvie said. "Any boost from that?"

"And that," Wales said. "That's another layer. Another ritual. It has nothing to do with deflecting Tepeyollotl. I don't know why he's doing it. Humans don't need souls."

"You use them to sneak into hotels," Sylvie said.

Wales shifted. "Not the same thing. Ghosts aren't souls.

Ghosts are the dead, personality warts and all. Souls are . . . They're pure. Distilled."

"Powerful?"

Wales shrugged. "Not to us. A soul doesn't *want*. Can't bribe them or make them afraid. They don't care about the living."

"But he devours them—"

"Devour. It's only a word. He's doing *something* to them; I just don't know what. Souls are god business, not human."

Sylvie said, "Maybe it's just an act of contempt. You know, he's taking Tepeyollotl's would-be people, using them to counteract the curse, then destroying souls that would have been the god's? Azpiazu's bastard enough for that type of spitefulness."

"I don't know," Wales said. "I don't. But we have to stop him, Sylvie. Before he takes someone else. Before he finishes."

"You're my best hope for that," she said. "You figure out what his goals are. How necromancy and alchemy and god-avoiding works out to something good for him. So we can turn it bad. Work fast, Tex. I think we've got a deadline, and I'm not sure if it's Azpiazu's or the god's."

"Sure," he said. "No pressure. That's my hotel you're passing."

She slewed the truck over two lanes, did a U-ie, and brought him to the front doors. He popped the latch; she put a hand on his arm, curling her fingers around the thin sinew of it. "Tex, we did good tonight. Mostly." She shook herself and started again. "We saved Maria. You saved Maria. I know I can count on you."

"Lose the pep talk," he said. "Doesn't suit you. We're screwed. But I'll work on ways that might make us less so. See if I can figure out what the layers are for. See if I can figure the best way to unpick them. What about you?"

"Azpiazu's shopping for a new girl now. That reporter, Cachita, had some ideas."

"It's . . ." He turned his attention to her dash, to the

dimly glowing clock. "It's nearly 3:00 a.m. I don't think Cachita's gonna give you anything but grief you go waking her up now."

"You and Alex, all about working hours. Too much can happen while you're sleeping."

"Sylvie, you're mean enough without sleep dep. Go home. Get some hours in."

"Who's the boss, here?" Sylvie said.

Wales yawned in her face, showing her all his teeth. "You're paying me for my advice. Might as well take it."

13

Remember Me?

THE NEXT MORNING, SYLVIE WOKE WITH A SCALDING HEADACHE, A body that protested, and a strange metallic taste in her mouth. She smacked her lips before opening her eyes and thought about lead poisoning.

A shift of displaced air, the scent of coffee, heavily laced with cream, and a scuff of slippers had her rolling over in time to accept the cup Alex handed her. She cracked an eye, stared blearily up at Alex, and envied Alex the seven-year difference between them. Alex was as short of sleep as Sylvie was, and it only showed because she was quieter than usual. Sylvie knew she'd have bags beneath her eyes like tarnished silver dollars.

Alex moved back to the kitchen, her act of mercy complete, and Sylvie heard the clicking of keys. Regular people got up, went outside, got the newspaper. Alex got up, turned on the computer, and started scanning news files.

A *thump-flap* of a stressed dog door birthed Guerro, and Sylvie rolled off the couch before the shepherd could investigate the person who'd taken his preferred sleeping spot. She fended his nose off, covered the top of her coffee cup as he shook, setting loose hairs into the world, then sipped her drink once he'd bounded off after Alex.

Sometimes, Sylvie looked at her empty apartment and thought she could get a dog. Something to greet her at the end of a crap day, to be a quiet companion. Then she visited Alex and saw the truth. A dog owned you as surely as a cat did, or a baby, requiring care, and time, and routine that Sylvie didn't have.

Plus—she fished dog hair out of her mouth—there was the mess.

She set down the coffee cup, staggered into the kitchen, and stole Alex's bagel, spoke through a mouthful of lox and cream cheese and fresh bread. "So, I'm going to see Cachita—"

"She's a total liar," Alex said.

And that answered the question she'd been about to voice. Alex had managed the time to look into Caridad Valdes-Pedraza. Look enough that she was visibly indignant and unhappy.

Sylvie leaned back against the counter space, fed chunks of bagel to Guerro, and said, "Hit me." It felt like waiting for a blow. She'd rather liked Cachita.

A total liar.

"First off? Elena Valdes? Not her cousin. Not by genetics, not even by proximity. I looked both of them up. Cachita's not a local girl. She just moved here, grew up in Louisiana, stayed there for college. Elena Valdes? Her parents emigrated here, left all their family in Havana, and Elena never left Miami. No way they intersected."

Sylvie snorted. "But it made it easy for her. Get my sympathy. Explain her interest in the Everglades women as personal not ghoulish. So, a reporter who lies. I'm surprised that I'm surprised."

"Not a reporter," Alex said. "Or at least she never took a single journalism class in her entire college career."

Sylvie blinked. "Okay. Wait. Now I am surprised."

"Told you. Total liar." Alex bit her lip, tried not to look smug, but *I told you so* was seeping out all over.

"So who is she?" Sylvie said.

Alex's smug deflated. "I don't know. I mean, I know who she is, where she was born. But she got out of school—anthropology, by the way—two years ago and hasn't had a job since. Not even the usual postgrad jobs like waitressing, bartending, call centers, et cetera."

That might explain the near-empty house. Cachita was squatting more than living in it. Living hand to mouth and still going after Azpiazu?

"I could ask her," Sylvie said. "Go straight to the source."

"Yeah," Alex said. "Just be careful. I don't know what her game is."

"Here's hoping she's on the side of the angels." Sylvie put down the rest of the bagel, wiped her hands on a Hello-Kitty dish towel, and said, "At least her information on Azpiazu was true." She paused, thought about it. "What about Azpiazu himself motivating her? If she's not a reporter, and she's not related to any of the victims, then it's got to be about Azpiazu."

Alex said, "Why don't you go ask her?" Crankier than usual, but Sylvie had roused her out of bed late to crash on her couch, stolen some spare clothing, and now stolen her breakfast.

• • •

AS HOT AS SHE WAS TO FIND CACHITA, SHAKE SOME ANSWERS FROM the woman, Sylvie had to make a stop first. She was out of ammo. Not that it had done any good with Azpiazu, but it was the principle of the thing. An empty gun was a broken tool.

The office safe yielded the bullets she wanted. She sat at her desk, slotting the clip in, listening to her little dark voice purring in contentment, when the sound of glass cracking reached her.

The downstairs window?

Not loud enough.

The front door.

Which meant it wasn't a car-spun rock making an unlucky impact.

Sylvie looked at her upper windows and thought, not
for the first time, that she really needed a back exit.

Instead, she eased herself onto the narrow landing, keeping to the shadows, peered downstairs. Movement, a long,
supple shape slipping out of her visual range, leaving a
drifting voice behind. "Don't be like that, Shadows. Come
on down! Patrice wants to talk to you."

The goth boy-witch, Aron.

Sylvie felt a peculiar triumph twisting her mouth.
Patrice had actually done her a favor. Broken doorway,
trespassing, and threatening her—Sylvie could shoot and
claim self-defense.

She slipped down the stairs, bracing herself against the
rail, hunching low, gun in hand. Aron launched himself at
her, a surprisingly physical attack for a witch, and they
tumbled over each other, Sylvie kicking away, firing blind.

The window spider-cracked, her bullet dimpling the
center of it. Aron laughed in her face, said, "Are we having fun yet?" and leaped away. "Patrice is waiting."

He darted through the broken door, and Sylvie wiped
the blood from her split lip, hesitating only briefly before
bolting after him.

Foolish, her little dark voice hissed. Aron wasn't a normal witch, all talk and sneakiness. Aron, Sylvie thought,
was crazy.

Ahead of her, Aron paused to wave—encouragement, a
taunt, god only knew—and detoured from the main drag
toward the oceanfront. Sylvie moved steadily after him,
dodging joggers, vendors setting up, tourists looking shocked
awake, and her mind noted that this wasn't right. A man
running down the street, chased by a woman with a gun?
No one was noticing them at all.

Witch, she reminded herself. Their invisibility some
type of elaborate spell, triggered when they touched.

Witch? her dark voice echoed. It didn't sound certain. She slowed her steps. They'd tangled in the nightclub, and she'd felt the burn of magic against her skin, strong and sharp, an electrical current dancing through her bones.

His laughter drifted back, edgy and close to manic, deep-toned like the roar of the surf.

Seeking a confrontation.

Trap, her little voice said.

No duh, she thought. She slowed her chase, trying to figure this out. It felt . . . strange. Her brain said trap. Her instincts said it wasn't that clear-cut.

They'd tumbled against each other in her office, and that magical burn still lingered, sensitizing her nerves. Either every piece of tacky goth jewelry he wore was laced with spells, or there was something more here.

A gaggle of tourists wandered down the shady path toward the sea, putting themselves between Sylvie and her target, unaware of either of them. Aron, a black streak against the sun-dazzled sea, beckoned Sylvie on.

Sylvie let her gun hand slacken, slowed her pace to a bare crawl, giving the tourists the chance to get out of the way. But instead of moving on, the tourists, two men, two women, an assortment of bickering teens, swayed in her wake like driftwood on the tide and ended up following her toward Aron.

"Why don't you stretch yourself?" she said. "Use some of that spellwork to clear us some space." She needed to get the tourists gone.

He grinned back, a slow smile. "Nah. I like 'em. Keeps you on your best behavior."

Kept her gun useless. With this much magic in the air, Sylvie was loath to just start shooting. She'd have to have the barrel snugged up against Aron before she fired it, and she doubted he'd allow it.

"So Patrice let you off your leash? I thought you were only her bodyguard. Not her attack dog."

"I'm no one's dog," he said, his grin fading.

That hot temper, that fierce rebuttal, they dredged something like memory out of her, woke a vague sense of déjà vu. "Patrice sent you after me. You do as you're told."

He shook his head. "Only sometimes. Only when it's right."

"Enough talk, Aron," Patrice said. She stepped out of tree shadow, petulant and puffy-eyed. A week in Bella's body, and she was using it harder than Bella ever had. It looked like she'd aged five years. A corrupt spirit corrupting what it had claimed.

"Patrice," Sylvie said. "Looking tired. Life not as easy as you thought?"

"Aron, kill her already," Patrice said.

Aron's feverish gaze ran across Sylvie's skin, shoulders to toes and back up again. "You sure?"

Sylvie, clenched in readiness to fight back, to flee a spell or another attack, to crack the morning open with bullet fire, felt her body jerk in shock.

Patrice twitched also, a bizarre body echo. "Of *course* I'm sure! I paid you to—"

Aron's chest shifted, moving fast with his quickening breath. "I know. I just thought. Sometimes, there are things you want to do yourself. For the satisfaction of it. No matter who you've hired."

Patrice's expression was pure distaste and Sylvie found herself laughing, hard-edged and furious. "You killed for that body, and now you won't even fight to defend it? Afraid of scratching the finish? Or are you afraid you don't have what it takes?"

Her voice was shrieking warning; this was not how any confrontation with a bad-magic witch was supposed to go.

"Kill her now, Aron."

Aron hesitated, his eyes bright on Sylvie's, amused still. "What do you think, Shadows? You think you can get to her before I get to you?" There was a hunger in his voice, a fierce vibration that suggested this was what he'd wanted all along: some type of cage match that he could enjoy.

"I can try," Sylvie said, moving even as she spoke, heading straight for Patrice. Hesitation was fatal, no matter the

situation. She aimed—sighting at Patrice's startled face—
pulled the trigger. The sound was loud, louder than their
voices had been. It cracked the illusion around them. The
tourists scattered like a flock of wild birds, still blind to
the players, but not to the danger. One of them cried out,
clapped a hand over her calf.

Bullet wound.

Patrice simpered at Sylvie, but her eyes showed the
whites all around. Her hand clutched nervously at one of
her oversized earrings.

Protection charm.

Deflection.

Sylvie had just shot the tourist.

Fuck.

But Patrice had betrayed herself with that one gesture—
showing Sylvie where her protection lay. Sylvie tackled
Patrice, slapped her hand over the earring, and yanked
at it.

It didn't come off; the flesh around it didn't yield. Invulnerability, then.

Aron began to whisper, his husky voice drawing tighter,
lighter, and strangely familiar. A chant. A spell. Something.
It lacked the focused energy she had come to expect from
magical workings, but it diverted the attention Sylvie's
shot had drawn.

Patrice squalled like a skinned cat, shrieking Aron's
name. He broke off the chant and threw himself into the
battle.

He wasn't a witch, Sylvie realized abruptly, taking the
brunt of his weight across her shoulders as she twisted away.
She elbowed him sharply in the nose, and he jerked back.

Holding back, she thought. Playing with her? Or . . .

He wasn't an enemy.

Or was he?

There was real rage in his eyes. It didn't seem directed
at her, though. Didn't seem directed at all, just free-
floating fury.

She slipped free from his grasp, his hands like steel but

failing to close tightly enough on her bones. Patrice scrambled toward the sidewalk, through the grass; lizards and a quick black scuttling scorpion fled her.

Sylvie slammed into the girl, using her longer reach, her heavier weight, knelt on the woman's back. Patrice screeched and clawed, tore gouges in Sylvie's wrists, but Sylvie undid the clasp on the earring and yanked it away.

Patrice screamed loud and long, shrill enough to make Sylvie recoil. The woman staggered upright and ran. Aron caught her in three swift strides.

"I paid you!" she shrieked.

"Someone else hired me first," he said. His hands closed over her neck and face; he drew her close as if to kiss her, then wrenched.

A wet, gristly sound and Patrice's body dropped, knees folding, torso slapping wetly into the grass. Her head, eyes still fluttering, fell a moment later. Aron licked blood off of his fingers and turned back toward Sylvie.

Definitely not a witch, not even a sorcerer, Sylvie thought. Her heart raced; her gun was tight in her hands.

"Gonna shoot me? Again?"

A Power in the city as well as a god. A Power that was looking at Sylvie expectantly. Eagerly. Hungry down to the core. She thought she recognized it. Impossible as it seemed.

"No praise?" he said. "I did it for you."

She licked dry lips, studied the gothy clothing, the simmering hunger, and took refuge in words. "Seems to me, I did more than my fair share. I got the charm off."

"I could have done it," he said. "But I thought you'd want to participate. You like your vengeance, Sylvie."

"I'm not the one yanking heads off in a public park. With children present."

"Children should know that monsters can be killed," Aron said. "Patrice killed two children for her selfish purposes, an infant and that girl whose body she wore. But if it makes you happy, I'll keep her invisible until you clean her up."

"Me?"

"I cleaned up after you in Chicago."

If Sylvie had any lingering doubts about who Aron was, they were fading fast. Especially when he slumped, crossed his arms across his narrow chest, and sulked, spiky black hair loosening and settling like storm clouds over his brow. "You don't even recognize me, do you."

"I do," Sylvie said.

"Yeah?"

"Erinya," Sylvie named her. The youngest of the Fury trio that worked for Dunne. She was rewarded with a quick smile that bared those vampiric veneers again. Wait. Not veneers after all, not if this was the Fury.

"Took you long enough. I thought you'd know me at the club. I even rubbed up against you, and you couldn't tell? I came when you called, and you weren't there. You didn't even leave me instructions! I had to figure out what you summoned me for all on my own."

"Cut me some slack," Sylvie said. "I thought Dunne destroyed you. I saw him devour you when he needed your strength."

"He absorbed us," Aron said. "And when he didn't need us any longer, he spat us back out. *Refined* us, he said. I hunt specific types of murderers now."

"Child-killers," Sylvie said. Of course. It explained the other murders in the city. All people who'd killed children.

Erinya grinned. "It's a fertile field to play in. Alekta couldn't wrap her mind around change, so she's still dealing with matricides, patricides, families gone bad. And Magdala got stuck with crimes committed against society. *Bo*-ring, just like her."

"Reshaped you, too," Sylvie said. "Guess he always wanted a boy?"

"What? This? No," Aron-Erinya said. "I thought Patrice would like it, and I wanted to get close to her, wanted to draw out the hunt. What about you?"

"Me?"

"Do you like this shape?"

Sylvie opened her mouth to say something in response to Erinya's violent and unsubtle flirtations and failed. She forgave herself; there was a lot to process—that through a scratchy symbol drawn on a doorstep based on instructions Sylvie'd given herself in a dream, she'd called Erinya down to Miami. That there was anything to call . . . the Furies not gone.

A brief spurt of terror touched her. *Demalion.* If the Furies were alive and hunting, Demalion's safety was precarious.

"Refined, my ass," Sylvie muttered finally. "It's your body, your choice. My preference is irrelevant."

"Doesn't have to be," Aron said. He shook all over like a wet dog, flipped gender. Took on the more familiar form, the punk gothette. It really wasn't that much of a change. Aron had been long and lean, androgynous. So was Erinya. "So. The body?"

Sylvie's head ached. She looked down at the blood-spattered grass. Bella Alvarez hadn't been a big girl. It wouldn't be much effort to cart her body away. Or they could just leave her. An unsolved murder, committed impossibly in broad daylight.

Even if the murder hadn't happened practically in her backyard, Bella/Patrice could be linked to Sylvie easily enough through Lio. And Lio thought poorly enough of her at the moment that he might do something rash, something like talking to the ISI. If Bella disappeared, Lio'd be unhappy but unable to get the justice system rolling.

Sylvie said, "You get the body. I'll get the head."

Erinya shifted foot to foot. "But I did all the work."

"I'm the one who summoned you to do it," Sylvie said. "Cleanup's part of the job."

"Fine," Erinya said. She bent, scooped up the body; blood dribbled down her shoulder. "Where's your truck?"

Sylvie said, "Give me your jacket."

"Again?" Erinya dropped the body, shrugged off the jacket. "You're hard on my clothes, Sylvie. It's a good thing I like you."

"It's a good thing you like bloodstains," Sylvie said. She spread the jacket on the ground, toed Patrice's head into the center, and made a neat bundle of it. "Can't you just magic her away?"

"Not and keep us invisible," Erinya said. "I'm not really good at the magic part. I'm good at the killing-things part."

"Yeah, I get you," Sylvie said. Her mouth stung; she realized she was smiling, straining her split lip. Smiling over a dead body. She stopped.

Erinya sighed. "I'm going to ask Dunne to make you a Fury when you die. You and I can hunt forever. I know he worries about what he should do with you."

"Nothing," Sylvie said, "I'm not his."

"You fight for justice," Erinya said. "You could be his, no matter your lineage. When it came to it, when you asked for help, for vengeance . . . you drew the scales of justice on Patrice's doorstep."

"Tell you what," Sylvie said. "We move the body now. And God and Dunne can fight over my soul when I'm dead."

"But that could be such a very long time," Erinya said.

"Not the way my life is going," Sylvie said.

"Yeah," Erinya agreed. "You should be more careful. Tepeyollotl's skulking around, and he's a real bastard god. If he hates you, you get your heart ripped out. If he loves you, you get your heart ripped out. Oh! You should take Patrice's invulnerability charm. It's not as good as Lilith's was. It's only a temporary one, but it'll help you."

"No," Sylvie said. "Those things have hidden costs. I wear it, and someone else suffers, right? Like the tourist who got clipped by a bullet meant for Patrice?"

"Could have been a bad ricochet," Erinya said. "Guns are no fun. Always best to fight teeth to teeth."

"That's not an answer," Sylvie said.

"Always so suspicious," Erinya pouted.

"Am I right?"

"Fine. Yes. The talisman would bounce your injuries, your death, to someone else."

"No," Sylvie said.

"But you're more fun than other people," Erinya said. "You're sneaky and you're dangerous and you brought me good sport. A ghost that changed bodies to escape death. I didn't know humans could do that."

Sylvie's breath stuttered in her chest; she stumbled. Patrice's head squelched nastily inside the jacket. Erinya paused, predatory instincts firing. "Sylvie?" It was a growl.

"Tripped," Sylvie said.

Erinya's dark-eyed gaze narrowed; her eyes burned out, leaving black pits in her head. Her hair shifted and spiked toward feathers, losing control of the quasi-human form and taking on the pure aspect of Fury. Sylvie jerked her eyes away, focused them on the safer sight of the lumpy jacket in her arms, growing steadily damper and darker. Looking a Fury in the eyes led to nightmares at best, madness at worst.

Her day was too full for either option.

"You smell like . . . secrets," Erinya said, keeping pace with her. Her feet on the pavement were clawed; leathery boots shifted into sinewy legs and strong paws.

"It's my job," Sylvie said. "Lots of secrets."

Warmth along the side of her face, and the pinprick of needle teeth closing gently, warningly, along her nape. Sylvie stopped. Her heart rocketed. Erinya would be tasting fear, along with sweat and adrenaline and secrecy.

Sylvie dropped Patrice's head, punched Erinya in the muzzle as hard as she could. Her knuckles split; the skin of her neck stung as Erinya's teeth were jarred free.

"Get off me," Sylvie said. She drew her gun, turned to face the monster. "Look, Eri, I'm probably happier than I should be that you're not gone, not dead. That doesn't mean I won't do my best to make you that way if needed."

"Something . . . important," Erinya said. She turned her head this way and that, that strange nightmare creature, half dog, half bird, all hunger. Her forked tongue tasted the air, cleaned the thin smear of Sylvie's blood from her curving teeth. "I'll find out."

"You know what?" Sylvie said. "Leave the body. I'll take care of it. You, go back to Dunne."

Erinya laughed, shifting back toward her human guise. Her smile had no warmth in it. "You're not the boss of me, Sylvie."

"I summoned you; doesn't that count?"

"That's the trouble with calling in mercenaries," Erinya said. "They're hard to control. They like to be paid. Give me something, and I'll leave your secrets alone."

"And here I thought you were on a god-given mission," Sylvie said. She picked up Patrice's head again, grimacing at the splotch it had left on the pavement, and headed for the truck. She focused her thoughts on practical matters, tried to soothe the worry from her mind and body. Erinya's senses were sharper than any animal's, and she coupled that with rudimentary mind reading. Sylvie thought hard about whether she'd left the tarp in the truck lockbox, whether the olive fabric would be enough to hide stains, whether the tide was right to drop a body, and when all of those didn't ease the suspicion on Erinya's face, she went for the sure shot. She thought of Patrice, dead. Sylvie's own guilty satisfaction that Patrice wasn't going to prosper. That her enemy was destroyed.

A sated smile curved Erinya's lips; her lashes came down, changing anger to pleasure. "I did good."

"Yeah, you did," Sylvie said. She gave the praise without hesitation. For one thing, a happy Erinya was an Erinya less likely to pry. For another . . . Well, it had been a job neatly done.

Sylvie had hoped for a more subtle way to kill Patrice. She'd hoped for something that could pass for a medical condition. As far as the world was concerned, Bella Alvarez had already had one serious medical episode. But, once Patrice had started throwing witches Sylvie's way, it could only end violently.

Erinya slung the body into the back of the truck without even a shrug of effort, wrapped it with the tarp, and climbed into the cab humming tunelessly. Sylvie shivered. It was a human thing to do, and it sounded nothing like human at all. She put the truck into gear and headed out.

Erinya stayed with her long enough to see Patrice's body slip beneath the deep waters, weighted down with broken concrete and rebar, before vanishing. Sylvie hoped the Fury had gone back to Dunne, to Olympus, to anyplace other than Miami. She didn't even let a wisp of Chicago cross her mind. Erinya's disappearance was a bullet dodged. Made Sylvie crazy, though. If she hadn't been carrying that dangerous secret, she might have been able to recruit Erinya to fight against Azpiazu.

Sylvie ran the truck through a car wash, rinsing off any blood that might have seeped into the back, and called it done.

14

Mirror Mirror

SEEN IN FULL DAYLIGHT, CACHITA'S HOUSE SEEMED ALL THE MORE out of place in what was otherwise a nice old neighborhood. Sylvie parked the truck in front of the massively overgrown lawn, scattering lizards and spotted cats. Feeling eyes on her, she turned. Cachita's next-door neighbor stood in the doorway, staring over at Sylvie. When she realized she had Sylvie's attention, she beckoned imperiously.

Sylvie gritted her teeth but adjusted her path. The woman, dressed neatly in jeans and a silk shell, looked like the type to get difficult if thwarted. Sylvie wasn't in the mood for difficult. She forded the grass and stepped onto the neighbor's close-clipped lawn.

"Are you with the city?" the woman asked. She was younger than Sylvie had thought. In her fifties, not the seventies she had imagined when Cachita had mentioned her cat-crazy neighbor.

"Nope," Sylvie said. "Just visiting."

"She's your friend?" The woman's mouth wrinkled in disgust.

"Not that either," Sylvie said.

"Well, tell her I've called the city. She needs to get her

house cleaned up. It's an eyesore. It's always been an eyesore, but we were assured the new tenant was going to fix it up."

"Your cats seem to be enjoying it," Sylvie said. "Isn't there some limit to how many you're allowed?"

The woman's brows rose sky-high. "My cats? They're not mine. They came with her."

Sylvie absorbed that with a spark of strangely potent anger, nodded once, and stalked off the woman's lawn.

"Where are you going? I'm not done."

"Don't care," Sylvie said. She stormed up Cachita's front path, pounded on the door. When there was no answer, she studied the warped front door, the gap that let AC bleed out. She kicked hard just beside the latch; the door groaned. She shifted her weight, braced herself better, and kicked again. The latch ripped through the humidity-rotted wood frame, and the door slammed open.

Sylvie kicked it shut behind her, found Cachita scrambling out of her bedroom, Taser in hand, bare feet, and panicked.

Recognition blossomed as Sylvie snapped on the overhead light, but her expression stayed wary.

"Did you lie about absolutely everything?" Sylvie asked. "Even your goddamned cats?"

Cachita's shoulders drew tight, then dropped. She said, "You going to shoot me? Or you going to wait for answers?"

"You're the one with the Taser," Sylvie said.

"You're the one with the gun," Cachita said. Her eyes flickered downward.

Sylvie followed her gaze. One thing Cachita was right about. Sylvie didn't even remember unholstering the gun.

Fallout from killing Patrice, from hanging out with a Fury. Her temper burned hotter and faster than usual. And that was saying something.

"How 'bout we both put our toys away," Cachita said. Her voice quivered.

Another act? Or honest fear? Sylvie hated that she didn't know. "You first."

Cachita bit her lip, running calculations.

"I've got the gun," Sylvie said. "I've got the advantage here."

"Yeah, but I've got nosy neighbors."

"Put it down," Sylvie said.

Cachita sighed, let the Taser drop. "Happy?"

"Not even close." Sylvie gestured Cachita closer, edged around her, picked up and pocketed the Taser; only then did she holster the gun.

"So your little assistant looked into me, I guess," Cachita said.

"She did. Elena Valdes isn't your cousin. You aren't a reporter."

"Hey, I could be," Cachita said. It was a feeble rebuttal. The young woman looked suddenly tired. Burdened. It was more than just the sleep disruption; it was ground-in stress that she had managed to cover up with her act.

"Sit," Sylvie said.

"I'm the host here," Cachita said. "Just so you remember."

"Sit," Sylvie repeated.

Cachita flounced into a seat, a little of her previous attitude surfacing. "If this ends with bondage, I'm going to be pissed."

"Who are you?"

Cachita laughed. "That's your question? Isn't that obvious? Sylvie, I'm you."

. . .

SYLVIE LOOKED AROUND THE ROOM, THE GLOOM OF IT, THE FILES stapled to the walls, the disorder and chaos of a life, and grimaced. She pulled up the only other seat in the living room, a rickety ladder-back chair with a cane seat, perched on it. "You're a PI?"

"I'm a god's bitch," Cachita said. "Just like you and Justice."

"I'm no one's dog," Sylvie said.

"Then you're lucky. Or deluded," Cachita said. She put her face in her hands. "Or your god is kind."

"Gods aren't kind," Sylvie said. "Not their nature."

"Tell me about it," Cachita gasped. Laughed again. "Oh god."

"So you're Tepeyollotl's—"

"Yes."

"He hired you? To find Azpiazu?"

"Hired is a human word," Cachita said. "I'm not sure there was anything human about what happened to me."

Sylvie said, "Tell me?"

Cachita shuddered.

"C'mon," Sylvie said. "You've latched onto me. You've studied me. You've been hunting any excuse to talk to me. You're dying for an audience."

"Your girl looked me up? She tell you I was an anthro student?"

"Yeah."

"Latin American culture," Cachita said. "I went down there. I worked there. In Mexico. I went down worried about *los narcos*. About my health. About making something new and noteworthy academically out of plowed ground. I didn't worry about gods. I didn't even believe in them."

"Atheists are fair game," Sylvie said.

"Know that now." Cachita rubbed her face. Her lashes were spiky with tears that didn't quite fall. Too controlled for that. Too tired for the catharsis of it.

"So instead of finding a study topic, you found Tepé."

"He found me. My dreams first, then my waking hours. Until every moment of every day was filled with his presence. He's not . . . He's not very good at communicating," she said. "It was like being forced under a waterfall while someone yells at you. Except the waterfall was blood and screams and knives. I thought I was going insane. I *was* insane after a month of it. Then I started waking up with a jaguar in my room."

"Off-putting," Sylvie said.

"One word for it," Cachita said. "'Terrifying' was another. But it shocked me sane again. It wasn't in my head, you get that? Something there. Something impossible. But real. Something I could touch. Something I could smell. Other people saw it. I could tell by the screaming." Cachita shrugged. "The last time I saw it was in a hotel, and it had stopped first to eat some woman's dog.

"So the next time the yelling started, I yelled back. It was that or crumble. It helped. He stopped sending jaguars and shaking things. Still get house cats and uncontrollable kudzu. And a lot of anger. He wants Azpiazu found. He wants Azpiazu dead."

"He give you any ideas on how to accomplish that?"

"I just need to summon him," Cachita said. "That part's easy. It's finding Azpiazu that's fucking things up."

"Been there, done that," Sylvie said. "Let's back up. Summon Tepeyollotl? That's not going to happen on my watch."

"You found him? And you didn't call me?" Cachita wailed it, a woman who learned her chance at freedom might have escaped her.

"You lied to me," Sylvie said. "I didn't have any reason to think you'd be useful. Your own damn fault."

Cachita panted, brought herself under control. "I thought we were going to be partners."

"You researched me," Sylvie said. "You know I don't do partners."

"What happened?" Cachita said. "With Azpia—"

"I know what you mean," Sylvie said. She closed her eyes briefly, the better to shut out Cachita's burgeoning hope. "We found his lair. We saved one of the women. Then he came back and caught us in the act."

"No," Cachita said. "No, dammit, he'll have moved by now! He'll be gone. You ruined our chance. He'll be in a new state."

"He's not going anywhere," Sylvie said. "Stop panicking. He wants something, and he's close to getting it, Cachita. Stop reacting and start thinking. Why did Tepeyollotl change his mind?"

"What?" Cachita said. She shifted uncomfortably in her seat, dared to rise and start pacing. Sylvie watched, but didn't try to make her sit again. Cachita looked like she was the kind who thought on her feet. "Tepeyollotl changed his mind. . . . You mean the curse?"

"I do," Sylvie said. "First he curses Azpiazu with uncontrollable shape-shifting and immortality. Then he . . . decides no? To kill him instead?"

"Azpiazu controlled the curse," Cachita said. "That was never Tepeyollotl's intention."

"But it took him this long to decide to send someone after him? A human agent? No. That doesn't make sense. Something changed, Cachita. You're not a reporter. But you were a student, and you've done decent research. Take yourself out of the equation and think about it. Why kill him now?"

Cachita said, "I'm the first human he's reached out to in centuries. I knew that. His language. His thought patterns. He's archaic and totally uninvolved with this modern age. He's violent and simplistic. He wants. He takes."

"So what does he want?" Sylvie said. "You can't tell me you didn't research him. Not if he's holding your leash."

Cachita shook her head, not a rebuttal, but a sort of exasperation. "You want to talk about Tepeyollotl now? Azpiazu's the problem."

"Yes and no," Sylvie said. "Azpiazu's pissed off the god. He's outthought Tepeyollotl's curse and punishment. But if we don't know how Tepeyollotl thinks—"

"He doesn't," Cachita said. "He's broken. Badly broken. Look, Shadows, here's a history lesson. Tezcatlipoca was one of the primary gods in Aztec culture. He had . . . aspects, like a mirror. He showed different faces, different things, to his people depending on their needs. He juggled personalities. He reshaped himself, over and over and over. He was clever. He was cunning. He was . . . everything."

" 'Was' being the operative word," Sylvie said.

"When the Aztecs crashed. In the sixteenth century, when the Spaniards came, complete with sorcerers as well as soldiers, Tezcatlipoca was spread thin across his region. Focused in different directions. I'm not sure what the sorcerers did—Tepeyollotl doesn't remember—but he shattered. Became only the parts, separate and fading. Tepeyollotl, the jaguar god, the earthquake bringer, is all that's left of Tezcatlipoca, and he's mostly animal instinct."

"So Azpiazu can outthink him," Sylvie said. "Tepeyollotl's curse was powerful but simple. A reaction to a slight—"

"Killing of his acolyte by a sorcerer," Cachita said. Her pacing slowed. "Yes. He reacted at once. He didn't think about it. He hates sorcerers." Outside in the yard, in the overgrown grass, cats howled. Cachita flinched.

"He can hear us?"

"I'm not sure if they're his spies or just reacting to his interest in me," Cachita said.

"Assume spies," Sylvie said. "Safer that way."

"Well, I've no secrets from him," Cachita said. "He's been in my head, in my dreams, in every thought I ever had. Go ahead and speculate. Why not? It's not like he's easily offended or something. Not like he curses those he thinks are betraying him."

Sylvie got up, found a can of soda in Cachita's barebones kitchen, and passed it over to the woman. She was close to hyperventilating. Cachita pushed it away, and Sylvie said, "Take a sip or two. Calm down. You're not betraying him. You want Azpiazu dead. So do I. We're just trying to spare Tepeyollotl from making the trip to this plane."

Cachita said, "It'd be easier if we just called him when we found Azpiazu."

"No, Cachita," Sylvie said. "No, it really wouldn't. There's nothing easy about a god's presence on earth."

She looked mulish, and Sylvie fought down the urge to argue. She could press that point later. The more urgent problem was Azpiazu. "He's going to need another woman," Sylvie said. "The spell is broken, right now."

"You don't think he's just running," Cachita said, coming back to the topic Sylvie needed her to focus on. "You think something else is happening."

"Yes," Sylvie gritted. "Wales, my consultant, says the magic he's using is too strong, getting stronger."

Cachita licked her lips. "Magic is like any force. Struggle with it, and you get stronger. Isn't that all it is?"

"The weight he's lifting is a godly one," Sylvie said. "Not exactly easy to build up to. Even if it's a broken god."

Cachita stepped to the papered-over window, leaned her head against it, then slunk toward Sylvie, as wary as one of the feral cats outside. She crouched near Sylvie's chair, and said, voice a bare whisper, "Thing is. I thought. I thought I was getting used to him. To his words. The feel of him in my mind. In my dreams. But maybe"—another glance toward the walls of the house, another pitch lower in tone—"maybe he's getting weaker."

Sylvie let her breath out, not in the hiss of epiphany she wanted but a slower thing, soundless, careful as Cachita was careful. But it would explain Azpiazu's strength. And it matched with what Wales had told her, what she knew herself.

Magic was a shifty kind of thing. Most magic was about creating a link between two objects, the better to manipulate one. But the thing was, the binding went both ways. If Azpiazu had been less clever, he'd be suffering as the god had intended. But instead, he was a tricky, malevolent bastard, used to transforming materials he had to hand.

She and Wales knew he was using the women to filter the curse power that was pouring out of the god's intent. Turning it to his purpose. Maddening enough to Tepeyollotl. But if he was doing more. If the filter also *pulled* . . .

Tepeyollotl was bleeding power to his enemy.

Azpiazu was sucking up the strength of a god.

Sylvie's blood cooled in her veins. The humid air in Cachita's house seemed suddenly as clammy as an underground crypt. She wiped at the nape of her neck, stole back the soda, and pressed it to her face.

"Sylvie?"

If Azpiazu was siphoning off a god's power, bit by bit by bit, that was bad enough. That could turn a human magic-user into something very horrific indeed. It should be a self-correcting problem. A human had limitations, couldn't control a god's power, couldn't bear its weight.

But Azpiazu was an immortal. And more. He had a plan.

An immortal who shared a god's power became a demi-god. Like Erinya. A Fury in the cause of Justice.

Azpiazu didn't seem like the kind to take orders.

Sylvie felt the last piece drop into place. "Soul-devourer." They'd bandied the term back and forth enough. Now she understood what it meant. Azpiazu wasn't just taking power. He was taking souls.

Back in Chicago, she'd stopped Lilith from stealing a god's power, from replacing him as a god. The easiest way to become a god: kill one, replace it.

Sylvie thought that with filtered god-power, with his own store of souls, Azpiazu might have found his own way to budding godhood. He wouldn't be Tepeyollotl's servant. He'd be his rival. His enemy. His equal.

• • •

THE SILENCE IN THE ROOM LINGERED, BROKEN ONLY BY THE COOLING hiss and pop of the carbonated drink in Sylvie's hand, by the rustle of cats moving through the high grass outside. Chasing lizards, Sylvie thought. Recalled the two-headed reptiles she'd seen around Azpiazu, in the 'Glades, and in the city.

A god's power, bent in two directions. A god's power bending to two wills. No wonder the smaller animals were warping around it. It was only a matter of time before bigger changes were apparent. Before the world started yielding in a massive way to Azpiazu's will.

"You know something," Cachita said. "You know what he's doing."

"Fucking up the world," Sylvie said.

"That's not an answer," Cachita said. "Share and share alike."

Sylvie wanted to keep Cachita out of it but doubted Tepeyollotl would allow it. "What do you know about gods?"

"Mythologically, or practically? 'Cause I don't know how standard Tepeyollotl is."

"Gods have power," Sylvie said. "Varying amounts, but all of it more than a human can ever hope to touch. Under normal circumstances."

"Azpiazu—"

"Yeah," Sylvie said. "But there's more to gods than power. That's a lot of it. That's the shiny part. The thing people always think about. Power. Omnipotence. Give or take a few degrees. But they're also about collecting souls. It's so important to them that all the pantheons have an agreement not to touch each other's people. To divide up the nonbelievers. We're more than property to them. We're assets of some kind. Gold bullion.

"The curse laid on Azpiazu was supposed to do more than just make him suffer. It was supposed to mark souls for Tepeyollotl to claim. He's a forgotten god mostly. Broken. He needs souls to heal. To regain his strength. His place in the worlds. He's dependent on the atheists. The unclaimed ones. But Azpiazu got fancy."

"He's stealing Tepeyollotl's power *and* the souls," Cachita said. Her cheeks blushed hot with rage. "You should have called me, Sylvie. I should have summoned Tepeyollotl. It would all be over. And instead, you fucked this up and went it alone, and now you're telling me Azpiazu's trying to be a god? He's a serial killer, Sylvie. Is that really someone we want to deify?"

"We're not summoning Tepeyollotl. No matter what," Sylvie said. "I will shoot you dead before you can if it comes to that. And he'll have to find another agent."

Cachita reeled back. "I don't understand—"

"In Chicago," Sylvie said. "A month or so back. You read about the hurricane midcountry."

"Yes."

"The freak accidents. The weird shit that people don't want to talk about."

"Over a hundred people died, I remember," Cachita said. "Wait."

"Gods," Sylvie said. "Ready for the kicker? That was a squabble. One god restraining himself as best he could, and some petty infighting. The sky rained blood, Cachita.

"If you bring Tepeyollotl down, and Azpiazu's as close as I think he is to godhood . . . It'll be all-out war. They might not be as powerful as the ones in Chicago, but they won't have any intention of playing nice. If god presence can create a hurricane on a landlocked lake, you want to see what warring gods can do in Florida?"

Cachita wrung her hands, knotted them in her hair. "I don't know what to do, Sylvie."

"Listen to me. Trust me."

"You let Azpiazu escape you." .

"But we saved Maria Ruben."

"She doesn't matter!"

"She matters to her family," Sylvie said. "Just because you're dealing with gods doesn't mean you can give up being human. Trust me. I can stop him. I can kill him."

Pure bravado. She didn't have a clue. Wales would have to come up with something. She'd hurt Azpiazu before. Minor injuries. But it was only a matter of getting the right degree to make them major ones. Mortal ones.

We kill the unkillable, her voice murmured.

Cachita's voice left all trace of frightened vibrato behind. "All right. You're in charge. But I'm sticking close. If I think you're wrong, you'll have to shoot me."

The answer quivering on Sylvie's lips, burning like salt in a wound, gave way to startled cursing when her phone rang shrilly in her pocket. She yanked it out. "What!"

"Sylvie," Alex said. If Cachita had found her nerve, her iron core, Alex had lost hers. Tears drenched her voice. "Sylvie. You gotta come now. Back to the office. Please."

"Alex," Sylvie said. "Are you hurt? Are you—"

The phone disconnected on a whimper.

Naked terror.

Not the ISI, then. Not the police.

Sylvie thought of Maria Ruben, safe and sound in the hospital. Out of Azpiazu's reach. But Alex . . .

"Time to move," she told Cachita. "I think Azpiazu's come calling."

Cachita dithered unexpectedly, gesturing at her PJs, at her bare feet, her face blanching at the sudden call to arms.

Sylvie said, "My office. As soon as you can."

"Shadows, wait!"

She didn't. In the *Magicus Mundi*, patience was rarely a virtue.

15

Negotiations

THE TRAFFIC BETWEEN CACHITA'S QUIET SUBURB AND THE SOUTH
Beach strip was dense enough that Sylvie honestly regretted not buying a motorcycle instead of a truck. Her hands
danced on the wheel; her stomach soured.

She should have made sure Alex didn't go to work until the office was magically secured again.

She jerked the truck through a gap, changed lanes in
a flurry of horns, and put the pedal down. The first sight
of her office made her heart jump; she'd forgotten about
the bullet she'd put into the window. For a single moment,
Sylvie thought maybe that was what had Alex so upset.
The cracked window, the signs of violence. That happy
image couldn't hold.

If Alex had been concerned about the violence, she
would have asked about Sylvie's well-being. Not begged
her to come home.

Sylvie stopped the truck, left it skewed in front of the
office, heedless of traffic. The blinds had been drawn down;
sunlight reflected off the front door, turning it mirror opaque
when she needed it to be clear. To give her even that tiny
warning as to what she might find.

She put one hand on the holster, another on the latch. Pushed. The door wasn't locked.

Alex looked up, face pale to her very lips. Her bright makeup looked garish on her bones. "Sylvie—"

Her attention was already drawn elsewhere, to the unexpected presence in the room. Not Azpiazu after all. *Erinya.* The Fury stood with her back against the wall, her claws leaving deep gouges in the plaster. Curls of paint and plaster dust made bright confetti on her dark boots.

"I didn't mean to," Alex blurted. "I'm so sorry. She surprised me, and I was on the phone with him. I said his name."

Sylvie closed her eyes. *Demalion.*

Erinya bared all her teeth. "He ghost-jacked a body. Just like Patrice. Trying to escape the inevitable. Where is he, Sylvie?"

"I'm not telling you."

"I'll find him myself."

"Then why are you still here?"

Erinya's eyes burned bloody and bright; Alex ducked her head and whimpered.

"Yeah," Sylvie said. "That's right. You aren't as good at scenting humans as your sister. And his scent's changed."

"Tell me."

"No," Sylvie said.

"I won't tell you either, so you can just . . . just . . . go away!" Alex's defiance—brave, but stupid—started out strong, went shrill when dark feathers spiked along Erinya's spine, when her head lowered and went bestial.

"Oh god, please!" Alex yelped, and before Sylvie could move to step between them, Erinya backed down. Shook the Fury aspect off, looked . . . chastened.

"I'll get it out of Sylvie, then," Erinya said.

"You know you won't," Sylvie said.

Erinya threw a chair at the wall; it slammed into the plaster and stuck for a moment, dangling by a leg thrown with enough force to become a spear. When the chair landed, Erinya crashed onto it, shredding the heavy wood and leather to matchsticks.

"You all right?" Sylvie asked Alex. Let Erinya destroy the furniture, keep her occupied. "Not hurt?"

Alex shook her head.

It was an unlooked-for boon. Sylvie had seen Erinya yank information from a woman's mind, leaving trauma and coma behind. But she hadn't hurt Alex.

Sylvie doubted it was out of respect for her. "Go home, then. Lock the doors. Be careful, Alex. I thought Azpiazu had come to get you. He still might. He still needs another element to his spell."

"Atheists," Alex said, "right? Unclaimed soul. I'm safe, then."

Erinya snarled, a vibrating hum in her throat something like a growl, something like a swallowed howl. Pure frustration.

Was *that* why?

Alex believed so deeply that the Fury couldn't interfere with another god's worshipper? Sylvie couldn't believe it. Alex had never been religious, gently mocked those who were.

"She's *marked*," Erinya said.

That said it all. Alex hadn't chosen to believe; she'd been chosen. And it had happened under Sylvie's nose.

"Marked?" Sylvie asked. "How. When. Who." It came out rapid-fire. Furious. Gods were too damned greedy.

"None of your business," Alex said. Her chin came up. Her color slowly returned.

"Eros," Erinya said. Slapping back at Alex the only way she could. Spilling her secrets. "He touches something, then he wants to keep it. Greedy boy. When he saved her life, he claimed it for his own."

"Can I break the mark?"

"I don't want you to!" Alex snapped. "Okay, Syl? It doesn't hurt me. It doesn't hurt anything. It doesn't do anything. It's just there. And hey, it's apparently protecting me."

"You want to be someone's possession?"

"We all are, one way or another," Alex said. Erinya skulked around behind her, trying to get access to the laptop. Abruptly Sylvie realized why Alex hadn't run from the Fury in the first place. Not just because it was a fool's instinct to run from a creature who chased. But to stay and protect the data. Demalion's contact info.

Alex slid the laptop under the desk, shielding it as if Erinya's setting eyes on it would be enough to give her the information she sought.

All of Sylvie's borderline rage at Alex fled. Scared nearly witless and still thinking. Still trying to do the right thing. "The mark doesn't hurt?"

Alex bit her lip, rubbed off some of the foundation at her cheek. A blushy bruise, like the press of a fingertip, lay at the crest of her cheekbone. "Where he kissed me to heal me."

"It doesn't hurt?" Sylvie asked again. More intently.

Alex blushed, obscuring the mark altogether. "No. It . . . I get dreams sometimes."

"Nightmares?"

Erinya scoffed. Alex's lips curved. "No. Very definitely not nightmares."

Sylvie raised a brow. "Oh."

"Oh, yeah," Alex said. The blush on her cheeks spread downward, and Sylvie turned back to Erinya.

"So you're sticking around until I give you the information you want, right?"

"Yes," Erinya said. "I can be patient."

"Got a mangled chair and a bunch of memories that say otherwise. How 'bout I give you something else to do. We're hunting a would-be god."

Erinya laughed. "I should strip-mine your mind, take the information. You refuse to belong to any god. You're fair game."

"But not easy game," Sylvie said. "I kicked you out of my head before. And that was when I didn't have some-one to protect. C'mon, Eri. Help us hunt."

"No," Erinya said. "I don't get what I want? You don't get what you want."

She and Sylvie bared teeth at each other in unwilling stalemate.

• • •

THE DOOR OPENED, AND CACHITA CAME IN, HEAD DOWN, MUMBLING something urgent, rummaging through her purse, utterly oblivious. Sylvie hung her own head in exasperation. She'd warned Cachita they might be facing Azpiazu, and this was how the woman entered the room?

Cachita looked up, and Sylvie's disgust faded. Cachita's eyes had gone from warm brown to panic black. When she brought her hand out of her purse, it came clutching a shark-tooth-shaped dagger, black obsidian, gold handled, and sharp enough that her fingers were already bleeding from brushing up against it.

The blood against the blade changed the feel of the room. Tiny tremors traveled the walls; beneath Sylvie, the floor seemed to rise and fall as if the office were suddenly asea.

"Hey, no!" Sylvie said. Cachita hadn't come in distracted. Cachita had come in halfway through her Tepeyollotl-summoning ritual. "Cachita, stop it. It's not Azpiazu! It's not—"

Too late, really. The room shifted and blurred, took on the thick, heady scent of tropical jungles; a jaguar's cough roughed the air. Erinya morphed so quickly, Sylvie found herself shoved into the wall to make room for Erinya's full Fury shape.

Four-legged, big as a bear, long and lean and supple. A creature designed to chase and kill, feathers and scale, beak and teeth and rage. Erinya shrieked defiance. Sylvie clapped hands over her ears, tried to figure out the odds of the coming fight taking out all bystanders.

Gods of different pantheons chose not to interact, a mutual-avoidance pact. Erinya . . . she wasn't a god. Just a demigod. Sylvie had the sinking suspicion that meant a brawl was inevitable. Erinya was threatened, and a threatened Fury was a violent one. And Tepeyollotl, summoned by his human agent, would come ready to kill. If not Azpiazu, anything that threatened his agent.

Sylvie put one hand on Erinya's spiky back, felt the scales rip at her palm, and scrambled over Erinya, slamming Cachita into the door, spilling them both through it and onto the curb, scattering the passersby who'd stopped, gawking at the office. Erinya's curses still blistered the air. The front window, already cracked by the bullet, started to chip away, to patter bits of glass downward like hail.

Sylvie clapped a hand over Cachita's mouth, still moving, though Cachita's eyes showed the woman had checked out. Around them, people cried out, the hunt for someone to *do something*.

The sidewalk juddered beneath them, an undulation of concrete as hard on their human skin as shark scale. Sylvie grabbed Cachita's wrist, shook the knife out of her grip. It skidded away, smoking where Cachita's blood had touched it.

A woman shrieked as it butted up against her flip-flop, drawing another bead of blood. Sylvie lunged, grabbed the screaming woman's bottled water, ripped the cap off, and dumped it over the blade. The smoke dwindled, disappeared.

Sylvie held her breath. The trembling in the world slowed but continued.

"Tell him not to come," Sylvie said. "Tell him you made a mistake."

Cachita gasped for air, fumbled her way upright, reached for the blade. Sylvie fielded her off. "No. Tell him, Cachita. Tell him we don't need him now."

"I can't—"

"All spells run in two directions," Sylvie snapped. "A door opens, but it also closes."

She looked at their audience, some familiar faces—her mercantile neighbors more aggravated than frightened—and some not. A cop car turned onto the street.

"Fuck," Sylvie muttered. She dragged Cachita to her feet, dragged her and the blade inside, shoved Cachita straight into Erinya. "Look!"

Cachita did. Her eyes rolled up in her head, and she went down as if Sylvie had coldcocked her.

"Fuck," Sylvie said again. There was a . . . hole . . . forming in the ceiling of her office, a place where the earthquake warp was strongest. Where Tepeyollotl was investigating Cachita's call. She drew her gun.

Erinya leaped upward, slashing, biting, shrieking at the gap. Sylvie's heart rocketed. This was all going to see them turned into meaty gobbets of godly cat chow. She couldn't see Alex, could barely see Cachita; all her instincts insisted she keep Erinya in her view.

A good thing, too, as her barbed tail lashed across the space Sylvie had just vacated.

Sylvie rolled, grabbed Cachita, shook her back to consciousness.

"What—what is that?" Cachita asked.

"*That* is less trouble than the god you've called," Sylvie shouted. "Send him back!"

Tepeyollotl shimmered partway into existence—a world-warping blur of cat and man, spots and gold, sweltering heat and jungle scent and growling. Where his body touched, smoke rose.

Sylvie felt his presence like a scalding wind and shuddered. The worst part of it all was that this was just a precursor. Some type of scout—a thinned-out shadow of the god; Tepeyollotl responding only halfheartedly to Cachita's aborted call.

Still didn't mean his shadow wouldn't kill them.

Erinya charged him, fearless, furious.

The sound they made as they collided wasn't anything as simple as two bodies in motion; their collision rang like imperfect metal just before it shattered. Cachita sobbed; Sylvie crouched low, gun clenched uselessly in her hand.

It was over as fast as it had begun. Tepeyollotl protested once more, a petulant roar of surprise and pain, and disappeared. Erinya spat out a piece of hide large enough to make a coat. It smoked and stank like burning blood and herbs.

Erinya's tail lashed and lashed; her back rolled in waves of spikes.

A gentle touch wrapped itself around Sylvie's wrist; she jerked and found Alex creeping up beside her. Un harmed. Eyes wild and wide, but unharmed.

"Alex--"

"We don't need a closet," Alex breathed out. "We need a safe room. Magically and physically reinforced. I don't care if we empty the savings account."

"Agreed," Sylvie said.

"All right, then," Alex said. She slumped against Sylvie's side. "You gonna do something about that?"

"That" being the Fury, still smashing the office furniture to bits, still climbing the walls, gouging holes in the terrazzo, in the ceiling struts, snarling, drooling bloody spittle across the floor.

"She's pissed at me already," Sylvie said. "I think we're going to sit here and let her work her way down to sane again."

Cachita whimpered. "Can we run?"

"Last thing we'd do," Sylvie said. "Sit tight, Cachita."

"What is it?" Cachita whispered. She shrank back when Erinya whipped her head around to look at them all, then huffed in disgust.

Cachita put her hand over her mouth, trying to hide even her breath. The tiny cuts on her hands left blood on her cheeks. Erinya looked like she wanted to investigate, slunk off the wall, crept across the floor, claws *screek*ing, and Sylvie said, "Uh-uh, Eri. You got lucky. You surprised the god. Don't bring him back by trying to eat his chosen one, okay?"

The front door swung open; a patrol officer put his head in, saying, "Everything all righ— Holy fuck!"

Erinya pounced, pinned him between her front paws, and Sylvie said, "Eri, please!"

The Fury tasted the man's neck, hesitated, breathing heat and hunger that Sylvie could feel all the way across the room. Then she pushed him back. "Go away, good man." The patrolman took the dismissal as the command it was and ran.

A virtuous cop, Sylvie thought. Nice. The relaxation rolling through her body was making her dazed with it.

Erinya shook her entire body, shedding agitation like a dog shedding water, slowly dwindled inward, until there was nothing but a crouching goth girl snarling, incongruous in human-shaped vocal cords.

Cachita shook harder. Sylvie said, "Caridad Valdes-Pedraza? Meet Erinya. One of the Eumenides. A Fury. And if you think she's dangerous? If you think she's piss-your-pants scary? You'd be right. But you know what she *isn't*? She's not even a full god. Think about that before you shout for Tepeyollotl again. Think about how much worse it would be to deal with a full god in a rage. That's what you're wanting to bring down to earth."

· · ·

THE OFFICE WASN'T QUIET YET: TOO FULL OF THEIR RAPID BREATHS, OF the ringing patter of falling glass, and furniture breaking down further under its own weight. Even the walls were creaking, settling as if Tepeyollotl's earthquaking appearance had left them perched above a sinkhole.

"It's too late," Cachita said, finally, her voice a rasp. "I've called him. He's primed now. He'll be checking in."

"Then we need to get Azpiazu sorted before—"

"Deal with me first," Erinya said, interrupting them. "I want Demalion."

"I want peace and quiet," Sylvie said. "I want supernatural guests who don't shred my workplace."

Erinya slung herself into Sylvie's personal space, a smooth lunge and crouch, black-painted lips peeling back to show red gums and sharp white teeth. "I want Demalion dead."

"He died," Sylvie said. "You killed him."

"He didn't stay that way. His soul should be languishing, tormented for his misdeeds."

"Then go hunt for him and leave us alone," Sylvie said. "I've got bigger problems."

"I'll help you," Erinya said abruptly. "This Azpiazu. I can find him for you. And you'll give me Demalion—"

"I won't," Sylvie said.

"I could take it from you."

"You could try," Sylvie growled.

Alex and Cachita protested at the same time, their fright like a dash of cold water to her own rising temper.

"Let's make a deal," Sylvie said. "I won't give you Demalion. But . . . I can make it worth your while."

Erinya gave Sylvie her back, heading toward the door, bootheels clicking.

"Erinya," Sylvie said. "Dunne can have me when I die. I'll hunt with you."

Alex squeaked, and Sylvie slashed her hand down, shutting off further protest from without and within. Her little dark voice was a drowning cry of objections. Negotiations didn't work with interruptions.

The Fury stopped in her tracks. "You'll be a Fury?" She came back toward Sylvie, all slink and hunger and quivering hope. She got close enough to sniff reluctant sincerity from Sylvie's flesh and mind, but hesitated. "When you die . . . That could be such a very long time away."

"You're immortal. Be patient," Sylvie said.

"You're the new Lilith," Erinya said. More objections. "The Christian God might have plans—"

Alex looked intrigued, and Sylvie grimaced. She didn't want Alex poking into the "new Lilith" business. Not until Sylvie'd had the time to do some investigating on her own.

"I make my own choices," Sylvie said. "Always have."

Erinya rolled her shoulders as if settling the idea into her skin.

"Would you help us for that? Help us kill Azpiazu?"

"I can't," Erinya said. "Find him, okay, yeah. But he's

Tepeyollotl's chosen. I can't just step in between them and rip his head off any more than I could shake the truth out of your girl."

Sylvie said, "I'm not sure I want to give my soul over for tracking abilities. I can find Azpiazu on my own."

"Mortals have time constraints."

"I can work fast—"

"Sylvie!" Alex interrupted their bargaining. Her hands were tight on Sylvie's forearm. "Sylvie, listen!"

The street outside had grown quiet. No more bystander noise. No traffic. No cops. Nothing. All the hairs on Sylvie's body stood up. "Something's coming."

"Hunters," Erinya said. "Human hunters."

The remnants of the plate-glass window shattered as a smoking cylinder crashed through it, streaming . . .

"Tear gas?" Sylvie gasped out. Regretted it as the movement of her breath brought the gas billowing into her face. It was like inhaling an angry jellyfish. Her nose stung, her mouth burned, her eyes spat tears in a vain attempt to soothe the irritation. She coughed, clenched her hands by her sides, controlling the urge to rub at the burn, to scrub it off her skin. She knew it wouldn't work.

Alex had ducked, turned away, had covered her face by yanking up her shirt. The cotton mesh wasn't fine enough to protect her for more than a few moments. Sylvie, sobbing helplessly, letting the tears go, trying to flush out the toxin even as the smoke still eddied in the room, dragged Alex closer, dragged her under her jacket. Alex's fingers clutched Sylvie's side, tight bands of panic and fear.

Cachita had rolled sideways, was vomiting feebly, her face streaming tears and snot.

Gas-masked men bulled in after the tear gas, and Sylvie heard the first one scream, his cry ending bloody and wet, when Erinya tore into him with talons extended.

"Erinya, go!" Sylvie said. "Just go. Find us later." Each word was hard to get out. Each word felt like an eternity between a panicking heart and challenged breathing.

Erinya's growl echoed through the room; she dropped

the first man, and the others slowed. She turned once, red-black eyes shining like lanterns, and snatched Alex away from Sylvie so quickly, Alex's nails left gouges through her shirt.

Erinya vanished.

Sylvie, fighting to breathe, to stay in control of herself, fumbled her gun from her holster and slid it away from her.

The last thing she wanted was to be shot by the trigger-happy ISI SWAT team. They couldn't be anyone else.

Their timing, as usual, was utterly, world-endangeringly, awful.

16

Enemy Engagement

TWO HOURS LATER, SYLVIE HAD BEEN DETAINED, DETOXED, STRIPPED, scrubbed pink, and given a pair of white cotton pants and a tee to replace her clothes. Her clothes were gone down to her boots. She wiggled her bare toes on the cold tiles, wiggled her ass on the cold, plastic bench, and thought dark thoughts about the goddamned ISI, and the surveillance team who'd decided they'd had enough of watching.

"Get up," Agent Riordan said.

It'd only been a day since she'd dealt with him, and already his shiny was wearing off. He looked ruffled, rumpled, and pissed. His suit jacket was gone, and his white shirt showed sweat stains at chest and pits.

She leaned against the slicked, easy-to-wash wall, and held back her shiver at its chilly touch. Small defiance. Enough to make his cheeks flush, to make his head jerk sideways to see if the men in the doorway noticed her refusal to respect him.

If they did, they were either too polite or restrained to show reaction to it.

"Up!" Riordan said, and gestured them forward. They hesitated.

"Uh-uh," Sylvie said. "Bad form to make your men put down their guns to come wrestle with a prisoner. How new are you to this job, anyway?" She stood, stretched. "So where are we headed? Cells? Or interrogation?"

"Just walk," Riordan said.

"So bossy," Sylvie said. She moved anyway. She wasn't up for a fight. Or at least, not a pointless one. Azpiazu was still out there, still glomming up power.

The hallway was clean, crisp, tile-floored, white-walled. Not the hotel this time. Some other facility. Still in the city, but where? Would anyone know to look for her?

Sylvie felt the first trickles of real worry creep into her blood. She mocked the ISI often enough, and they did earn her scorn, but . . . they were still the government, with government resources and the laws on their side.

All she had was Alex. And maybe not even her. Memory flashed; Erinya yanking Alex away.

The two silent men sandwiched her, a wall of armed muscle on either side. She might not respect Riordan, but he respected her enough to hem her in.

They moved her along at a quick pace, trying to deny her the chance to cause trouble, trying to keep her off balance. The tear gas might have been cleared from her system, but she still felt shocky and sore.

An elevator took her upward, and, stepping out, she got a view through a narrow window. The downtown skyline, up close. They were probably in one of the newer condominiums, barely finished and foreclosed on. Snapped up cheap by the government.

Sylvie had expected, given the scrubs, the bare feet, the escort, to be shoved into a room turned cell. Instead, she was marched through a reception area and into one of the single most ridiculously opulent offices she had ever seen, all white marble and dark, glossy furniture. The man behind the mahogany desk didn't raise his head, just jabbed his stylus at one of the steel-and-leather chairs. "Sit."

Riordan leaped to attention and Sylvie evaded him, taking a seat herself and propping her dusty bare feet on the edge of the desk. "I'm seated. Now what?"

The man raised his head briefly, flipped his attention back to the tablet before him. He matched his office. Steel grey hair, black eyes, all hard edges and gloss. The nameplate on the edge of the desk read DOMINICK RIORDAN, and Sylvie looked back over her shoulder. "Aw, you joined the family firm."

The younger Riordan shifted uncomfortably in the doorway, and Dominick Riordan set down his tablet with a click. "Ms. Lightner, you're here for serious reasons, not to harass my son." His voice . . . was unfair. Mellow, rich, exactly the kind of voice to elicit trust and contentment in his listeners. Sylvie, looking at that cold gaze, thought it was a warmth as deceptive as a succubus.

"What would those reasons be?" she asked.

"You've been consorting with monsters."

"Is that a crime?" Sylvie said. "No, really, I'm curious. Is that going to be a crime in your new rule book?"

Riordan hmmed quietly, and said, "I'd forgotten. Demalion was your man. He shared information with you."

"Shared more than that," a woman said, eeling under Riordan Jr.'s arm, and dropping into the seat beside Sylvie. "They were quite a power pair from everything I hear." She gave Sylvie a bright, insincere smile.

She was familiar. The agent who'd given Adelio Suarez his ride home. The agent who'd mentioned Demalion with easy familiarity. The agent with the strangely marked hand.

"Ms. Stone," Riordan said. "You're late."

"Things to do," she said. "You know how it goes. I was checking up on Chico in the infirmary."

"He make it?"

"No," Stone said. "Sylvie's friend ripped his head off. Kind of impossible to reattach."

Sylvie let her feet drop from the desk. Dammit.

"Still feeling smart-mouthed?" Riordan asked.

"Didn't ask you to break into my office. You're the one who—"

"Be realistic," Riordan said. "What did you think would happen? You made enough ruckus that the police were called. Of course we sent someone in. You're a trouble-maker, Shadows. A barometer of things going wrong."

Sylvie leaned forward, clenched her hands on the edge of her chair. "Such a waste of your time. There's going to be a massive smack-down happening somewhere in the city that makes the ruckus at my place seem like a fender-bender. What are you going to do about that? You've seen the signs. I saw your people in the Everglades."

"Is it you we have to thank for our men missing time?"

"Focus!" Sylvie said. "A god coming to Miami. Sooner, rather than later—Kind of on a time line, here. If you lock me up, what can you do in my place?"

"Do you expect a meteorologist to stop a hurricane?"

Her breath caught in her throat, a thousand words try-ing to escape at once, gagging her. Beside her, Stone cocked her head as if she could sense even a fraction of Sylvie's outrage.

"That's your plan? To run around telling people to get out of the pool. That a thunderstorm is coming?"

"What can we do against gods? Nothing. Statistically, it's irrelevant. Deaths caused by gods are massive, but the real casualties are the deaths caused by witches and sor-cerers, by monsters. By people like you." It all sounded so reasonable in his newscaster voice.

"You think I'm a part of the *Magicus Mundi*?"

"You're telling me you're not? That being *the new Lil-ith* means nothing? That it's a human thing?"

"It's the quintessential human thing," Sylvie said. "The ability to say *fuck you*." Whatever else it meant, whatever expectations the title came with—Sylvie knew that much was true. She was still human, still had free will. Every-thing else was just details.

He leaned across the desk, and said, "What was the creature in your office?"

"No one you want to tangle with." Sylvie sneered at him. "She's one of your hurricanes. Too much for you to handle. Maybe you should just . . . report on her. Tell people to run for their lives."

"Caridad Valdes-Pedraza said it was a Fury," Stone said beside her. "One of the creatures who turned Chicago inside out."

"And you wonder why we name you an enemy," Riordan said. "One city through turmoil's not enough for you? You want to go for two?"

"I want to save my city," Sylvie said. "You're the ones who're jeopardizing it." She turned on Stone. "When you talked to Cachita? Did she tell you that she's got a god waiting on her words? That he's not a patient god? That he's not even a particularly bright god? He's been manipulated by a sorcerer he meant to punish. He's not happy."

"And you can make him happy?"

"Nothing can," Sylvie said. "At best, we can keep him . . . elsewhere."

Riordan tapped his stylus thoughtfully on his desk. "Convenient that it requires you to be set free."

"And Cachita," Sylvie said. "Just to be clear."

Riordan said, "And Ms. Valdes-Pedraza."

"She was carrying an obsidian knife," Stone said. "A nice weapon. Sharp. For ritual use, I'd imagine." She gestured obscurely; her red-mottled hand held an imaginary blade with a deadly competence.

"The kind that might carve symbols in dead women's skin?"

Sylvie let out another careful breath. "If you're trying to suggest that Cachita is the Everglades killer, you're dangerously off target. If you're planning on using her as a scapegoat, it won't last. Azpiazu's appetite is too big."

"Take her away," Riordan said, shaking his head. "It's late. I'll deal with her tomorrow."

"Am I charged with anything?" Sylvie snapped. "Are you sure you can keep me?"

"Bella Alvarez went missing earlier today. I think we can keep you until she shows up. As a person of interest. Actually—" He paused to smile. It was a nice smile, showed just the right number of teeth, made his eyes crinkle with laugh lines. Whatever he was going to say made him happy. "We're the ISI. We can make you disappear. With no questions asked."

"Here I thought you were going to study the supernatural for years before you started carting people off. What was the plan? Five years of study, three years of legal tests, and two years of preparing the world? You're in year four. Jumping the gun a bit, aren't you?"

"Demalion talked too much," Riordan said. "We've had to accelerate the ten-year plan. Because of you."

Stone leaned close as the guards moved in. "Should have had that chat with me, Sylvie. I could have given you a heads-up." Her whisper was a brush of warmth against Sylvie's cheek.

That whisper lingered even once Sylvie had been dragged back down into the cold, sterile hallways below, a reminder of a political current she didn't understand. She hadn't paid enough attention to the ISI, and she was paying for it. The problem was keeping the city from paying the price as well.

. . .

THE CELL THEY PUT HER IN WAS CLOSER TO A HOSPITAL WARD'S SE-cure room than the steel and concrete cage Sylvie had expected. Four walls, a solid door with a wire-mesh glass panel, a number pad beside the door. Sylvie watched the guards punch in the release code—six digits long, easy to understand, that day's date—but the knowledge wouldn't do her any good when she was on the wrong side of the door.

They shoved her in, and she staggered a few steps, stubbing her toes on the bare floor and cursing. When she looked up, she found she had a roommate. Cachita, looking small and huddled in her white scrubs, sitting knees to chest on the lower bunk.

There was one flickering fluorescent light pressed close to the ceiling, a toilet, and a sink. The walls were high-gloss white, shiny enough that she could track almost-reflections in it.

"Spartan," Sylvie said. "But at least it's new and shiny."

Cachita's eyes were red-rimmed; but then, Sylvie was sure hers weren't much better. Tear gas was wicked stuff. She knuckled an eye in reaction to phantom pain and peered out the window. There were more doors in the hallway, at least three that she could see, but none of them had keypads beside them. Guess she and Cachita were roommates by necessity. The ISI wasn't prepared for the full-time jail business yet.

She wandered back over to the sink—ten steps at a tight stride—and slurped some water from the faucet. Mineral strong and chlorine rough on her throat, but it felt good going down.

"Well, this sucks," she said. "You think we're being monitored? I don't see anything. No mikes, no cameras, but they're making them so small these days."

Cachita let out a strangled sob, and Sylvie turned. Maybe her eyes were red from the tear gas. Or not exclusively. "Hey, you okay there? They hurt you?"

Cachita knotted herself tighter, wrapped her arms around her knees, her hands around her shoulders. Her hair was loose and messy and dark, stringy from the chemical shower they'd been put through. Tears leaked steadily down her cheeks.

Sylvie ducked her head, sat down beside Cachita. The mattress gave, springs squeaking with newness, still smelling of the plastic it had been wrapped in. "Huh. Bet they outfitted this room today. IKEA, you think?"

Cachita dropped her head into the tangled cradle of arms and knees; her shoulders shook. Not with laughter. Even her feet were trying to huddle up into her scrubs. Utter terror and retreat.

"It's okay," Sylvie said. "It's going to be o—"

Cachita raised her head, found a spark enough to express her fear. "I've been to Mexico, Sylvie. People disappear there. If the government doesn't like you. If *los narcos* don't like you. It's not supposed to happen here."

"We're not here forever," Sylvie said. "It's just gonna feel like it."

"Sylvie, no one will miss me."

"Maybe not, but you know? I'm a big pain in the ass. They'll miss me. Besides," she said, feeling her mouth stretch in a grim smile, "we'll get out. There's no doubt in my mind."

"Yeah?" Cachita asked. Skeptical. Wanting to be reassured.

"Yeah," Sylvie said. "You said it yourself. Tepeyollotl's impatient. Sooner or later, he'll be checking up on you, and we can get out during the—"

"Slaughter," Cachita said. She didn't look reassured.

"Hey, on the bright side, maybe Erinya will come instead?"

"Not funny," Cachita said, but she relaxed her defensive posture, stretching her legs out before her.

"No, not funny," Sylvie agreed. She started pacing again, too antsy to be still even when she knew she should be reserving her strength. Too many worries. Azpiazu and the god, of course. But Alex, also. Was her memory right? Had Erinya abducted Alex in the midst of the chaos? Then there was the ISI and their call to arms, which meant, apparently, arresting her.

She wasn't ready for the ISI to get aggressively involved with the *Magicus Mundi*. She didn't think *they* were ready, kept imagining new recruits like Riordan Jr., stumbling into a firefight like today's, facing a Fury with technology and expecting it to do the job.

To be fair, Erinya probably could be brought down by bullets. But could she be kept down?

"Sylvie?"

"Yeah," Sylvie said absently. She shivered; the room was chilly. They were going to have an uncomfortable time of it if they were stuck there. The ISI had bought mattresses, but no sheets, no blankets.

"The woman who interviewed me took the knife."

"Good," Sylvie said. "Less temptation for you to summon him." She peered at the narrow window inset into the door. It was slowly going as white as the walls. She touched it, jerked her finger back.

Cold.

She licked her lip, nervously, sudden images of government "interrogation" techniques coming to her. Environmental discomfort was just the start.

Except—she held her hand toward the air vent. The air coming out of it felt . . . warm in contrast. The cold was centered outside the door. Then at it. Then *inside*.

Sylvie stepped back, shuddering all over. She knew this type of cold. Something beyond physical. A chill of the spirit. A tiny piece of death moving through the living world.

A ghost walking.

Cachita hissed and pointed toward the glossy white walls. A third shadow had joined theirs, a narrow human-shaped blur, and when it swayed closer to the wall, it grew grey-shaded and sharper; the wall frosted over.

"Marco," Sylvie said. The shadow ducked its head in a nod.

Cachita shot her a wild-eyed glance. "Who?"

"Wales's . . . pet." But what was he doing here? Sylvie jerked her gaze from the wall to the spot in the cell where Marco stood and saw nothing at all. Damn ghosts. Even when they wanted to communicate, it couldn't be easy.

At least, not for her. Not for a non-necromancer.

Why was Marco here?

Sylvie shook her head abruptly. Stopped asking herself a question she couldn't answer and asked Marco instead. "Why are you here?"

Only after she asked did she realize it wasn't an easy question to answer if all they had for communication was a ghost shadow that could nod or shake its head. But it seemed to be what Marco was waiting for.

That bitter cold, that chilled rot swooped in on her again, something biting at her mouth, her lips, a bitter, deathly kiss. She tried to push him off, but only pushed through the gelid unseen mass of him.

His fingers wrapped her skull, an icy cage around the back of her neck, her cheek, and a freezing fog pressed into her mouth. She gasped, choked. He backed off, and she coughed the fog out.

It came out, warmed by her living breath, and created sense out of ghostly silence. His words. Her voice. *"Wales needs you."*

Sylvie shivered. "Why?"

Their shadows merged again, and Sylvie shuddered through another onslaught, growling even as he fed her his frozen words. There was necessity, and there was Marco, and his misogynistic history. And an icy hand that was sliding down her throat toward her breast.

She tore herself away, sprawled on the tile; the words gusted out on impact, strained, but clear.

"Sorcerer found him."

"Sorcerer. Azpiazu?" Sylvie held up a hand. "Nod yes, or no."

The shadow on the wall swayed, grudging her that, but his need to communicate was too strong. He nodded.

"Killed?" Sylvie asked. Her throat felt sore, stretched by its brush with death.

The shadow swayed, a twist at its top like a small tornado. Dizzying to watch, to focus on that pale shadow on a white wall.

"Taken."

Another nod, slow so there could be no misunderstanding. It should have made her feel better. Taken was a long way from dead. But taken, when she was trapped here, felt a whole lot like dead.

"For his binding spell."

The crash of shadow and cold against her, within her, pressing inward, an invasion. Marco pressed into her skin, into her body, climbed inside, and pushed a nightmare of images into her brain.

Wales/Sylvie, bent over his/her computer, reading spells

*by tech light, stretching absently, lifting an empty soda can
to their lips, brief burst of warm dregs dropping onto their
tongue. Long ache in their spine and a yawn, cold coins
in their palm, the kiss of cool air as they passed the ice
machine, the sudden stink of animal in the hotel's wide
halls, strong as skunk, turning too slow, the blow crashing
down, the impact and crackle against the soda machine,
then black.*

*Waking underwater, lungs straining for air, with claws
ripping patterns into their skin, blood swirling upward, so
hypnotic, so sleepy, bubbles rising, find Sylvie . . .*

Sylvie jerked away from the memories, from Marco's
invasion, from the physical sensation of being drowned,
of being frozen, of being afraid. She lunged for the sink,
hung over it, gagging.

Sweat sprang out all along her hairline; her neck felt
swampy with it.

"Sylvie?" Cachita pulled the belt from her scrub pants,
wadded it up, wet it with cool water, and sponged at Sylvie's face. "What's happening?"

"We're getting out of here," Sylvie said, when she felt
more in control. "We're not waiting for Tepé or Erinya or,
hell, for Alex to call us a lawyer. We're getting out. We're
getting Wales, and we're kicking Azpiazu's ass all the way
to hell."

"How?"

Sylvie leaned against Cachita's human warmth, soak-
ing it in. "Marco's a free ghost now. But he used to be a
Hand of Glory. I'm betting he still has it in him."

"What does that mean?" Cachita asked. "Hand of Glory?
A free ghost?"

"It means," Sylvie said, "we're walking right out the
door."

. . .

AS SOON AS THE LAST OF THE SHAKES HAD LEFT HER BODY, THE LAST
of the ghost-repulsion fled, Sylvie gave Marco the go-
ahead. The shadow drifted toward the door, and after a

moment, the door popped open. An alarm buzzed, an annoying electric whine like a swarm of mosquitoes. Cachita tensed, but Sylvie said, "Marco can handle it. Just stay behind me."

They followed the ghost into the hallway, their bare feet leaving marks in the frost caused by his passage.

Three ISI agents appeared in the hall, talking rapidly into their headsets, and balking at the sight of them escaped from their cell

Pausing, Sylvie thought, was definitely their mistake. They crumpled one after another, falling so fast that they didn't even have time to draw their weapons.

Cachita squeaked beside her. "What just—"

"Don't ask."

Marco might be biting into their souls, putting them into soul shock, but hell, they were still getting off easy. Erinya, Tepeyollotl—the white walls would be bloody by now.

By the time they neared the front door, word had gotten out, and Marco had taken down so many agents that he had lost his translucency; he pulsed with stolen pieces of soul, a false heartbeat that glowed dimly in the building's bright lights.

Sylvie collected two holstered guns, yanking at buckles and webbing and slinging them over her shoulder. She'd want them later. Even if they wouldn't work against Azpiazu and his oh-so-talented ability to change metal into something harmless.

Another agent appeared, blurry behind the luminescent mirage that was Marco, and for once, Marco paused. Sylvie edged out behind him, found Agent Stone standing a cautious distance away, her red-stained hand held up before her face like a shield.

"Call off your ghost," she said. "I've got your stuff. You can get gone. We won't stop you."

"Cachita," Sylvie said.

Cachita took the unspoken command and met Stone halfway, careful to stay out of the woman's reach, to keep

an eye on her holstered gun. But Stone seemed more concerned with keeping her one hand held before her.

Marco thrummed and pulsed but held steady. Afraid to
attack, Sylvie thought. Stone might be more than he could
take.

If the red-stained hand was like Zoe's, Stone could
have gained it through killing a ghost. Enough to make
Marco cautious.

"Got it," Cachita said, retreated back to Sylvie's side, a
rough bundle of clothes and shoes in her hand.

"Get dressed," Sylvie said. "Hey, Stone . . ."

"Marah," the woman said. "My name's Marah."

"Don't care," Sylvie said. "You got car keys?"

"You don't need mine," she said. "The cars in the garage have keys in the ignition. Just pick one."

"Thanks. Now go away before Marco decides to snack
on you after all."

"I could help you—"

"No," Sylvie said.

Marah nodded once, and backed away. "Just remember. I offered."

"Brownie points noted," Sylvie said.

"What about this?" Marah held out the obsidian summoning knife. Cachita collected it; when she returned to
Sylvie's side, Sylvie took the knife herself.

"Thanks," Sylvie said. "Now go away."

Marah held up both hands in mocking surrender, turned
as if putting her back to an armed escapee was nothing,
and sauntered away.

"It's mine," Cachita snapped.

"You can't be trusted with it," Sylvie said.

Cachita was dressed now, khakis and sneakers and
slightly less crisp blouse; she had the advantage over Sylvie, whose hands were awkwardly full with gun, knife,
and clothing. But Cachita was—*incompetent*, her little
voice suggested—used to obeying others, Sylvie thought,
and made no effort to take the knife by force.

Sylvie skinned out of her prison scrubs, trading them

for her own clothes, dressing awkwardly with the gun in her hand and belatedly aware of the ISI cameras.

Vanity, her voice muttered. More likely they'd be occupied with the blur that was Marco.

"C'mon, Cachita," Sylvie said. "Let's go."

"Go where?" Cachita asked. "Out's good, but you lost your tracker. How are we going to find Azpiazu?"

Sylvie laughed. "Cachita. Pay attention. Lassie's come all this way to tell us Timmy's down a well. We follow Marco all the way to Azpiazu's front door. And as a bonus? I don't owe Erinya my afterlife."

17

Simple Plans

THEY HAD TO BACKTRACK TO GET TO THE ISI GARAGE, AND IT MADE Sylvie's nerves prickle every step of the way. Marco was powerful, but he wasn't an infallible weapon. A single necromancer in the building, or an agent who understood some basic protection spells, and their ghost-shield could be neutralized in a heartbeat.

Cachita's breath warmed her ear; she was getting too close again, blocking Sylvie's range of motion, and Sylvie shoved her off.

Marco moved before them, an icy fog shot through with roiling motion, endless hunger, endless appetite. He took out the agents on guard in the garage, leaving Sylvie free to pick and choose among the car keys on the peg board.

She chose a black SUV, wanting as much space between Marco and her as possible while they hunted for Wales. He drifted into the passenger seat, and Cachita crawled into the back without a single protest.

Marco raised an arm, a bar of cold shadow pointing south. Sylvie took the SUV into the twilit streets of Miami, streaks of neon beneath the freeway flickering to life.

Cachita leaned forward, her hands tense around Sylvie's seat. "You really think the ghost can find Wales?"

The question hurt. A sudden sharp pinch of awareness. She didn't want to lose Wales. She had grown to like him. Was one long lunch away from calling him friend.

He might be a necromantic Ghoul, but Alex was right: Wales was a good guy.

She forced calmness. "I think Marco's better than nothing. I think Marco's the only game in town. I never got a chance to give Erinya Azpiazu's scent."

"But I have *yours*," Erinya said from the backseat.

Cachita shrieked. Sylvie grappled with the wheel; the SUV slewed just enough to elicit a series of horn blasts and multilingual curses.

"Eri," Sylvie said. "Don't. Do. That."

"Better than Alekta," Erinya said. "She would have appeared in front of the truck and been surprised when you hit her. Not that it would have stopped her from climbing aboard." She poked her head forward, shoved Cachita back with a careless hand. "Why do you have a killer's ghost in your car? Is it for me? Can I eat it?"

"No," Sylvie said. "He's our guide to Azpiazu."

Erinya snarled. "*I'm* your guide."

"You've been replaced. You took off," Sylvie said. "And not that I'm not grateful—the ISI's going to be on my ass enough about one dead agent—but what the hell did you do with Alex?"

"Alex?"

Sylvie stared at her, cold horror crawling down her spine at the utter confusion in Erinya's voice. If Erinya hadn't taken Alex, then . . . had they left her in the ISI's untender care? "My assistant? Blonde? Eros's chosen—"

"Oh. Her. I took her to Eros. He wouldn't want her hurt, and I like to make him happy."

"Of course you do," Sylvie muttered. *Everyone* wanted to make the god of Love happy. "Wait. You took her to him? You took her *off earth*?"

"Just for a little bit. Eros'll send her back, soon. Probably. Unless he really likes her. He gets bored. Justice is busy busy busy trying to straighten things out up there and fighting with Zeus."

Sylvie swallowed. "Erinya. The moment we are all done with Azpiazu? *You will bring her back.* In one piece. Not transformed, enchanted, or lovesick."

Erinya shrugged. "Whatever."

Sylvie changed lanes at Marco's prod, a cold spur into her shoulder that made her fingers tremble as if he'd shocked her. "Jesus, all right. Turn here. I get it."

Cachita shivered. "Sylvie, we need to hurry."

"I'm aware," Sylvie said. There were time strictures all over their little plan. They had to race Azpiazu's spellwork. They had to race Tepeyollotl's impatience. On top of it all, sooner or later, the ISI agents would start waking from Marco's soul shock, and they were going to be pissed. The SUV would be easy enough for them to track, what with the government GPS a standard part of its equipment. "Eri, you still going to be part of this?"

"Can't kill another god's chosen," Erinya said. "Even if the god wants him dead. Can't hunt Demalion, 'cause you won't tell me where he is." She slumped back into the shadows of the car, the very picture of a teen who'd been unfairly grounded.

"I'm sure there'll be things you can fight," Sylvie said. "Stick around?" She took the next road Marco suggested, irritated at the slowness of his navigation. For all she knew, he was taking her the slowest route possible. But short of pulling the car over and trying that memory merge again, she didn't know another way.

Wales had been beneath the water. Not deep. Tiles at his back, slimed with algae that tore under his struggles. The water just above his reaching hand. Not a swimming pool, not a natural pond. Large enough for five adults. Isolated.

She studied the roads they were on, the slow changeover from full city skyscrapers to smaller shops and slower

streets. To old-fashioned streetlamps and shady walks. Coconut Grove.

And water everywhere. Biscayne Bay butted up against
the seawalls there. But he wasn't in salt water; his eyes
hadn't been stinging. Not the ocean.

Erinya cocked her head, sniffed the air, and Sylvie
said, "Eri? You getting something?"

Erinya sucked her lower lip into her mouth, pouting as
if she were nothing more than the twentysomething goth
girl she appeared. "You gonna come work for Dunne if I
tell you?"

"I think I'll just wait for Marco," Sylvie said. Safer, but
less informative. Erinya twitched, ran her claws down the
leather seats, fidgeted. Sylvie hid a grin. Erinya wanted to
tell. All Sylvie had to do was wait.

"Close to the sea," Erinya said. "Something's twisted.
Something's rotten. Cruel. I can taste prey and fear."

"Azpiazu," Sylvie said.

Marco pressed closer just as a familiar landmark began
to appear on Sylvie's left. Vizcaya Gardens.

Sylvie choked back a laugh. It fit in a terrible way. Lots
of water features, shallow ponds, lots of archaic luxury.
She just wondered what he'd done with the tourists. Here
was hoping he'd set up after hours.

She pulled the SUV to a halt, let her strange passengers
unload into the tree-dark lot—Erinya bounding out, animal grace in a human form, Cachita clambering out on
shaky limbs, and Marco oozing through the door.

Sylvie hadn't been to Vizcaya since her high-school
days, remembered it as a green expanse of blind grottos
and ponds, of stone stairways and carefully patterned gardens. A safe place to play.

Now, while the sky purpled about them, closing them
into darkness, the gardens felt anything but safe. The air
pressed close to her skin, dark, hot, humid like an animal's fetid breath. Hungry and predatory, giving her the
sense of something larger moving behind the darkness.

The gardens themselves felt *dead*, suffocating in silence and stillness. There were none of the sounds Sylvie expected from tropical night settling in—no frog creaking, no bird wings rustling as they perched and preened, no owls calling through the dark—only silence and weight.

Erinya sniffed the air, wrinkled her nose. "It smells like rot."

"What does?"

"*Everything,*" Erinya said.

Cachita shivered and her shiver was echoed by the world, a tremble in the gravel pathway they stood on.

"Hold it together," Sylvie said. "You lose it, we get Tepeyollotl's attention." She wanted Cachita to wait in the car, to stay out of the conflict, stay calm. Given the way Cachita clutched Sylvie's sleeve, leaving her behind would only send her into panic faster.

"Cachita!" Sylvie snapped. "C'mon. I expect more from the woman who was trolling the streets for a sorcerer armed only with a Taser."

Cachita blinked, released Sylvie's arm, put her chin up. "Right. Right. I'm sorry."

"Erinya," Sylvie said. "You smell Azpiazu?"

Erinya shook her head, dark hair flying. "Only death."

Cloaked by spells, Sylvie wondered. Some type of sensory illusion hiding him? It would be well within his abilities and his predilections.

Sylvie looked ahead. From the parking lot, there was only one entrance, one way in. The gardens lay beyond that, but if Azpiazu was set up where Sylvie imagined he'd be—at the main reflecting pool—he was going to see them coming long before they could get to him.

Marco jabbed her with cold fingers at her spine, shoving her forward. A clear urging to move.

Sylvie checked her borrowed guns, reassuring herself that the clips were full. She stepped forward; the ground crumbled at Sylvie's feet, grass withering where it should have held the soil together. Earthworms lay slack and dry; the ancient sinkhole beside the entry gate shifted, pulling dirt downward. "Eri, the gate?"

Sylvie squeezed out of Erinya's way, brushed up against a hand-lettered sign on the iron gate: *Closed for alligators.* She shook her head. Only in Miami was that an excuse. She wondered if they were real gators encroaching on tourist land or some illusion Azpiazu had created. For once in her life, she hoped for magic.

Erinya ripped the entry gate from its hinges, a metallic shriek in the quiet night, and flung the twisted iron into the brush. Leaves fell like rain.

Maybe the stink of rot was no illusion. Maybe everything was dead. Sylvie touched a fallen leaf, and it smeared beneath her fingers, its cellular integrity gone, a pulpy mass of rot.

Not a good sign.

Azpiazu had to be on the very edge of god-transition. Close enough that Tepeyollotl's power, filtered, warped, changed, was bleeding out through him.

Sylvie headed through, keeping to the trembling stone path, her gun before her.

Five steps in, something enormous hissed and roared out of the bushes, scattering branches and pebbles. Sylvie jerked back, firing directly through Marco. Her hand went cold and numb. Bullets did no good. Not when you were faced with a two-headed bull alligator in full charge.

Sylvie focused on the grey-green-black blur, aimed at the gaping mouth on the right, and realized abruptly what was bothering her beyond the two-headed nightmare of it. The alligator had no eye shine on either head. Four eyes at twilight? Should be full of shine.

"It's dead," Cachita said, gagging. "Your Fury was right. Everything's dead." Her lips trembled.

It was worse than that. Sylvie got a quick glance of the alligator's legs as it lumbered toward them for another try. Instead of claws, it had hands. Human-style hands. At least they slowed the gator, buckling and breaking under its weight, made evading it a possibility.

Azpiazu's fight for shape-shifting integrity was warping the world around him.

Erinya changed form, grew claws and thick scales to rival the alligator's hide, and attacked with an eldritch screech. The alligator snapped furiously, even as Erinya tore gobbets of dead flesh away, sent reeking bits into the air like piñata stuffing.

Erinya shook the alligator in her mouth until its bones snapped, until it broke, shrieking the entire time.

So much for the element of surprise.

• • •

MARCO PRESSED UP AGAINST SYLVIE'S NECK, A COLD, URGENT touch, and she jolted into movement, thinking flashlights. She should have brought flashlights. The alligator had been hard to see, had been lurking just beneath the shadows. What else might be there? Not breathing. Eyes invisible. Soundless until it attacked.

Shoot to kill and don't worry about what it is, her dark voice suggested, and Sylvie took its advice. Soothing. Simple.

"Erinya, you see all right?"

"Yup," Erinya agreed. She flicked alligator off her leather jacket and wiped her boots on the gravel path.

"Go first," Sylvie said. "Clear the path."

Erinya rolled her eyes. "Bossy. Who'll watch your back?"

"I watch my own," Sylvie said. "Cachita, follow her. Not too close."

Marco drifted by her, an ice-cube shiver along her side. "And Marco does whatever he wants as long as he stays away from Cachita," Sylvie finished.

It all made her edgy. Erinya was help. Sylvie didn't have to worry about her, didn't have to protect her. Cachita, on the other hand, was a liability. Vulnerable and worse. Gateway for a god.

Holding the knife was a nice reassurance that Cachita couldn't call the god but probably a futile one. Tepeyollotl was paying attention, would come at Cachita's first whisper of his name, whether she had the knife or not.

Erinya trotted swiftly along the limestone path, heading toward the main garden, sniffing. "I smell blood."

Sylvie's heart picked up pace. Convenient that it was already racing when, a moment later, another dead reptile fell heavily across her shoulders.

Dead, but quite active.

The python, twice her length, and as heavy and hard to move as sandbags, wrapped around her shoulders, its two heads hissing, showing a pair of leprous mouths ringed with curved teeth.

"Get off!" she yelled, like it could listen or obey. She shoved at it. Heads hissed and struck, stunning, bruising blows against her thick jacket. Cachita jumped in, wrapped her hands tight around softening scales, grimacing. Erinya cocked her head, decided the zombie snake was too small to interest her, and kept moving.

Sylvie cursed, her hands barely wrapped around two thick throats. Scales slimed off in her hand, rotten and flaking from dead meat. It was even odds for a moment whether she was going to be choked by the snake or by the stink of it. Then Cachita got her hand beneath the heaviest coil, and the two of them levered it off, dropped the python hissing and striking on the pavement.

Sylvie blew off its two heads, panting, wasting ammo, and wondering if it would go hydra on them—regrow and double its heads and attack again. She'd never dealt with zombie animals before. After this, she never wanted to do so again.

Cachita swallowed hard. "Tepeyollotl *can't* be worse—"

"*Oh yes he can,*" Sylvie said. "Right now, we're dealing with small shit. Warped reptiles."

"Two-headed zombie reptiles are small shit?"

Sylvie thinned her mouth, nodded brusquely. She didn't want to get into it. But yeah. Small stuff. Worse, she didn't even think the zombie reptiles were arranged as deliberate traps. Anger spiked. Outrage at being ignored.

Even though he had taken Wales, taken her ally and friend, even though he knew Sylvie would be coming after him, Azpiazu didn't care enough to try to stop her. It argued extreme confidence. Sylvie wanted to make him eat that confidence.

Sylvie yanked Cachita back into movement. "Less gawking, more moving."

"Give me a gun," Cachita said.

"Should have picked up your own," Sylvie said.

"Sylvie," Cachita said. "You have more than one."

"Fine. You know how to use—"

"Yeah."

"Just remember who you're aiming at," Sylvie said. "We're fucked enough without friendly fire."

Any response Cachita would have made was buried under Erinya's growl, a soft, moaning rattle deep in her throat. Sylvie'd heard that sound once before; a Fury laying eyes on an enemy. Even directed elsewhere, it made the hairs on her neck stand up and take notice.

Azpiazu.

* * *

THE GARDENS STRETCHED OUT BELOW THEM, AN EXPANSE OF DARKness broken by Azpiazu's setup. He'd set up his ritual exactly where Sylvie had thought he would: the squared-off reflecting pool at the base of two stone stairwells leading up to a hilly balustrade.

Torches marked the stone surround of the pool, cast bloody light over the darkness, over the shapes drifting in the waters, over Azpiazu's hunched and inhuman form. The firelight reddened the stone stairs, made Sylvie think of Tepeyollotl's reign and human sacrifices in such numbers that the stairs to the altars ran dark and wet with blood.

Azpiazu raised his head and snarled. She steadied her gun, studied the distance. Thirty feet or so. Easily in range.

She sighted along the barrel, aimed.

He didn't even bother to get out of her way, just laughed as she sent one, two, three shots in his direction. Didn't even jerk as they touched him. In her earlier confrontation, she hadn't seen how he'd survived what should have been lethal heart shots. Here, lit by torches, with the hiss of magic in the air, she did. The bullets rusted, crumbled as they touched him, dusted his fur with powder. Ineffective.

Her little dark voice echoed Erinya's growl.

"Eri, can you?" Sylvie asked.

"No," the Fury said. Her body quivered with the urge to hunt, long shivers rattling her spines. "He's still the god's chosen. His god's whipping boy. But . . . soon."

Soon would be too late. By the time Azpiazu was free from Tepeyollotl's claim, he'd be a god.

"Shadows," Azpiazu said. "Come to watch?"

He dragged one of the bodies out of the water—long, lanky, too thin to be anyone but Wales.

Cachita stepped up beside her, fired with a satisfying competence. Not at Azpiazu directly, but at the stone coping. Ricochets spattered sharp shards of limestone and old coral, and Azpiazu flinched. "Get away from him."

"Tepeyollotl's agent," Azpiazu said. "I felt you sniffing around on my tail. If I'd known you were so attractive, I might have let you catch up with me sooner, so I could carve out your heart and soul from your living flesh."

Sylvie and Cachita fired as one, aiming at the stone, and Azpiazu gestured sharply. The women rose from the water, a living shield; Sylvie jerked her gun up.

As the water streamed over their skin, limned scarlet and orange, the women changed shape, growing monstrous. Snarling. Preparing to defend their captor.

Beyond them, Azpiazu lost control of his human shape, bulked into the mangled chimera, and dragged Wales toward his makeshift altar, the base of the stairs.

Sylvie rushed forward but found her way blocked. The two women-wolves—Lupe Fernandez and Anamaria Garcia—closest to her turned, heads lowered, eyes trained on her throat.

Not dead—Sylvie saw their sides heave and flutter—but dead-eyed. Zombies by default if not fact. Rita Martinez rose up, warped, until a bear rose upward to full dismaying bulk, water streaming, red-tinged, like shedding lava.

Erinya snarled back and pounced just as the fourth woman—Elena Llosa, by default—in jaguar form, lunged at Sylvie. They tumbled over each other, a snarling, tail-lashing blur of spots and scales. Erinya shook the cat by its scruff, flung it into the far trees. The cat groaned as it landed, tried to stand, sprawled again, shaking its head.

"Don't hurt them!" Sylvie shouted. "They're innocents." Hard to remember, but under that spotted pelt was a high-school girl. Sylvie should have thought, should have planned better. If the ISI hadn't snatched her, maybe she would have. She needed tranquilizer darts, not bullets.

Erinya swapped end to end with the wolves, taking on two at once. Her hindquarters thickened, ran stiff with heavy scale just as one of the wolves tried to hamstring her.

The bear charged Sylvie, and she turned and ran. What else was there? She wasn't willing to shoot her—single parent, she remembered—wasn't willing to just stand still and let the woman kill her either. She leaped upward, snatching at a tree branch, and had it betray her, puffing rottenly loose, dropping her right before the bear.

Cachita screamed. The cat had staggered to its feet enough to lash out at Cachita. It raked her calf with savage claws, set blood spurting into the night.

The world started to shake; dirt dancing like water on a hot skillet. Tepeyollotl on his way. Cachita's blood call enough.

Sylvie rolled out of the way of the bear's clumsy first strike, saw that the fur on the heavy brow was patchy, revealing the binding sigil that linked Rita to Azpiazu. She seized a handful of sharp gravel, ignored all common sense, and lunged into the bear's reach. She scrubbed the gravel over the mark, a tumble of jagged edges, bear's scalding breath on her skin, and thought if this didn't work, if it didn't at least slow the bear, the last thing she was going

to see was the spurt of her arteries as her throat was torn
out by a woman she was trying to save.

The world shuddered around her; the cough of an angry jaguar sounded. Bigger, louder than the shadow Erinya had scared off. Tepeyollotl heading to the scene. The
bear staggered, and Sylvie forced her focus back.

Be damn stupid to die because she got distracted.

She lunged upward, climbed the bear's thick coat, and
slashed. The binding sigil, a silvery leaden mark in the bear's
skin, spat blood. The bear collapsed backward, convuls-
ing, slime and saliva spewing.

It lay still, sides heaving, and Sylvie counted it a win.

Or as close as she was going to get. They were both
alive. For now.

She shuddered. The ground trembled with her. But
Tepeyollotl . . . wasn't here yet.

Gratitude washed over her, even if it was short-lived.
She didn't have time to wonder why. Didn't have time to
think.

Erinya had put down one of the wolves with a vicious
slash that had taken out the sigil by chance, but the jaguar
had rejoined the fight, had leaped onto Eri's back, jaws
locked tight on the Fury's neck.

A faint sound carried to Sylvie. A voice that had screamed
so much it was shredded, but still continuing. "No. No.
No." Cachita was hunched, tight and tiny, her hands flung
up above her head, tight with tension, tight with effort, as
if she were pushing on a door that was trying to open.

Holding back the god.

Sylvie blinked, read the determination in her face.
"Cachita . . ."

"Kill Azpiazu," Cachita husked. "I can do this. You
said it. A spell goes both ways. A door that opens can
close." Tears lined her face like war paint, reflective in the
light; her jaw locked tight around her words. Her body
shook.

She couldn't hold Tepeyollotl for long; it was amazing
she could hold him back at all.

Time was running out. Not just for Cachita. Not just for Sylvie. For the city.

Erinya and the jaguar tumbled and snarled, a whirlwind of mindless rage. The remaining wolf snapped at any flesh it could reach.

Around Azpiazu, the world bent and shuddered, drawing inward. Sylvie could sense it like a sound out of human range, a stressed vibrato that made her skin tingle, made her want to duck her head and howl like a frightened animal.

One more soul, one more taste of filtered god-power . . . and she'd be front and center at a god's birth. Wales would be that last bite, the final thing that filled Azpiazu to bursting and beyond.

But Azpiazu had Wales draped over his lap, his knife held lax between paws, watching. Waiting.

Waiting for what?

A skiff of frigid air slicked her skin, welcome in the putrid heat. Marco blew past her, strong and furious, filled with energy stolen from the ISI agents' souls, heading straight for the sorcerer. Marco crackled with determination; his ghostly skin rippled and flashed as he moved, like the firelight on the water.

He hadn't bothered to help Erinya or Sylvie or Cachita. But Wales was his.

Sylvie tried to grab Marco as he passed, understanding all at once why Azpiazu had waited. Why he hadn't sacrificed Wales while Sylvie and Erinya fought the bespelled women. Why he had broken a lifetime of habitual misogyny.

Marco's attack was a calamity waiting to happen. A miscalculation that was going to cost them everything. Sylvie lunged forward, but her grasping at Marco was literally grasping at air. She fell, scraping her knees in the dirt, got her head up in time to see Marco rush against Azpiazu, enveloping him like fog.

Marco tried to take a bite out of Azpiazu, tried to put the sorcerer into soul shock, and Azpiazu only threw Wales's limp body aside, laughing; his arms went wide, allowing Marco to come closer.

Marco ignored her calling him back, moved forward even more aggressively.

Azpiazu drove his knife into Marco's ghostly shape. Instead of passing harmlessly through him, steel through smoke, it pinned him like an overlarge butterfly. Marco jerked, light and color flashing within him, a shimmering oil slick comprised of more than a dozen stolen pieces of soul. Azpiazu grinned, baring sharp teeth, and turned the blade, baring the necromantic sigils carved into the steel blade.

Azpiazu might just be the most adaptable villain she'd ever faced.

How long had he been planning this? Since he first saw Marco's handiwork in the Everglades? The soul-nipped cops, and realized that if he took a soul-eating ghost, it was more bang for his buck? When he realized that Marco would defend Wales to the death.

Wales *wasn't* the final soul Azpiazu needed. A necromantic soul might be a powerful one, but it could fight back. Death, a familiar battlefield.

Marco's ghost, on the other hand . . .

Marco was not only vulnerable; his was a soul completely suited for Azpiazu, a serial killer and a misogynist. And to make his soul even more palatable?

When Azpiazu took Marco, he laid claim not only to the ghost, but to the ISI agents lying senseless in their white halls, their souls nipped and made a temporary part of Marco.

Sylvie raised her gun, emptied the clip into Azpiazu, not trying to hurt—she knew that was impossible—but trying to distract. To disrupt the ritual. To stop Azpiazu from taking those threshold souls.

The bullets were less than useful. They actively worked against them. Marco, pinned by a magically infused sacrificial knife, had gone tangible enough that each bullet danced him like a puppet, tore him into shreds.

Azpiazu sighed, and all that humming energy in the air, the electrostatic charge that danced over them all, an unseen aurora, shifted and settled over Azpiazu's shoulders like a mantle, drawn in by Azpiazu's easy absorption of Marco's soul.

He raised his head, shook the animal from his flesh, shed Tepeyollotl's punishment like it was nothing at all, a mist of water on a warm day. Around his feet, the grass withered, going blackish at the roots and spreading upward like ink.

"So, Shadows," he said. "You couldn't stop me before. Think you have any chance now? I am the god of Death and Change. Be sensible, little Lilith. *Run.*"

18

Two Gods, No Waiting

VIZCAYA GARDENS WERE TEN ACRES OF MANICURED LANDSCAPES and grottoes, butted up against Biscayne Bay, capped with a turn-of-the-century manor house—it was a spacious place. With Azpiazu exuding energy, bleeding deathly rot into the night, he loomed large enough to her senses that the gardens felt tightly claustrophobic, a tangled jungle of rotting vegetation.

In the background, Cachita's exhortations had gone hoarse; she was down on her knees, head craned back, arms crossed above her face. Agony in her bones. Still trying to keep that door closed, trying to cage Tepeyollotl with nothing more than the letter of their bargain, that he would come *when* she called. And not before.

"Can't leave," Sylvie said. "You've got some things I want."

"What? Them?" Azpiazu gestured at the bespelled women, still challenging Erinya, gestured at Wales's limp body. "No. They're mine. They're going to be my first true souls. The first chosen ones to be part of my godhood."

Erinya rolled, dislodged the jaguar from her back and neck at the expense of blood and scale and chunks of feathered hide, and flung the squalling, limping cat across the courtyard. The wolf, racing in to take advantage, was slapped hard enough to spin into the reflective pool with a bloody splash and howl. Sylvie winced.

Erinya cocked her head, put her burning gaze on Azpiazu, and growled, "*Your* godhood."

Azpiazu laughed, and it was a disconcertingly gorgeous sound, a man thrilled with himself and his new lot in life.

Erinya grinned, her lips split wide, wider, widest until the entire lower half of her face seemed comprised of needle teeth. "New gods are fair play. Especially if they don't have anyone to watch their back."

Sylvie chimed in. "Who's feeling like running now?"

"She's nothing to me," Azpiazu said. "A flunky for a softhearted—"

Erinya flew at him, talons on all four legs extended, wings curving over her back to end in sharp-edged spikes. Azpiazu stood his ground, and her claws shredded his clothes, but not the skin beneath.

A god.

Sylvie's little dark voice made itself heard over the tumult, over Cachita's defiant cries and the thundering groan of the earth, the howls of an angry wolf deprived of prey. *Not a god. Not yet,* her voice whispered. *Not quite yet.* It gifted her with one word further. A word that gave her a tiny flare of hope.

Transitioning, it said.

Azpiazu might have been immortal, but even an immortal body needed alteration to take full advantage of godhood. To allow him to access the kind of power that would turn a human body, no matter how durable, into ashes and dust.

For a few minutes more, Azpiazu was both god and man. And while Sylvie would pit herself against a god, if needs must, she was happier with a man.

The problem was, Erinya wasn't making headway. Azpiazu slung her into a tree, smashing it like glass. Erinya staggered, rose up, her skin oddly leprous. As if death were touching an immortal creature.

Sylvie jerked her gaze away. If Azpiazu was transitioning, she still had a shot. He had a weakness. He had to. She just had to figure it out.

But first . . .

A low growl chilled her spine; she turned. The woman-turned-jaguar slunk toward her on three legs, one dragging. Erinya's idea of not hurting the unwitting left something to be desired. At the moment, with the jaguar dragging hand leftward, with the leg slowing its inevitable course toward Sylvie, she couldn't regret it.

The bear was still down, still unconscious, the broken bond releasing it from Azpiazu's order to attack. The wolf whose face Erinya had torn was down. Freed from the binding sigil.

The binding sigil. The thing that bound Azpiazu to the women. Let him control them.

Sigils ran two ways.

Sylvie shifted stance, trying to keep an eye on the jaguar while keeping Azpiazu in her view. He was playing with Erinya, breaking a hind leg, ripping a wing off; her efforts were doing nothing but stripping him of his clothes. The jaguar crouched awkwardly, one leg crooked, her eyes glowing, teeth dripping blood and feathers.

Sylvie bared her teeth and snarled back. The jaguar hesitated, slunk back into the underbrush, gave her breathing space.

Azpiazu's binding sigil had been carved into each woman's forehead. For the symbology to work, Azpiazu had to have a matching sigil to influence. Sympathetic magic at its most basic.

Somewhere on his skin, hidden in the darkness, in his fluid movements, in the shadows racing his body, there'd be a sigil to match the one he'd carved onto each woman's forehead. Onto Wales's.

That binding link would be the last thing to change, the last piece of him that would be mortal. He was holding on to it, still controlling his "harem." It would be small, the size of a quarter. Easily overlooked in the dimness of firelight and thundercloud. She couldn't shoot it. Even if bullets worked on him. Even if she had bullets left.

But if she could wake Wales, he might have magical means to help. She crept toward him, trying to keep Azpiazu from noticing. Playing with Erinya just wasn't holding his attention the way it should, though Erinya was doing her bloody best.

The jaguar lunged out from the underbrush; Sylvie dodged the killing blow but still tumbled backward, hitting the ground with a painful, breath-stealing thud.

Something slammed into her kidney with the near-familiar pain of a gun crushed between her body and the ground. But she'd discarded all the guns once they'd emptied.

She kicked the jaguar in the chest, kicked hard at the damaged leg, and the cat screamed and retreated for easier prey. Sylvie rolled, put her hand on the source of the pain, and found Cachita's knife. Metal handle.

Obsidian blade.

The jaguar, burdened by Azpiazu's will, kept fighting, turned her attention toward the only remaining prey. Cachita. Still contorted, face grey with exhaustion, still chanting, *No no no*, still locked in her struggle with Tepe-yollotl.

"Erinya!" Sylvie said. "Protect her—"

"Not fair," Erinya gasped, even as she moved Cachita's direction with a horrible, broken stagger. She was ragged, savaged nearly past mending. "You'll hunt without me." Azpiazu let her run, then grabbed her remaining wing, and dragged her back. Playing.

A single moment. That was all it took. Erinya spun, clawing; Sylvie lunged after the jaguar, but was too slow.

. . .

CACHITA SCREAMED, HER VOICE SPIRALING UPWARD, THEN RIPPED into silence. The jaguar's jaws closed down hard on Ca chita's straining neck, white teeth going black with arterial blood.

Azpiazu's jaguar had broken the wildly uneven stalemate between Cachita and her god. No agreement could hold through one party's being mauled. The jaguar shook Cachita; she dropped limply, eyes empty and dead.

The world shook; trees shattered all around them, earthquakes and rot mingling with disastrous results. The reflective pool cracked, let stagnant water grease the stones around them.

Azpiazu stopped stalking Erinya, paused, waiting for his chance at the god who'd given him so much, waiting for Tepeyollotl to see what he'd become. That wicked smile was on his face once more, the bubble of laughter in his throat.

"You are enjoying yourself way too much," Sylvie said.

Tepeyollotl breathed himself into the world, an enormous concussive force that knocked her sprawling, knocked the breath from her lungs. Her ears stung as if wasps had crawled inside and attacked. When she touched them, her fingers came away wet with blood.

Erinya's despairing moan was a fractured whisper in Sylvie's traumatized hearing.

Enough.

They were going to lose.

They were going to lose *everything*.

Beneath Tepeyollotl's looming arrival, Cachita's body faded, drifted to smoke. Obliterated. Dead without even a body to mark where she had fallen.

Sylvie wasn't going to lose anyone else. Not the women. Not Wales. Not even Erinya. She clutched the obsidian knife with white knuckles.

Tepeyollotl slunk down from the raised balcony, his heavy bulk overwhelming the wide, stone stairs. His smoky shadow flowed before him like a river, eating away at the stone, a destructive, intangible river. The earth trembled and rippled. Trees fell with the sound of torn fabric, of reality altering in the reflection of the god's anger.

A sharp avalanche heralded an entire wall sliding down, hitting the shaking ground and puddling outward. Sylvie nearly lost her footing all over again, and, in regaining it, made the mistake of looking at Tepeyollotl. She couldn't look away.

Tepeyollotl was the shattered remnant of Tezcatlipoca, Cachita had said. The god moving ponderously through the world *looked* shattered. He was four times human size, his flesh scarred and battered and studded with what looked like broken glass. Some of his skin wasn't human flesh at all but a tattered and decaying jaguar pelt, equal parts black spots and char. It sagged unhealthily. He crawled on all fours, yellowed nails curling over his massive fingers, sharp enough to leave gouges in stone; his eyes were blood-red from lash to lash, and scars ran down his cheeks and throat.

Despite his bulk, his bones jutted, pressing against the jaguar pelt, against flesh that seemed parchment thin, in angular, agonizing protrusions. He raised his head, sniffed the air, nose wrinkling, human mouth drawing up into a cat's whiskered cheek pads. His huge tongue was white-spined. A single lick would flay a man.

Still blind to Azpiazu.

That last bit of mortality, that binding sigil, hiding him. His only weakness saving him from his enemy.

Tepeyollotl's bloody gaze locked on Sylvie. His lips peeled back. He coughed, a jungle cat's hunting call. It rattled her bones, raised the hairs all over her body. It was all she could do not to retreat to basic mammal instinct and curl up, hoping to be unseen.

"Should have run, Shadows," Azpiazu said. He held his hands out before him; oily darkness dripped from each palm. It flowed outward toward her like tar, spreading rot.

God of Death, indeed. And if he was accessing his new powers, her time was running short.

Sylvie lunged forward, dragged Wales's deadweight out of the path of the rot, picked up the necromantic blade in her free hand. She kept the obsidian one behind her back, hoping he hadn't seen it. Dark hilt, dark blade, dark night. Erinya dropped heavily down beside her, panting, coughing up something smoky and dark. Demigod blood.

Azpiazu said, "Caught between death and . . . death. What are you going to do, Shadows? *Nothing*. You're just a human woman. And I'm a god."

Sylvie's retort died on her lips. There. On his chest. Dead center. The binding sigil—the fusion symbol that held the rest of the spells together, the last bit of human in him. The flesh there rippled, muscles straining from an exertion the rest of him managed effortlessly.

"Not yet," Sylvie said.

"Close enough," he said. "And that knife won't help you." He spread his arms. "I can be generous. If you want to try . . . one last blow before I eat your heart and soul. Make you my sacrifice."

Arrogance, she thought. Had to love it.

She grinned, dropped the silvery blade, and brought the obsidian knife up, hard, fast, and on target. It lodged right where she wanted it. Right through the spell link he had carved into his skin. The one that blinded Tepeyollotl to his presence.

Azpiazu, impaled, staggered forward, clutching at Sylvie's arms, slipping death under her skin. Her skin grew cold and heavy, unresponsive. Nerves withering, death creeping in. Her numb hands slid on the knife's handle, losing grip. She compensated with a full-body shove; the blade had already penetrated, its glassine edges sliding through skin, muscle, and bone as if it had been designed exactly for that purpose. She would push it deeper with her last effort, lodge it in his black heart, if that was what it took.

Sylvie didn't think it would come to that.

Azpiazu coughed, his stolen power bleeding out, his eyes showing shock and betrayal.

"I kill the unkillable," Sylvie whispered.

"I'll outlast you," he gasped, coughing.

"No," she said. "You won't." She yanked the knife out, a slippery leap in her hands, and jammed it through his throat.

. . .

AZPIAZU SCREAMED, AND TEPEYOLLOTL ROARED, A CAT'S RAGE IN A human-shaped throat; a hundred or more years of his prey's eluding him ended all at once.

He leaped forward, crashing through the remnants of the pond, into the feeble shield Erinya made. Erinya blindsided him, clung fast, and sent them both tumbling.

Sylvie felt the numbness in her body spreading, death spreading, and scrabbled at it, not physically—her hands were unresponsive—but willfully. She'd fought off Azpiazu's curse before; she could do it again. She pushed at the creeping death, rejecting it, refusing it, finding that alien magic and shoving it back toward Azpiazu. The easier target. The dying god.

Like called to like, the balance tipped steadily. The creeping rot sank down her arms, her hands, crawled up and into Azpiazu's chest. The air around them grew smoky and dull, heavy with the taste of burned blood. It itched along her skin, clung to her hair, her throat, her panting mouth, trying to find a way back in.

Tepeyollotl backhanded Erinya into the underbrush. The Fury rolled, a disjointed spill of limbs and wing, and lay still.

Sylvie wanted Tepeyollotl gone, needed him gone. He'd gotten his vengeance, even if not by his own hand: Azpiazu was slowly going to death. But Tepeyollotl kept prowling, growling under his breath. Sticking around, pacing tight circles when he could be hunting new souls, new followers—a swift and blatant display of power to regain his kingdom. Why? Awaiting his chance to kill her?

No, she thought. If he wanted her dead, she'd be dead. The struggle to push out Azpiazu's dying curse was making her stupid. Tepeyollotl wasn't going anywhere without trying to regain the power that Azpiazu had stolen. The power that swirled around Sylvie and Azpiazu like steam trapped in a lidded pot, hotter and hotter, close to exploding.

It must be driving him mad, she thought, forcing herself upright, leaning her weight on the knife, on Azpiazu's body. Tepeyollotl was so close to his stolen powers, and yet, Azpiazu's filtering had altered them just enough that he couldn't reach out and take them. They didn't fit right anymore.

He'd figure it out soon enough, poking and tasting the new flavor of his stolen power. Sylvie's lashes drooped under the weight of it; her skin was smudged with Azpiazu's last bloody breath.

Thing was, Azpiazu's death hadn't solved the imminent problem. Freed the women, yes, but Tepeyollotl and loose god-power . . . Tepeyollotl threw back his head and screamed frustration. Lightning lanced from the sky, started the trees burning, tangled snarls of fire leaping from branch to branch. Sparks spattered the shaking ground, singed Erinya's fur, spurred her to bare consciousness.

If Tepeyollotl got his power back, they'd be standing at ground zero for the god version of a nuclear blast. If the power just . . . dispersed, every bad cess witch in Miami would suck it up and spit it back out in a thousand malicious ways.

Sylvie's body ached. Shuddered with the magic winding around Azpiazu's body, around her throat. It felt like that zombie constrictor again, all malevolence and injury just waiting to strike.

Tepeyollotl lowered his gaze from the sky, looked at Sylvie. She met those huge, blood-lit eyes, and knew she was out of time. He was coming for his stolen power, and coming for it now. If she wanted to keep it from him, keep it from the witches and sorcerers . . . she was going to have to take it for herself.

Her little dark voice screamed warning. She knew what happened to people who grasped magic beyond their abilities, knew that Azpiazu's death would look gentle in comparison and yet . . . it seemed so easy to just reach out. To put her hand on Azpiazu's rotting chest and bones and pull instead of push. To seek out the source of that char-smoke-blood power and cup it into her palms.

It was like putting her hands into the heart of a fire. They went from numb to scalding in a heartbeat. She'd expected the god-power to fight her.

It didn't.

At her first touch, her first tug, the lurking god-energy leaped toward her and poured itself into her skin.

The world was

White-hot.

Her skin was

White-hot.

Her eyes—

She saw *everything* around her. The violent blurs of power-life-hunger-will that were Erinya and Tepeyollotl, the faltering hiccups of humans forced into animal shapes, so unnatural it made her teeth itch and burn, her nerves scream. She knew them, felt them all, their fears, their hopes, their dreams.

Tierney Wales, so scared, yet trying to do the right thing. A man who mourned his murderous ghosts like some men mourned their children.

The women—Lupe Fernandez, Anamaria Garcia, Rita Martinez, Elena Llosa—their tangled lives ran kaleidoscope through her mind, college student, schoolteacher, bartender, high-schooler, all their wants, and desires. She knew them down to their cores. Knew which animal shape was which, saw the overlay of their spirits in animal flesh. Saw the wounds that she and Erinya had dealt in defending themselves. Felt each wound like a brand on her skin. The jaguar who'd been blown into the trees, its back broken when Tepeyollotl came. The last wolf still crouched, slavering and terrified, in the underbrush.

Tepeyollotl lunged forward, nails clawing at her; Sylvie desperately missed her guns, and the thought was enough.

Bullets sprayed in Tepeyollotl's direction, created and

fired by her will instead of a gun. Each one felt like it ripped something out of her, replaced it with more magic.

Sylvie's little dark voice shrieked sheer disgust, utter repulsion at the power burning inward, boring into every cell of her, seeking a home. Her body was flame.

She couldn't contain this power.

She was.

She shouldn't be able to. She was only human.

But more than that—

She didn't *want* the power. It revolted her, this giant seething mass of magic crawling around, curling through her veins, out her fingers, through her hair. It invaded and tainted every breath she pulled into straining lungs, reinforcing every bone in her body like a coating of molten steel, jacking her heart rate to hummingbird speed. Her skin hissed with energy, a living force trying to remake her every molecule into something more. Something greater.

Something inhuman.

She burned in the night like a bonfire, and snake patterns slid over her flesh, red, black, yellow—serpent colors. Sylvie groaned, tried to hold the power at a distance, but it was as hard to shake off as lava.

Erinya staggered to three feet, flesh sloughing off with creeping rot, her exposed core smoky and scarlet, and Sylvie saw a sudden escape from an inhuman future as an unwilling god.

"Erinya!"

．．．

THE FURY WAS TOO SLOW TO DODGE TEPEYOLLOTL'S REFLEXIVE AT-tack, and Sylvie reached out and yanked the Fury toward her with all the aimless power smoldering in her soul. Erinya disappeared from beneath Tepeyollotl's grip, re-appeared skin-close to Sylvie, sprawled at her feet, so broken, still angry, still wanting to fight. Sylvie wanted to give her the means to do so.

Sylvie reached down, and said wildly, "I owe you? Come and get it!" and pressed her hands down into Eri's

wild hair, into her scaly skin, and kicked the power outward. Evicted it with prejudice. Forced it into a new home.

Erinya arced under Sylvie's hands, struggling even as
Sylvie force-fed her strength and that unwanted power.
Erinya's false flesh sealed up around the gaping wounds;
her scales smoothed to obsidian; her feathers grew thick
and glossy and scarlet. Her teeth lengthened, grew sharp,
grew white, near glowing in the dark.

Sylvie's heart slowed, her skin cooled, pinging like an
overtaxed engine. The patterns crawling her flesh slowed.
Retreated. The glow oozed away from Sylvie, lit every
single scale and feather on Erinya's body.

"What did you—"

"You owe *me* now," Sylvie said. "Get rid of Tepeyollotl. You're a match for him."

It was the best thing about Erinya, Sylvie thought, col-
lapsing, her legs gone numb and shaky beneath her. Give
her the whiff of a violent command, and she was all over
it, no hesitation. It was also the worst thing about her—
that endless appetite for violence.

Erinya and Tepeyollotl collided physically and magically with an impact that made Sylvie think of an avalanche.
The ground shuddered, trembled, cracked wide. The ponds
and fountains split, spilled their water deep into the screaming earth. The air sounded like high tide coming, crashing
against a rocky shore. Sinkholes gaped, and Sylvie grabbed
Wales and dragged his deadweight away from a sudden
edge.

Sylvie's stomach churned—a remnant of god-magic still
working away in her, trying to rebuild her, to claim her.
She tried to push it out, but it lingered, making itself at home.
Fine. If it wanted to be owned by her, she would use it.

She gave it purpose, sent it pouring out to rupture all of
Azpiazu's remaining spells, waking Wales from his stu-
por, healing the wounds on the shape-shifting women. It
was barely enough to do the job, sputtered out within her,
ripping itself out by the root as she forced it to obey. Us-

ing that power, even that fragment of it, felt like she was renovating her body using razor blades.

Erinya rolled Tepeyollotl, pinned him, knees and wing tips on his loosely slung pelt. "Stay down," she growled.

Sylvie dumped Wales out of her lap and started talking fast. "You lost, Tepeyollotl. Your empire's long gone; your enemy is dead—"

That elicited a snarl, more earthly upheaval. Windows shattered in the main house; she was surprised they'd lasted that long, and Sylvie hastened over that point. Reminding a god that a mortal had taken his prey? Not a good way to make friends.

"You're damaged goods," she said. "You're *weak*. If you stay on earth, you won't attract new followers. You'll attract hunters. Not just the Fury. But sorcerers and humans who want a bite of your power."

"And you," Tepeyollotl said. "You would kill me if you could."

His voice resonated in her bones, a beehive rumble that carried the threat of pain. She breathed steadily through the aftershocks, and said, "Yes. I don't want your power. I want you dead. Or gone. The choice is yours."

Tepeyollotl jerked in Erinya's claws, a mindless, surprised twitch. Sylvie bared her teeth, met that red-tinged gaze, and said, "Make the right one. Look at the shape you're in now. Imagine what I could do if I was trying to kill you instead of just stopping you."

Erinya laughed, leaned close, and licked Tepeyollotl's scarred cheek. "She could do it, too, I bet."

"Gone?" he said.

"Retreat and wait for your time to come 'round again," Sylvie said. "You've got time. Who knows? Maybe there'll be a new interest in you. You'll find new followers, grow strong again."

It was an effort to sound in control, like this was the best solution for him. Tepeyollotl might be reduced, a shell of what he once had been, but he was still a god. His influence radiated outward, and the world around him adjusted to his will.

Right then, luckily, he was confused and focused on fighting Erinya and listening to Sylvie. Even with that, though, there were changes.

Vizcaya's crumbled stones had shifted, changed from French-styled gardens to the beginnings of pyramids. Bright sparks lit the underbrush, shadowy shapes of cats in all sizes from tabby to Florida panther. Calling like to like. His own allies approaching.

"Go?" he said, tasting the idea for palatability. "But not forever." He groaned, threw Erinya off him in a long ripple of contorting sinew and tendon.

Erinya crouched, wings mantled, neck arched, teeth bared.

Tepeyollotl vanished without further words, and Sylvie jerked her gaze to Erinya. "Is he gone, or just gone somewhere else in the world? Are we going to have to hunt him down?"

"Gone," Erinya said. She sounded disappointed.

Sylvie didn't share that disappointment at all, felt dizzy with relief.

"What just happened here?" Wales asked. His voice sounded so frail after listening to gods. It made it easy to ignore him.

Her wary attention was all for Erinya.

In the heat of the battle, drowning under power she didn't want and didn't know how to use, giving it to Erinya had seemed a no-brainer. Now Sylvie worried. The Fury had been powerful enough as a demigod—willful and violent, but under the god of Justice's control.

Now that Sylvie had made Erinya his equal?

Erinya shook herself, shook off the monster aspect, trying to fit back into her human guise. It wasn't working very well; she couldn't seem to shake away the razor-edged wings.

She flipped them back finally, sharp feathers rasping like blades in the night and paused. Her eyes widened. "Oh."

Erinya had caught up with the rest of the class.

"Yeah," Sylvie said. "Guess no one's going to be bossing you around any longer."

"I can taste them all," Erinya said. "All those evil souls—"

She threw back her head and shrieked.

Sylvie jerked, stumbled to the ground, clutching her ears. Dark shapes scattered out of Erinya's mouth, a swarm of . . . something. One-winged bats, shadowy daggers, silent locusts.

Sylvie ducked and covered and listened to the echoes of Erinya's cry bouncing off the stone walls.

"That's that," Erinya said. "I can find anyone. Anywhere." Sudden triumph laced her voice. "I know where Demalion is. I know *who* he is."

Sylvie leaped, her body reacting before her mind knew to do so. She caught Erinya's wing in her hand as she started to vanish. "No," Sylvie said. "You leave him alone. You owe me, Eri. *I made you a god.* What's one escaped soul to that?"

Erinya bared her teeth. "Like to see you try to force me. I'm not Tepeyollotl. I'm not damaged."

"Erinya," Sylvie said, then her throat dried. Threats wouldn't work here, and entreaty would be seen as weakness.

"You like hunting," Wales said. He pushed himself upright, held himself there even when the Fury-god's gaze landed on him. "You're a merciless hunter but not an indiscriminate one."

Sylvie said, "Demalion's already been punished for his crime. He's lost his body, his talents, his life. He remembers his death. His every nightmare belongs to you. Let him live. He'll live in fear of you."

Erinya shifted her wing out of Sylvie's grip, stayed silent and sullen and *here*, and Sylvie knew she'd won.

"Thank you," she said.

Erinya said, "I'm just leaving him alone. I don't make promises for Alekta or Magdala."

"But you won't tell them he's alive either," Sylvie demanded.

"Won't talk to them at all," Erinya said with a toss of her head. Sylvie closed her eyes, thankful that Erinya was such a bad-tempered creature that she didn't get along with her sisters.

Wales made a soft sound of surprise, a tiny, startled gasp that turned to a smile, as he saw Lupe Fernandez stir. He darted over to her, reassuring her that she was going to be all right, that they had been rescued, that they would be taken home.

Sylvie sank down on the broken stone wall and watched Wales corral the women, wondering vaguely if the ISI van was still waiting, or if it had been swallowed by the earth, crushed by a flaming tree, or just eaten by zombie alligators. Be a hell of a time to have to call a taxi.

"It's there," Erinya said, reading her mind effortlessly. "But so are the ISI. They think they're laying an ambush."

"Wanna chase 'em off?" Sylvie said.

"How many favors are you going to try to collect?" Erinya asked.

"As many as I can," Sylvie said.

She should get up, get moving. The ISI wouldn't lurk forever, and despite what her battered watch said, the skyline was brightening, heading inexorably toward dawn and discovery. She should be sore; she'd been thrown around, brawled with a baby god, and fought off a death curse. Instead, all she felt was tired. Worried.

Erinya disappeared, and Sylvie twitched for her gun in automatic reaction, making Wales, who was approaching her, fling his hands up automatically.

"Sorry," she said. "You ready to get out of here?"

"Only too," he said. "How long did Azpiazu have me? It felt like days."

"Hours at most," Sylvie said. "Marco found us damn promptly; I'll give him that."

Wales licked his lips. "Marco?"

Sylvie shook her head. "Azpiazu ate him." There'd be

time later to tell Wales how Azpiazu had planned it.

"We're not all going to fit in your truck," Wales said, looking back at the women. For kidnap victims who'd been bespelled, manipulated, shape-shifted, and used as weapons, they looked damn good. For regular people, they looked shell-shocked and terrified, crowding close to Wales like impressed ducklings.

"Got a different ride," Sylvie said. "We'll fit."

"What are we waiting for?" Wales asked.

Distant gunfire rattled, chattering in the dawn. Shouting. Screaming.

Sylvie nodded in that direction. "For Erinya to clear our path."

19

Taking Stock

SYLVIE FELT LIKE CHRISTMAS MORNING, PLAYING SANTA, DROPPING
Lupe, Anamaria, Elena, and Rita off at their homes, watching them seized up by happy families. It was a good feeling. She wanted to bask in it.

Wales climbed forward from the back bench seat, took
shotgun, and said, "So, I'm going to need to go back to
Vizcaya sometime soon and make sure Azpiazu is gone."

So much for her happy feelings, Sylvie thought.

"He's *dead*," Sylvie said. "You were unconscious, but I
killed him pretty thoroughly." It was protest for the sake
of it. She started the ignition, waved at Rita and her family, and pulled back onto the streets. "You think he laid in
a contingency plan?"

"Necromancers, for all they deal in death, tend to cling
to life like limpets. And he outthought a god, manipulated
Tepeyollotl. . . ."

"Manipulated *me*," Sylvie murmured, thinking of Wales
being taken solely to get to Marco. "All right. You need
help?"

"I could stand for you to watch my back," he said. "I'm
down some power with the Hands destroyed."

"Deal," she said. "You have any of the Hands left?"

"A couple," Wales said. He wrinkled his nose. "I don't like them much. And they don't like me. I'll miss—" He shut up, didn't finish the sentence. He didn't need to. She knew what he was going to say.

"You know, missing ghosts of convicted serial killers is why you get called the Ghoul," she said. "If you're going to hang around, you could work on that."

"I didn't say I was hanging around."

"You didn't say you were leaving."

"Maybe I've learned my lesson," he said. "Tell you I'm leaving town, and you show up with reasons I shouldn't. Maybe I'm just going to split this city all sneaky-like."

"I got your stuff," Sylvie said, finding a tiny smile. It felt good to have this mindless banter after she'd nearly written him off as dead.

She turned the van automatically for her office, and Wales waited long enough for the route to become familiar before saying, "You know the government's tracking this van."

"You're just full of sunshine, aren't you," Sylvie said. "Yeah. I know. Of course I know. Hell, they had my clothes, and I'll have to shake those out for bugs. Probably my apartment also. But right now, the ISI is busy with Erinya, and besides, there's no point in ditching the van, finding a new ride, and heading directly to the office. They know where I work."

"That's a problem," Wales said.

"I know," Sylvie said again. "It's one I'm thinking about."

• • •

AS A TINY ACT OF SPITE, SHE PARKED THE ISI VAN DOWN THE STREET from her office in the most isolated area and left the keys in the ignition, the doors unlocked. Wales said, "If I tried to leave town, you'd sell all my stuff on eBay, wouldn't you."

"Petty revenge is a skill," Sylvie said. As they entered

her office, she sighed. "And oh, do they deserve it."

The office had been in bad shape before the tear gas, before the ISI raided it. Now it was a total wreck, and probably looted as well. The broken storefront window and shattered front door had been left unguarded.

Alex's laptop was gone, the filing cabinets—dented from Erinya and Tepé's earlier spat—gaped emptily. And over the broken furniture, the glass that crunched underfoot, her ransacked kitchenette, Wales's cardboard boxes dragged out from the closet, lay a layer of whitish dust: tear gas residue.

Sylvie moved gingerly through the room, trying not to stir the dust. She peered up the stairs, noted booted footprints stamped into the residue, and prepared herself.

The upstairs office was cleaner than below, the tear gas not so thick on the ground. Tracked in, but not over every surface.

The ISI had taken her computer also, rummaged through her desk, the upstairs filing cabinet that dealt with the *Magicus Mundi*. They'd even cracked open and robbed her safe.

"Fuckers," she murmured, but it was hard to be angry when she was so worried. They hadn't shown her a warrant, or really given a reason for her arrest. So either they had a warrant and hadn't taken the time to show her, or they were running without rules. Either way, it made Sylvie twitchy, and certain she hadn't heard the last of them.

Hopefully, their escape and Erinya's aid at Vizcaya would move Sylvie to the pile of *things we don't mess with*, and her life could go back to normal.

Her little voice scoffed, and she echoed it. *Normal.*

"Sylvie!" Wales called from below.

"Yeah," she responded absently. She moved the desk aside, covering her face with her shirt when dust swirled above the floorboards.

They'd found her safe, but not her hidey. Sometimes caution was a good thing. She popped the floorboard, took out the emergency cash. Maybe it was time to buy those fake IDs.

Money crammed into her pockets, she wandered downstairs, pace picking up as she heard Wales talking to . . . "Alex!"

Alex caught Sylvie up in a spine-crushing hug. "You're all right?"

"You?"

"Oh god, Sylvie, I'm awesome," Alex said. Her smile was bright and huge, glowing. Beautiful. Guess Olympus had treated her well. "But god, what a mess! I called Etienne. He's going to come and board things up. Who do you call to get rid of tear gas?"

Sylvie didn't answer, struck anew by the mess. The cash in her pockets didn't seem like enough. New IDs all around or repairing the office where the ISI could walk in and touch them at any time?

"It's okay," Alex said. "We can fix it."

"We could," Sylvie said.

Wales perked up. "I hear Fort Lauderdale's nice."

Alex raised her head, catching the whiff of "maybe we won't" in Sylvie's tone. "What are you thinking?"

"The ISI doesn't like me. Never has. But now they've slapped a label on me. They think I'm one of the monsters." She held up a hand, forestalled Alex's rebuttal. "Not looking for reassurance, Alex. It's a fact. The ISI doesn't trust me. I can't afford to trust them. I don't want to be an ISI test subject."

"You're going to give up. Quit?"

"Not so much. But I might set up shop elsewhere. At least I'll make them work if they come for me."

"For *us*," Alex said. "If you leave, I'm coming, too."

"You have family here."

"So do you. It's not like you're trying to drop off the grid completely, right? Just slow 'em down a bit. It's not like we're entering witness protection. I can call my family."

"The ISI might tap—"

Alex wrinkled her nose. "I'd like to see them try."

Sylvie found a smile. She'd nearly forgotten. Alex's hacking skills came directly from her family. She was just the only one who did legit work with them.

"And you know Zoe would nuke anyone who tried to listen in on her calls," Alex continued. "Of course, if you start thinking about it that way . . . Syl, we'd be crazy to leave Miami. Our support's here. Zoe, Val, Tierney." A quick flick of her lashes in his direction, a curving smile.

Wales said, "You're assuming they're coming at you legally."

Alex scoffed. "You are way too negative."

"I don't like running," Sylvie said abruptly. "I really don't like running when I haven't planned an effective retreat. We're staying. There's no point in running, anyway. The ISI has branches everywhere, a lot of money, and a long arm. I'm staying and trusting that Erinya scared them off. They don't like gods? I've got one in my pocket. At least for now."

Alex said, "You what?"

"Long story," Sylvie said. "The important thing is, the good guys won, the women are home safely, and Azpiazu's dust."

"Almost dust," Wales said. "We're going to lay his spirit."

"I'm coming with you guys when you do. Ooh, hey! You and me," Alex said, gesturing at Wales. "Time for a celebratory breakfast burrito run. You in?" Her smile widened; Wales seemed dazzled.

"Yeah, all right," he said. Breathless.

Sylvie watched them go, watched Wales catch Alex's arm, stilling her. He stooped, awkward but determined, kissed her quickly, shyly. Alex linked her arm through his and dragged him off. Sylvie smiled.

• • •

BANGING SOUNDS FROM THE ALLEY GOT HER ATTENTION, AND SHE went out to find Etienne dragging hurricane-proof plywood toward her store. She grabbed the other side of the board, and said, "Thanks, Etienne."

They got the first few planks up, screwed in tight, and were working on the last, Sylvie concentrating on the sheer physicality of it. Nice to have something mindless to do. Something that let her shut off her brain.

If Erinya had scared off the ISI, that gave her time to think.

She didn't want it.

The last board up, Etienne thanked with a smile and a hundred dollars in his pocket, Sylvie found herself sitting on a bench in the sunlight, flipping her phone from one hand to the other.

The ISI had had it in their clutches. They'd have the numbers she dialed; they'd probably set spies on it so they could listen in. She put it back in her pocket, and went to harass Etienne again.

The phone rang on the other end, and a woman answered, throwing Sylvie off a bit. In the age of cell phones, it was so rare to get the wrong member of the household, but that was what she had. Wright's wife on the line.

"Who is this?" she asked.

Sylvie spun a quick line about being a collection agency, got an exasperated huff, and a shout for "Adam" to take the call.

"It's me," Sylvie said the moment she heard his breath.

Demalion huffed quietly, something approximating wry amusement. "Fun. All the guilt of cheating, and she's not even my wife. But you're okay? You sound postcase."

"Bad guys vanquished," Sylvie said. Her throat was tight.

"Casualties?"

She closed her eyes. "Yeah."

"Not your pet necromancer," Demalion said. "Alex has a crush."

"No, thankfully. They're off courting over bacon. But the intrepid mini-me didn't make it."

"You liked her."

"Yeah. She was smart and brave when it counted. Anyway, that's not why I called. You're safe from the Furies. Or at least, reasonably safe."

Another betraying breath. A mingled intake of relief and shock. When had she learned his language so well that she could read his mood over the phone? "How'd you swing that?"

"Erinya called off her hunt, and the other two think you're still dead."

"That must have cost you." He was hedging his gladness, refusing to give in to it just yet.

"Nothing I wanted to keep," Sylvie said. "Hey. You still planning on rejoining the ISI?"

"If I can get an entry point, yeah. Why?" His relief was short-lived, giving way to wariness. She pressed the phone closer to her cheek and smiled. Probably wrong, but she liked Demalion suspicious. Kept her on her toes.

"I need eyes on the inside," she said. "They've stepped up their interest in me."

Demalion said, "Stepped up how? More surveillance? Phone tapping—" He faltered. "Do you think they're listening now?"

"I'm on Etienne's phone," Sylvie said. "And more like tear gas and sudden detention."

He swore, something angry, quiet, and hissed. "You all right?"

"Not going to mark tear gas as one of my top experiences, but I think I came out of there in better shape than they did." She hunched over the phone, tried to sound tough. Her hands shook. She hadn't been afraid then, too caught up in worry about Azpiazu and Tepeyollotl. Now she had the time.

"You want me to fly down?"

"If you're going to rejoin the ISI, better have as little contact with me as possible. It's going to be iffy enough when they research Wright and realize he . . . *you* were a client. Luckily, I never cashed his check. He . . . you can be dissatisfied with my services."

"Ah," Demalion said on a sigh. "The good old days. Careful backstories. Disposable cell phones. Coded calls. Secret rendezvous in strange cities. Sounds like fun."

"Spy junkie," Sylvie said, and knew he could hear her smile across the distance. She heard Alex and Wales returning, Alex chattering lightly and Wales's slower drawl interrupting. Near-death experiences, or perhaps Eros's recent presence in Alex's life, seemed to whisk away his shyness.

They walked toward her, shoulders bumping companionably, and Sylvie sighed. Chicago was a long way away.

"I have to go," she said. "Hey, D? Be careful. I don't trust the ISI."

"I'm the careful one, remember?"

"Seriously," she said. "Watch yourself."

"Always," he said.

She folded the phone closed as Alex approached, bag in hand. Alex said, "We're going elsewhere to eat. The office is a health hazard. My apartment?"

Sylvie felt her smile falter. "Actually, I have something I need to do."

"Something risky?" Alex said.

"No," Sylvie said. It was even the truth, though it didn't feel that way. Alex studied her, turned, and handed the bag of food to Wales.

"I'm going with her. I'll catch you later, all right?"

"I'll wait," he said.

Sylvie said, "You don't need to come, Alex."

"Yeah, but I'm going to."

"Fine," Sylvie said. Arguing with Alex was a fool's game; she preferred to save the fights for when she really cared about the results.

Her truck, when she opened it, was scaldingly hot, a lion's breath of sun-baked metal, and her entire body flushed. Alex swore as she clambered into the passenger seat. Sylvie cranked the windows down, blasted the air, and headed off. Her hair snarled and tangled in the breeze, and Alex's attempts at conversation—at prying—were lost to the roar of the engine and the buffet of wind.

Alex subsided, made herself comfortable in the seat, and rubbed briefly at the god mark on her cheek. Sylvie wondered suddenly if that touch of Eros had anything to do with Alex's ability to make people listen to her. To make people like her. Alex had always been amiable and clever, but . . . when had Sylvie started confiding in her to such an extent?

Sylvie shook her head, shook the suspicion off, well aware that she was dwelling on other things than the source of her discomfort.

She turned the radio to local news, listened to a report that occupied her mind quite nicely. Apparently, prison had lost nearly a hundred convicts to sudden death this morning. They just dropped where they stood, their hearts rupturing.

Another report said the police were taking calls about other sudden deaths in the city, trying to map if there was any single cause. They were dancing around the idea of some new type of gas. Sylvie had a good idea that it was something other than that. Especially when the information started trickling in that the prisoners had all been in jail for child-related offenses.

Erinya didn't need to make personal stops any longer.

If she hadn't been dealing with morning traffic, Sylvie might have closed her eyes, shut out the looming sense of responsibility she felt. She'd wondered what kind of god Erinya was going to be; now she was finding out. Violent, deadly, but still sticking to the guidelines the god of Justice had set her.

Alex shifted in her seat. "Weird, you think?"

"Hopefully controlled weird," Sylvie said, let the conversation lapse again. She shoved a CD into the deck, cranked the volume.

When she stopped the truck, the air was cooler outside than it had been at the beach. Early hours still, and the tree shade kept the neighborhood dim and silent.

"Where are we?" Alex asked.

"Cachita's house," Sylvie said. "I want to pack it up, put her files in order."

"Okay," Alex said. "Why?"

Sylvie shrugged. "Respect? She was—"

"*I'm you,*" Cachita had said.

"No, you weren't," Sylvie murmured. "That was the problem."

"Sylvie?"

Sylvie got out of the truck, ignoring Alex's query, headed for the door. The house was as overgrown as before, but the cats were gone, and they'd taken all vestiges of life with them.

Sylvie jimmied the lock, let them in. Less than twenty-four hours, and it felt like the house had been empty forever. Alex looked at the papers stapled all over the living-room walls, the detailed reports, the sheer amount of information she'd gathered. "She did this?"

"Yeah," Sylvie said. "Once a research student, always a research student, I guess. You see any boxes?"

"Paper bags," Alex said, finding a stack of them. She opened the first one, started layering file folders in. Sylvie flipped open Cachita's computer and a password prompt greeted her.

Tepeyollotl, she typed. The password was accepted. Sylvie wasn't surprised. Tepeyollotl had been the biggest event in Cachita's life as well as her biggest secret.

There was a journal. Sylvie opened it, then shut it down before her eyes could take in any of the words. Not hers to read.

"So, you going to tell me what's got you so shaken?" Alex said.

"Dead friend not enough? Tepeyollotl obliterated her."

"Don't try that," Alex said. "You didn't know her. You might have liked her, but she wasn't your friend. Don't use her death to stave me off. It's disrespectful."

"Ouch," Sylvie said.

Alex shifted a shoulder but didn't back down. Just waited.

"The ISI thinks I'm a monster," Sylvie said. "They've lumped me in with sorcerers and the like."

"Yeah, you said."

Sylvie swallowed. "That's not the confession part. This is. I'm not sure they're wrong, Alex. I'm not sure I'm human standard any longer. The new Lilith."

"I hate to break it to you, Syl, but a little voice in your head makes you crazy, not inhuman."

"Thanks," Sylvie said. "I wasn't talking about that. The voice is actually calming down. Being helpful. I'm talking about Azpiazu sucking up a god's power. He was able to contain it."

"He was immortal. Barely human at all."

"*I* was able to contain it. Hell, I was able to *use* it. For one moment, Alex. For one moment, I was teetering on being a god." The words were ragged in her throat, hard to say, hard to admit. That lingering repulsion still echoed in her bones.

Alex said nothing at all, only licked her lips and sat down on the windowsill, peeling old stucco away with shaking fingers.

"I should have burned to ash," Sylvie said. "And the pins should have done more damage. And Odalys . . . The ghost she sicced on me couldn't devour my soul."

"So, you're saying you think that you could maybe be . . ." Eventually Alex ran out of qualifiers and came at it from a new angle. "Lilith was immortal."

"She was," Sylvie said.

"And you?"

Sylvie shrugged, suddenly uncomfortable in her skin, edgy, as if it had changed sometime ago, and she was only now noticing. "I don't know. But I'd better find out what being the new Lilith means before the ISI does."

Alex leaned her head back against the paper-covered glass. "Okay, I'm rethinking the running plan."

"No," Sylvie said. "You were right. Running only encourages things to chase you. I've fought gods, Alex. I'm not scared of the ISI."

"No," Alex said. "You're scared of yourself."

"Maybe," Sylvie admitted. "But think about it this way. If I scare myself, imagine what I do to the ISI. If they're foolish enough to want a fight, I'll give it to them."

Penguin Group (USA) Online

What will you be reading tomorrow?

Patricia Cornwell, Nora Roberts, Catherine Coulter,
Ken Follett, John Sandford, Clive Cussler,
Tom Clancy, Laurell K. Hamilton, Charlaine Harris,
J. R. Ward, W.E.B. Griffin, William Gibson,
Robin Cook, Brian Jacques, Stephen King,
Dean Koontz, Eric Jerome Dickey, Terry McMillan,
Sue Monk Kidd, Amy Tan, Jayne Ann Krentz,
Daniel Silva, Kate Jacobs…

You'll find them all at
penguin.com

*Read excerpts and newsletters,
find tour schedules and reading group guides,
and enter contests.*

Subscribe to Penguin Group (USA) newsletters
and get an exclusive inside look
at exciting new titles and the authors you love
long before everyone else does.

PENGUIN GROUP (USA)
penguin.com